SPARROWHAWK

Book Two
HUGH KENRICK

A novel by

EDWARD CLINE

MacAdam/Cage Publishing
155 Sansome Street, Suite 550
San Francisco, CA 94104
www.macadamcage.com

Library of Congress Cataloging-in-Publication Data

Cline, Edward
    Sparrowhawk—Hugh Kenrick / by Edward Cline.
        p. cm. — (Sparrowhawk ; bk. 2)
    ISBN: 1-931561-20-6 (alk. paper)
    1. Great Britain—History—George II, 1727-1760—Fiction.
2. Young men—Fiction. I. Title: Hugh Kenrick II. Title.
PS3553.L544 S63 2002
813'.54—dc21   2002006483

Manufactured in the United States of America.

10 9 8 7 6 5 4 3 2 1

Book and jacket design by Dorothy Carico Smith.
Cover painting "Entrance to Fleet River" by Samuel Scott 1702—1772

SPARROWHAWK

Book Two
HUGH KENRICK

A novel by
EDWARD CLINE

MacAdam/Cage

CONTENTS

The special province of drama "is to create... action... which springs from the past but is directed toward the future and is always great with things to come."

— Aristotle, On Drama

Prologue: The Peace Makers

I N July, 1748, the merchantman *Sparrowhawk* was piloted up the York River, Virginia. Her first stop on this deep-water gateway to Chesapeake Bay and the Atlantic was Yorktown, a thriving port that boasted several piers, boatworks, tobacco and crop warehouses, palatial homes on the hill overlooking the waterfront, and, of course, several hostelries and taverns. It was one of the vessel's last calls before she sailed farther up the York for De La Ware Town at the headwaters of the river to begin taking on cargo for the voyage back to England. She had already discharged most of her paying passengers in Charleston, South Carolina, together with most of her inanimate cargo—barrels and crates of British-made merchandise, farm and household implements, pipes and casks of various liquors, books, furniture, and even a few pieces of marble. There also her captain and part-owner, John Ramshaw, sold the indentures of the English and Huguenot redemptioners, and the indentures of his sentenced felons. In Hampton, Virginia, closer to the Bay, he had paused long enough to exchange a portion of his vessel's ballast of Newcastle coal for one of saltpeter.

Only a few paying passengers remained on board the *Sparrowhawk* as she sailed up the coast to the York River. Among the men and women who filed down the gangboard with their bundles and bags at Yorktown on the hot mid-July afternoon was the McRae family. Ian McRae was the new factor for the firm of Sutherland & Bain of Edinburgh, tobacco importers, and had journeyed these three thousand miles to replace another Scotsman who had died six months before. His store was located in Caxton, Queen Anne County, another port town and tobacco collection point some miles farther up the York. McRae had brought his wife, Madeline, and their five-year-old daughter, Etáin, with him. He expected to live out the balance of his life here.

Ramshaw had other errands to run up-river, and decided to leave the *Sparrowhawk* in Yorktown so his crew could empty the holds of the last of the merchandise and finish proper repairs of the damage she had sustained during an encounter with a French privateer months earlier. He shared with the McRaes the cost of renting a wagon from a local merchant and rode with them to Caxton.

Accompanying him also was the one remaining felon, fourteen-year-old Jack Frake, who had seven and a half years left to serve of his sentence for smuggling in Cornwall, England. He was a hero to the McRaes and Ramshaw, for in the heat of the sea fight he had fired the swivel gun that killed the captain of the predatory French privateer and caused his crew to call off its attack. In Caxton, Ramshaw called on an old friend, county militia officer John Massie, owner of Morland Hall, a large plantation near Caxton. He introduced Jack Frake to him, and sold that man Jack's eight-year indenture for a penny.

"Can he read, or cipher?" asked Massie, looking out his study window at the boy, who waited on the spacious porch. Sitting at Jack Frake's feet was a bundle of possessions, including a green suit, a few things he had acquired from other passengers during the *Sparrowhawk*'s voyage, and some books that Ramshaw had given him, including a copy of a novel, *Hyperborea; or, the Adventures of Drury Trantham.*

"*Can he read?*" scoffed Ramshaw, puffing on a pipe. "My friend, he has copied out whole books, and helped me with my accounts on the way over! Found some errors I was blind to. Some day, he'll read His Majesty and Parliament their own Riot Act, you mark my words." He studied his host for a moment. "Treat him like a son, John, as Skelly and O'Such did, and you'll win his loyalty. He's rough at the edges now, but with a firm hand and some fine honing, he'll become a devil of a man, and then there will be no stopping him! You'll want him at your side, and on it!"

With earnest farewells and promises to meet again, Ramshaw left Jack Frake behind at Morland Hall two days later. In August the *Sparrowhawk* left Chesapeake Bay and sailed back into the Atlantic.

*   *   *

In October, 1748, French privateers were still harrying English merchantmen, even as the ink dried on the second Treaty of Aix-la-Chapelle, which formally ended the War of the Austrian Succession. Nothing momentous was settled by this treaty. The Pragmatic Sanction, established by Hapsburg Emperor Charles VI in 1720 to define the line of succession to the throne of Austria, was guaranteed, and Maria Theresa's husband, Francis Stephen, Grand Duke of Tuscany, could more easily occupy it. Lands conquered were restored, except for Silesia, which was grudgingly ceded by Austria to Frederick's Prussia, an article of the treaty that would contribute to the resumption of hostilities in the Seven Years' War. Parts of Italy were added to the possessions of the Spanish Bourbons, which already included Naples and Sicily. The House of Savoy, or Sardinia, was awarded a portion of the Duchy of Milan. The Republic of Genoa, the Duchy of Modena, Bohemia, Hungary, and Holland were also signatories to the treaty. The privateers, however, were not, and for at least a year pretended to have no knowledge of the peace. When the convoys of warships and merchantmen ended, merchant captains ventured out on the high seas at their own risk. The Admiralty turned a deaf ear to stories of the privateers' numerous depredations.

England's only gains were some tenuous border adjustments and concessions in North America from Spain and France. These articles, including the one returning Louisbourg in Nova Scotia to the French in exchange for the return of Madras in India to the English, would serve to precipitate the Seven Years' War as well. Assurances were also provided that the House of Hanover, to which George II belonged, and whose political status in Germany was of constant anxiety to him, would retain its right of succession in the German states and on the English throne. George II, Elector of Hanover, both feared the designs of his brother-in-law Frederick the Great on Hanover and other German states; and envied his standing army of 80,000 men. English law prevented the sovereign from having such a toy. George II was not a keen political observer, but at least he knew that a king with a large standing army at his disposal would always be tempted—even driven—to do something with it. The cost of maintaining such an instrument of power could always be offset with the conquest by it of a rich and influential state. Hanover was such a state.

The peace was a vehicle of mutual convenience for all the signatories, an extended cease-fire tacitly contrived to allow them to catch their wind before continuing the contest seven years later. No one familiar with the byzantine, treacherous tangle of Continental politics, with its maze of treaties, pacts and alliances, with its smoldering jealousies, codicilled secret agreements and xenophobic court protocols, culminating in Aix-la-Chapelle, was fooled or beguiled by the Treaty of 1748, especially not the diplomats and statesmen responsible for it. At the same time, however, everyone wished most earnestly to believe in its beneficent longevity.

As if to augur the impermanence of the peace, George II commissioned George Frederick Handel, another Hanoverian more happily and busily ensconced in London than was the sovereign, to compose music with which to publicly celebrate it, specifying that the opus employ martial themes, allow for the prominence of wind instruments, and feature as few stringed instruments as possible, preferably none. The fiddle admittedly is not a warlike instrument, and George II, hero of the battle of Dettingen and the last British monarch to lead troops into battle, wished to stress that the peace owed much to England's military prowess, even though he withdrew his army from the conflict four years earlier to combat the Jacobite menace at home.

Handel, offended at having esthetics dictated to him, at first balked at the royal stipulations, then acquiesced, after this performance. The Duke of Montague, in the meantime, out of his own purse, had built in a corner of St. James's Park a great Doric pavilion to accommodate one hundred musicians and from which to launch a dazzling array of Italian fireworks once the orchestra had played Handel's overture. The pavilion, conceived by a famous Italian stage designer, was an imposing structure four hundred feet long and one hundred high, boasting plaster copies of Greek gods, a bas-relief of George II himself, and, from the center temple, a two-hundred-foot column crowned with a sunburst, in the middle of which were inscribed the words Vivat Rex. The Duke of Montague wished it to be known that, where his fealty to the king was concerned, he had no scruples, esthetic or otherwise.

A rehearsal of Handel's *Music for the Royal Fireworks*—sans fireworks—was held at Vauxhall Gardens across the Thames in mid-April, 1749, and was attended by the Duke of Cumberland, hero of Culloden, for the purpose of ascertaining that the music was martial enough for his father the king's tastes. The rehearsal attracted some twelve thousand paying subscribers, causing a three-hour traffic jam of carriages on London Bridge and a number of fights among footmen competing for their employers' rights-of-way. A week later, on the unseasonably warm and humid evening of the 27th, the king attended the official celebration in Green Park. He, his son the Duke of Cumberland, and other notables, toured the pavilion, then retired to the nearby Queen's Library to hear the music and observe the display. One hundred and one brass cannon were scheduled to be fired in salute to His Majesty, a sound more to his liking, perhaps, than was the overture. In a lamp-lit cordoned area facing the pavilion, lords, ladies, viscounts, and important commoners sat uncomfortably in the stifling air under special shelters to audit the event. The ladies fluttered their fans, the lords scratched their itchy hose. In the park itself, beyond the flower-bedecked railings and a cordon of grenadiers that secured the pavilion, milled many thousands more spectators.

Chapter 1: The Brass Top

I N THE PARK, BENEATH AN OAK TREE, STOOD SEVERAL GOVERNESSES AND their charges, children either too young to appreciate the select gathering at the pavilion, or too much of a care for parents distracted by the scintillating company gathered in it. With them were manservants of other families, assigned the duty of guarding the women and children from footpads and other criminals. Near the tree an altercation occurred between two of the boys, ages six and eight, just as the orchestra began to play Handel's overture. The cause of the dispute was a top belonging to the younger of the boys, Hugh Kenrick, son of Garnet Kenrick and nephew of Basil Kenrick, the Earl of Danvers. It was coveted by the older boy, John Hamlyn, son of a Sussex baron and nephew of an important man who was a member of the king's Privy Council.

It was a brass top, a beautiful, lustrous solid thing that hummed and that was powered by a finely made silk cord with a special brass grip on the end. Hugh's father had bought it for him the day before in a Strand shop at his excited urging, once he espied it among all the other possibilities. Hugh Kenrick did not so much play with it as study it. He spun it over and over again and peered at it as it whirled and hummed, trying to imagine what physical properties it had and what forces were at work that caused it to sit on one end and spin so long, much longer and much more smoothly than did any of the wooden tops he had in his room at home. The hum, he had concluded, was caused by little notches artfully carved on the flat top of the tapered disk, and he had deduced that his role in its spinning ended when the cord disengaged and left the tiny hole in the shaft, leaving the thing to turn by its own rules. He had mastered the art of launching it so that it spun on exactly the point he had set it on, instead of traveling across the floor and bumping haphazardly into things. He had also established the policy of stopping the top when it began to wobble dramatically, so that it would not topple to an ignominious end and scratch its surface. He had even turned it over and launched it upside-down so that it spun on the knob on the end of the shaft, but this was more difficult to do and it did not spin so perfectly, and so he had concluded that the weight and shape of the top governed how well it performed. It was a small thing which barely fit into the palm of his hand, and the smallest of the things he owned, but it fascinated him as nothing else ever had. He loved it and respected it.

Hugh had arrived at the park in the company of his governess and his father's valet hours ago and joined the governesses, children, and manservants of other families. With them, also, was his mother's wet nurse, who carried his one-year-old sister, Alice, wrapped in swaddling clothes, in a woven basket. After a while he tired of watching the endless throngs of spectators pass by the tree. He tried climbing the tree for a better view of the pavilion, but was prevented from doing so by Bridget, his governess, who was worried that he would spoil his blue suit or ruin his immaculate white wig by getting it tangled in branches, damages for which she would be held accountable. He watched the other children play games—Blind Man's Bluff and Hot Cockles—but was not interested in joining them. Eventually he knelt in the grass not far away, took the top from his frock pocket, and launched it on a flat stone. Bridget was grateful that he could amuse himself, for now she could both keep an eye on him and trade gossip with the other governesses about their employers. Owen, the valet, had joined the manservants on the other side of the tree for a game of dice.

John Hamlyn did not join the other children, either, and they were glad of it, for he was a notorious fun spoiler who either threw tantrums if he did not win a game or bullied them into changing the rules so that he would. He was a thin, sickly-looking boy with a face scarred by a bout with smallpox. He sulked and roamed about the grass, undecided about whether to listen to the women's gossip or to watch the men play dice, approving of neither diversion and resolving to report both to his parents. But he felt restless chiefly because he envied Hugh Kenrick. The other boy seemed not to need the other children, either, but for a reason he sensed was different from his own. And the other boy had something he did not so much wish to have for himself, as to take for the pure pleasure of challenging his right to it. After all, he was someday to be a baron—his parents never tired of reminding him of that—and this was a future baron's prerogative.

Hugh Kenrick was oblivious to everything around him. It was only when the distant orchestra pronounced the first slow, regal notes of the overture that he became aware of someone standing near him. He looked up and saw John Hamlyn.

"I want it," said the older boy, pointing down at the top.

Hugh Kenrick frowned in disdain, shook his head, and glanced back at his spinning top. Only his father or his uncle had a right to speak so arrogantly to him.

"I want it," repeated John Hamlyn with finality.

To Hugh Kenrick's amazement a bony hand reached down and grasped the top.

Hugh Kenrick rose and faced the barbarian. "You shall not have it. It's mine."

"It's mine now," replied John Hamlyn. "My uncle will speak to the king about it, and then it will be mine."

From Hugh Kenrick's perspective, this reply had no bearing on the matter. "Give it back," he said quietly, "or I will thrash you."

"If you touch me, my footman over there will hang you from that tree, and your father will be forced to pay damages." John Hamlyn added with a smirk, "And I will still have this top."

"So be it!" replied Hugh Kenrick, who kicked one of the boy's shins, then smacked the surprised face with a fist, and then dove onto him, knocking him down. In a wink he was astride the boy's chest, pounding the scarred face repeatedly, shouting "Let it go! Let it go!"

He snatched the top from his bawling enemy's hand just before his valet and the other boy's footman pulled them apart at the panicked urging of the governesses. "That's no way for gentlemen to behave," berated Bridget, "especially when His Majesty invited us all here to mark the peace! Peace! What am I to tell the master? Look at you!"

Hugh Kenrick dusted off his suit and readjusted his wig. "Gentlemen don't steal from other gentlemen!" he replied.

"I didn't steal your damned top!" shouted John Hamlyn. "I *took* it!"

"Men are hanged for stealing less value, John Hamlyn," replied Hugh Kenrick, "even barons-to-be. Whether or not I saw you take it, it was still theft!"

This sophisticated rejoinder surprised both John Hamlyn and the adults, who had been ready to argue among themselves about which boy was at fault. But the younger boy had articulated an unanswerable moral position, and against this the adults had nothing to say.

"Keep your damned top!" shouted John Hamlyn, wresting himself from his footman's grip. "My father will get me a bigger and better one than yours!" And he stormed off. The boy's footman and governess followed, glowering at the back of their young master, whom they did not like, wondering how they were going to defend his and their conduct to his parents.

With a silent signal from Owen, the valet, Bridget rejoined the other women around the tree. Owen put a hand on Hugh Kenrick's shoulder and bent to say, "It would seem that I have the better of two possible masters. Well done, young sir. Now, let us listen to Mr. Handel's tune."

They found another, larger rock farther away, and sat to listen to the music. Before Hugh Kenrick was a quiet, vast mass of people, some of whose heads he could see in the lamplight. Far above them, atop the column, shimmered the sunburst in a circle of its own lamps.

When the overture was finished, even before the audience had time to applaud the music, the air rocked with the concussion of the royal salute as one hundred and one cannon were fired, one after another, by artillery men deeper in the park. A great cloud of white smoke rose beyond the pavilion from the blank discharges. After another moment, the first rockets soared into the sky from the pavilion and burst over the crowds. The crowd gasped and noisily approved, while some children began to cry, frightened by the abrupt presence of the unnatural light. Then the great fireworks machine roared into life as conical towers, vertical suns, Roman candles, and giant pinwheels flared all at once, while more rockets whooshed high into the air and exploded in so many patterns, as though touched by some invisible power. Only a brilliant glow and part of the illuminated face of the pavilion were visible over the heads of the crowd.

It was a phenomenon Hugh Kenrick had never before seen. He stood up to watch the multicolored bursts of fire far above him as they lit up the roof of clouds that threatened the festivities. He chanced to turn around, and through a break in the trees, saw the reflection of the violence flash off the dome of St. Paul's Cathedral far down the river, and reveal even London Bridge, and the rooftops and steeples of the city. If he had been able to artic-ulate his thoughts then, he would have said to himself: What a vast city! It is a great city, where great things have been done, and where great things can and will be done. I shall live here someday, as a great man, and cele-brate all the splendid things men are capable of. *I* shall do splendid things! This is a proper place for me.

It is not important that someone so young be able to express his deepest thoughts so precisely at the moment he has them; if he clings to the thoughts, and to the feelings they cause, he will someday have the words. Hugh Kenrick did not forget the feeling. He preserved it, and later was able to express it. Nor did he think it presumptuous to think of himself matching the greatness of the city; his response to it was a smile of joyful benediction. He did not challenge it; he approved of it.

It was a night of a nation's celebration of peace. For six-year-old Hugh

Kenrick, it marked the beginning of a war, for what he saw and heard, together with what he thought and felt, ignited another series of explosions as spectacular as fireworks, and would put him at odds with most men he would encounter. For while many men would experience the same things, but would let the glow fade and the fire fizzle out, Hugh Kenrick would not. Just as the fireworks lit up the spires and domes and roofs of the city and even the clouds above it, something lit up the peaks and valleys possible within himself. He was held rapt by the sights and sounds of that night, enthralled by some inchoate vision of his own make-up, by some tantalizing vista of the landscape of a soul that could be his. These things, he would realize in time, came from within himself, not from outside. He would grow to know, founded and sanctioned by the vision he would not release, that he owed nothing to anything external in terms of what he was, could be, or was to become, that nothing outside had a claim on him, except for what he chose to swear loving allegiance to.

*   *   *

With attentive though distant courtesy, Hugh listened without comment to the conversations of his parents, his uncle and aunt the Earl and Countess, and other guests at a long table at Ranelagh Gardens as the party was served dinner that night. The talk dwelt on the peace, on the fireworks, and on the absence of Countess Walmoden from the event. It was spiced with gossip about other notables, speculation on how the Duke of Montague was to be rewarded for his ostentatious loyalty to the king, and complaints about the weather. There was also ribald amusement over the likely fate of the Chevalier Servandoni, designer of the pavilion, who was arrested for drawing his sword and verbally castigating the Comptroller of the Ordnance for his negligence; an errant rocket had started a fire that destroyed one wing of his exquisite structure.

Owen, the valet, had dutifully reported the fight between his charge and John Hamlyn to the boy's father. Garnet Kenrick spoke to his son about it in the study of the Earl's terraced house that overlooked the Thames in Westminster before they departed for dinner. "Couldn't you have shared your top with him?"

Hugh Kenrick had shaken his head. "He wanted to keep it," he said. "And I didn't want to share it with him. You bought it for me. It is mine."

"It doesn't do to go knocking down the sons of barons, Hugh. Doubtless we will receive a note from Baron Hamlyn. Your uncle will smooth things over, but it will cause him some annoyance. He does not like to be distracted by trivial matters." His father paused to sip some sherry. "However, we are fortunate in this matter. Baron Hamlyn is a particularly favorite enemy of your uncle's."

"Does it do for the sons of barons to behave like footpads?" asked Hugh.

His father scowled at him with mock seriousness, and bent a little closer to him from his armchair. "Does it do for a future earl to be so un-Christian in his thoughts and deeds?"

His father would not relent on the impropriety of his son's own behavior, but the son noticed a twinkle of pride in his eyes. This caused Hugh to wonder why his father did not express what he felt, and why propriety was of more importance to him than was proprietorship.

But he did not think of these things now as he sat quietly in the gay, boisterous company. There were hundreds of guests at other tables all around him, and in the scores of boxes that ringed the promenade, and across the crowded space a small orchestra played gentle music as loudly as it dared, so much of his table's conversation was drowned in the hubbub that rang under the great dome of Ranelagh. For all the festivity, he felt a curious emptiness, even an indifference. He was excited by something else, and did not know by what, but he was certain that it had little to do with the people and events of the day.

In an unconscious need for affirmation that something important had happened tonight, he slipped his hand into a pocket of his frock coat and felt the cool shape of the top.

Chapter 2: The Enfants Terrible

TWO DAYS AFTER THE FIREWORKS, THE KENRICKS LEFT LONDON. WHILE the Earl owned the house near the York Stairs, he disliked the city, and leased the house to men and women of rank more often than he used it himself. Home for the Kenricks was a great mansion near Danvers, in Dorset, on the south coast close to the fishing and quarry town of Swanage. It would be more correct to say that the estate was Danvers, for the little collection of houses and shops was enclosed by a manor of five thousand acres. Danvers—originally called D'Anvers—began as a settlement of Norman tradesmen and artificers, but over the centuries the nobility's growing dominions encircled it. All roads passing through the Earl's lands to Danvers could be tolled by him. The village drew its fresh water from wells on lands bought or seized by the Earl's predecessors, and so he could charge the village for water. Much of the village's sustenance was grown, bred, or fattened by cottars and free tenants on the Earl's lands, and so the Earl profited doubly. The man sent by the freeholders in the neighboring town of Onyxcombe to Parliament was always the Earl's man.

The Earl of Danvers was a power to contend with.

It had not always been so. After the Norman Conquest, an earl had little or no power; the title was honorific. Dukes had power. Marquises had power. Even lowly barons and baronets had power. In the Middle Ages earldoms proliferated as kings bestowed the status in reward for services rendered them. An earl was presented with a letters-patent, signed by the sovereign, which described the lands, privileges, obligations, and exemptions attached to the title. An earl acquired power by purchasing it from those who wielded it, or by performing some urgent service which left the beneficiary indebted to him.

If Hugh Kenrick was unruly, his ancestors were cravenly duplicitous. An early Kenrick, then a minor Welsh-Saxon nobleman and former vassal of King Harold, recently slain at the Battle of Hastings, was awarded a baronetcy for helping the Normans subdue other Saxons, which necessitated laying waste to villages that did not swear submission to William the Conqueror. There were many such villages in Dornsetta, and Kenrick so thoroughly erased their names from memory that they did not occur in the exhaustive Domesday Book, compiled by William's army of roving commissioners to record every taxable entity in the country. He was crueler than even the Normans, for he could live only if no other Saxons were left who had the courage to challenge his treason, and this added a ferocity to his scourge. For the Normans, he exacted tribute from the dependable survivors—the meek, the humble, and the dutiful—and for himself and his descendants, the unquestioning obedience of the yeomen and serfs. For two centuries, no commoner in Danvers dared christen his son Harold.

The baronetcy was inheritable. The first Kenrick's heirs languished for centuries in complacent obscurity until the Wars of the Roses in the fifteenth century demanded public commitment. In this thirty-year struggle between the houses of York and Lancaster for the throne of England, Baron Kenrick and his son swore allegiance to whichever side seemed on the verge of winning. The Kenricks rode as men-at-arms with the Yorkist knights at Blore Heath, and together slew six royalist knights. When Yorkist morale collapsed at the Teme River and men began deserting, under cover of darkness the Kenricks went over to Henry VI and the Lancasterians, and had the white rose on their banner dyed red. At Mortimer's Cross, the Kenricks again threw their lot in with the seemingly unbeatable Yorkists. At dinner one evening, another baron suggested to his colleagues that the Kenricks should replace the white rose on their banner with an impaled chameleon. The baron was found dead in his tent the next morning, his throat cut. Baron Kenrick himself died soon afterward on the Aire River at the battle of Ferrybridge. His son assumed the title.

In the end, Richard III, because of his audacity and ruthlessness, won the allegiance of the new Baron Kenrick and his one hundred foot soldiers, but then lost them when Kenrick, riding with the Earl of Northumberland and other nobles at Bosworth Field, also elected to stand neutral when their king was betrayed by the Stanley brothers and overwhelmed by Henry Tudor's forces. It became a family fable that young Baron Kenrick found the slain Richard's crown in a bush on the battlefield, though the witnesses he claimed could attest to this fillet of glory were all fortuitously dead.

The Kenricks' fortunes rose and fell over a century, until another Baron Kenrick, an impoverished country gentleman and hanger-on at the court of James I, and whose lands and manor were more a burden than an asset, oiled his way into the conspiracy of Lords Cobham and Gray to dethrone the king in favor of Arabella Stuart. He then joined the ranks of others who "confessed" the plot to James. He was rewarded with the

earldom of Danvers. The earldom was created from the dissolution of two
rival Dorset baronetcies, whose title holders were also implicated in the
plot but permitted to live in exchange of a payment to James of one hundred gold Dutch guilders each. He enjoyed the title for six months, then one
winter day died. The letters-patent signed by James allowed a male issue to
inherit the title. His son, the new Earl of Danvers, was attacked by the dis-
enfranchised barons, who were defeated in a skirmish. The young earl
killed one baron and had the other beheaded by royal decree. After all, the
Kenricks had been awarded Danvers by the king himself, and it was a capital offense to oppose the sovereign's will.

A later Kenrick took no sides in the Civil War, nor for the duration of
the Commonwealth and Protectorate, but gave succor to whichever side,
Royalist or Roundhead, happened to encamp on his estate. His only active
role was to give information to a Roundhead officer about the location and
strength of a local unit of the Dorset Clubmen, a militia formed to deter
depredations committed by both sides. This information led to the annihi-
lation of the unit by a company of Cromwell's New Model Army. His suspected sympathies were with Charles II, but the Earl vehemently denied
that the king had hidden in Danvers at any time during his six-week flight
to the continent.

A grandson of the first Earl, Baron and heir apparent Kenrick, rode
with the Duke of Monmouth, nephew of James II, in 1679 and helped to
defeat the Scottish Covenanters at Bothwell Bridge. Six years later, as Earl,
he helped to rout Monmouth, now a protégé of the late Earl of Shaftesbury
and John Locke, at Sedgemoor. The king ordered his nephew beheaded, and
Kenrick gave evidence of the rebels' treachery at the Bloody Assizes, which
hanged over two hundred men and sent some eight hundred to Barbados to
die in servitude. Many of these men had rallied to Monmouth's cause when
the Duke landed at Lyme Regis, in Dorset, and Kenrick had once quaffed
port with them and called them friends. Kenrick was rewarded for his
fealty with a writ of perpetuity for his earldom and a majority interest in a
rechartered merchant company formerly owned by one of the executed
rebels.

The Earl of Danvers labored, as many others did, to persuade philosopher John Locke to come out of exile in Holland and receive the king's
pardon for his role in the rebellion and for his critical remarks on the character and purposes of James II. If Locke could be lured back to English
shores, the king's gratitude would have been boundless, whether or not he

actually intended to pardon the man. His return would have sanctified James's tyrannical actions and indirectly acknowledged the Stuart's right to sit on the throne and assume all the absolutist powers he wished to have. But the Earl of Danvers had no better success than had his competitors. His messengers at first could not locate the elusive thinker, but when one did, the man returned to Danvers with a sealed envelope containing a courteous note to the Earl. In it Mr. Locke said that he did not think he had done anything he needed to be pardoned for, and that the Earl's generous offer of intercession on his behalf was therefore moot.

The stature of the man who could write such a note was beyond the Earl's ken. He recognized only the slight, the absence of gratitude, and a lost opportunity. From that day on, the Kenricks remained resolutely monarchist, obsessively anti-republican, and only barely tolerant of Whigs.

When James II abdicated the throne under pressure from the Whigs and his nephew William (Prince of Orange and husband of Mary, James's daughter), the Earl of Danvers lobbied vigorously among the lords and members of the London Convention—there was no sitting Parliament, as there was no king to call one—to have William's sovereignty legitimized. For this work, Kenrick was appointed to the Board of Trade, and made a lieutenant surveyor of the Cinque Ports.

Clearly, it had been established as a Kenrick family tradition not to risk death, banishment, or insecurity for anything so insubstantial as a belief or a principle.

"Mine has been an unscrupulous family," remarked eight-year-old Hugh Kenrick to his tutor, who had been assigned the task of teaching the boy his family's history. The tutor frowned; nothing in his dry recitation of the chronicle could have been interpreted as judgmental. "You may say that, sir," he said. "I may not." He paused. "What causes you to reach such an...opinion?"

"My uncle often gets drunk at dinner and talks. And I hear things. And I don't like the men I see in the portraits in the hallways. You provided me with information. I formed an opinion of it."

"I see," said the tutor. "Well, I would advise you not to communicate that opinion to the Earl."

"I shall restore the family's honor," said the boy thoughtfully. "No. I shall introduce it to the family, for the first time."

"Your father is an honorable man," broached the tutor, hoping that he was not inferring that the boy's uncle was in any way dishonorable.

"Yes," answered Hugh Kenrick tentatively. "Perhaps he is."

The boy seemed to be reserving an opinion on his father. Still, the tutor decided to drop the subject and move on to the boy's arithmetic lessons. This kind of talk had a way of reaching the wrong ears, and he could not afford the risk of offending the Earl.

The Earl's mansion was a great house of granite, roughly shaped in the form of an H, and sat in the middle of ten acres of landscaped grounds. The Earl and Countess and their retainers occupied the eastern half of the H, and his brother and family the western. The segment connecting the two parts contained the offices, libraries, and studies of the brothers. The facade of the eastern length was the front of the mansion, serviced by an immaculately kept cobblestone road a mile in length, flanked by Italian cypresses, which ended in an oval courtyard decorated with a fountain and copies of Roman statues.

The Kenrick brothers were born at Danvers, the Earl three years before his brother, Garnet. Garnet Kenrick was nominally a baron, but neither used nor advertised the title. They did not resemble each other in the least; local gossip had it that they did not share the same father, for while the previous Earl was a bookish man and a model husband—an anomaly in the Kenrick tradition—his wife indulged her fancies for dashing young officers and the vigorous sons of neighboring nobility. The Earl bridled at the notion that his mother was anything but noble and virtuous, and had whipped and banished from Danvers any servant caught repeating the rumor. He had not liked his parents, but that was another issue.

Against his will, the annoying canker of a suspicion sat in the back of his mind that perhaps there was some truth in the forbidden gossip. It was inflamed by boyhood memories of the odd, surreptitious behavior of his fair mother and her gentlemen visitors, especially when his father was away on business or had locked himself in his library to write another tract. If it was in the least true, then it was entirely true, and either he had no legal claim to the title, and his brother had, or his brother had no claim to his, which would leave the earl without a successor. Or, much worse, neither of them had a claim to any title at all. The letters-patent signed by James I specified that, in the event there was no male issue to assume the title and take possession of Danvers, the reigning sovereign had the right to appoint a new earl. The specter of strangers dispossessing the Kenricks haunted Basil Kenrick's mind and mocked his sense of permanence and posterity. But that was only when melancholy affected his thinking; he allowed himself

no further thought on this subject beyond these simple but terrifying syllo-
gisms.

Garnet Kenrick also harbored the same suspicions, but did not permit
them to fester in his mind. It was one of the few subjects he and his brother
did not discuss; it was a gentlemen's understanding not to be named. There
had been no instances of attempted blackmail. He knew that their father
had had to purchase the silence that surrounded a handful of his and Basil's
youthful indiscretions, but there was otherwise no potential for scandal.

The Danvers servants, among themselves, discreetly referred to the
brothers as "Lord Fox" and "Baron Box." The Earl was tall and thin almost
to the point of emaciation, and had a saturnine face that no one ever
expected to see smile. He moved quietly, like a ghost, down his mansion's
halls and through his garden paths, and had the unnerving habit of
speaking before anyone knew he was present. Garnet Kenrick was also tall,
but moved with a robust energy and a sense of purpose. His face was hard,
broad, and angular. He smiled with an unaffected benevolence uncommon
among the nobility then. He could share a joke with the servants, on occasion solicited their views on practical matters, and generally treated the
Earl's staff with a respectful humanity that granted them some dignity; a
notion utterly alien to his brother's sensibilities.

While Basil Kenrick was an earl, and had a keen, aggressive interest in
preserving and extending the influence of his rank, he had not much bothered to develop the faculty for the task. A nobleman, he had been taught,
could not be expected to demean himself with the physical and mental
labor required to maintain his rank. "We *wear* swords and finery, young
Basil," his father had once told him. "It is not within the definition of a
gentleman or a lord to soil his hands or his soul in the *making* of these or
any other things." This attitude did not apply to the writing of books.
Basil's father authored many tracts on such subjects as *The Necessity and
Superiority of Nobility*, *The Clergy's Duties as the Sovereign's Spiritual
Watchmen and Criers*, and *The Planning and Pleasure of Private Parks in a
Search for Eden, with Epistles and Analogies on the Flora of the Christian
Soul*. The vicar of St. Quarrell's, the parish church, borrowed liberally from
the Earl's many published tracts for his services. For this flattery, the parish
of Danvers was richly endowed by the family. It is no mean compliment to
have one's scrivenings treated on a par with Scripture. Basil Kenrick
viewed his father's authorship of the tracts on his study shelves with
respectful, sometimes fearful awe, superstitiously believing that the old

Earl had been bequeathed with a gift of moral knowledge quite beyond his own ken.

The death of his wife from pneumonia affected the old Earl in a strange way. It was as though her passing dissolved his self-imposed bonds of mature respectability, and he was seized by all the vices he had once inveighed against. He abruptly abandoned his dilettantish excursions into theology and moral philosophy and became as profligate and promiscuous as the late Countess. He gambled away enormous sums at the gaming tables and in the cock-fight dens in London. He became a regular patron of the *Folly*, a floating brothel on the Thames, and once bought each of its whores a new broadcloth gown, a pair of silver slippers, and a Dutch watch. He was rarely seen entering his once precious library, except on ill-concealed trysts with a servant girl or one of the more notorious local baronesses. He began to drink the wine cellar dry, and to eat more at one meal than a servant did in a week. His doctor could only attribute his embarrassing behavior to a "choleric imbalance of mental fluids caused by grief for the late Countess." He followed his wife into the family burial vault in St. Quarrell's church a mere three years later, having died under scandalous circumstances in a Weymouth inn. His carefree mode of living brought the family to the brink of financial ruin.

Basil Kenrick left the task of sustaining Danvers to his brother, who did not share their father's once-chaste sense of aristocracy. Garnet Kenrick wished he had been able to lead a life independent of his older brother. But he gravitated to a career in commerce, chiefly because, on their father's death, he was the only one capable of sorting out the financial shambles left behind. It was not a chosen career, but it consumed his time and immediate interest, and so it became his career. His late grandfather's connections on the Board of Trade, and the still thriving merchant company from his great-grandfather's day, gave him an edge and allowed him to compensate for his brother's occasional extravagances. He managed the Earl's business from Danvers and traveled frequently between there and the family company's offices in Poole, Weymouth, Bristol, and London.

The Earl left his brother alone in business matters, but harbored a secret envy of him for being able to master them, coupled with a peevish condescension. He resented the special, peer-like relationship Garnet granted to his business associates and even sea captains. Garnet Kenrick did not think himself indefinably superior to anyone.

The Earl had another reason to distance himself from his brother:

Garnet and his wife had children, while he had none. He and his wife, the Countess, almost had one—who would have been heir to the title—but the child was stillborn, and the Countess could produce no more. This was a closely kept secret. Further, Effney, his brother's wife, mother of a son and a daughter, was a gracious, amiable woman who also lacked airs and whose handsomeness would endure well past her child-bearing years. The Earl's wife, on the other hand, had allowed herself to grow fat, shrewish, and tyrannical. The Earl was bitterly aware of his wife's shortcomings, but she was the Countess of Danvers, and he would brook no insolence from anyone about her.

Once, at a ball he had thrown years ago, he overheard a young squire say to his companion, "The Lady Danvers, I know, is a painfully virtuous woman—virtuous, I dare say, from fear. She wouldn't think of risking a son not of the Earl's passion." The companion had answered, "I own that this must be true, friend, but, you must credit it, her virtue is greatly assisted by her ungainly visage." The Earl, surprising them in the midst of their laughter, had taken a cane to both men and beaten them bloody in front of the throng of horrified guests, and then had his servants toss them outside and down the mansion's broad stone steps.

Garnet Kenrick could not say that he hated his brother, or merely disliked him. Their frequent consultations on family and business matters were informal and cordial. No love grew between the siblings, and none was lost. Each regarded the other more as a family intimate than as a brother. The only evidence of a close link between them was that they addressed each other by first name. And the only personal feelings they would tactfully reveal to each other was that Garnet thought his brother overbearing and baselessly arrogant; Basil thought his brother *déclassé*, if not outright plebeian. "My dear Basil, had you the mind of Newton, and the physique of Ganymede, perhaps we should see the world running to you, instead of you after it." "My dear Garnet, it does not do to behave as though you preferred to be familiar with the coachman's daughter, rather than with those of your own station." This was the limit the brothers would permit their curious, mutual acrimony to go.

Basil Kenrick held the upper hand. He had power. His man in the Commons voted for every protective, mercantilist measure that came up for debate on the floor. The Earl himself was a peer, and journeyed to London, when it suited him, to sit at sessions of Lords.

There was, however, one matter in which the brothers were in full agreement. The Baron saw to it that the family's coffers were filled with the profits of smuggling into the country the very things the Earl voted to ensure were heavily taxed.

Many smuggling gangs offered shares in their enterprises, which were bought anonymously by aristocrats and gentry along the south coast of England, from Land's End to Ramsgate. Garnet had seen to it that the Earl owned shares in half the principal gangs in each coastal county, except Dorset, where the Earl controlled one of the biggest gangs. This gang was known as the Lobster Pots for its practice of landing, hiding, and transporting illegal goods in lobster pots deposited near the shore by Dutch, English, and French partners. The chief of the Lobster Pots, once a fisherman, owned a great house and twenty acres near Lulworth Cove, the gang's main point of operation. The Earl had never met him and refused to meet him; the task of negotiating with commoners was left to his brother and his intermediaries.

When the Skelly gang in Cornwall was crushed and its leader hanged in Falmouth, Garnet Kenrick tied a black satin ribbon around the neck of an Italian bronze statue of Hermes that loomed from a corner of his vast study desk. The Skelly gang had repeatedly rejected his careful overtures of partnership in the gang, and shown no interest in the capital he could have provided to expand their scope of activities. Still, he had admired the gang and its leader, and was sorry to see them vanish.

The ribbon remained, after almost two years. The Baron was reluctant to remove it, for he had read many newspaper accounts of what was said and done at both Marvel and the trial in Falmouth. Something unusual had happened in these places, something significant, and he felt that if he removed the ribbon, the incidents would vanish into the anonymity of his mundane affairs, and he would never know what was special about them.

When Basil Kenrick entered his brother's study one evening, he cocked an eyebrow on sight of the black ribbon, and asked in challenging jest, "What means this eternal mourning, dear brother? Did Hermes fail to persuade Prometheus to coax Athena from Zeus's head?" He took pleasure in needling his brother for what he considered over-sentimentality.

"No, dear brother," answered Garnet. "A son of Hermes failed to coax reason from the skulls of cretins. He was extinguished by them and, like Prometheus, chained to a rock."

Hermes was the Greek god of commerce, invention, cunning, and theft. The brothers, who had both excelled in classics at Eton, had years ago fallen into the habit of discussing the Skelly gang and related matters in these allusive terms, and Garnet, on an inspired whim, removed the statue from the dining hall and placed it in his study, "So that he might bless all the unimpeachable and crafty things done here in his name," he had explained then.

The Earl sniffed. "Prometheus was alive when he was chained. This son of Hermes is tarred and very dead."

"Still, someone's liver is being eaten."

"Well, thank God for that, nevertheless. You will remember that some of the things said by these brigands at their trial were unsettling. Treasonable!"

"Revolutionary," remarked the Baron.

"*Leveling*," added the Earl with rancor. "This son of Hermes was shown mortal justice!"

"But someday, I fear, Hermes himself will make an appeal to his friend Apollo, and then we shall know Olympian justice."

"What do you mean?"

"That only the gods are immortal." Garnet studied his brother for a moment. "Suppose they all went to the colonies—these sons and daughters of Hermes—and one day refused to deal with us mortals?"

"We should teach them an awful lesson," scoffed the Earl.

Garnet shook his head. "One does not teach gods or their offspring lessons, dear brother."

Chapter 3: The Rebel

EIGHT-YEAR-OLD HUGH SAT IN SHADOW NEAR HIS FATHER'S DESK, listening intently to their cryptic exchange, but understanding little of it. He recognized the names from his tutor's classics instruction, but could not grasp how his father and uncle were using them. His uncle had nodded curtly to him when he came in, then ignored him.

Hugh had been summoned here to receive advice from his father on how to best conduct himself at Eton College, where he was to be sent in a few days on the stern recommendation of the vicar of St. Quarrell's.

"He's a bright lad," the vicar had said to his parents a week ago during an unexpected call, "but he needs the tonic of society of boys his own age. He is too, well, *imperial* for his own and others' good. I cannot help but imagine that he leads a somewhat solitary life here, in his home, and I believe that this has had an unfortunate effect on his moral character." The vicar paused to sip some of the sherry he had been offered, and continued his nervous pacing before the seated parents. "True, the masters of the College would better be able to impart the knowledge and mental exercise his keen mind needs and yearns for—better than a single tutor. At the same time, the rigors and demands of school life may work as an *aqua regia* on a peculiar, unattractive aspect of his character."

"What aspect?" Hugh's mother had asked.

"I would say rebelliousness, but then, every boy has that in him. This particular aspect defies category. I know only that if it is not restrained, it will bring him and you both a quantum of pain and unhappiness. A turn— perhaps even a career—at Eton may spare everyone concerned the nurturing of, well…an *incubus*."

The Baroness had gasped. Garnet Kenrick had risen from his chair. "*Incubus*? That's a drastic term, Vicar," he said with unusual sharpness. "You are speaking of our son!"

"Indeed, I am," replied the vicar with airy confidence. "It is the nearest thing I can think of." Then he had lowered his voice and in menacing, embittered sympathy said, "Last Saturday, I saw him outside the vicarage, before he was to report to the curate for his Scriptures lesson, on his hands and knees on the church lawn, inviting a *hare* to eat some clover he had in his hand. The hare came and ate it, and he let it go off without trying to kill it, as other boys would have tried. As *he* should have tried." He turned his back on his listeners. "Subsequently, he could not recite the Thirty-nine Articles of our Church, as he had been able to just the week before."

This was ominous news to the otherwise sane and practical parents, for in Dorset, hares were regarded as transformed witches.

The vicar need not have said more. Still fresh in all their minds were the incidents, only days apart six months ago, involving two village children. One, the son of a cobbler, had cornered a hare and was bitten by it. He had gone mad, and after a terrifying sickness, died. Another, the daughter of a seamstress, had tried to cage an injured hare for a pet, and had also been bitten. She had gone mad, too, but did not die. Instead, she lost the power of speech and the ability to control her facial expressions. The magistrate of Danvers had forbidden her to appear in public, except in the company of her mother, and then only on a leash and wearing a hood.

Obviously something inside their son enabled him to be friendly with the dreaded hare. And so, embarrassed by lending the superstition any credence, but convinced of the esteemed vicar's reasoning and concern, the Kenricks agreed that a turn at Eton might do the boy some good.

Hugh knew nothing about the conversation. He knew nothing about Eton, except that it was a school far away, and that his tutor, Mr. Hales, spoke almost enviously of the time he would spend there.

"Why *is* he here?" asked the Earl now, indicating Hugh.

"He is going to the College next week," explained the father. "He needs instruction on how to best deal with his instructors and fellow pupils."

The Earl turned and wagged a finger at Hugh. "Mind your masters and get along with the other boys, except if they are sons of gentry. Those you may cuff. But I want no more business like the Hamlyn boy. Is that understood?"

"Yes, Uncle."

The Earl promptly forgot Hugh. "Now, what is this about a schooner?" he asked his brother. "Why do you need to see me about it?"

"The *Ariadne* is for sale. She is in dry-dock in Weymouth. She was impounded by the Revenue some time ago and her captain and most of her crew tried for smuggling. She was sold to another captain, who took her to Boston. On her way back she was badly mauled by a Spanish pirate, but she got away and limped home without further incident. The captain does not wish to spend more time or money repairing or refitting her. His cargo was mostly orange trees from the Floridas, and half of these either perished in the fight or died from attrition. He is short of funds." Garnet Kenrick smiled. "She can be had for a mere eight hundred guineas."

"What would we want with a schooner?"

Garnet placed a sheaf of papers in front of his brother. "Talbot thinks, and I concur, that we should have our own conveyance, now that the war is over. He has been urging me for some time to secure a merchantman of modest size." Otis Talbot was the family's commercial agent in Philadelphia.

"The *Ariadne*?" interjected Hugh.

Garnet turned to his son. The Earl frowned. "Yes, Hugh. That is the schooner's name."

Hugh beamed. "Ariadne was the daughter of King Minos, a son of Zeus and Europa, and of Pasiphaë, a daughter of Helios and Persë. Ariadne gave Theseus a sword with which to slay her father's Minotaur and a length of thread with which to find his way out of the beast's labyrinth. Then she left Minos with him."

Garnet Kenrick chuckled. "And what happened then, my proud cygnet?" he asked with affection.

"Theseus deserted her on Naxos, but she married Bacchus." Hugh turned and addressed his uncle. "Prometheus did not coax Athena from Zeus's head, sir. He cleaved it with an ax, and then she sprang from it. He was not a coaxing kind of hero, and she was too wise to be persuaded of the benefits of such a birth. She already knew them."

"Anan?" replied the Earl. This flagrant contradiction of his words added another particle of dislike of the boy. But he stretched his lips in what most men would not recognize as a smile, but which was one nevertheless. "You will do well at Eton, if you can correct me. But the next time you hear me fiddle with myth, be gracious enough to allow me my amusement. Is *that* understood?"

"Yes, sir."

The Earl turned in his chair and addressed his brother again. "Now that my privilege has been *cleaved* by this young Titan of yours, dear brother—have you taken into account that we should have to pay a crew?"

"Of course. However, we would be more than compensated by the erasure of many of the extraordinary arrangements we now need to make with other merchantmen, not to mention by the commensurate degree of independence we should gain. The schooner can be repaired, refitted, and crewed in three months. I have inspected her. She does not need careening, and she is eminently seaworthy. Full cargoes both ways in two years would cover the initial outlay of her purchase and refitting. That is a modest outcome. Extraordinary cargoes should halve that time. I know of two or three captains for hire, presently idle but known to be amenable to our kind of business."

This conversation lasted for another half hour. Hugh Kenrick had been present during many such meetings between his father and uncle, as a silent observer, and learned much about commerce and the family business. He listened with the same fascination that he experienced when he read the legends of the Greeks and Romans.

*   *   *

When the Earl was gone, Garnet Kenrick gave his son his advice. The Baron was innovative in business, but his inventiveness did not extend to questioning the received wisdom of his time. Thus, his advice was a litany of contradictory maxims, adages, and homilies.

"Above all," he concluded, "submit to the spirit of compatriotism among your peers. If they are gentle, be gentle with them. If they are cruel, be cruel, for if you exhibit the least amount of reluctance to resort to cruelty, it will be turned against you. I made that mistake myself, you see. Fashions in manners and sentiments change, but all aim to mould the proper comportment of a gentleman. You must learn that you are not alone—did not Mr. Donne write so wisely that 'no man is an island'?—and the best way of assuming the dignity of nobility is to learn early in what I hope will be your long life that you must defer your person and your desires to the sanctity of your present and future station. You *will* be the Earl of Danvers, someday. Observe the posture and actions of your peers and superiors, and emulate them to the best of your wits. Keep in mind that your instructors and masters at the College are not quite gentlemen, but that they have knowledge to impart to their charges, so do not tease them with inordinate curiosity, and do not bait them, as you will see other students will be wont to do. They are the only commoners in the kingdom who may with impunity birch a knight." The Baron studied his attentive son. "You have a quick mind, Hugh, and it would be easy for you to commit that venial sin."

The Baron paused again. He could not be sure that anything he was saying was finding a niche in his son's mind. "Err…Vicar Wynne informs us that on Saturday last you were not able to recite the abbreviated Articles. Yet today, you are able to regale your uncle and me with a portion of a complex pagan legend. Can you explain this, Hugh?"

The boy frowned. "I remember the legends better, Father, because they are more interesting than are the Articles."

The Baron was willing to concede this. Had he not, when he was his son's age, reveled in the adventures and epics of gods and mortals, and lost himself in the worlds of *The Iliad* and *The Odyssey*? The mighty struggles, the alliances and betrayals, the exotic lands! But he could not confess this to his son. "The gods and the Titans were lawless, Hugh. Humility and generosity could not be observed in a single one of them, good or bad."

Hugh Kenrick's face brightened. "That is because they were not Christians, father. They could not have tolerated the saints of our church. The gods and the Titans fought for possession of the earth, while the saints forsook it. How could the meek and the humble inherit the earth, as Vicar Wynne claims they will, when the gods and the Titans were so powerful? They would have laughed, and evicted the saints and the humble!"

The Baron raised his eyebrows in alarm. Here was a formulation he had never heard before in any sermons, and he doubted it had ever occurred in his son's catechism. On one hand, he was intrigued; on the other, the Vicar's evaluations and warnings seemed much more ominous. "Do you approve of the saints, Hugh?"

The boy grimaced. "They are sometimes droll, but mostly dull. I know that the Romish church makes much of the saints, while ours does not. Is it because Englishmen have martyred the most illustrious of them, such as Thomas Becket and Joan of Orleans?"

The Baron laughed involuntarily. "No," he said, "that is not the reason—or, at least, not the whole reason. I am not an authority on the subject of our church's history, and I would not think it wise to ever put that question to Vicar Wynne. I may assure you, however, that the schism between ourselves and the Papists had little to do with an embarrassment of such riches."

Hugh Kenrick laughed at the jest. The Baron merely smiled. He felt a compulsion to hug his son, to laugh with him, and to encourage through these actions the spirit he was beginning to see emerge in the boy. There was something right about that spirit. After he dismissed his son, he thought, also, that there was something dangerous in it.

Children tend to explode, when set free of their parents or tutors, especially when their parents' or tutors' notions of character building consists of pounding into their charges' heads a plethora of undifferentiated maxims, adages, rules, and moral concoctions that had little or no relation to the world as observed by children. Hugh Kenrick's difficulty lay in this phenomenon, also, though what was pounded into his head was, more often than not, ejected with a violence that frightened his wardens. If something did not make sense to him, he questioned it relentlessly, and if no sensible or credible answer to it was given, he dismissed it.

Hugh Kenrick was spoiled. He had six pairs of shoes, all with silver buckles. He had riding boots to wear when he exercised his pony. He had several suits of clothes of the best cut; fine shirts and lace cravats; more toys in his room than possessed by all the middle-class children in Swanage and Danvers combined; three meals a day, none of which he ever finished; a succession of governesses and tutors before he was sent to Eton. He had a sumptuous allowance of ten guineas a year, to spend as he pleased. He had books, or rather his father and uncle had books, and if books were missing from his elders' libraries, they could usually be found in Hugh's room.

Therefore, Garnet Kenrick could not say that he was completely surprised when, a week after delivering his son to the College of Eton, he received an urgent letter from the headmaster requesting that he remove his son at his earliest convenience. Hugh Kenrick had seared the hands of a senior boy with a red-hot poker when the older boy attempted to make him his fag. The Earl was scandalized, for the injured boy was the son of the Marquis of Bilbury, a political ally in the House of Lords and sometime guest and companion when the Earl spent time in London.

Some days after his return, Hugh's parents escorted him into the Earl's study, and in their presence Basil Kenrick interrogated him. The Earl had been kept ignorant of Vicar Wynne's revelations and speculations about the boy's behavior. To him, his nephew was beginning to take after the king's oldest son, Frederick Louis, the Prince of Wales: sullen, rebellious, spiteful, and frivolous. The Prince, who was hated by his father the king, was in the Earl's eyes a witless fool who had no good reason to reciprocate his father's detestation. Hugh stood before the Earl's desk, while his parents sat to the side, almost in shadow. "Why did you do this cruel and cowardly thing, young sir?" asked the Earl.

"Because he was trying to humiliate me, sir," answered the boy.

"Were you the only boy levied in this ritual?"

"No, sir. There were three others."

"Tell me what happened."

Hugh Kenrick narrated the incident. Two days after arriving at Eton, in the dead of night he and the other new boys his age, still in their night-shirts, were roughly spirited from their cots by older boys and taken to a small wooden structure somewhere off the school grounds. There he was told by the young Marquis of Bilbury that he was releasing another boy from his obligations as a fag or servant, and that henceforth Hugh would fill that role, acting as the Marquis' valet and cook. "Your handsomeness also recommends itself to occasional, special companionship, when the village tarts are otherwise engaged," added the aristocrat, and the other older boys giggled. Hugh Kenrick did not understand the import of this last remark, but he noticed, after he had related it, his parents exchanging quick glances with his uncle, whose nostrils flared slightly in distaste, but whose expression otherwise remained stern and unmoved.

Then he had been told that as part of his initiation, he was to hold a tin bowl of hot coals from the den's fireplace while the young Marquis tickled his bare feet with a twig. If he dropped the coals, he would be punished with a birching that would leave the back of his legs raw for days. Hugh refused to pick up the bowl. When the Marquis rose and forced it into his hands, Hugh flung it at his tormentor. Angered, the Marquis approached Hugh, screaming that he would break all the fingers on his hands. Hugh picked up the fireplace poker and stabbed at the Marquis' outstretched hands, which grasped the hot end of it. The Marquis roared in an unearthly scream of agony as the metal fused his palms and fingers.

In the meantime, the glowing coals Hugh had thrown at the Marquis had fallen on some of the dilapidated cushions that littered the den floor, started a fire and a panic, and the den was consumed by flames. Hugh and the other younger boys had fled in the confusion and sought refuge in the headmaster's quarters.

When Hugh was finished, the Earl asked, "Did the other boys submit to their initiation?"

"Yes, sir."

"Could you not, like they, tolerate a spell of humiliation?"

"No, sir."

"Why not?"

"I saw no point in it, sir. I will *not* be anyone's lackey."

"It is the practice in such circumstances to submit to the wishes of senior students, sir," replied the Earl. "The sole persons exempt from such customs are the members of His Royal Highness's immediate family, who may not be touched by anyone except by waiver and leave. *You* are not of royal siring. You had no right to refuse to submit or to question the right and prerogative of any older student to impose service on you."

"The Marquis' son wished to harm my person, sir," replied Hugh. "He wished to harm my soul."

The Earl snorted. "He would not have inflicted mortal injury on you, sir. But *you* have apparently so mangled his hands that he will be denied the use of it for the rest of his life."

"*His* intention was harmful, sir," answered Hugh.

"How so?"

Hugh could not answer. He could not find words for the evil thing that seemed to govern the events in the Marquis' den.

The Earl said, "*Your* person is not so *precious* that it cannot be taught to brook a modicum of servility, sir. It is not your prerogative to set yourself or your soul apart from the concerns and standards of your fellow men. It is disturbing to me that such a basic Christian precept has not already found a permanent cranny in your conscience. It applies to all men, humble and great. And the Marquis, regardless of his intent or purpose, is one of your fellow men."

His uncle's words awakened something in Hugh's mind, and he stared at the Earl with amazement.

The Earl took the glance as a frown in the affirmative. After a long, withering scrutiny of the boy, he reached for a book on his desk and lifted it. "Take this," he ordered, and when Hugh had stepped forward and obeyed, the Earl continued. "You will read that labor of your grandfather's and write for me an essay agreeing with its thesis. This will be in addition to attending to the duties assigned you by your new tutor, whoever that may be."

Hugh glanced at the book in his hands. It was a richly bound tome, entitled *The Many Ways to Sainthood*, by Guy Kenrick, the 14th Earl of Danvers.

"That is all," said the Earl. "You may return to your room. I wish to speak to your parents."

Hugh's parents placated the Earl by denying their son the liberty of the estate for a month. The Baron agreed to pay the elder Marquis of Bilbury a sum of money in compensation. The Baron and his wife were confused by their responses: they were secretly proud of Hugh for having defied what they both regarded as a silly, brutal tradition; yet they sensed the seed of a character trait which they were certain would eventually ostracize the boy from normal human society. They wished to see the trait corrected; but they did not possess the cruelty in themselves to crush it. They would not nurture it; but neither would they starve it. Hugh, they concluded, must make his own rules and reap their rewards and penalties. Garnet Kenrick resolved never again to advise his son on what he should do, be, or believe in.

Hugh Kenrick read his grandfather's work, and composed an essay on its virtues and values. It was a dry, unconvincing essay, but it satisfied the Earl, and no more was said about the incident at Eton College.

Chapter 4: The Heart of Oak

IN MARCH OF 1751, THE PRINCE OF WALES DIED, AFTER A BRIEF ILLNESS, OF a burst abscess caused by a rebounding cricket ball.

The Earl and the Baron and Baroness were having tea over a game of faro in the orangery one early spring evening when a messenger arrived at Danvers. A servant handed the Earl a sealed envelope. He opened it, read the contents, then glanced up at his brother with a face that was expressionless but for a twinkle in his eye. "It is from Hillier," he said. "Poor Fred is dead." Crispin Hillier was Danvers' representative in the Commons. Not only was it his job to protect the Earl's interests in that house of Parliament, but to gather and relay political intelligence. The Earl rang a table bell, and the servant reappeared. "Pay the man who brought this a guinea," he said. "Put him up in the stables, and attend to his needs. I shall have a reply ready for him to take on the morrow."

The Earl leaned to support the king's oldest son, Frederick Louis, Prince of Wales and Duke of Cornwall. The Prince, he reasoned, was very likely to be the next king, or at least Regent.

Still, the Earl, on advice of his brother, had maintained a delicate neutrality between the king's two sons, the Prince of Wales and William Augustus, the Duke of Cumberland, liking neither but ready to return overtures of friendship from either, should they occur. He forbade Handel, the king's favorite composer, to be played at concerts and banquets at Danvers, requiring his hired musicians to learn the compositions of the Prince's favorite, Giovanne Buononcini, who managed Lincoln's Inn Fields Theatre in London until he was discovered to be a plagiarist and forced to leave the country in disgrace. For years, the Earl had sent the Duke a birthday present of five pounds of sweetmeats in a bentwood box adorned with military tableaux painted by the best illustrator in London; and to Augusta, the Princess of Wales, a birthday present of a silver brocaded quilt of flowers stuffed with the finest Dorset wool and swans' down.

The Prince left more turmoil in his wake than he had caused in his lifetime. Leicester House, the Prince's domicile in London, ceased to be the fulcrum of parliamentary opposition to the king, and the enmity once focused on Frederick by his parents—his mother, Caroline, had so hated him that she even refused to see him on her deathbed—gradually shifted in the widowed king to William Augustus. Cumberland, in the event of his father's death or incapacitation, could become either king or Regent. There were many in all strata of English society who feared that Cumberland would seize the reins of power from the heir-presumptive, George, son of the Prince and Princess of Wales, before the latter reached his majority, and establish a military kingship not unlike that of Frederick of Prussia's.

Cumberland was at this time Captain General of the Army, and busy reforming it. At the same time he was still living under the shadow of recrimination for his and his staff's depredations in Scotland following the quelling of the Jacobite Rebellion, and even his most obsequious sycophants and admirers had ceased proclaiming his name. The merciless and often indiscriminate execution of Highland Scots and the brutal uprooting of their clans had shocked even Englishmen, most of whom had no love for the Scots. It was said that, when the Livery Companies of London were contesting each other for the privilege of granting the Duke the status of freedman in the City (for English kings and their immediate family could not enter London except by permission of the Lord Mayor), someone caustically suggested that he be made a member of the Company of Butchers. The newspapers subsequently nicknamed him "the Butcher."

Nevertheless, the Earl and his brother the Baron knew that the Duke would be courted now by many of the men who had once flocked to Leicester House and the Prince of Wales and plotted with Frederick Louis to bedevil the king in and out of Parliament.

"Billy," remarked the Baron, "will need friends."

"He is sure to be pressed to take the lead," said the Earl.

"He might be persuaded to, but he heeds his father's every wish and whim."

"True," conceded the Earl with a sigh. "If his father ordered him to give up women and horses, he would. He has proven that he will do nothing that will antagonize *Mr. Lewis*."

"So it would need a strong man—one more persuasive than his father—to get him to move, to take the right actions, to make the right friends."

"Do you know of such a man?"

"No," said the Baron. "And I know that it is neither of us."

"He strikes me," broached the Baroness, "as a man who is content with the back bench. He would make a poor and indifferent pawn, and a worse

sovereign. His toy soldiers, horses, and dice are all he wants from his rank."
She paused to take a sip of her tea. "He has no ambition."

The Earl hummed pensively. "There are men who would act in the Duke's interests," he said. "Fox, for example."

"And men who would oppose them with equal vigor," said the Baron. "Pitt, for example."

The Baroness smiled. "Do not discount the determination of the Princess to secure the succession for her son, George."

The Earl scoffed. "I cannot seriously entertain the notion of Augusta in the role of Regent," he said. "If she is anything like her late husband, she must share his gift for tactlessness and spite, and will scotch any chance she might have."

"I must agree with you, Basil," replied the Baroness. "But you both neglect an important factor here, one which will nullify all other considerations. The Princess is a mother, and she will fight for her son. In this fight, she will wield two unsavory, frankly tactless and spiteful, but powerful weapons."

The Baron and the Earl looked at her expectantly.

The Baroness smiled again in triumph. "His Majesty's shame for his treatment of his late son—and his younger son's present unpopularity."

The Baron thought about it for a moment, then chuckled in appreciation of his wife's perspicuity. His brother, who did not as a rule ascribe intelligence to women, merely grunted in acknowledgment. "On these points," said the Baron, "it would seem that ambition is now feasible. The Duke may not be ambitious, but there will gather around him men who are. These, though, will be less skilled than the allies the Princess will very likely recruit in the Commons and Lords. The albatross of unpopularity will flit from her and alight most unceremoniously on the shoulders of the Duke and his supporters. Newcastle, I have it from reliable sources, is also leaning in Pitt's direction. It is quite clear to me now how His Majesty will weigh the matter."

"Nevertheless," replied the Earl, "it would seem the prudent thing to cultivate the Duke, gaining entrée into the Princess's beneficence, to be sure, but at the same time assuring *him* of our sentiments." He paused to stare into his tea for a moment, then put the cup and saucer down. "You will compose our condolences to the King, the Princess, *and* the Duke, will you not, Garnet? And if there is to be a largish funeral, we should of course wish to be in attendance."

"Of course, dear brother." The Baron shook his head. "But all three parties seem insensible to our sentiments, one way or another."

"True," agreed the Earl. "But insensibility is at least better than ignorance. It is of no consequence to me whether we are on any of their minds, just so long as we are on the opportune side."

There was no "largish" funeral for the Earl and his family to attend. George II, the Prince's brother the Duke, the Prince's sisters, all the bishops, and all but one Peer from Lords were conspicuously absent from the dismal, rain-soaked procession that wended its way through London's streets to Westminster Abbey. There the Prince was put in Henry VII's chapel near his mother and his illegitimate son. Everyone had been warned away from the occasion. In the Abbey, the organ played no dirges, and the choir sang no hymns. Enemies of the king rankled and bit their tongues; his friends chuckled up their sleeves.

But the Princess of Wales triumphed in the end. Pitt's influence worked; the Princess was named in the Regency Bill of 1751 to act for her son in the event of the king's death or incapacitation, while the Duke was stung with being appointed to a contingent regency council of advisors. If the Princess of Wales had become Regent, no doubt whatever advice he had to offer her would have been spurned, for she despised her "great, great fat friend" and brother-in-law. The matter being settled, the Duke, now that he had been cut out of the picture, was freed of the necessity of channeling his energies into political machinations, and refocused his attention on women, horses, gambling, and the army.

*   *   *

Children of the aristocracy were kept in the background of their parents' lives, and brought out only on extraordinary occasions. In this background, boys were taught practical, worldly subjects and what passed for wisdom; girls were trained to be useful ornaments.

Following the incident at Eton College, Hugh Kenrick's parents found what they thought was a perfect solution to their worries about their son's seeming antisociability. Not far from Danvers was the estate of Squire Drew Tallmadge, who had hired a clutch of tutors to educate not only his own sons but those of the local gentry and lesser nobility. Parents paid the tutors, and also Tallmadge for the "rental" of his house for instruction.

This option had not previously been considered, for many of the patrons of the "grammar school" were minor irritants to the Earl. Squire Tallmadge had refused to sell the copyholds of lands adjacent to the Kenricks' estate, had introduced alien agricultural practices to favorite leaseholders, and had begun to enclose his lands, allowing troublesome copyholds and leaseholds to expire, and resorting to rack-rents to discourage obstructive and unproductive tenants from staying. But Tallmadge had acquired the estate from his lord, whose family was practically extinct, who sold it to pay off debts and later disappeared in London among the growing ranks of titled bankrupts. The Tallmadge family had served this baron's family for centuries; it was at least a known, established name.

Squire Tallmadge had also wished to be elected to the Commons, but lost the election because it had been established almost as a tradition, by the 40-shilling electorate of neighboring Onyxcombe, to send Crispin Hillier, the Earl's favorite, to the Commons. There was one contest, which occurred almost a generation ago, but the Earl had never forgiven the Squire for challenging his hegemony.

The Brunes, however, were strangers altogether, new to Dorset by a single generation. Old Squire Robert Brune, still living, had won the estate in a still talked-about game of hazard from its owner, another minor baron, at the Kit-Kat Club in London. The Brunes had introduced new wool-processing mechanisms and installed them in special buildings on their estate, and built a new mill house over the narrow Onyx River, which meandered through the three estates, to grind their corn and wheat. Like the Tallmadges, the Brunes were able to buy the prestige and status of their predecessors without the encumbrance of fealty to the Earl of Danvers, which was not transferable. The Earl regretted that the law courts had not in the past ruled on this oversight.

The Brunes and the Tallmadges wished to be associated with the Earl; the Earl did not wish them to be neighbors at all. He had never visited them, and looked upon them and their novel management of their affairs with alternating disgust, petulance, and outrage. Baron Garnet Kenrick, however, out of necessity of business and sheer curiosity, had visited the families and once had even dined with them. The Earl would never himself have invited either family to his banquets or balls, except on the practical advice of the Baron, and to avoid pointless conflict. The relationship among these three families was the epitome of eighteenth-century social mores: coldly cordial, cunningly civil, and exaggeratedly gracious.

And so Hugh was driven by a footman in a dogcart to the Tallmadge house six days a week. A relay of resident tutors drilled the young baron and his classmates in Latin, Greek, French, drawing, mathematics, and rhetoric; in Greek, Roman, and modern history; in geography and navigation. "Science" was taught by Squire Tallmadge himself, for he was a committed Newtonian and an ardent agriculturist who experimented with the means of making his 500 acres of tillage more productive. At first Hugh was reluctant to attend this school, then he warmed to the idea, for the tutors were good teachers. The tutors were at first leery of their new charge, the nephew of a powerful and notoriously temperamental earl, but Hugh was a bright and eager pupil, and they in turn warmed to him.

And here at the school, Hugh did not so much make a friend of Roger Tallmadge, as he was befriended by the youngest of the Squire's sons. It was the rumor of his rebellion at Eton which drew the boy to Hugh. "Is it true that you burned a marquis's hands?" he asked breathlessly in private. He was the frequent butt of his older brothers' pranks, and the notion of fighting back appealed to him.

*   *   *

Two tragedies befell the Danvers household that same year.

The Earl's wife, the Countess, had been suffering from an ailment which one local and two London physicians had been unable to diagnose, though for which the trio unanimously prescribed a daily remedy of one part snail's broth, one part ground mistletoe, and one part camphor. After a month of imbibing the bitter potion, the Countess was found dead in her chair while sunning herself on the south lawn. The funeral, the special services at St. Quarrell's, the solemn interring of the Countess in the family vault, and the stream of visits by local nobility and townsfolk to express their sympathies all struck Hugh as empty formality. He had not liked his aunt, and was certain that no one else had either, including his parents and his uncle. Everyone, especially the servants who had had to endure her sharp, mocking tongue, seemed relieved that she was gone; and yet everyone behaved as though she had been a beloved mistress and personage whose passing deserved marking. Hugh could not generate within himself such sham piety, and went through the motions with a blank face. His parents noticed his demeanor, but said nothing; how could a ten-year-old boy understand these things? The Earl noted it, too, but was more perceptive than the boy's parents about the cause of Hugh's naive and barely disguised disdain.

Two months later, a brother to Hugh was stillborn, and Effney Kenrick nearly died in labor. The boy insisted that he be allowed to be at her bedside until she recovered. He waited on her as a servant would, amused her by playing games with his three-year-old sister, Alice, on the bedroom rug, did tricks with his brass top, and read to her poems from her favorite authors. To cheer her up, he once read humorous passages from a volume of *The Spectator*, by Addison and Steele, but stopped when he saw that her laughter cost her strength. Garnet Kenrick was present at many of these sessions, first and foremost out of concern for his wife, and then because he had never seen his son express such care for anyone. This made him happy. He was so touched by the phenomenon that he at times permitted himself to pat his son's shoulder in gratitude and camaraderie, out of sight of the Baroness.

And when she was in pain, Hugh would hold her hand. On one of these occasions, when the Baron was not present, she said to him, "I would not discourage the devotion you have shown me, Hugh. But it is more love than I have seen you demonstrate for your father and uncle. Is there a reason for it?"

Hugh smiled at her. "You are a beautiful, kind, and wise lady, Mater, and no misfortune or agony should ever darken your life. It is a personal offense to me that you should suffer." He paused. "My devotion to you is not from duty, but from affection."

The Baroness studied her son for a moment and stroked his hand. "Do you frown on duty, Hugh?"

The boy put down the book he had been reading from—a collection of poems by Thomas Gray—and thought for a moment. "It is of less value to me than is sincerity, Mater. I cannot understand its importance in the scheme of things." He paused. "I am truly sorry that you lost a son."

The Baroness smiled sadly. "Are you not sorry that you have lost a brother?"

Hugh looked perplexed, then his brow cleared. "I did not know him at all, Mater," he replied, "and so he cannot be so much of a loss. You were better acquainted with him than I could ever be."

The Baroness smiled again and squeezed his hand. "My dear, precious Hugh," she said with warmth. "Stay with me while I rest for a while, and then send for Bridget."

*   *   *.

When the Baroness had fully recovered, Garnet Kenrick took his son on a postponed inspection tour of the Danvers estate, a weeklong sojourn, accompanied by Owen, the valet. They spent their nights at local taverns or as guests in tenants' cottages. On the tour they encountered trains of pack-horses laden with agricultural produce, coal, and wares bound for London, Bristol, Southampton, and other major towns. These trains also carried wool, cloth, and any other manufactured goods that could be lashed to the ponies. While on the road, they stopped to talk with chapmen, men who sold penny books, utensils and patent medicines. The Baron bought a chap-book from one of these men for Hugh, who read while he was riding his own pony, and saw that it contained some news, anecdotes, biblical say-ings, and folk wisdom. They also met with "riders," men employed by city merchants to visit tradesmen in the towns with samples of cloth patterns and other household goods, and who took orders and filled them. The idea so fascinated Garnet Kenrick that he on several occasions bought the riders lunch in nearby taverns in trade for information on the workings of this new profession.

Danvers was five thousand acres. The Earl took no active role in man-aging them, other than approving his brother's decisions. Much of Danvers was tilled or occupied by leaseholders, or tenant farmers, who paid rent to the Earl in money or in kind, or a portion of their harvest or produce. In exchange for farming for the likes of the Earl and the Baron, the tenants were allowed small private plots on which they grew or pastured what they pleased. But largely they acted on the Baron's instructions.

Garnet Kenrick owned a much-thumbed copy of Jethro Tull's *Horse-Hoeing Husbandry*, a classic in the science of agriculture, and kept a journal thick with his own observations and endeavors. And he had long ago entered into a correspondence with a Norfolk gentleman farmer, trading ideas about how to mix soils, about paring and burning fields, the best way to abolish rack-rents, the efficacy of various kinds of manure and dung, the novelty of burying clay trunks to drain marshy soil, and improving the stock of Dorset red cattle. At one point on their venture, the Baron stopped atop a hill and waved to the panorama below them, which was a third of the Kenricks' holdings, and lectured Hugh on the breeds of sheep and cattle they could see dotting the rolling meadows. "Ryelands and Herefords yield superb wool for fine broadcloth, Hugh. Sussex and Southdowns have a fine soft curly wool, you see, highly prized by the factors in London. Other sheep I have introduced from the north are long-wooled Cheviots, Northumberland Muggs, and the Lancashire Silverdales, which, incidentally, account for over one-third of the country's annual clipping." His father stopped speaking, and took out his journal to make some notes.

Hugh looked from the panorama to his father. "It is a grand enterprise! You are a great man, Pater."

His father leaned on the pommel of his saddle to study his son. There was a set, subdued smile on his face, a smile that wished it could be more. "Thank you, Hugh. However, you mustn't forget that all this is your uncle's."

Hugh's face turned red. He had forgotten the Earl, and he wished he had no reason to remember him. "No, Pater. I shan't forget it."

When they came to farms, the Baron said, "Turnips, you see, do not deduct from the soil. They add healthiness to it. My plan is to have all the tenants let crop fields lie fallow and sown with turnips, and instead of feeding the cattle by letting them wander over a fallow field, require the tenants to harvest turnips and feed their stock in pens and stables. This will prevent damage by stock to the fields. It will also simplify the care of stock in winter. I plan to eliminate untreated dung from the fields—and with it flies, which are thought by some to cause certain ailments."

His father, Hugh learned, encouraged the cultivation of clover, sainfoin, and lucerne grasses for fair-weather cattle grazing, and mandated the practice of sowing seed by hoe and drill. The Danvers sheep population was evenly divided among the Cheviots, Muggs, and Silverdales. In the town, the Baron had established a "factory" which used a fly-shuttle and hosiery frames, to which the tenants brought their shearings. Danvers produced some of the finest serge in the south of England, which found ready buyers in Exeter, a closer market than was London. Garnet Kenrick carried with him a little book of notes in which was itemized the tasks he had given each tenant on previous tours. Hugh noted that while many of the tenants greeted his father with some cheer and familiarity, their inquiries after the health of the Earl were more a reluctant afterthought than genuine concern. It was as though his father were a respected Apollo, and his uncle a feared Zeus.

One evening, while they rested in a tenant's cottage, Hugh said, "What wonderful material those sheep are! I shall write a play!" Owen, the valet, had just finished serving them a meal at the rickety table, and was busy with chores by the fire he had lit. The tenants, a man, his wife, and three children, had retired to the stable to share straw with their cattle. The Baron had invited them to stay, but the tenant, out of respect for his master, had insisted on spending the night with his livestock.

The Baron exchanged interested glances with Owen, the valet. "About sheep?" asked the father.

"No," said Hugh. "About men. I mean, about families. They shall be the Cheviots, the Muggs, and the Silverdales. It will be a farce."

"A farce?"

"About *our* families." Hugh paused. "We will be the good family—the Silverdales," he assured his father. "But they will all act like sheep."

The Baron laughed, and Owen grinned. "I don't know as I like being cast as a sheep, Hugh."

"You will be the smartest Silverdale. The Muggs will be the Brunes, and the Cheviots will be the Tallmadges. I will make people laugh!"

"Well," said the Baron, not certain of the seriousness of his son's ambition, "you may also make others angry. Has your tutor not yet taught you the misfortunes of John Dryden, and of Defoe, and John Gay? Near-death at the hands of an offended statesman's ruffians—for satirical remarks on that man's character—gaol and the pillory for mocking the government's policies—and enforced literary eclipse. Ah, the pugnacious phrase, the skewed allusion, the hurtful rhyme!" exclaimed the Baron with a shake of his head. "Riskier business than piloting a leaking merchantman into port in a storm!" He noticed the curious look on his son's face, and added, "But, I'm sure that *you* would compose nothing of that ilk."

Hugh leaned across the table anxiously. "You would not be offended by it, would you, Pater?"

"I? Heavens, no, for I would know that you meant me no malice. Your mother might even feel flattered by the attention, and I'm sure you would do her justice. But if you wrote such a fable, you must have some object in mind, some custom, or foible, or hypocrisy that you wished to mock, and some character in your opus must be a paragon of it. And he must be confounded in the end, and made the object of contempt. And though you may cloak your cast in several varieties of wool, it would be less the verse or the prose that would cause people to laugh, and more the sly inspiration for that object. Your 'mocked man' must deserve his *shearing*, if you will allow the analogy. Nothing is so silly-looking as a sheared sheep, and sillier-looking still is a sheared ram, and many of *his* biped kin have the run of society. The foolish and the corrupt may be audacious in their actions, or blind or indifferent to their foolishness and corruption, but never so blind or foolish that they would not savor vengeance. For, you see, Hugh, mirth and mockery can be more stinging than an undisguised truth, and outlive both their author and his object."

"By your leave, your lordship," interjected Owen, who was cleaning the Baron's muck-covered boots by the fireplace, "if I might construe your epistle? How many poets have purchased immortality at the price of their lives?" He paused and turned to address Hugh. "That is what your father the Baron is telling you, milord."

"Why, Owen!" exclaimed Garnet Kenrick with a laugh, "How perfect a way to putting an end to my blather! I could have gone on for hours! I'm in your debt!"

The valet raised his eyebrows and smiled with half-serious emphasis. "A shilling a month more in my wages would make me happy, your lordship."

The Baron replied without hesitation. "You shall have two, Owen."

For a reason he could not then fathom, Hugh learned more about men, from this short exchange between his father and the valet, than he did from his father's epistle.

*   *   *

When they returned from the tour, they found that the Earl had gone to London. "Urgent business that needed his special attention," explained the Baroness to her husband. "He would not say what it might be, although another of Hillier's men arrived with a message. He said he may have a surprise for you when he returns."

The Baron grinned. "Danvers will be ours for a while."

The Kenricks had a placid week during the absence of the Earl. They did not acknowledge the peace, but it was real to them all the same. When the Earl returned, he was beaming after his own fashion. He immediately called his brother into his own study and poured them both glasses of port. "We want a guaranteed purchaser of our serge," he explained. "That would be Fenwick, in Exeter. Fenwick wants a share of the contracts to supply the army with clothing. That would be Wraxall, in Army Supply. Wraxall has the close ear of the Duke. I have been to see Wraxall—and the Duke, who granted me a short audience, thanks to Wraxall. I have convinced him of the quality and dependability of Fenwick, who would never be granted an audience, as he is a mere commercial commoner. The Duke will grant him a large contract, once he has seen our sheep and our serge." The Earl drained his glass of port, and helped himself to another. He fell back into his chair and seemed to gloat.

The Baron stood with his untasted port. "He is coming *here*?"

"In three months. In January, to be precise. Not exclusively to visit Danvers. He will be making a tour of the south coast to evaluate defenses in the larger port towns. He will be accompanied by a modest entourage. He will stop here for a night or two. We must prepare for this occasion."

"A royal visit...," murmured the Baron.

"I know what you're thinking, dear brother. I can picture you despairing over the chaos in your neatly kept ledger books. You should see the look on your face! How costly an affair! The entertainment, the food, all the incidental expenses of putting up a *large*, important man and his train. But—think of the benefits, think of the gains! A contract to supply the army with its jackets, breeches, and blankets! The contract would be two-fold: one with Fenwick, and one with Danvers. Fenwick is part-owner of a dying establishment in London."

"I know," said the Baron, sitting down on the edge of an armchair as though it was too delicate to take his weight.

"Yes, you know." The Earl grunted once. "But it was an opportunity *you* neglected."

The Baron put his glass aside on the table. "How did Hillier come upon this opportunity?"

"He has friends in the ministry, and he heard about it. He introduced himself to Wraxall."

The Baron thought for a moment before he spoke again. "Is there to be another war?"

The Earl shrugged his shoulders. "Not that I know of," he replied. "Neither does Wraxall, nor the Duke. It's a matter of laying up supplies."

"How is the Duke?" asked the Baron abstractly.

"In the best of spirits, despite the albatross of unpopularity nesting on his shoulders."

"Did he thank you for the birthday gifts you sent him?"

"I did not think it opportune to jog his memory of them. It seems he chose to see me in the middle of an impromptu meeting of the Jockey Club at his lodge, in Windsor Park. The subject was some sickly Arabian studs he bought from another member, and he was so fit to be tied that I thought he might be short with me. But he was most gracious and accommodating, and we had a very amiable chat."

"Have you discussed this with Fenwick?"

The Earl frowned. "Good lord, no! *You* deal with the man, not *I*. You've talked about him often enough."

"I shall have to talk to him again and soon. It would have been wiser to await my return before you acted on Hillier's message, dear brother. Fenwick shall be more surprised than I at this news."

"Why?"

"If there are fruits borne of your efforts—if we are granted an exclusive contract—it will mean less serge for Fenwick to sell to the colonies…to Talbot in Philadelphia, for example, though Talbot is not our only purchaser. Fenwick has other commitments. The material has been spoken for by other factors. If he breaks his contracts with them, he may never see another."

"Why should that concern us?" replied the Earl sharply. "We will be dealing directly with the Crown." He shook his head in consternation. "Does this cornucopia displease you, dear brother?"

The Baron sighed. "It disturbs matters," he said.

"If you are so concerned about Fenwick, we can purchase wool and serge from Tallmadge and Brune. You told me they must send their material to Bristol and London. We can purchase it from *those* people here—and they'll thank us for the chance—and resell it to Fenwick, so he can meet his blasted commitments."

"Perhaps," said the Baron, who rose and began pacing. "But they have commitments of their own. We should have to make it worth their while to break them."

The Earl poured himself another port. "There is no *honor* in commerce, dear brother. I don't know why it should trouble you so. Good lord! If there were any, we should not be giving the Lobster Pots a living, or even Talbot or Worley, for that matter." Benjamin Worley was the Kenricks' commercial agent in London.

"It is honor that makes commerce possible, dear brother. And the law courts, when men lack it."

The Earl merely sniffed at this truism. The brothers said nothing for a while. The candles burned steadily in their lamps, and the Dutch wall clock ticked away, measuring the Earl's growing satisfaction and the Baron's galling resignation.

Then the Earl said, "We shall need to hire extra servants for the occasion, Garnet. And tidy up the place. And the staff will need to be refreshed in royal deportment. *That* is especially important. We want no discourtesy shown the Duke. All courtesies paid the king must be paid to him as well. Fawkner, his secretary, has promised he will dispatch a chamberlain to instruct us more carefully in the proper etiquette. He will also send us a list of those to be in the entourage, so that we may prepare rooms." The Earl paused to study his pensive brother. He seemed to derive some pleasure from having shaken his sibling's certainty about business. "The town must be jollied up somehow, to greet the Duke. I shall prevail upon the Lord-Lieutenant to loan us some militia for the occasion. I read somewhere that he has a company of unemployed musicians. No doubt the Duke will be escorted by some cavalry. Billeting for them must be found, or constructed. The grounds could do with some pruning. What do you think? Should we have fireworks? That would be grand." Then he remembered something. "Oh! How was the tour?"

Chapter 5: The Extraordinary

SIR EVERARD FAWKNER KEPT HIS PROMISE; A CHAMBERLAIN ARRIVED BY packet in Swanage two weeks later and drilled the Kenricks and their household in the courtesies required of them in all situations governed by a royal presence. For the Baron and Baroness, this was a tedious exercise, for they had already met the king and his family, in London at the celebration of the Treaty of Aix-la-Chapelle. But the Earl insisted that everyone participate. On the advice of his brother, the Earl reluctantly informed the Brunes, the Tallmadges, and other local notables of the Duke's scheduled visit, and invited them to receive the same instruction, for no one else in Danvers had ever met or even seen royalty. On one hand, the Brunes and Tallmadges were envious; on the other, relieved, for such a visit, scheduled or surprise, would have impoverished them, and they knew that they could neither count on nor discreetly prompt the Duke's generosity for compensation.

On the Earl's order, the great Palladian house was cleaned and scrubbed inside and out, the portraits that lined the hallways and adorned the rooms were dusted and rearranged, the grounds pruned, the estate road replenished with new stones crushed by the workers in a Portland quarry in which the Kenricks owned a part interest. The Earl paid for bolts of red, white, and blue ribbon to be hung from the village's windows and the single steeple of St. Quarrell's church, and even ordered a new banner bearing the Kenricks' coat-of-arms to be made; it would be flown from a staff near the mansion's cupola. The Kenricks' coat-of-arms was a stale thing concocted by an ancestor in the fifteenth century. It featured a shield with a griffin and wolf rampant, a bramble flower and a rose respectively clenched in their mouths, the creatures clinging to the bend in the shield. On a scroll beneath the shield was the Kenrick family motto: *Vires facit veritas.*

The excitement was so infectious that even Hugh Kenrick, usually aloof from the concerns of his uncle, felt a swell of anticipation. He, too, submitted to the chamberlain's drills, and surprised the man and even his parents with the quickness of his learning. The chamberlain, in a droning, condescending tone, imparted the rules of royal decorum in an informal setting. "Unless otherwise waived by the Duke, all courtesies must be observed, without exception... At a dinner or other table, no one may eat or drink, or initiate a meal, until the Duke has begun his repast... No one may contradict or interrupt the Duke in any discourse or conversation on any whatsoever subject... The subject of Culloden Moor will not be mentioned in the Duke's presence, nor will any questions, either supportive or mischievous, be entertained by His Grace on that subject... Ladies and children will not address the Duke, except in answer or reply to him... All persons must rise when His Grace enters a room, and sit again only if and when His Grace sits or he waives the courtesy... No person shall wear a white rose or ribbon in the Duke's presence; a breach of this rule will be interpreted as a treasonous gesture, and the offender will be removed from the premises... His Grace is not his father the King, and so one may meet his glance, though not in an insolent or reproachful manner..."

Hugh memorized these and other rules, and excelled in the physical demonstration of deference. He had never before had to bow to anyone; the meaning of it was not lost on him. Curiously, he looked forward to the chance to bow to someone admirable. His parents and his uncle had painted such a glowing picture of the Duke in their dinner table conversation that the impending episode had a quality of magic for which he wished to be prepared. He imagined that a heroic god was coming to visit.

Hugh's parents were secretly pleased that their son seemed to be happy, happy at home, happy with his tutors. He was even oblivious to the chronic disapproving scrutiny of his uncle. One day, after a footman brought him home from his lessons at the Tallmadge house, he rushed into his father's study and handed him a sheet of paper. "Pater! It ought to be your motto!" he exclaimed.

His father read the single sentence on it that was written in a fine, elegant hand: *O Fortunatas Mercatores!* He grunted in appreciation. "Oh, happy traders!" he said. He looked quizzically at his son. "*My* motto?"

Just then Hugh heard a rustle of silk, and the Earl came out of the shadows cast by the candles on the Baron's desk. Hugh turned and glanced at his uncle, then at his father. "Yours," he answered, "and Uncle's."

"Hardly the motto of a great family, Master Hugh," remarked the Earl, who sat down in an armchair within the light.

"Under what circumstance did you come upon this idea?" asked the Baron.

"Mr. Cole gave us some sentences to put into Latin, and that was one of them."

"Is not our motto *noble* enough for you, dear nephew?" asked the Earl.

Hugh remembered that his uncle was having a new banner with the family coat-of-arms prepared for the Duke of Cumberland's visit by the best seamstresses in the village. "It is not a proper sentiment for commerce, sir," he replied in his defense.

The Earl merely hummed in answer.

The Baron chuckled. "I won't deny that our business could use a motto to celebrate its success."

"It's from Horace's *Satires*," said Hugh.

"It's a very formal language, Latin," mused his father. "Don't you think?"

"No one speaks it, Pater," observed Hugh, "yet so much wisdom can be found in it."

"True." His father glanced sharply at his brother, and as though he were expressing some secret defiance, smiled and said, "Henceforth, Hugh, you may address me as 'Father.' And your mother, 'Mother.' My teeth gnash every time you address me as 'Pater.' It's much too formal, you see."

"Yes...Father."

"All right, Hugh. Get along. Your uncle and I are discussing our status as fortunate traders."

Hugh began to turn, but hesitated.

"Is something else on your mind, Hugh?"

"Yes, Father." Hugh paused, then spoke. "Why may not one mention Culloden Moor when the Duke comes?"

The Baron shrugged. "It is a...sensitive subject," he replied.

"I have heard—from Mr. Cole, and Squire Tallmadge—that it was a great battle, and a great victory."

"Perhaps the Duke is too modest to wish to discuss it," suggested the Earl.

The Baron looked again at his brother, then smiled. "There are those who say it was a great battle and victory, Hugh, and that he wept when he rode onto the battlefield and saw all the dead Scots. And there are some who claim that the Duke ordered the execution of a wounded Scot who smiled at him, and that he established a cruel policy of punishment in that luckless country."

"What is the truth?" asked Hugh.

The Earl answered impatiently, "What it will be when the Duke has passed to his final judgment."

On another occasion, Hugh sat in his room late one evening, when the house was quiet and the fall wind beat against the lead-paned glass of his window. The candles on his desk flickered nervously over a page in his school notebook and twenty Latin sentences he had been assigned by Mr. Cole to "render into plain, unembellished English." They were difficult sentences, but an hour's effort had conquered them.

Two of them fascinated him for a reason he could not yet explain. He had even read them out loud to himself, in Latin and in English, so that he could hear the words in a place other than inside his head. "Though you lose all, remember to preserve your honor." "Freedom with danger is preferable to peace with slavery." These dictums attracted him; he felt like a moth near a candle. He did not fully understand honor, for so far he had none to preserve. Perhaps, he thought, it had played a role in the incident at Eton; something like honor was in peril then, though the notion of it which most people seemed to ascribe to was of a passive nature. He knew that his parents and uncle believed that his actions then had been dishonorable. He could not agree with them; they had forgiven him, but the forgiveness made him uneasy.

Neither did he fully understand the sentence about freedom and slavery; he was enough of an aristocrat that the ideas held little meaning for him in the world around him. Yet, he thought, there was some unseen connection between honor and freedom and slavery, and with what had happened to him at Eton.

The next day, Mr. Cole congratulated Hugh on all the translations but one. "Danger *seemed* preferable, Master Kenrick, not *is*. 'Poitor visa est periculosa libertas quieto servito.'"

Hugh was surprised with his error, and conceded the point, but preferred his error to the literal translation. He said, "It ought to read *is*, sir."

"You may not correct Sallust," said Mr. Cole. "Kindly keep in mind that the quotation is from his *History*."

"Yes, sir."

Mr. Cole assigned his pupil twenty more translations. He meant it to be punishment. His pupil did not know it.

This was an aspect of Hugh which caused his parents to smile and which confounded his tormentors and enemies: his amity with thought. He did not regard thinking as a painful, cursed exercise peripheral to his life. Thought was as much an appendage to his being as an arm or a leg, and more: it was a constant, inseparable, welcome companion, as much an automatic reflex as using any of his limbs. Puzzles, problems, and conundrums did not last long under his purview. The behavior of many adults and of other children who did not think perplexed him for the longest while; he was growing to be intolerantly contemptuous of anyone who resisted or dismissed it. He neither nurtured nor dwelt on this contempt; it seethed at any chance encounter with resistance, then ebbed when the cause was no longer present.

Another tutor, Mr. Rittles, instructor in rhetoric, asked his pupils to parse two selections from Cicero, and to write an essay on the logical connection between them and on the moral inference to be drawn from them. Hugh obeyed, but tested the tutor's patience when he questioned the truth of the second selection. When Mr. Rittles noted the statement in his pupil's essay, and bid him to explain its brevity, Hugh said, "Cicero wrote: 'Every judgment is an act of reasoning. Of good reasoning, if the judgment is true. Of bad reasoning, if it is false.'"

"Have you any difficulty with that, Master Kenrick?" asked the tutor.

"Some," answered Hugh. "You see, sir, he goes on to say that 'Reason underlies all our vices and is the seed of injustice, intemperance, and cowardice.'" Hugh paused and laid down his notebook. "I cannot connect the two logically, sir, because I do not believe that reason can be a partner in vice, injustice, intemperance, or cowardice."

Mr. Rittles scoffed, and with a discreet glance at the other boys—there were seven other pupils—invited them to join him. All but Roger Tallmadge chortled. The tutor asked, "Then to what would you attribute the cause of vice and all those other failings, Master Kenrick?"

"I am sure that it is not reason, sir, or any kind of thought at all. Reason is too noble an endowment to sire stupidity."

"How would you explain false judgments, if not by bad reasoning?"

"Perhaps by...counterfeit thought, sir!" exclaimed Hugh. "Or just... emotion. Whimsy. A man can *pretend* to think, to reason, but it is not actually *reasoning*. If reasoning is concerned with only truth, it cannot be employed to create a lie, or an untruth." He spoke, and his bright eyes seemed to reflect the light that had flared up in his mind. He derived an almost feverish joy from following a course of logic, from putting his thoughts into words, thoughts that were his own, and words that were his own. "So there cannot be such a thing as *bad* reasoning. Bad *thinking*, perhaps, but not bad reasoning. But men do lie, they do put over untruths. They use words and logic, but do not report truth, they have not employed reason, they have only erected a *subterfuge*, or a facade." Hugh paused to catch his breath. "Bad thinking is either intentional, or proof of lack of wit."

Mr. Rittles had leaned forward on his lectern, engrossed together with the boys in the impromptu speech. Then he realized that Hugh was waiting for a reply. He snapped to attention, patted his wig once, then cleared his throat and said, "My apologies, Master Kenrick. It seems that you have propelled us, prematurely, into the realm of *sophistry*. For that is the name of what you were laboring to identify." He gave his pupils a broad, all-inclusive grin. "Sophistry may be called the antithesis of reason."

Roger Tallmadge smiled in celebration of his friend's victory. The other boys granted Hugh a grudging, if envious respect. And Mr. Rittles said, "Thank you, Master Kenrick. Someday, when you assume the ermine of your office, you may speak with such passion in Lords. I earnestly hope to audit that moment." He never baited or mocked Hugh again.

Hugh cemented his friendship with Roger Tallmadge inadvertently, but inevitably. The boy was mystified by Hugh's self-possession and aloofness, which seemed to both reject companionship and at the same time invite it. He observed that Hugh's bearing provoked hostility or wary respect. He could not understand the older boy's character, but he was attracted to it.

Roger Tallmadge was given a clue to understanding it when, one afternoon, he had difficulty delivering an oral description of two countries to the geography and history tutor, Mr. Galpin. Mr. Galpin was the lowest paid and the least liked of all the tutors in Squire Tallmadge's pay. His colleagues avoided him and his pupils feared him. He compensated for his unpopularity by being a prig to his colleagues and a tyrant to his dozen charges. He regularly failed a pupil's otherwise competently written paper for the misspelling of a single word, and badgered anyone who displayed the least hesitancy in answer to a question in class.

Hugh Kenrick was the only pupil who had never been subjected to the tutor's abuse, because he always knew his lessons, and because he was the nephew of an earl.

Mr. Galpin, on this day, called on Roger Tallmadge to recite some of the differences—cultural and geographical—between Spain and Ireland. The boy, stammering out of fear, confused the locations, the languages, and the climates. Mr. Galpin lit into him, and called him all the derogatory names he could think of. He did this because he was a miserable man, and because he had explicit permission from Squire Tallmadge to be as harsh on his

sons as he thought necessary. "If Francis and Roger do not take to knowledge," said the Squire to his new tutor some years ago, "then they must be
taken to it—in harness if necessary. Do not spare them. Be rigorous."

Roger Tallmadge, standing at his desk, sobbed under the stream of
invective, and was barely able to hold back his tears. Then Mr. Galpin
stopped shouting, and laughed. The other boys felt free to join him,
including Francis, Roger's older brother, aged twelve. "And," added the
tutor with another bellow, "you are a *blubberer*!" The boys laughed even
harder, and Francis picked a pebble stuck on the bottom of his shoe and
flicked it at his sibling.

Hugh Kenrick rose from his desk and addressed the tutor in a clear
voice. "Perhaps, sir, Mr. Tallmadge is at a loss because you yourself have
not clarified well enough the distinctions between Iberia and Hibernia."

The laughter ceased, and all eyes, including Mr. Galpin's, turned to
look at Hugh. "Excuse me, Master Kenrick?" asked the tutor.

Hugh did not repeat himself. He stood waiting for an answer.

Mr. Galpin drew himself up with some dignity and looked down his
nose at the boy. "While I do not need to justify myself or my methods,
young sir, I will say only that Master Tallmadge was not prepared for the
question, as he should have been. He was not prepared, because he did not
listen closely enough to my lecture yesterday afternoon."

"Begging your pardon, sir," replied Hugh, "but you devoted a mere five
minutes each to Iberia and Hibernia, and concentrated on Russia, Sweden,
and Persia. You did not ask us to take notes on Iberia or Hibernia."

This was true. Mr. Galpin scoffed. "Perhaps *you* can tell us about *Iberia*
and *Hibernia*."

Hugh did so. He recited from memory what little the tutor had said the
day before about the two countries, and added: "Ireland is a Celtic country,
and mostly Catholic. So is Northern Spain, parts of which are also Gaelic.
'Gaelic' is a variation of 'Gaul,' the Roman name for France, which was
once a province of Rome, as was Spain. Southern Spaniards are of a different complexion and temper than Northern Spaniards, because of the
long Moorish occupation. The Moors were thrust from Spain three centuries ago. Ireland has a fair climate, except in the fall and winter, when it
is terribly wet and damp. It is notorious for giving men the ague. Spain, too,
has a fair climate, but its summers are hot and fatiguing."

Mr. Galpin raised his eyebrows. Francis Tallmadge muffled a laugh, but
the tutor heard it and threw him a wicked glance. Then he smiled. "No

doubt you have taken your studies seriously, Master Kenrick—unlike some of my other pupils. You are to be commended. Thank you for the enlightening recitation."

Some of the boys gasped. They had never before heard him compliment a pupil.

But Mr. Galpin read something other than acknowledgment in the boy's eyes: not merely bravery or the knowledge of his lurking power, but contempt. His smile still fixed, he nodded to his pupil to take his seat again, then turned, and without looking at Roger Tallmadge, said, "I will quiz you again tomorrow, Master Tallmadge. You may be seated."

Hugh's fellow pupils wondered at the precedent. It was not just a matter of confronting and contradicting Mr. Galpin; some of them had done it before, out of boredom or bravura, and had been punished. They knew that the tutor would never again taunt Roger Tallmadge, thanks to Hugh Kenrick. They were beginning to believe that the future earl had a special power that made unjust and cruel men cringe and crawl.

When the day was over, Roger Tallmadge took Hugh to the family's kitchen and gave him a pastry one of the cooks had baked. "Thank you, Hugh, for what you did today," he said. He smiled tentatively. "You are more of a brother to me than is Francis," he added with bitterness.

Hugh smiled. "You shall be my brother, when we are together," he said.

"A brother? *I*, to you?" asked the other boy incredulously.

"If you wish."

"Why?"

"Because you have never laughed at me, or mocked me. Because you try harder in your studies than does anyone else."

"Yes! I do wish it!" laughed Roger Tallmadge.

Hugh smiled. "You ought to have known about Spain and Ireland," he said. "Mr. Galpin often pulls that trick on us—mentions something one day, and examines us on it another. And Spain and Ireland are in your geography book."

"I'll be ready for him tomorrow!" laughed Roger.

For Hugh Kenrick, the idea of adopting Roger Tallmadge as his "brother" was a sudden impulse and a brainstorm. Since the stillbirth of a brother months ago, he had occasionally wondered about the value of a sibling. His sister, Alice, was too young, the other boys in his school too old for him or too preoccupied with concerns that were not his, and the boys in his uncle's and father's employ were too fearful of his rank to respond naturally to his overtures, and risked little more than gruff, almost hostile acknowledgment of him. But in Roger was a perfect model for experimentation, someone a little like himself, an outsider, a scrappy maverick, enthusiastic about many things—someone with a sense of his own importance.

And so they kept each other company in the intervals between their tutors, more often than not in silent preparation for their lessons than in games or conversation. Hugh appreciated Roger's unobtrusive presence when he wanted time alone for his thoughts; Roger appreciated the respect granted him by the older boy. Hugh saw in Roger a friendly, patient sounding board for his ideas and even for his presence; Roger saw in Hugh an almost regal mien which curiously was neither arrogant nor arbitrary nor an affectation, together with a cool approach to almost everything. Hugh broadcast a self-possession that Roger found intriguing, and so he felt worthier for having befriended him, though he never completely resolved the question either of why Hugh tolerated him or what about himself was worthy. Hugh unconsciously set the terms of their companionship; Roger submitted to them in deference to everything that was Hugh, and in doing so learned the value of unanxious solitude.

He also learned that virtually the only thing that commanded Hugh's unreserved respect was knowledge, both in what was to be learned and in what degree it was demonstrated in others.

It was only in the social arts that Hugh exhibited extreme rebellion. All games bored him, and when pressed to participate in cricket and rounders, he played indifferently. Squire Tallmadge, who usually supervised games for the pupils in between their time with tutors, spoke to the Baron about Hugh's laxness. And the Baron admonished his son. "You will encounter politics someday, Hugh. Games are a crude introduction to that most crucial sport of all."

Hugh sighed. "I'll try, Father."

And he did try, but the games became now an exercise in duty.

On another occasion, he rode with his father one early winter day into the village of Danvers and observed how rents were collected from the shopkeepers. Riding through the cobblestone streets, Hugh saw a number of men, women, and children, sometimes together, sometimes singly, clothed in mere rags and shoed in scraps of leather, carrying bundles on sticks over their shoulders, trudging through the newly fallen snow without purpose or hope of finding any, but still with an almost tangible slyness that was both pitiable and repulsive. His father gave these creatures a grave eye, but said nothing to them. These were paupers, and Danvers had no almshouse for them. The Baron rode to the constable's house, and informed the man of the strangers.

"'Pon my word, my lord, I didn't know they was about! So help me! They all know, these beggars, there ain't no comfort for them here!"

The Baron frowned. "Refresh their memories, Mr. Stobb, or we'll appoint a new constable. I don't want to see a single ragged body loitering in this vicinity tomorrow."

"Yes, my lord."

As they rode back to the estate, Hugh said, "Father, I want to learn a trade."

"What?"

"I want to *be* something."

"*Be* something?"

"Yes."

"You *are* something, Hugh," replied his astonished father. "You are a knight banneret. You are to be a baron. And someday, an earl."

Hugh turned his head to hide his grimace. "Like Uncle Basil?"

Garnet Kenrick raised his eyebrows. He knew what his son thought of him—he was grateful for that. And he suspected what his son thought of his uncle, and was grateful that his brother was too arrogant to sense his nephew's estimate of him. The Baron sighed. "Hugh, what would you become? A coal-heaver? A silk-thrower, or a wool-puller like the men in our factory? A mudlark? An apprentice higgler? If you went to London or Bristol to apprentice a trade—with no support from your family—you would find yourself sharing a miserable, cold, rat-infested cellar with twenty or so other souls who called it home. You would spend all of your time working your trade, and the time you didn't spend scrambling for pittance, you would spend scrambling for food. You would have no time for books, no time to make neat observations. You would be too tired, too hungry, too distracted. The mental energy you expend now on construing Latin wisdom and appreciating the prose of Milton and Dryden would be wholly diverted on the time, place, and composition of your every meal."

The Baron paused to gauge the effect of this description on his son. Hugh was looking at him expectantly.

"Hugh, the men and women who must have trades are born with poor, dim candles for souls, made of the most adulterated, cheap tallow, which they spend all their lives keeping from sputtering out. One could say that it is their sole purpose for living. Even so, their candles are stunted and do not illuminate much. You, however, were born with an untaxed candle, made of the finest, purest tallow and beeswax. It is tall and it burns brightly. In London or Bristol, that candle inside you would be snuffed out in a wink by the brutal exigencies of life, and you would become dross, like those paupers back there, or philistines, like those shopkeepers. You would see, but have no vision. You would become like them—able to appreciate a political cartoon, laugh at a puppet show, or marvel at an engraving by Mr. Hogarth, but be blind to a canvas by Titian, or deaf to a chorus by Mr. Handel."

"The shopkeepers seemed to have some dignity. And cheerfulness. They must be happy about something. What?"

Garnet Kenrick chuckled. "Oh, I imagine the same thing that makes me happy, on occasion—the solid jingle of a fat sack of coin. We have that in common, at least."

Hugh urged his pony to keep pace with his father's bay. "Some men of vision have had humble origins, Father. And they seemed to have fashioned their own candles, and kept them lit through the most brutal exigencies. How can one account for them?"

The Baron shrugged his shoulders. "They had the help of God, Hugh. There is no other explanation for their existence. They are extraordinaries outside the plan of things."

This answer did not satisfy Hugh's curiosity, but he asked no more questions. He sensed that his father had no other answers. Instead, he said, "I could apprentice a trade in the village, and learn how to make the things we wear, or use, or eat. We put a value on these things, so there must be no natural disgrace in working in their manufacture."

Garnet Kenrick smiled sadly at his son. He said, "Even if I agreed to such a scheme, Hugh, your uncle would never permit it. No, my boy, you must content yourself with nobler diversions." He dug his heels into the sides of his bay. "Come! I'll race you back to the house!"

Hugh knew that this was a closed subject. He obeyed his father, and used his heels to spur the pony into a gallop. The silence was broken only by the double tattoo of hooves on the dirt and pebble road as the two riders rushed up the quiet slope through the swirling snowflakes.

Chapter 6: The Test

THE WEATHER, USUALLY FOUL WITH WIND, SNOW, OR GALE AT THIS TIME of year, was perfectly placid, with a mild temperature and a blue, cloudless sky. The Earl had hired a man and horse to watch for the Duke's approach in Todd Matravers, a village some miles northeast of Danvers on the King's Highway, to alert the town of the Duke of Cumberland's progress. Late on the morning of the twentieth of January, the messenger galloped through Danvers and up the estate road to the mansion with the news that from a hilltop he had seen the train of coaches and cavalry approach Todd Matravers. The household jumped to life, while the militia in town assembled to quick-march to the estate. A crowd of excited townsfolk followed the militia soon afterward up the immaculate estate road, thronging past the gatekeeper, stopping to marvel at the tall cypresses and sculptured boxwoods. The crowd stepped aside to allow the carriages and phaetons of the Tallmadges, Brunes, and other notables to pass; this, too, was something for the villagers to marvel at—Whig families eagerly paying a visit to a Tory citadel. A holiday spirit moved the townsfolk, even though they were recently satiated by the celebration of Twelfth Night.

The Kenricks had been ready for the Duke's arrival since sunrise. It was the servants and the kitchen staff who hustled about their chores. The Earl and his family waited in the orangery, which had a view of the estate road. The Earl, watching from a window, grimaced at the sight of the townsfolk streaming up the road to trample promiscuously over the great lawn; the gardeners would need to make many repairs once the event was past. He dutifully left the sanctuary of the orangery to greet his guests as their carriages came to a stop before the fountain below, and instructed his servants to keep them happy in the drawing room with tea, punch, chocolate, and sweetmeats.

The Baroness, in one corner of the bright green-papered room, played with her four-year-old daughter, Alice, showing her how to dress and undress a doll. Hugh Kenrick sat idly in another corner, patiently spinning his brass top on a wing table; its distinctive hum competed with the ticking of the tall floor clock nearby. The Baron stood in another corner with two special guests, one of whom was here by design, the other by chance, though they had arrived in Poole together on the same fast London packet two days before. The first was Benjamin Worley, of Worley and Sons of London, the Kenricks' chief commercial agents. Worley had had a small hand in arranging the Duke's visit; he and Wraxall of the army commissariat were inseparable card game partners in their London club. The second guest was Otis Talbot, of Talbot and Spicer of Philadelphia, the Kenricks' colonial agents. Talbot had voyaged from the distant port on his biannual business visit to Worley and the Kenricks, only to be bundled back onto a boat by Worley for a sooner-than-expected journey to Danvers.

Hugh Kenrick glanced occasionally at the colonial agent, whom he had never met before. The man was about his father's age, but he seemed younger. The face was ruddier, his bearing natural—almost reminiscent of the manner of the townsfolk, but with a regal element of certainty. He was as well-dressed as Hugh's father, and wore a powdered wig beneath his hat, and spoke with a kind of confidence and presumption Hugh had never heard before. The man was English, yet his Englishness did not seem to be an actual part of him. Some indefinable difference existed in the man, an unnamed quality that set him apart from all the other men Hugh had encountered.

Another messenger rode up the estate road; Cumberland's train had entered the other side of the village of Danvers, led by Constable Stobb, who had been assigned as guide for the cavalry escort. The Earl herded his guests and the household outside to take their places on the broad front steps.

No children under the age of five were permitted by the Earl to be a part of this reception, for they could not be trusted to act with dignity and deference in the presence of royalty. Thus Alice was sentenced with her nurse to watch the arrival of the Duke from an upper-floor window. Nor were any working children of the staff allowed to be present if they did not own the proper formal attire. Thus the scullions, stable boys, cooks' helpers, and such had to be content with watching the reception from the roof.

Hugh Kenrick stood with the children of the guests and their governesses, in between eight-year-old Roger Tallmadge and ten-year-old Reverdy Brune. He wore a green suit under a black cape, and a black tricorn with gold braid. Reverdy Brune had taken his hand and squeezed it with excitement when the lead squad of the Duke's cavalry escort came into sight far down the estate road, a column of scarlet bobbing under a golden banner flapping in the wind. "Look, Hugh!" exclaimed the girl. "The *Duke* is coming!" Hugh had glanced at her, and saw the wild excitement in her eyes. "Hugh," said Roger Tallmadge on his left side, "my father says that you will be presented to the Duke personally, and allowed to sit with him and the men when the ladies leave the room. Promise you'll tell me what they talk about!"

All chatter and nervous movement ceased when the crowd in front of the mansion could hear the hooves of the cavalry escort, and then the crack of stone as wheels rolled over the pebbled road. And all eyes became fixed on the magnificent six-horse gold and blue carriage when it loomed into sight and rumbled around the oval lawn and fountain of the courtyard. The major of the cavalry stopped to doff his hat to the Earl, who merely nodded in acknowledgment. And then the great carriage slowed to a walk, and halted at the foot of the wide flagstone walkway that led to the steps. A train of seven other carriages, less ostentatious, pulled up behind the Duke's.

A footman leapt from the back of the post-chaise and ran to open a door and place a gilded stool beneath it. As the Duke descended from the carriage, the bandmaster struck up the "Dorsetshire March." Possibly the Duke had never heard it before, for he winced; no one dared to inquire whether it was because he was startled or because he found the raucous cacophony unbearable. He stood for a moment, watching the band, with an enigmatic but respectful smile, then turned and handed out a woman in a hood and cloak. This was Maud Harris, a London actress, and his current mistress. She was in her early twenties, and had a vaguely beautiful face and a permanent smirk made more pronounced by her flaunted liaison with the Duke. She was introduced by him to strangers as Miss Harris; in fact, she was Mrs. Harris, wife of the owner of a theater company from which she had taken a leave. Her leave had been bought with a handsome, discreet endowment from the Duke that would allow the company to play to empty houses for two years.

Miss Harris, too, glanced in amazement at the band. She touched a rolled fan to her lips to stifle a laugh. "Milord!" she said under her breath. "Not even Mr. Handel's baton could salvage *that*!"

"Perhaps not," replied Cumberland. "Still, it has some martial charm."

Miss Harris giggled. "I know, milord! The next time you face the French, you could have *this* band play that *agony* in the field, and give them so thorough a fright that their ranks would drop their arms to hold their ears! And the day would be yours!"

Cumberland chuckled. "Miss Harris, you are *too* droll!"

The Earl stood a few feet away, with his brother and the Baroness, waiting for the right moment. He stepped forward now as Cumberland offered his arm to Miss Harris and turned. The Earl bowed low to the Duke and faultlessly doffed his hat in a broad sweep. "Welcome to Danvers, your grace. You honor us with this visit."

"Thank you, Lord Basil," replied the Duke. "Your hospitality is gracious." Cumberland smiled. "But, my word, sir! You *do* make a man feel at home! I had not expected such a commotion!"

The Earl nodded. "I would be pleased if you regarded it as a hero's welcome, your grace. It is rare that we see men of your eminence in these parts." He then introduced his brother and the Baroness. The Baron bowed in the same manner as did his brother, while the Baroness performed a low, solemn curtsy.

Pleasantries were exchanged. In time, the principal members of the entourage left their carriages and joined the Duke. More introductions were made: to Rear Admiral Sir Francis Edward Harle; to twenty-five-year-old Lieutenant-Colonel James Wolfe, seconded from the 20th Regiment of Foot and temporarily rescued from a binge of dissipation in London by the Duke's need for his military advice; to Major General Sir John Ligonier, the Duke's personal advisor; to Everard Fawkner, his secretary and chief-of-staff. A gaggle of aides, adjutants, secretaries, servants, including the Duke's own barber and valets, debouched from other carriages and stood in the background, waiting for Cumberland to enter the mansion. The troop of cavalry had formed in two lines on the Danvers lawn and was also waiting. A number of townsfolk had also gathered on the lawn and stood in awe of the event. Some of them, women, wore a white rose or ribbon pinned discreetly to their hats or cloaks. And the band played on, this time laboring through a rendition of Handel's "See, the conquering hero comes."

The group then turned and, led by the Earl, made its way up the broad walkway to the steps of the mansion. On one side of the steps were lined the Earl's staff, on the other guests and notable neighbors, including the vicar of St. Quarrell's. Otis Talbot and Benjamin Worley stood rigidly with frozen smiles. As Cumberland, with a slight limp from a wound he received at Dettingen, ascended the steps, the women dipped in abbreviated curtsies and bowed their heads, and the men bowed their heads and bent their backs. The Earl, his eye sharp for the least departure from the courtesy by guest or servant, walked a step or two ahead of Cumberland and Miss Harris, for he was, after all, a host welcoming a great personage into his home.

Hugh watched the arrival of Cumberland with an expectant reverence. His uncle the Earl preceded the Duke, who had a woman on his arm. His uncle's mouth was a thin band of nervousness.

When the Duke came to the children, he paused to bestow a smile on them. The children emulated their parents, and the governesses their employers. The Duke even smiled at the laggard boy who did not bow, but stood looking at him with a mixture of curiosity, muted astonishment, and disappointment. Cumberland paused imperceptibly to allow the boy to cor rect this faux pas and when the boy did not bend and incline his head, moved on. The Duke's glance shifted to the Earl, whom he saw glaring at the boy. The Earl seemed to feel this scrutiny, and turned briefly to hold his eyes. In the Earl's look he saw anger, fear, and apology.

Hugh Kenrick was both oblivious to the others around him and fully conscious of them. As the Duke had come closer, he became less aware of the figures that preceded the man, figures that acted like the depressed hammers of a clavichord, and more aware of the bulky figure that caused the phenomenon. This figure was corpulent, the face bovine, the pale blue eyes cold marbles of inanimation, dull, unseeing, devoid even of the arrogance of station. The Duke went by and entered the mansion. Hugh remained insensible to the stares of those around him.

Cumberland did not wish to delay a rest from his arduous time in the coach by making an event of the anomaly. The Earl, who did not wish to call further attention to the incident, passed by with him, his face redder than anyone had ever seen it. The Baron and Baroness were aghast, but did not dare to stop and make a scene with a reprimand. They disappeared with the Duke inside.

Hugh felt a hand on his shoulder, and was roughly turned around. It was the vicar, whose face was purple with wrath. "Master Kenrick, you are in *grave* straits! I have never seen such...such impudence!"

*   *   *

The Earl escorted Cumberland and Miss Harris up the grand staircase to their quarters, while servants showed the other members of the entourage to their rooms. He quickly returned to the great hall, where this evening's banquet was to be held, and took his brother aside. The Baron did not need to ask why.

"*Where is he?*" hissed the Earl.

"I sent him to his room."

"Is he addled?"

"I don't know, Basil," replied Garnet Kenrick helplessly.

"I *do* know that I would enjoy forcing a bottle of Daffney's Elixir down his throat, followed by a more than ample helping of licorice to purge him of whatever bile is clogging his mind!"

"He has caused a fine tardle this time, my son Hugh," conceded the Baron.

The Earl paused to throw an evil look at a passing servant who might have been eavesdropping, then said, almost in a whisper, "Do you realize that this incident will be reported in the *London Gazette* and God knows how many other newspapers? That it will be the subject of conversation and gossip at all the balls and dinners? Do you know what must be done?"

"No, Basil, neither I nor Effney know what must be done."

"Your son's action could cost us this contract, dear brother. In fact, I'm certain of it. That contract is the only reason we have His Grace here!"

The Baron sighed. "I can't think of a remedy, Basil."

"*I* will think of one!"

The Earl called on Sir Everard Fawkner in his room. Fawkner asked his valet, who was unpacking his employer's trunks, to step out of the room.

When the door was shut, Basil Kenrick wrung his hands. "Please convey my humblest and most urgent apologies to His Grace, Sir Everard."

Fawkner removed his wig and propped it on the bedpost. "Who *was* that boy?" he asked.

The Earl took a deep breath, then said, "It was my nephew, Hugh."

Fawkner barked once in amusement. "Oh! Well, that's awkward! I suppose we couldn't ask you to flog him and terminate his employment!" He paused and grinned at the anxiety he saw in the Earl's eyes. "Well, Lord Basil, something must be done, some gesture must be made. A mere apology won't do. His Grace must be offered a substantial demonstration of regret."

"Yes, I realize that."

"You must let me know what form that demonstration will take, Lord Basil, before His Grace can dine with you this evening. Before you leave this room, in point of fact. Otherwise, he will take his dinner in private, in his quarters."

The Earl went to a window and gazed out. He did not wish Fawkner to see the raging anger in his face. "I could flay that boy!" he exclaimed.

"Ah!" said Fawkner. "There's a solution! Whip him. A hundred whacks with a cane!"

The Earl turned in genuine astonishment. "Sir Everard! This is not the *army*!"

"Nor the navy," chuckled the secretary. Fawkner looked pensive. "Well, let us reconsider an apology, Lord Basil. Written in the boy's own hand, and read by him to His Grace—in the company of some of those who witnessed the error. That would satisfy His Grace and heal his wounded dignity—and the incident will be forgotten."

Basil Kenrick blinked. It was a simple enough remedy, but he could not imagine his nephew apologizing to the Duke. His knowledge of the boy made him doubt the likelihood. Something about Hugh forbade the scenario from ever taking place. He said, tentatively, trying to sound as though it were a mere rhetorical question, "And if an apology proves...infeasible, what may be accepted in its stead?"

Fawkner clucked his tongue and sighed. "Forty strokes with a birch rod," he said. "Or with a cane. It matters not which. No, wait! We'll be inventive *and* merciful at the same time! Thirty-one strokes! One for each of His Grace's years! He'll appreciate that!" He paused to smile at the Earl. "Witnessed by me, of course. And then I must have the rod to present to His Grace as proof of his avenged dignity—and the incident will be forgotten. But—such a drastic measure, I'm sure, need not be resorted to. A brief apology will do. The boy must compose it himself, and present it without assistance from his parents. Are we agreed on these details?"

The Earl nodded and walked to the door. "I will go now and explain the situation to my brother."

Fawkner shrugged and began unlacing his shirt. "And when all this is past, Lord Basil, we might discuss the terms of this *wool* business. After dinner tonight. Can you have a plate of something sent up now? I'm famished!"

*   *   *

Basil Kenrick stood in the middle of his bedchamber while one valet dressed him in an afternoon frock coat, and another busily combed and powdered a wig at the dressing table. "Send for my broth...Send for the Baron, Clayborne. I wish to see him immediately." The valet gave one last smart tug at a sleeve, and went to the fireplace to pull on a tasseled velvet rope beside it.

Minutes later Garnet Kenrick appeared in the vestibule of the Earl's bedchamber. They were alone. The Earl told his brother what had been discussed with Everard Fawkner, and added some of his own thoughts. When he was finished, he glanced away from his brother's stolid face, because he did not need to guess what thoughts were hidden behind it. "Those are my conditions, dear brother," he concluded. "Your son has disgraced me, his family, and this house. It is only right that he should bear the brunt of that disgrace. If it were humanly possible, I would see him bear all of it." Then he turned and entered his chamber, and closed the door behind him.

*   *   *

Garnet Kenrick stood at his desk with his hands behind his back. Hugh stood before the desk, almost at attention. "You are not ill, sir, or light-headed," said his father. "Explain yourself."

"It was not a willful act, Father," said Hugh. "I simply forgot."

"How could you *forget*? After all the instruction, after all the examples set for you to see—how could you *forget*?"

"He...did not prompt me to bow."

"What?"

"I...saw nothing divine in him, sir. He is a noxious man." Hugh paused. "It did not occur to me to bow." He paused again, searching for words that would explain his actions even to himself. "He is not a great man. I did not feel compelled to bow, or to grant him any more courtesy than I would the village drunkard." He shook his head. "Still, Father, it was not willful."

Garnet Kenrick paced in back of his desk. "You may disrespect the man, but not his station and status, which demand your immediate and unquestioning deference." He paused. "You carry reason too far, Hugh. In this instance, reason applies to neither your action nor your estimation."

"It must apply to everything," protested Hugh. "To things natural and made by man, and to men themselves."

The Baron shook his head. "In most things, Hugh. Not all. There are exceptions. Some very mighty exceptions. This is one of them."

"I cannot honor a man who I think has no reason to receive it...from me."

The Baron furled his brow. "We are speaking of the King's son, Hugh, and of a prince! Of a hero of battles! Of a generous and magnanimous person! How can you compare His Grace—His Royal Highness, I might remind you—with a village drunkard?"

"I saw a very ordinary man today, Father. No magic or special power or intelligence emanated from that person. That is why I did not bow."

The Baron shook his head in exasperation. "I told you, Hugh—this is beyond reason! As beyond it as is God, and to question the honor one must pay to the Duke is tantamount to questioning one's devotion to God." He raised a finger and shook it at his son. "Hugh, men have been imprisoned, tortured, deprived of their property and livelihoods for the kind of inso-lence you showed today! Can you not appreciate the gravity of the matter?"

Hugh did not reply.

His father paced in back of his desk for a moment, then pointed to a chair. "Sit down, Hugh."

Hugh obeyed.

The Baron planted his hands flat on his desk. "Your uncle and I want you to write a note of apology to His Grace, which you are to read to him in our company. In it you will explain why you neglected to pay the respect due him—something, to the effect, that you were so struck by his presence that you...forgot. His Grace will continue on his journey the morning after tomorrow. Your apology must be ready for him by tomorrow midday." He paused. "I cannot overemphasize the gravity which seems to have eluded you, Hugh. Apart from the gross infraction of courtesy, there is the matter that your uncle went to great lengths to arrange this visit, and great sums of money were spent preparing for it. There is more at jeopardy here than our standing or His Grace's offended honor."

Hugh at first felt an icy shot of fear, then a strange aura of calm. He looked up at his father. "I cannot author an apology, Father."

The Baron's jaw dropped. "What did you say?"

"I cannot author such an apology." Hugh furled his own brow this time, hoping it would help him articulate his stand. "It would be a fraud."

"A *fraud*??"

"I would not mean it, sir. I could not mean it. I would know that, the Duke would know that. Everyone would know that." Hugh paused. "The Duke would know it best of all, that my apology would be a false one. You see, Father, *our eyes met*, and he knew what I thought of him, and I knew what he thought of me. And so, if he honors truth at all, the Duke would know that I did not mean anything, and the apology would mean nothing to him—as it would mean nothing to me."

Garnet Kenrick stood erect and stiffened his shoulders. "Fraudulent or not, Hugh, an apology is required, and an apology will be composed and addressed!" he commanded. "You are not being asked to apologize to the man, but to the person of his station! This is not a matter of personal offense, Hugh! It is a matter of *state*!"

Hugh glanced at the rug. He could say nothing in answer to this formidable fact.

Garnet Kenrick pursed his lips and said, "The alternative is a birching, Hugh, administered by me in the presence of your uncle and Sir Everard. Satisfaction will be had, in one form or another. The punishment is to be severe enough to draw blood. The instrument with such blood on it must be offered to His Grace as proof of punishment. Those are your *uncle's* demands, in lieu of an apology." The Baron stopped to sigh. "An apology, sincere or not, would seem the least painful course for you to choose."

"Father...I cannot author one."

The Baron turned and pounded the silk-clad wall once with a fist. The sconce nearby rattled and the flame in the candle flickered. "Why not, for heaven's sake?"

"Because...it would kill me, Father," replied Hugh, "inside, and nourish a wrong." The words seemed distant, almost as though another person had spoken them, because overriding the issue of the Duke and the terrible punishment was the first glimpse of something immeasurably more precious than remaining loyal to his conviction that the Duke did not deserve his humble recognition. He felt the faint glow of a self-awareness that muted the importance of everything around him, including his father, the house, Danvers, even the Duke. It was an emotion that made everything, even his stand, seem irrelevant. Yet, at the same time, his stand, while diminished now in his mind, was the catalyst for the emotion, and he knew that somehow the two phenomena were mutually, inexorably dependent. His stand acted as a kind of door to a greater, cleaner awareness of himself and everything else around him.

His son's last words echoed in Garnet Kenrick's mind. If he had heard a note of desperation in his son's reply, he might have relented and written and delivered the apology himself, pleading the illness of his son as an extenuating circumstance. But Hugh had said it with an unshakable conviction that seemed unconcerned with consequence; there had been no begging in his manner, no petulance, no plea for pity—no bow to the power and prerogative of his elders.

For was not the act of bowing a combination of submission to the majesty of power and of offering one's neck to the pleasure of the person endowed with that majesty? Was it merely a physical gesture, governed by strict rules of courtesy and protocol? The boy seemed more concerned with the life of his pride than with the dire consequences of not having performed that act. His refusal to write an apology was another form of that act, though this time it must be willful—Garnet Kenrick believed his son on that point—for it was a more conscious decision than his neglecting to bow.

Garnet Kenrick wanted to ask his son: "Are you saying that bowing to the Duke would bend more than just your spine, or that an apology to His Grace would bend more than your mind?" But he did not ask it. He knew the answer. Instead, he said in a low, tired voice, "Great men have paid their sovereign proper respect, Hugh, and assumed the entitled decorum, and still remained great *and* men. Can you do no less than they?"

Hugh did not answer.

"Why, the Duke of Monmouth made a private confession to Charles the Second of his complicity in a plot to assassinate his king. *He* bowed with the best of them!"

Hugh averted his father's eyes for the first time, not from shame, but because a word had entered his mind, an ugly word that he did not want to associate with his father: extortion.

Garnet Kenrick studied his son. Outwardly, he bristled at his son's defiance. Secretly, he was pleased, even envious, though he would never admit these things to himself. He thought: "I wish him to be what I was never brave enough to be." He thought: "We—Effney and I—have a monster for a son, and he will bring us grief—or much pride." He thought: "My son will not live long enough to be the Earl of Danvers. He will be struck down by God or by the Crown, for he seems not to pay either of those powers any mind." He thought: "My son will be a great man—or he will never reach manhood."

These thoughts drove him on. The Baron said, "Birching will be but the beginning of your punishment, Hugh—if you do not do this thing. In the absence of an apology, your uncle has insisted on this, also: that, for a

year, you be banished from the dining table. That you scrupulously avoid
the presence and sight of your uncle. That should you encounter him in his
house, you are not to expect him to either speak to you or acknowledge
your presence. That you not enter either his library or his quarters. That
you not be asked to join our company in the evenings. That you not attend
any ball, concert, or ridotto that may be held in this house. That you take
your meals in your room. That the servants treat you like a leper. Finally,
that we—your mother and I—not speak to you in the presence of others,
particularly your uncle's, except in the most dire circumstances."

The Baron paused to study his son's face. He hoped to see some sign of
wavering. He also hoped to be spared a punishment that would be no less
cruel for him and his wife than it would be for Hugh. Instead, he saw a
flicker of pain, then a fleeting beat of defiance, and then, again, that odd
sense of calm. He went on. "Those are your options, Hugh. Thirty minutes
devoted to composing an apology—versus a year of shame and solitude. A
transient gesture of humility, or a year of ostracism." He paused. "What say
you?"

Hugh was more perplexed by his father's willingness to acquiesce to his
uncle's demands than by the severity of his punishment. He saw the
strange expression on his father's face, an inexplicable mixture of hope and
stoically muted pain. Hugh, though, was governed by his own conviction,
and these observations were subordinate to it. A test was being set before
him. He tried to imagine a year of enforced loneliness; a huge question
mark filled it. He did not know if he could endure it. But his estimate of the
Duke was an absolute that forbade him any action but loyalty to it; it would
not be cheated of its ineluctable finality. It was a wall erected by his own
hand, and nothing would persuade him to loosen or remove a single brick
of it.

Hugh stood up, took a step from the chair, and shook his head. "I will
not author an apology."

The Baron shut his eyes for a moment. "Very well, Hugh," he said with
a heaviness Hugh had never heard in him before. "Your punishment will
commence tonight. You will be birched before dinner, which you may not
attend. Then you must go to your room and not leave it until His Grace has
departed."

Chapter 7: The Punishment

A WORD OR TWO ABOUT WILLIAM AUGUSTUS, DUKE OF CUMBERLAND, who was also Baron of the Isle of Alderney, Viscount of Trematon in Cornwall, Earl of Kennington in Surrey, Marquis of Berkhamsted in Hertfordshire, and Knight of the Bath. The Duke began his life with a fair appearance and a sharp, absorbent mind. A poet once referred to the young prince as "Adonis." As an infant and a growing boy, he was hailed as "the darling of the nation." He was an assiduous learner, and displayed signs of potential for becoming either a Latin scholar or an engineering genius. He had the benefit of instruction by the best tutors his father the king could hire, including close personal association with Isaac Newton and Edmund Halley; he so esteemed Newton that he insisted on attending his funeral. He became fluent in French, German, and Italian. He had a quick wit and was noted for his repartee. He was physically active and cut a trim, handsome figure for the adoring newspapers and court biographers to report.

But a sharp, absorbent mind is not necessarily a critical one. In his elevated, privileged station, the Duke failed to develop a mind of his own in the things that mattered. His rank at the top of English society spared him the absolute necessity of forming his own judgments, a crucial task shirked often enough even by those who must make their way on their own skills and intelligence without benefit of royal promotion. The Duke left the moulding of his character to the chance influences of fashion, royal protocol, and the banalities of the moral wisdom of his age. He was not born to be the caricature of profligate dissipation that he was eventually to become, but he neglected to think for himself, and so he became that caricature. Nature will not tolerate a vacuum, neither in the physical world, nor in men's souls.

It would be unfair to say that Cumberland had formed no evaluative powers. He had developed a shrewdness for appraising horses, women, sportsmen, and games of chance. He introduced the unpopular notion of promotion by merit for army officers, and assumed the equally unpopular and thankless task of standardizing the army and removing large segments of it from hereditary control by noblemen and from larcenous colonels rich enough to buy whole regiments from vanity. Obviously, he judged the army ripe for improvement.

Early in his life, the Duke showed a penchant for things military, and he pursued a military career. As this career progressed, his mind dulled, and his appearance seemed to register the growth of the dullness with complementary degrees of obesity. The slim, sharp young prince became a stocky middle-aged man with a large, commanding, but insipid face. He moved heavily, and later in life with difficulty. He loved horses, and owned and raced stables of them. He loved women, married or not, and the aristocracy of gossips counted his conquests. He loved boxing, and promoted the careers of some of England's most famous pugilists. He loved gambling, and bet, lost, and won small fortunes on everything from dog races to cards to the course of a raindrop down a windowpane.

He loved war, too, but because war requires a man to be able to think on his feet, to know how to elude peril yet be one himself, to know how to assess the character and intentions of an enemy, and to act with imagination and initiative, the Duke's career was a lackluster, blameless one. It was only at Culloden Moor that he gained an upper hand over any enemy, chiefly by default of the Young Pretender, whose campaign during the Jacobite Rebellion was conducted by mood and whimsy. Elsewhere, the Duke proved to be a general whose military skills were limited mostly to a talent for withdrawing from an engagement in good order and with honor—that is, he was able to pull most of his chestnuts from the many fires lit by his thinking opponents. He displayed no special political leanings, other than whatever was right by his father the king; and so he developed no political talent, no shrewd acuity, and was easy prey to those who had leanings, acuity, and the requisite talent.

In short, the Duke of Cumberland was a tragic example of a man who became basely common because he did not need to think. A beat was missed by him some time in his life. Perhaps he knew this, though it is doubtful. It requires an introspective, critical mind to detect such a loss.

This was the man Hugh Kenrick saw.

Hugh Kenrick knew only a smattering of the details of the Duke's life; but not even these were necessary for him to form an estimate of the man he witnessed striding grandly up the steps of his home. The splendiferous figure could just as well have been an impostor, an impersonator, or a mannequin. It would have made no difference.

This was the man to whom Hugh Kenrick neglected to bow. Because he forgot all the power and glory that was appended to the figure, and saw only the figure. Because he sensed that even the village drunkard might have a pathetic excuse for being a drunkard, while the Duke, for all the spectacular benefits, advantages, and emoluments bestowed on him throughout his life, was essentially a nondescript blank.

This was as honest an observation for a child to make as that a king wore no clothes. The Duke was magnificently arrayed in the finest traveling garments, yet the child saw nothing in them.

The man who had no critical faculty encountered the boy who had. The boy paid the price.

*   *   *

Hugh Kenrick waited in his room until his pocket watch, ironically a gift from his uncle two birthdays ago, read six o'clock. Then he rose from his desk, left his room, and walked through the chilly corridors to the eastern wing and his uncle's study, as his father had instructed him.

Hugh spent the hours between the time in his father's study and this moment in his own room. His mother, responsible for preparing tonight's banquet, had stopped in to see him. She had never scolded him before, and did not scold him now. She did not say much to him; he could not remember what she said, except that it was brief, perfunctory, and regretful. He remembered only that she studied him with an expression oddly reminiscent of how she sometimes looked at his father.

He did not know it, but his father had furtively sought the advice of his valet about how to mitigate the severity of the whipping. "Can we somehow substitute rabbit's or chicken's blood?"

"No, milord," had answered Owen. "If the gentleman, Sir Everard, is to witness the punishment, then there is no way to simulate the wound." He offered to administer the birching himself.

"No, Owen, thank you, but this is my doing, I think. If he should hate anyone, it should be me."

Owen cleared his throat. "His lordship will insist that such a task is unseemly for a man of your rank, milord."

Garnet Kenrick's face became a mask of defiance. "And I will remind him that it is the prerogative of a father."

*   *   *

"I would die, inside, and nourish a wrong." Hugh reflected on these words while he waited in his room. But the thoughts came so quickly that he went to his desk, opened one of his school notebooks, and tried to write them down.

That thought, those words, had come to him like a divine revelation. The truth of the words was so brilliantly clear, almost as though he were describing a tree, or the shape of a book, that he could not help but utter them. Yet, the wisdom of the thought was a mere consequence of some other, more fundamental and intimate knowledge of himself, something that was so joyous that it made the wisdom irrelevant. Another boy, had he stumbled upon this wisdom, might have made it a core premise that would govern his character and actions for the balance of his life. He would have deserved the esteem of other men. But Hugh did not think it sufficient reason to cherish it that way. He did not know why, and he did not deny its ineluctable finality, but it was not enough. "It is a right thing to know," he wrote in his notebook, "but is it enough to make a religion of it? I would respect the man who wore it as the raiment of his soul, and never belittle him—I would thrash the person who did so!—but is there not some wonderful thing about oneself to which such a truth owes allegiance? It is an efficacious truth, but it is a servant to that thing. One does not live to starve wrongs, to deny sustenance to evil. It is important for a man—for his honor, for justice—to be able to judge when it is best to employ this servant—nay, to know that the servant is there to be employed."

The thing he had felt when pressed for an answer by his father, he might have called a touch by the finger of God, had he known what that phenomenon felt like. And though the knowledge and the concomitant emotion seemed to light up his mind and all the atoms of his being, he suspected that his experience had little to do with God.

The corridor walls were lined with the portraits of his ancestors through the centuries, men and women, as children and adults, some in equestrian settings, some with their pets, some in their gorgeous ermines. There was even a crude likeness of the first Baron of Danvers. He was on horseback, in full armor, brandishing a mace and shield, and in the background was a town in flames, a town which he and his thanes had erased for denying homage to William the Conqueror. Family legend held that when he was offered the baronetcy by an emissary of the Conqueror, on the condition that he deliver all the towns and villages in his own and the neighboring Saxon parishes, he had replied: "The town that does not swear fealty to my liege lord does not exist." This became true. He made it so. *Vires facit veritas.* Force makes truth.

That ancestor's name was Hugh Kenrick.

His far descendent realized that he had stopped to study the picture. The sight of it had triggered the memory of an afternoon years ago when he told a tutor that he would bring honor to his family for the first time. He was discovering now, as a deliberated action, the meaning of honor.

*   *   *

The rod that was to be used in the punishment was taken from a branch of a birch tree on the grounds. On the vicar's advice, the Earl had the rod thawed, shaved, and soaked in water and vinegar. The advice was given by the vicar during a confidential interview granted by the Earl in the afternoon. "This treatment will make the instrument supple and increase the sting," he had said. "Some blood may be drawn—if this is what is required to restore your standing with His Grace—as you say it is."

"As Sir Everard says it is," answered the Earl. He studied the vicar. "Have you written a treatise on corporeal punishment, my good man?" he asked. "Surely, this is not the spiritual advice you led me to believe you had wanted to offer me on the matter."

"No, your lordship," replied the vicar with uncertain amusement, "though I imagine that some thoughtful man has. There are books now on so many unlikely subjects. My father, who was a humble smithy, had he been literate enough, could have written you one. He was a master of wood. I was a frequent subject of his many rods, when I was your nephew's age, and older." The vicar paused to smile. "The rod in its many manifestations has helped make me a good Christian."

The Earl smiled wryly. The vicar did not recognize the twist in the mouth as a smile. "No doubt you can recommend a technique of wielding the rod," remarked the Earl with veiled sarcasm.

The vicar was not certain that he was being mocked. "No, your lordship, I cannot." He blinked once, then asked, "May I witness the punishment, your lordship? The event may inspire a sermon."

"You may witness it, but not preach about it, except in the most general terms."

"Thank you, your lordship. I take my leave."

*   *   *

A servant opened the doors to the Earl's study. Hugh went in, and the doors closed behind him. His uncle sat at his desk. His father, Sir Everard, and the vicar rose from their seats. All were dressed for dinner, which would begin at eight. Owen, the valet, stood by the doors, holding the rod.

Hugh approached his uncle's desk and stopped.

The Earl's eyes drilled into him. "Has the matter been clearly explained to you, sir?"

"Yes," answered Hugh.

"And you are cognizant of your choices?"

"Yes."

The Earl leaned forward a little. "I grant you one last opportunity to make amends with an apology."

Hugh shook his head. "I waive the opportunity, thank you."

"So be it. The remaining conditions of your punishment will come into effect once you leave this room."

"I understand that."

The Earl rose to glare down at his nephew. He drew in a breath. "What will be done now will atone for the humiliation and abject disgrace you have brought to this house." He pointed a finger at the edge of the desk directly in front of Hugh. "You will prepare yourself, sir." When the boy was ready, the Earl nodded to his brother.

The Baron held out a hand. Owen stepped forward and placed the rod in it.

Hugh heard his father's steps on the rug. And then the whoosh of the rod through the air.

At first, he felt the pain, which, by the third stroke, seemed like a razor ploughing into his skin. After a while, he felt nothing but a dull, anonymous force that came at the end of each swish. His nerves had become as insensate as the polished wood gripped by his hands. He refused to cry out, and bit his lip. A pair of tears escaped from his eyes, as when a blast of winter wind would hit his face.

At each stroke, the men in the room winced. All but the vicar. Hugh could not see their faces, but he knew somehow that his father's was shiny with sweat. Then someone in the room gasped at the same time he felt a peculiar, warm sting, and he knew that blood had been drawn.

Some time after that, Sir Everard's voice said, "Thirty-one, Sir Garnet."

"I can count, Sir Everard!" replied the Baron sharply.

"I beg your forgiveness," muttered the secretary.

The rod stopped whistling through the air. It was finished. Hugh turned and saw his father looking at the rod, which now had smears of blood on the end of it. His father did not look at him when he said, "When you have made yourself presentable, Hugh, you may leave." He turned to address the valet. "Mr. Runcorn, you will see that my son returns to his quarters."

"Yes, milord."

Owen held one of the doors open for Hugh, and they went out together.

The Baron first approached Sir Everard, but then changed his mind and walked over to his brother. He held out the birch rod. "Here is the proof of repentance required for His Grace. Please, present it to his...factotum."

The Earl's eyes narrowed, but he shrugged off the insult to himself and the secretary. He drew himself up, took the rod, and smartly presented it to Sir Everard. "Your evidence, Sir Everard—and my apologies."

"All duly noted, I'm sure," said the secretary. He examined the rod, bowed his head, and left the room without further word.

Garnet Kenrick turned to the vicar. "Unless you are apprenticing for a position in hell as Satan's lackey, vicar, the spectacle is finished, and there is no more for you to see."

The vicar blushed, sputtered an incomplete word or two, and glanced at the Earl, who stood looking at him with an expression as stony as the one with which he regarded his nephew. The cleric said to the Baron, "I forgive you the jest, milord, under these most stressful circumstances." Then he quickly left the room.

The Baron next turned to his brother. "Are you satisfied, Basil?"

The Earl started at the use of his Christian name. He could not remember the last time it had been used. "Dear brother, well, you see what the situation is, and I—"

"We will discuss this no more, Basil," said the Baron. "Ever." And he left the room.

*   *   *

The pain suddenly seized his legs like a douse of scalding water. Hugh buckled, and violently clutched at a table they were passing, almost knocking over a candle. He leaned on the table with both hands, able to stand, but unable to move his legs. His eyelids fluttered, and the hall seemed to spin.

"Allow me, milord," said Owen. The valet bent and picked up the boy, heaved him over one shoulder, and walked calmly to the western wing. In Hugh's room, he lay the unconscious boy gently face down on the bed and removed his coat, breeches, and shoes.

The Baroness came into the room and rushed over to her son. Owen let her inspect the swelling red stripes and the blood on her son's body. The woman let go an awful cry of pain that had not come from the boy. Then the valet inclined his head, reached into a pocket of his coat, and held out a small round tin box. "If you will permit me, milady," he said.

"What is it, Owen?" she asked, not taking the box.

"It is balm, milady. Apply it liberally to all the affected parts. Expose the wounds as little as possible to the air, which will aggravate the wounds and prolong the pain."

The Baroness frowned, but took the tin.

"The balm was prepared by Mrs. Jervis in the kitchen, milady, at my request. It is composed of herbs in an aspic of buttered cream. It is most effective. Master Kenrick should be able to move about in a day or two. With discretion, of course."

"Thank you, Owen."

The valet paused, swallowed, and went on. "It may be impertinent to say so, milady, but while the staff of this house, and that of his lordship the Earl, will obey his lordship's instructions regarding the treatment of Master Hugh henceforth, I feel it…important to convey to you and to the Baron— through you, at your pleasure, of course—that our actions will not reflect our true hearts."

"Oh…?"

"For myself, milady, I feel obliged to say that if circumstances occur which require me to choose between my dismissal and regarding Master Kenrick as a leper, I should choose dismissal."

The Baroness nodded her head once in acknowledgment. "Thank you, Mr. Runcorn. Take care to see that such a choice is not necessary. The Baron and I value your service."

"Thank you, milady. Will that be all?"

"Yes. Please send for Bridget."

Bridget came in a moment later, and found the Baroness gingerly applying the balm to her son. "I will be detained by the dinner this evening, Bridget," she said to the governess. "You will come back here at ten and apply Owen's salve anew."

"Yes, milady. How is he?"

"He will heal. Go about your duties now, Bridget."

The Baroness remained for a moment, stroking Hugh's damp hair. After a while she rose and went to her son's desk. She saw an open notebook and idly read one page, then another. She read the first sentence: "I would die, inside, and nourish a wrong." And she read the last sentence: "I have brought honor to my family, and to myself, for the first time." She put a hand to her mouth to stifle a cry. For the first time, she understood her son. She guiltily took the notebook and left the room.

* * *

The dinner was a brilliant, gay affair, as the Earl had hoped it would be. The Duke, his companions, and the guests behaved as though nothing untoward had happened. Bons mots lit up the glittering company's conversation, competing with the candles that flickered magically on the silver and china service that was laid on the fine cambric. The Baroness had made a gift to all the women guests of blue silk fans on which had been painted sweet Williams, and these fluttered in time with the bons mots. She had even had delicate vases of carnations and blue auriculas from the greenhouse placed on the table and sideboards. The conversation shifted from the Duke's adventures on the tour, to the popular discontent with the adjustment of the calendar in the coming September, in which eleven days were to be skipped in order to bring England into conformity with the Gregorian calendar, to a miscellany of other, triter subjects, all governed by the Duke's careering interests.

The Earl was in his glory, while the Baron and Baroness were subdued. The empty chair between the couple was to have been occupied by Hugh. Everyone noticed the vacancy, but coldly averted their eyes. Rear Admiral Harle alone sympathized with the couple's reticence. Fortunately, the Baroness had seated him next to her husband, and the admiral was able to communicate his thoughts under all the chatter. "His Grace is becoming rather boorish, I must admit," he remarked in a low voice. "I have been on the road with him for a week now, and his company has grown tiresome."

"I can see how that might be true," ventured the Baron with caution.

"However, that does not excuse my son's actions."

The admiral smiled. He had not known his motive was so transparent. "Perhaps not," he replied without conviction. "Although I myself have lately mistaken His Grace alternately for a Drury Lane clown and a Smithfield cattle-drover."

The Baron merely smiled, also without conviction. "How do you plan to spend your day tomorrow, Sir Francis?" he asked in a tactful change of subject.

The admiral took a sip of claret. "We shall tour the Poole Harbor. I will propose to His Grace that we hire a boat that will take us out to the Channel, so that we might appraise the vicinity from an invading enemy's vantage point. I had intended to ask you or the Earl for assistance in the matter."

"I know of several men in Poole who would lend you their smacks." The Baron gladly put down his knife and fork, and finished his glass of Madeira. He had no appetite, and had been eating for appearance' sake. "Poole Harbor is sandy. We have a schooner, but it puts in at Weymouth more often than it does Poole, on account of the shifting bottom, which often is made impassable by the tides."

"So the Admiralty maps tell me."

"As for fortifications, I've always thought that either the Purbeck or Poole neck would be ideal for them. Or Brownsea Isle itself."

"My thoughts precisely," said the admiral. "Will you accompany us?"

"It would be my pleasure, Sir Francis," said the Baron. "Unfortunately, I must accompany Fawkner on an inspection of our herds."

"Ah, *that* business! Then, his lordship, your brother?"

The Baron shook his head. "My brother does not like the sea. It rollicks his stomach, and he will not risk the indignity of the consequences."

Later, after a dessert of blancmange and Pomfret cake, the company at the long table grew restive. The servants hastened to keep the epergnes refreshed with sweetmeats and the silver wine fountains flowing from the stock in the cellar. Cumberland consulted his pocket watch, then rose abruptly and proclaimed: "Leave us, dear ladies, so that we mere men may knock back a sinful ginful, and discourse on the disreputable without risk of offending your dainty lobes!" He nodded and bestowed a smile on Vicar Wynne. "You, too, sir, if you fear the profane."

Miss Harris giggled.

The vicar blanched. "I have, in my time, Your Grace, heard seamen swear, and harlots catalogue their arts. Profane talk is no stranger to my callused ears."

The Duke laughed. "Ah! A man of the world and the cloth, whose collar and station require him to warn us against cussing and knocking-shops! Behold, company, a veritable St. Augustine here! No doubt it was this God's gillie—forgive the Scottish term!—who prescribed the chastening of the Childe Aristides!"

The allusion to Hugh Kenrick's whipping was unmistakable. Everyone understood it, even the servants standing at the ready beneath the paintings, who, having little in the way of a classical education, knew nothing about Aristides the Just, the ancient Greek general and jurist who was banished from Athens for shaming its law courts. The Baron, the Baroness and the Earl did not know what to make of the remark; it could have been an inadvertent compliment, an offhand insult, or the tactless consequence of too many draws from the wine fountain. Sir Everard Fawkner sat immobile, staring at a painting on the wall.

"Forgive me, Your Grace," answered the vicar nervously, "but you have been ill-informed. *I* did not prescribe the punishment. I had the mere honor and duty of *refining* it."

"Much the same thing," quipped the Duke with a mischievous chuckle. "Your hand could be seen on the *reddened* rod of Mars—metaphorically speaking."

Garnet Kenrick looked up with new interest, first at the flustered vicar, then at the insouciant mien of Fawkner, and finally at the supercilious composure of his brother, the Earl. The Earl caught his eye, but glanced away. The Baron stared at him now with a venom in his glance that he disguised only with great effort.

At this point, because she did not wish to prolong the vicar's baiting—though she thought he deserved it—and because she suspected her husband's thoughts, because they were very likely her own—the Baroness chose to rise. All the other women rose on the signal. "By your leave, Your Grace," she said with a bow of her head.

"Retire, fair lady," replied the Duke with a wave of his glass. "And, I *must* say this: If I cannot esteem the good Baron there for his contumacious progeny, then I must envy him for his taste in alluring conjugality!"

The table laughed dutifully. Garnet Kenrick blushed, but inclined his head in acknowledgment of the crude compliment. The men at the table rose in courtesy, and the Baroness led the procession of gowns from the great hall. Maud Harris turned once and winked provocatively at the Duke.

When the women were gone, some of the men drew out their pipes and snuffboxes. The servants busied themselves with decanting harder liquor than what was acceptable at dinner. Cumberland fell back into his chair. "Well, Lord Basil, have you any good racers hereabouts?"

The Earl smiled apologetically. "Our steeds mostly pull hay, Your Grace, or uproot stumps in our fields with the oxen."

"Pugilists?"

"None to speak of, Your Grace," ventured Drew Tallmadge. "The fist trade among the population here is embarrassingly artless."

The Duke chuckled. "Then you must journey up to London frequently, to escape the boredom!"

"Often, Your Grace," said Covington Brune. "But on business, mostly."

"Too often," muttered Garnet Kenrick to himself, with a glance at his brother.

"Pretty country, Dorset," mused Cumberland. "Pretty holdings you gentry have here. Yours especially, Lord Basil. Your terraces are placid enough to inspire a poem or two. The sheep safely graze!—to borrow a notion from that Bach fellow!"

"It is prettier in the spring, Your Grace," said the Earl. "In all fairness, however, it is to my brother the credit must be given."

*　　*　　*

Later that night, the Baron, the Earl, and Sir Everard discussed the army contract. And when the Duke and his companions had retired, and the guests had departed, Garnet Kenrick walked wearily to his and his wife's bedchamber. Effney Kenrick showed her husband the pages from Hugh's notebook. "We have made a martyr of him, Garnet," she said.

"*I* have made him a martyr," replied the Baron. "*You* did not wield the rod."

The Baroness shook her head. "I sanctioned its use."

In silence, the Baron read the pages. He recognized the first sentence. And he understood the last.

"It is an alien thing he discusses there, Garnet," said the Baroness. "But I know it is right."

"It is not so alien a thing to me," mused the Baron. His wife wondered why his words sounded like a wrenching confession.

The Baroness sat down on the bed next to her husband. "I am certain of this much, Garnet: I shall no longer be afraid for Hugh. Such a thing as he observes about himself cannot ever be broken, or tamed, or made to submit."

Garnet Kenrick looked away from his wife, and merely nodded in agreement. Then he reached out and held her close, so that she could not see the tears in his eyes. He agreed with her, but not entirely. He hoped he could some day. Then he held her away and told her what he had learned, and what he must do.

A   ᴡ   ⁂

Still dressed for dinner, and silver candleholder in hand, he called on his brother in his bedchamber after the Earl's valet had gone. The Earl was dressed in his nightgown and day cap. "Yes, my tireless brother?" he inquired, amiably stepping aside. "What can I do for you?"

The Baron passed without word through the anteroom and into the bedchamber. He set down the candle on a wing table, faced his brother, and asked, "Do you hate my son so much that you wished to see him bleed?"

"What?" replied the Earl.

"I have spoken with Vicar Wynne and Sir Everard. The vicar states that you claimed that Sir Everard required the rod to draw blood. Sir Everard, in turn, asserts that he demanded no such thing. Moreover, he said that His Grace did not demand it. Ergo, it was your assertion alone— your desire." The Baron paused. "Not that any one of them was *displeased* with the blood."

The Earl sniffed. "It was my duty and privilege to require it," he answered, turning his back with nonchalance on his brother.

"It was a lie, and I was made the instrument of it."

"It has secured us a lucrative contract."

"That remains to be seen," said the Baron. "Sir Everard and his friends have a large gallery of applicants for their largess. And the contract means nothing to me. But you, Basil, lied to me, and through me, injured my son. Why?"

"I do not hate your son."

"You were eager to see him punished."

"He offended the Duke, and me as well, and embarrassed this family."

"*Why*, Basil?" insisted the Baron.

The Earl would not answer. He drifted to the fireplace and held his hands in the emanating warmth.

The Baron said, "You have the Duke to thank for this interview, dear brother. In his own thick way, he put me on to the lie. You may thank His Grace—if you dare."

The Earl jerked around to face him, his face wrinkled in ugly petulance, and spat out the words, "*He is a son I cannot have, and you are raising him wrong! He needs correction!*"

The Baron smiled and shook his head. "Hugh is a prodigy of unknown stamp, dear brother. And he is raising himself. Neither I nor Effney nor any tutor we may hire is equal to that task. He will be a stronger man than either of us. And he will be a great earl, someday." Garnet Kenrick smiled wistfully. "A *nobleman*, dear brother. Something, in fact, neither of us is, if we correctly parse the meaning of that word."

The Baron paced back and forth thoughtfully. "Besides, Basil, you *have* a son. Jared. Son of the late Felise Turley, once a maidservant in our father's household, then his occasional mistress—until our father's exertions with her in a Weymouth inn ended in sorrow. We blamed that hapless cook—I forget his name—to preserve the family's good name. And you retained the comely Miss Turley, and eventually also developed an appetite for her. A costly one, it has turned out. Where the father failed, the son succeeded. It would be an interesting tale to tell the Duke. He would be amused. The good earl owns not a racing horse, nor a pugilist, but a bastard son. He respects such...sport."

The Earl glanced at his brother with wicked indifference, and poured himself a glass of port.

"So do not tell me that Hugh needs correction, dear brother. A son of *yours* may not even enter Danvers, he is such a blot on our good name. He is being raised with money sent by the royal post through a third party, to a brother of his late mother's, a hard-drinking saddler in Lyme Regis, who gives him none of the advantages of your moral authority. I have observed your son from a distance, Basil. You have not. Jared is quite a nasty *bastard*. With luck—and your generosity—he should raise himself up to the level of a London Mohock. A bully. A wastrel. Gallows bait."

"I refuse to discuss him," replied the Earl, his words bitterly toneless. This time he smiled. "I have lied to you in the past, *dear brother*," he said, turning his back on the Baron. "And you shrugged it off, or even laughed."

"I did not mind being your dupe, so long as I was the only one duped.

This matter, however, is of a graver scale." The Baron stopped pacing, stood thinking for a moment, then turned to his brother. "I concede the offense to His Grace. But I will not concede your offense to me. I ask that you reduce Hugh's sentence to four months."

The Earl whirled around, spilling the contents of his glass in the movement. "I cannot do that!" he exclaimed. "Everyone knows that it is to be for a year!"

"Everyone will think you magnanimous. That is for you to cherish. But—it is either that, or I will shortly follow the Duke, when he departs. I shall remove my family and possessions from this house and from Danvers—and Danvers and the estate and the contract, and *you*, dear brother, can go to blazes—as surely it all will, under your enlightened guidance."

The Earl's glass slipped from his fingers and struck the carpet with a muted thud. "You would not leave!"

"I would, Basil," said the Baron. "I would not have come to this room if I did not think it absolutely necessary to be here."

The Earl stared at his brother with dumbstruck terror.

The Baron picked up his candleholder. "I grant you the night in which to entertain this concession, and to accustom yourself to it, Basil." He walked to the door, then stopped to face his brother again. "Oh…and I would be grateful if, on the morrow, when you speak again with His Grace and Colonel Wolfe, that you correct the anecdote you related to everyone this evening, about that cook and the haggis he served our late father. *We* did not beat him. *You* did. I merely wanted the fellow banished. He was a harmless, ignorant soul. Good night, dear brother."

Chapter 8: The Watershed

WHEN HE AWOKE THE NEXT MORNING, HUGH KENRICK LEARNED painfully that he could only hobble at a snail's pace, and not sit at all. Soon the pain ceased to be a personal affliction to him, and became a kind of external impediment, a nuisance like a pair of leg braces.

A number of incidents occurred that morning before he was taken to his tutors on the Tallmadge estate. When she had finished helping him dress, Bridget, his governess, pecked him on the cheek.

"Why did you do that?" he asked, surprised.

"You are a young man, milord," she said with a grin. "If you were a few years older, you'd see more than a kiss," she added playfully.

His mother came into the room to inform him of a reduction in his punishment, from a year to four months, and of the freeing of the servants from the requirement that they treat him like a leper. "All the other conditions remain. But you are not to communicate this news to anyone until His Grace has departed tomorrow. This is most important."

"Why did Uncle change his mind?"

Effney Kenrick smiled secretively, wanting to reply, "It was not so much your uncle changing his mind, Hugh, as it was your father making up his own." Instead, she said, "Your father can be very persuasive, and your uncle unaccountably lenient."

And when he went outside to the dogcart that awaited him by the door that he was to use from now on—for he was no longer to pass through his uncle's part of the house—he encountered Admiral Harle and Otis Talbot, pipes in hand, talking amiably in the brisk morning air. They stopped when they noticed him. The Admiral gave him a studied but cryptic grin, and doffed his hat once in a naval salute. The colonial agent regarded him more closely, and inclined his head, not in deference to Hugh's rank, but in apparent courtesy to an equal. Hugh nodded once in acknowledgment and passed on. He wondered, as the cart sped down the estate road, why the men had so behaved. He sensed that their actions had little to do with his rank. In classes that day, he stood the whole time at his desk. He defied the curious glances of his tutors and classmates, then grew inured to them. No one mentioned either his faux pas, or his condition, or the rumored punishment he had endured.

Only Roger Tallmadge spoke of it, during a spell between tutors. He had a black eye. "Francis called you so many names, and said you were a fool and a lurdane," he said excitedly. "And I said he had no right to judge you, and that he was the same! So we fought and he gave me this, and I bloodied his nose!"

"Thank you."

After an awkward pause, Roger Tallmadge asked, "Why did you do it?"

"Not pay courtesy to the Duke?"

"Yes. Everyone's talking about it."

"I forgot," replied Hugh, shrugging.

"You did not apologize, or express any regret?"

"No."

"Did you cry—when you were birched? Were you tempted to apologize?"

"No."

Roger Tallmadge sighed. "I wish I had your courage, Hugh."

"It was not courage."

"What was it?"

"I think it was justice," replied Hugh, after a moment of thought.

"It was justice that caused you to do it—I mean, not bow?"

Hugh again thought for a moment. "It was not a matter of what caused me to do it, Roger. Rather, it was a matter of an absence of a cause." He saw the perplexed look on his friend's face. "A man should bow at his pleasure, and not blindly. He should be able to choose his object of honor, one that complements his own."

"But...it is the custom to bow."

"It is not mine."

"He is the son of our king."

This Hugh could not deny. George the Second was indeed his king. Everyone's king. And the Duke, his son, could become king someday.

*   *   *

Garnet Kenrick sat in his study, content to be alone for a moment, before he dressed and prepared for this evening's dinner and ball. He had spent most of the day with his brother and Everard Fawkner, talking about

Danvers, its business, its history, local politics, and court gossip during a tour of the estate. Fawkner had expressed warm admiration for the organization and apparent prosperity of the Earl's possessions, and asked many questions about the herds of sheep and the wool they produced. It had been a tedious task, made more taxing by having to ride the whole day in a drafty post-chaise in a stiff winter wind. Garnet Kenrick did not think that his exertions had guaranteed him and his brother the army contract. He felt exhausted.

Not even his brother's capitulation this morning on Hugh's punishment could rouse the Baron. He knew that while it had been a victory, it would plague their relationship from now on.

For a reason he could not explain, his sight kept returning to the black ribbon tied to the neck of the statue of Hermes on his desk. He remembered that he had put it there to remind him of the mystery that surrounded the fate of the Skelly gang in Cornwall. It seemed so long ago, and he was no closer to solving it.

But the sight of it triggered another memory, of a pair of books hidden behind some others on a high shelf above him. In a spurt of energy he rose, climbed a stepladder, and retrieved the books. When they lay before him on his desk, he smiled. In a gesture of defiance, he resolved to do with them what he had first thought to do. Defiance against what? he thought. Against his brother. Against Fawkner, and the Duke. Against the thing that had made him a party to his son's punishment. He picked up one of the volumes and weighed it in his hand; it was mere paper and ink and tooled leather over pasteboard, but it seemed to be as augural as a hangman's noose.

It was a novel that lay before him. Its full title was *Hyperborea; or, the Adventures of Drury Trantham, Shipwrecked Merchant, in the Unexplored Northern Regions,* by Romney Marsh, Gent. Romney Marsh, he knew, had been an alias of one of the smugglers hanged in Cornwall so many years ago. The son of a prominent London merchant, too, he recalled. He had been at the Royal Exchange in London then, meeting with Benjamin Worley and other city merchants, when a king's man had posted the proclamation stigmatizing the book on a nearby pillar. Curiosity drove him to a bookseller's to purchase a copy of the novel. He read it on the coach trip back to Danvers. It had given him a strange, fearful pleasure. He could not imagine what could drive the man who could write such a book to a life of crime—unless it was an infatuation with the criminal and seditious actions that occurred in the novel, or something for which he had no name, but which seemed to animate his son, to whom he could attach no criminal motivation. He had heard his son's explanation for his actions; he had thought about those words; he could not digest them.

There was as much mystery in the novel's appeal to him as there was in the mystery surrounding the black ribbon. He could penetrate neither. He would give these books to his son. He did not know how this gesture could be defiance, but it was that. He felt as duty-bound to do this as he had felt duty-bound to punish his son. He knew that the gesture would be more for his own sake than for his son's; it would make his life more tolerable, and perhaps make his son's harder. In the books lay some inexplicable salvation, or redemption. He could not decide whether it was he or his son who was to be redeemed.

He loved his son, but could not now think of another way to express that love except to give him a proscribed book. It was almost as though he were contemplating giving a young Brutus the dagger with which to slay a future Caesar. He could fathom his motive no further. He was a highborn Englishman, and even the most thoughtful of his rank were noted more for their compulsions than for the depth of their introspection.

*   *   *

At the end of the day, when Hugh returned to his room, he found a pair of books sitting on his desk, accompanied by a note in his father's hand dryly cautioning him neither to take the books from his room nor ever to mention the books in the presence of his uncle. When he was about a hundred pages into the book, and had grasped the spirit of the story and the unleveled character of Drury Trantham, he stopped to wonder at the silent, unnamed purpose of his father in giving the book to him.

Garnet Kenrick called on him in his room that evening before the banquet and ball commenced. The Baron was ready to accept anything from his son. Even forgiveness. But Hugh behaved as though nothing had happened. Hugh turned to him from his window to greet him with a smile. "Thank you for the book, Father. It is a marvelous gift."

"Have you begun reading it?" asked the Baron, relieved and thankful.

"Yes." Hugh paused. "It is a compelling story. I don't know what to make of it. It's unlike anything I've ever read before." The boy's eyes lit up with excitement. "It's...it's like *The Iliad* and *The Odyssey* woven into a single, fantastic fabric, but the heroes wear cocked hats and carry pistols, and the Sirens lure men to their best, not to their deaths...and men have a different notion of themselves." Hugh shook his head, unable to express all that he recognized in the story. "It is a glorious tale, Father!"

The Baron permitted himself a slight grin. "I was sure it would entertain you." He sighed. "Well, I must attend to our guests. We shall talk later about the rascals you meet in *Hyperborea*. Your mother sends her regards. She may come by and watch the fireworks with you, but if she does not, please, forgive her."

"I could watch them with you, Father."

The Baron shook his head. "No, I am obliged to keep our guests company this evening." He paused. "Will you forgive me?"

Hugh nodded.

The Baron left the room.

That evening, Hugh listened to the music and laughter of the ball downstairs, the sounds only echoes to his thoughts. Owen brought him a platter of sweetmeats and other delicacies from the kitchen. Hugh asked him what music was being played. "Oh, the usual minuets and country dances, milord. And a bit of Mr. Handel, although the musicians play him awkwardly. Otherwise, it has been a grand affair."

Hugh tried to compose the comedy of sheep, but had no patience to invent the requisite humor for the things he wanted to say frankly and openly. He continued reading *Hyperborea*.

He was deep in his own thoughts when he noticed a silence. The music had stopped. Curious, he left his room and stole downstairs. He managed to avoid being spotted by the servants and got to the gallery that overlooked the ballroom in his uncle's part of the mansion. It was crowded with men in red uniforms, the band on loan from the Lord Lieutenant of Dorset. Their musical instruments were at rest. No one noticed him. The musicians, like the glittering assembly below, were listening to someone recite a poem. Hugh crept to the oak railing and looked down.

Lieutenant-Colonel James Wolfe, resplendent in his uniform, stood holding up a book, gesticulating with his free hand, reading a poem. He was a tall, rangy, almost homely man, but had an intent, expressive face as sharp as Hugh's uncle's. Cumberland stood to one side of the officer, Maud Harris on his arm, and the Earl and some of the Duke's retinue on the other. Hugh saw his father and mother in the attentive crowd.

"'The boast of heraldry, the pomp of power,

And all that beauty, all that wealth e'er gave
Awaits alike the inevitable hour—
The paths of glory lead but to the grave.'"

Hugh recognized the poem, Thomas Gray's "Elegy Written in a Country Churchyard," and remembered reading it to his mother after the stillbirth the summer past, but hearing it recited by another caused him to think of it now in a new light.

When Wolfe was finished and bowed in acknowledgment of the company's applause, Hugh withdrew from the gallery and walked back to his room. His mother must have given a signal to the musicians, for the halls now rang with a jaunty country-dance. He thought two things: first, he realized now that it had been an inappropriate poem to have read to his mother—even though it had been at her request—taking together the loss of his would-be brother and the subject of the poem, the death of a young man.

And he thought that while it was a touching comment on unrealized potential, it granted too much solace to the unsought-for potential that the late young man had never realized. He had the sense that the poem was an envious lament for the undifferentiated. He wondered why so many people who sought beauty, wealth and glory placed so much importance on a poem that denigrated those things.

When he reached his room, Hugh sat down and wrote in his notebook: "It is not the silent dust to which honor speaks. It is not the dull, cold ear of death that honor seeks to bend. A mind, pregnant with celestial fire, hurtles ahead, and will, in time, find its kith and kin."

This was to become the form in which he would address an insensate world—to himself, in a diary.

He watched the fireworks, which had been arranged by men his uncle had hired in London, from the balcony of his room. The explosions, though spectacular, lit up nothing but a ceiling of clouds and the crowd of townsfolk collected on the front lawn to watch them.

*   *   *

On the next morning, the Duke and his entourage departed with less fanfare than had marked their arrival. They were headed now for Weymouth. Hugh was awakened by the noise and clatter of men, horses, and carriages as preparations were made to depart. He stole from his room in his nightshirt to the roof and watched.

The Kenricks, Benjamin Worley, and Otis Talbot stood on the broad front steps and watched the great train retreat down the estate road. When it was out of sight, Effney Kenrick turned and went up two of the steps. She folded her blue silk fan, snapped it in half, let the halves drop to the stone, and trod on them as she went inside to give the servants instructions to clean up the house.

"It was a great affair," announced the Earl to no one in particular.

"It was," answered his brother noncommittally.

"The Duke is a magnificent man. Strange company he keeps, though. An officer who recites poetry! Mark me, he won't go far. No 'paths of glory' will be trod by that lad!"

"He recited the poem at the request of the Duke. Surely a recommendation. Besides, he frowns on flogging," remarked the Baron. "He would prefer to lead dedicated, not desiccated, soldiers. His very words."

The Earl merely sniffed at the allusion. "And that Harle—too high-minded for a commoner."

"Commoners usually exhibit more sense than their betters," said the Baron. "I liked him."

From that day onward, there existed a tension in the Danvers home, composed of muted animosity, on the part of the Baron and Baroness toward the Earl, and of resentment that clothed itself in studied arrogance and boredom, on the part of the Earl toward his brother. They dined together, traveled together, shared tea and played cards together, as usual, but never forgotten was the punishment. Hugh sensed the tension, did not understand it, but did not inquire about it, for these were adult matters, and he had little time for them.

One consequence of Hugh's punishment was that he was not permitted to sit with his family on Sundays during services at St. Quarrell's. He was sent, alone, to the second service in late afternoon. He sat by himself in the family pew box, across from the altar, a solitary figure in full view of the congregation. When the time came in the ritual to shake hands with one's company, there was no one for him to turn to. Hugh did not mind this; the sermons, the hymns, the groans of the organ all rushed past his consciousness like the water of a rapids. Vicar Wynne, aloft in his great gilded, canopied pulpit, observed Hugh's isolation with, at first, some satisfaction, then with disapproval, for while the boy looked attentive, his mind seemed to be elsewhere. His attentiveness seemed to be focused on things of his own concern and not of the congregation.

*   *   *

The London Gazette, the government's chief official organ, a week after
the event reported the injury to and repair of the Duke of Cumberland's
esteem at Danvers in a short notice buried in a flurry of other notices of
both graver and less-than-noteworthy importance. It generated some gossip
about the incident, but not as much as the Earl had feared.

The army contract, however, was pared from its original exclusivity to
half a dozen contracts doled out by the commissariat. In March, Danvers
received an order for enough wool that would, when factored, clothe a
mere regiment, not an army. The Earl wrote Sir Everard, asking for an
explanation. That gentleman's secretary replied that Sir Everard had gone
to the Continent for a rest cure. The Earl fumed and snapped at his servants, and even at his brother, for he knew that the other awardees even
collectively had not gone to a tenth of the bother and expense to win their
parts of the contract.

The Baron observed his brother's anger dispassionately and without
comment, for he had warned him about the likely outcome. While they
awaited word, the Baron's only other caution was "I reiterate my remark
on the Duke's gallery of applicants, dear brother. There are, as you must
know, more applicants than there are seats." While he was a loyal subject
of the Crown, Garnet Kenrick was pleased with the awards; he wanted as
little as possible to do with government obligations. He was more concerned with repairing the injury to the Earl's solvency.

*   *   *

It was a time when a desire for solitude was a mark of one of three egregious maladies: madness, genius, or eccentricity. Life, especially that of an
aristocrat, was governed by communal and public affairs. One did not shy
away from society; it was considered an inferred punishment for society to
shy away from any species of loner. This custom was lost on Hugh Kenrick;
solitude was not a punishment. He learned to savor it; to be alone with his
thoughts, with his own being. He was almost sorry that his uncle had
relented and reduced his sentence. For four months, his life became a routine, almost a ritual: he would rise in the morning, have his breakfast, be

driven to the Tallmadges, for tutoring, be driven home again, complete his assigned lessons, be served dinner, read on his own account, and sleep. His room for those four months became the core of his known universe. He was only partly aware of the value of his enforced solitude, of the unconscious gathering together of all the cords of his soul and their tying together into a knot that would never unravel and never be loosened by anyone. He would occasionally, idly launch his brass top, and watch it balance itself. It stood humming, turning, erect by its own rules. And though he read other books, he would reread *Hyperborea* many times, trying to glean the gist of its many facets. The novelty of the story led his mind down so many exciting paths, and opened up vistas of ideas that were tantalizingly sharp but somehow beyond his grasp. He came to regard *Hyperborea* as a personal possession, as something that had been written exclusively for him.

On the last day of May, he sat again for dinner with his parents and uncle. The occasion was marked by no mention of or reference to his former absence.

Hugh was never told of his uncle's role in the punishment, nor why its duration had been shortened.

*   *   *

"I read yesterday in the *Weekly Register*," remarked Garnet Kenrick, "that some colonial—a Quaker, no less—claims to have tamed lightning, bidding it to strike where he pleases it to, with the aid of a kite."

"There is a report in the *Daily Auditor*," mused Effney Kenrick, "that a farmer has discovered the remains of Pompeii, buried under a league of ash."

"Hillier reports," sniffed the Earl, "that the Parliament's journals are to be printed now. Now any cretin with half a skull can read them." He added, "They say in Lords that Clive will take Arcot some time soon."

"Lady Ornsby writes me from London that she has browsed through the new French *Encyclopédie*," said the Baroness, "and says that it will be superior to Chambers', once it is finished."

"The scrivenings of radical rogues," grumbled the Earl. "Even here, they can't be avoided. This Henry Fielding person, I have heard, basks in the scandal of this new history of his—*John Jones*, or *Tom Jones*—even the title is common and dull. Vicar Wynne has informed me that he shall preach against it soon, as his father preached against *Moll Flanders*."

The Baron and Baroness exchanged tactful glances about the irrelevancy of this comment. The silent remark did not go unnoticed by their son.

Hugh said nothing, and ate what was put before him.

Basil Kenrick rarely spoke to him, and when he did, spoke with obvious effort and control. The fact that the boy had elected to endure punishment rather than apologize to the Duke not only superseded his outrage at Hugh's behavior, but became the kernel of another species of odium. He could be persuaded to forgive forgetfulness and even ignorance; he would not countenance willful impertinence, and was closed to argument.

And in the deepest recesses of his soul, buried under an embarrassment for the barely acknowledged absurdity of the notion, and wrapped in a contempt for himself for harboring it, the Earl feared his nephew. One evening soon after Hugh resumed his regular place in the life of the estate, his valet heard the Earl mutter to himself: "I should have made him kiss the rod with which he was beaten. I wish to humble that boy. He will be Earl some day."

Chapter 9: The Portrait

"**M**AY YOU LIVE AS LONG AS YOU ARE FIT TO LIVE, BUT NO LONGER! Or may you rather die before you cease to be fit to live, than after!"

So wrote Philip Dormer Stanhope, Lord Chesterfield, to his illegitimate son in 1749. Hugh Kenrick might have pondered this frank bit of wisdom, and eventually concurred, had his father the leisure to compose such a thought.

A boy born into the aristocracy was driven against the very thing that was his milieu. The impetus was a multitude of assumptions that were to be taken for granted and never questioned. Such an aristocrat naturally presumed that all the privileges that he enjoyed were his by right. He could adopt his rank's vices and banalities, or be repelled by them. He could patronize those who wished to be aristocrats, but were not; or he could debunk or spurn them. He had the advantage of education, if he chose to use it; or he could become a notorious rake and profligate who perhaps had once read Pliny and mastered a complex mathematics, but to no observable consequence. He could be hurled against the wall of aristocratic demands like a meteor, and either be incinerated or deflected by the atmosphere of privilege and noblesse oblige. Either way, he would be destroyed as a man; either way, he was destined to become an aristocrat.

Hugh Kenrick seemed to take neither course, but still became an aristocrat—by his own definition. He had a notion of what it meant to be fit to live; that is, he sensed that a definition of fitness was necessary, but was certain that none would be offered by any adult. And he did not think in terms of fitness; rather of a purpose for living, a reason, or an end, and this purpose, reason, or end had to be fit first.

*   *   *

The Earl decided to have the family's portraits painted: one of his family, and individual portraits. Emery Westcott, a fashionable portraitist in London, was commissioned by the Earl and came to live at Danvers one summer while he recorded the likenesses of the family. The Earl also wished him to do renderings of the estate. "The portraits must be imposing, the grounds made more picturesque than they are."

Westcott assured the Earl that he would have difficulty improving on so picturesque a setting.

"None of your faddle, sir," rebuked the Earl. "I'm told you could make this grotesque Samuel Johnson creature look like a Greek god. Now, get on with you. I've spoken with you longer than I should."

Westcott set up a studio in one of the larger guest rooms in the mansion. Because he was a commoner, he was not permitted to dine with the family—at least not with the Earl, who spoke to him but never again with him. The artist accepted the slight; he knew he was a mere practitioner. Garnet Kenrick and his wife, however, shared frequent meals with him in his room, for they found him to be charming, witty, and a storehouse of gossip and information about London society.

The most difficult task for Emery Westcott was not the Earl, but the boy. There was the boy himself, whose piercing green eyes gave him the most trouble. He winced every time he saw them. They disturbed him in a way he could not name. But he bravely tackled them at every sitting. The face was mature and wise beyond its years. Then there were the objects in the picture—a stigmatized book, a brass top, and a plaque on a wall. The boy had had some instruction in composition from a tutor, and had recommended those props; had, in fact, insisted that his portrait be of him at his own desk. Westcott had originally intended a conventional out-of-doors setting for Hugh Kenrick, on the grounds of the estate, with the boy standing placidly with a hoop and stick, or some other toy suitably diverting for a boy of that age. But Westcott admitted to himself that the boy's suggestions were singular. He had asked the Baron and Baroness about their son's ideas, and whether they would insist on a standard setting. The parents had sided with Hugh, saying that it was their son's decision. "It is his wish to be remembered that way, Mr. Westcott," remarked the Baron, who spoke as though the boy was the Earl himself.

Westcott had painted many portraits of boys of Hugh's age and rank, but found this time he did not need to turn an insolent sneer or vapid indifference into something pleasant to behold by the parents. Hugh was unique. Westcott tried to ignore the eyes, to convince himself that there was nothing special about them. But he could not ignore them; the subject would not let him.

When he had finished placing the objects that would be a part of the portrait, the artist asked his subject, "Why do you wish to include the top, milord?" He paused. "I ask this so that I may better understand its place in the portrait."

"Because, when it is set in motion, it stands by its own rules. Then it is not an inert thing, like a tree or a rock."

Westcott had smiled. "Ah! But your hand must set it in motion, milord. So it cannot be as independent as you say."

"It is the symbol of a soul, Mr. Westcott. Or of a mind. Every man has one, and it is like a top, fashioned by himself. He must keep it upright, by his own hand. He must exert the effort. Otherwise it will topple, and lay inert and useless within himself, not a living thing at all. Or another hand may set it in motion, and then he will have no say in its motion or course." Hugh paused. "This top has sentimental value to me, sir, and I wish to remember it."

Westcott hummed thoughtfully to himself. "Interesting analogy, milord. It recalls a sermon I heard recently, about how Sir Newton's laws of nature confirm, rather than dispute, the actions of an all-wise Overseer." He paused. "Do you plan to take orders, when you have attained your majority?"

"Excuse me, sir?"

"Do you wish to become a shepherd of souls? A minister of our church?"

"No," replied Hugh, frowning. "Why would I wish to?"

"Your concern with souls, milord, invites me to believe that you ultimately may choose that path of occupation."

Hugh made a face of disgust. "No. I wish to become a man. One must become a man, first, before he can choose to be anything else."

Westcott did not again venture to discuss such weighty subjects with the boy. An unreasoning but accurate fear told him that to enquire further into the boy's mind would lead him to confront matters too disturbing to contemplate.

The boy also insisted on wearing a green frock coat. This Westcott could not argue against, for the coat matched the troublesome eyes.

*   *   *

Mr. Cole, who also tutored literature, assigned his charges the task of reading many famous authors, living and dead. He was particularly anxious that his students appreciate Alexander Pope's *Essay on Man*, one of his favorite literary paeans.

Hugh read the long poem, at first avidly, then with mixed feelings. On one hand, Pope exalted man and reason; on another, he derogated them. Hugh could not comprehend the dual purposes; he ascribed the composition to faulty knowledge, and said as much in a written critique of the piece required by Mr. Cole. In it Hugh would quote a line from the *Essay*, such as "Since life can little more supply, than just to look about us, and die" and then ask the question, "Does Mr. Pope mean that life is something like a Grand Tour, on which we see what great and wonderful and unusual things have been done, but that we should not presume to act to emulate them? How can Mr. Pope then hope for a 'kingdom of the just,' as he mentions in Epistle IV? Does not one act to attain justice? Just men are not mere spectators, but act to effect justice." The critique was masterful in its synopsis, but its analysis confounded Mr. Cole, who began to wonder if Milord Kenrick was an example of some species of idiot savant. He did not know how to answer such questions or appraise such commentary, for he refused to concede the contradictions.

Hugh found this phenomenon in much of the literature of the period: gems of reason, snatches of profundity, and eloquently expressed verities sunk in a tepid broth of humility, skepticism, and cynicism. He wondered at times about the purposes of these admixtures, or whether there was any purpose to them at all. But all attempts to make him humble, skeptical, and cynical struck his soul dully, and registered no palpable hits. He knew that there was an answer that would construe the pandemonium of ideas he encountered, and was certain that, once he knew enough, he would have the task of composing the answer himself.

Under Mr. Cole's tutelage, Hugh also sampled Montaigne, and rummaged through the great heap of skepticism and piety of that Frenchman's *Essays*, searching for nuggets of wisdom or insight, finding some, but ultimately leaving the rest behind, his memory of the task a gray stew of distaste and indifference. However, he took personal offense at one of the Frenchman's dictums, and grave exception to one of his stated purposes: "God permits no one to esteem himself higher," and "I make men feel the emptiness, the vanity, the nothingness of Man, wrenching from their grasp the sickly arms of human reason, making them bow their heads and bite the dust before the authority and awe of the Divine Majesty…" He rebelled against these statements to the extent that he paid a village craftsman to carve a plaque that defiantly proclaimed his single answer: "Reason is man's sole salvation; he is its sole and proud vessel," and had a servant fix it to the wall above his desk. He discarded everything else that Montaigne had said, because he did not think it was worth remembering.

He also read a translation of Baron de Montesquieu's *Esprit des lois*, and became fascinated by the politics revealed in the seminal work. He understood only a fraction of the thinker's observations, but enough of them to win his intellectual affections. The Frenchman's praise for English political institutions even awakened in him a smidgen of pride for his country; though when he heard his parents, his uncle, and their guests discuss politics, this pride was checked.

Hugh continued to wrestle with the conundrum that he was not permitted to be anything. A gentleman was nothing if he was something; to be something other than a royalty-conferred identity—an attorney, an engineer, a mechanic, or any variety of tradesman or merchant—was to be less than nothing, an object of scorn, pity, or condescension. A beggar could be given a penny or a shilling, and that would buy him a dram of gin or half a loaf of bread; a tradesman could be paid false civility, and that would buy him a humiliating kind of gratitude. This did not immediately concern Hugh Kenrick; it was his fate that all the avenues of occupation, of ambition were closed to him, other than conformity to his appointed station. He was fated to be an earl, which subsumed the rank of gentleman. A gentleman's identity was an ethereal thing, a mode of existence aspired to by those who connived to attain it. Hugh could afford the identity, but did not aspire to it. He was a gentleman, but did not attach any value to it. To be a gentleman was to be able to brush aside those who were something and indulge in one's whims or appetites. Many envied those who were nothing; Hugh envied those who were something. This was the society in which he was raised.

Hugh Kenrick was becoming something, even if he did not know it.

He assiduously absorbed the best of the wisdom of his age, prizing that portion of it which appealed to or nourished his sense of self, storing that portion of it with which he disagreed on the premise that it was better to know one's enemies than to be ignorant of them. Also pressing for his allegiance was a myriad of influences: the endemic skepticism that would shortly be exonerated by David Hume in his *Natural History of Religion*; the jealousy of Toryism; the nonchalance of Whiggism; the demands of the Dissenters; the posturing of Non-Jurors; the tolerance of the Latitudinarians.

In this chaos, his uncle the Earl remained a mystery closed to inquiry, moved by motives incomprehensible to him, while his father became more a friend and ally than a paternal mentor.

For all this, however, he did not turn into an annoying pendant, but became a vibrant young man.

And as he grew wiser, he grew lonelier. With each new insight he gleaned from a sage, or formulated by himself, he became aware of a curious, unsettling distance growing between himself and those for whom he cared, and of the gap between himself and strangers and those whom he disliked, which was widening into a chasm. He did not cherish indifference or contempt; there was no satisfaction in these things, even though they were what he justly felt. He accepted the phenomena as natural ones, and for which he presumed there would exist a corrective in the future.

He found more use for his father's library than for his uncle's. The libraries, he realized, were stocked with books that reflected his uncle's and father's frames of mind. His father's library was larger, and contained more titles that piqued his curiosity. The one book he valued the most came from his father's library, and was now his own. His antidote to the received wisdom of his age was Drury Trantham, the hero of *Hyperborea*.

*   *   *

A boy adopts a hero for two reasons: because a hero captivates his soul and serves as a projection of his innermost self; and because a hero seems to have solved many problems that may worry a boy, or at least demonstrates the capacity to solve them. The hero is an idealization of successful living, even though he may die in a story. The death may be gallant, brave, tragic, or perhaps even foolhardy. But living or dead, a hero is the stylistic embodiment of living on one's own terms—noble terms, grand terms, exciting terms—terms, in short, that complement any youth's uncorrupted, untamed, unabridged projection of what is possible to him in life.

Drury Trantham, shipwrecked merchant, became Hugh's model of manhood, his test for moral stature and successful living. His image of Trantham loomed large enough in his mind that it crowded out all other candidates of exemplars and became the exclusive touchstone of heroic worth.

Trantham, the tall, handsome, hardy, commanding gentleman rogue who was equally at home on the deck of his merchantman, *The Greyhound*, or in a raucous tavern, or on the floor of a great lord's ballroom; Trantham, who owned a magnificent estate in Sussex and a great house in London, purchased with the proceeds of a career of flouting the King's law; Trantham, a man who made no distinction between a common murderer and a Revenue rider; Trantham, the captain of a skilled and loyal crew whose members were willing to die for him, and often did, on land and at sea, and who would risk his life for any of them should an injustice be committed; Trantham, the ship's captain who boasted that his vessel had never come within twenty miles of London Bridge to be customed, inspected, or unshipped, but whose holds were the secret envy of all other merchants; Trantham, the scoundrel and the patriot, who spied and fought for the country he loved, but mocked the men who ruled it.

Drury Trantham, the discoverer of Hyperborea, a land of enchanting, seductive freedom—a "kingdom of the just"; Trantham, the outsider who won the love of Circe, the beautiful daughter of the land's wisest sage, and who became the best friend of his jealous rival for her affections; Trantham, who sailed with his crew on *The Greyhound* to fight an armada of pirates who had chanced near the unchartered straits that led to *Hyperborea*; Trantham, the laughing, defiant captain, who ordered his crippled, flaming ship to sail directly into the pirate chief's flagship, certain that he would sink the enemy only at the price of his own death; Trantham, who died happily with the rest of his crew, because he had seen something that he had always searched for, proof of his convictions; Trantham, who died to save Circe and preserve the secret of *Hyperborea*'s existence.

Hyperborea governed the course of his required reading. In his uncle's library were Robert Filmer's *Patriarcha*, Bishop Sherlock's works, Richard Allestree's *The Whole Duty of Man*, and Samuel Parker's *Discourses of Ecclesiastical Polity*—all rendered superfluous by *Hyperborea*. In his father's library there was James Tyrrell's *Patriarcha non Monarcha*, Sidney's *Discourses Concerning Government*, and all of John Locke's works—and Hugh thought he saw some connection between the novel and the philosophy he found in these works. He could not decide whether the philosophy inspired the novel, or the same vision of the novel had inspired the philosophers, long before the author of *Hyperborea* had been born. He could not help but think that some notion of Drury Trantham had existed in the minds of these men, and that their thoughts of the right political conditions friendly to that hero were the consequences of that notion. Yet, even though all these works appealed to him—and he could understand only a small portion of them—Hugh sensed that something was missing. Drury Trantham answered the best of them, and the worst. And in Drury Trantham lay the answer to that missing thing.

*　　*　　*

One day he startled Mr. Rittles with the question: "Why cannot moral questions be posed with the same precision as a mathematical equation, so that given x and y, z is the only possible answer?"

The tutor scratched his peruke, at a loss to answer. He had never heard the question posed before; and it had been asked by a mere boy. Finally, he ventured a reply, hoping that it did not precipitate another query. "Because many such questions do not require precise answers. Theology and the Scriptures do not invite reasoned inquiry. And moral philosophy only seems to."

"No, they don't," remarked Hugh. "But I believe they should."

Another time, in the middle of a dancing master's class, after the instructor had put the children through a strict rehearsal of gavottes and minuets, Hugh asked, "Sir, are there no dances for couples?" All the other children gaped at him, except Reverdy Brune, who smiled in the secret knowledge that Hugh had preferred her as a partner in dances that called for many partners, making sure that all their dances began and ended with her.

"Those are for plain folk, milord," answered the tutor, who did not know whether to be astounded or angry. "Gentlemen and ladies do not indulge in such…gross amusements," he added. "Dancing is a social grace, milord, and not a vehicle for personal diversion."

"It can be both," answered Hugh in a tone unconscious of its finality.

The dancing master did not pursue the subject, but peevishly instructed his students in the moves of a new country-dance.

Hugh and Roger Tallmadge had often donned stable boys' clothes and stolen down into the village to be among people who demanded nothing of them, to see how they lived and hear what they thought. Their most enjoyable times were when they would sit on the edge of a wedding party or other celebration, and watch the villagers dance to simple tunes played on flutes and fiddles. They felt more warmth and companionship in these gatherings than in the regal, stilted balls held in the Earl's home. "The plain folk in the village seem to have more fun," thought Hugh, "dancing with one another, instead of with everyone."

Westcott painted the family as a group first, then the individual members: Hugh and his sister, Alice, together and separately; the Baron and Baroness, together and separately; and the Earl. Hugh expressed interest in the art of portraiture, and often sat quietly on a stool to watch Westcott at work.

In early fall, Westcott completed his commission. Hugh's portrait was the last canvas he finished. Westcott had managed to mute the piercing green eyes, but they were still compelling. He was not at all certain that this particular canvas would be approved. But, to his relief, Hugh's parents were delighted with the portrait.

It depicted the boy sitting at his desk, the plaque on the wall above him, the top resting to the side of an open book, the first volume of *Hyperborea*. The second volume sat atop a pile of books elsewhere on the desk, its title clearly visible. Hugh's face was lit by a sconce on the wall and a candle on the desk. Because of Westcott's trouble with the eyes, they did not return the glance of the viewer, as was a common practice then, but rose above and beyond the viewer's, giving the face a curious uplifted, inward, and distant expression, as though the boy had been disturbed in the middle of a thought.

Much to Westcott's surprise, the Baron patted him on the back when he saw the finished portrait. "That's our Hugh!" he remarked. "Well done, sir." And the Baroness gave him a gracious smile of gratitude.

The portraits were hung on the walls. The Earl's was put in the dining room, opposite the Earl's usual place at the head of the table, in order that he could see it. The Baroness's went into the Baron's study, and the Baron's into the breakfast room. Hugh's portrait was also hung in the Baron's study. "I wish to mark the difference over time," he told his wife.

Basil Kenrick did not like Hugh's portrait, even though he agreed to pay for it. He was glad that he would not need to see it often. The animated, pensive face of the boy confirmed his certainty that the boy was not material for rule—neither to rule, nor to be ruled. "There's no dignity in it," he remarked to his brother. "Looks as though he might become a higgler of ideas, or a mere scrivener. What's that blasted book he's reading? I can't make out the title."

"*Hyperborea*," answered Garnet Kenrick.

The Earl looked at his brother sharply. "A blasphemous, seditious mass of verbiage!" he spat, his face reddening. "How did he come to acquire it?"

"I gave it to him," replied Garnet Kenrick with a slight shrug of his shoulders. He smiled. "How would you know so much about it, Basil—unless you had committed the sin of reading it?"

"I was told about it by some persons in Lords who had the distasteful, lawful chore of reading it and recommending its suppression."

"Poor souls. Well, you must own that Hugh will be the wiser for having read it himself. You will remain ignorant of its true potency for sedition."

Basil Kenrick scoffed. "Mark my words, dear brother: That book will warp his already addled brain! See here!" he added, wagging his finger, "I want no Whig puppies raised in this house! One word of compassion for the mob from him, and I'll brand his tongue!"

"The Whigs dislike the book as much as you do, Basil," sighed the Baron. "And I can't imagine Hugh expressing much sympathy for any mob." He chuckled. "But, then, of course, I have read the book, too, and must have a warped mind myself. Whatever I have to say is the spittle of a madman."

"Don't be flippant," replied the Earl. "You're an adult, and know better than to succumb to the allure of such trash. Does he know that it was written by an executed criminal?"

"No. I don't think it would matter if he did. Though I believe that if he did know, he would wonder why the fellow was hanged, and not awarded a royal pension."

The Earl sniffed.

The Baron smiled and said, "After all, dear brother, who are we to judge criminals and malcontents? If it happened that a member of the Lobster Pots penned a treatise on moral philosophy, I should probably subscribe to its publication."

The family portrait was hung on the dining room wall opposite the Earl's. Westcott was perceptive enough to feel the tension in the family, and to note that Hugh Kenrick was disliked by his uncle and that there existed a measure of coldness between the boy's parents and the Earl. Westcott had certainly heard of the affair round the Duke of Cumberland, and was certain that this was the reason for the tension. Because it was the Earl's commission, Westcott composed the group portrait so that the figure of Hugh was on the far right of the tableau, almost but not quite on the fringe of it. He chose a standard setting, the breakfast room in the orangery, and assembled the family around an oval table. The Earl sat prominently in the middle foreground; the Baron and Baroness sat to the side, little Alice, a look of sweet amazement on her face, on her mother's lap. Hugh stood at the edge of the table, looking bored but deferential. Above the group was the rendering of the first Hugh Kenrick, laying waste to a town so many centuries ago.

*   *   *

The Kenricks journeyed to London that fall, for both business and social reasons. Hugh was taken to many balls and concerts, and immersed in the haute culture of the times. He developed an appreciation for Gluck's ballet *Don Juan*, and discovered Vivaldi's "Echo" Concerto for Two Violins, the Concerto for Four Violins, and the Double Concerto.

He liked the "Echo" Concerto so much that he persuaded his father to pay the musicians to perform it again after the theater had emptied of the other patrons. The novelty of the answering, off-stage violin appealed to him for a reason he did not know. He sat forward, his arms crossed on the back of the seat in front of him, his chin resting on his wrists, his fingers moving in time with the melody. His face was set in a melancholy his parents had never seen in him before. They could not decide whether it was joy or loneliness.

Chapter 10: The Young Men

"**N**OW I SHALL HAVE NO MORE PEACE," LAMENTED GEORGE II ON the death of Henry Pelham, First Lord of the Treasury and Chancellor of the Exchequer, in March of 1754. Pelham, brother of the Duke of Newcastle, succeeded Robert Walpole in the "prime ministership," and for eight years channeled his energies into balancing the budget, trimming the army and navy, and reducing the land tax. The king was to be proven right. Pelham's passing inaugurated a political maelstrom that would last for decades between Tories, New Whigs, and Old Whigs— and between England and the rest of the world.

And in the following May, at Great Meadows Run in the wilds of Pennsylvania, young George Washington and a band of Virginians fired on a contingent of breakfasting French soldiers camped in a soggy bower of the forest and, after a short fight, compelled the survivors to surrender. On July 4, at Fort Necessity, Washington himself was obliged to surrender to a larger force of French, whose officer tricked him into signing a confession of murder before allowing him and his men to leave "with honor." The French reasoned that as a state of war did not officially exist, Washington's action in May was morally and diplomatically reprehensible. Washington did not realize that he had signed such a confession, which was written in French, until he reached Williamsburg to report to Lieutenant Governor Robert Dinwiddie, the man who had sent him on the "preemptive" expedition.

These brief clashes were to ignite a fuse of events that would ultimately lead to the beginning of the Seven Years' War, officially declared in May of 1756 and fought in theaters ranging from Europe to India. "The volley fired by a young Virginian in the backwoods of America set the world on fire," wrote Horace Walpole. It was to be the last struggle between the French and British for hegemony in North America. Pelham's death also signaled the rise of William Pitt, the Great Commoner, later Earl of Chatham, who would administer eventual victory.

Other events served to bridge the fuse and the actual explosion. Charles-Louis de Secondat, formerly Baron de Montesquieu, and intellectual stepfather to political theorist Edmund Burke, died in February, 1755.

He was England's favorite Frenchman, for he praised that country's political institutions. *The Dictionary of the English Language*, compiled by critic, essayist, and poet Samuel Johnson, was published in April of that year, after a nine-year effort. Young Jean-Jacques Rousseau published his first major work, *Discourse on Inequality*. Francis Hutcheson's *System of Moral Philosophy*, published posthumously that year, endorsed the tenets of David Hume's earlier *Treatise of Human Nature* and *Enquiry Concerning Human Understanding*; these three works derogated reason and posited the supremacy of "passion" in human action and values, and helped to put a seal of respectability on the cynicism, skepticism, and "sentimentality" that were the age's growing hallmarks. In Prussia, young Immanuel Kant published a paper on the formation of the solar system, proffering a theory that foreshadowed Pierre Laplace's, but his true fame lay in the future, in philosophy, not science. His series of *Critiques* would together comprise a body of philosophy for which Hume's and Hutcheson's would rank as mere advance valets. In Russia, Moscow University was founded to educate the young nobles. And in Austria, young Franz Joseph Haydn was busy perfecting the format of the symphony. But France, even though it was more politically oppressive than England, and whose freethinkers were more at jeopardy—often at peril—than their brethren in liberal Albion, remained the intellectual fountainhead of Europe.

The year 1755 was riven by great earthquakes. Thousands died when Quito was leveled in April. Forty thousand souls perished that June in Kaschan, northern Persia. Lisbon would be destroyed in November and fifty thousand of its inhabitants lost. Málaga in Spain and Fez in Morocco would be flattened by the same eight-minute quake, whose shocks were felt as far away as Scotland.

Englishmen were stunned when news arrived in late August of Major General Edward Braddock's death and defeat that July in Pennsylvania, not far from Great Meadows Run. Braddock, spending a small portion of the imperial treasury, was dispatched to accomplish what Washington, scantily paid and ill-supported by contentious colonial legislatures, could not: the capture of Fort Duquesne and the eviction of the French. It was especially galling for two reasons: first, that a force of nearly fifteen hundred regulars, supported by colonial militia, was defeated within shouting distance of Fort Duquesne by a much smaller force of very irregular French and Indians, who fought from behind trees and rocks; and second, the circulating rumors of the outrageous conduct of the British regulars, many of whom ran and even fired in panic on their own ranks. Almost a thousand English lives were lost to the victorious, nearly unscathed French and screaming, scalping Indians. Braddock was the first British general to campaign in North America. It was not an auspicious debut of British military prowess.

In England, and in the finer households in the colonies, gentlemen and ladies could not decide what was more contemptible: Was it the cowardice of the French, who in North America did not fight in the customary and honorable parade ground manner and tactics of Continental Europe, but behaved like cut-throats, footpads, and highwaymen? Or was it the disgraceful funk of the surviving regulars, who survived because they ran? Like many aristocrats in England who read accounts of the fiasco in the newspapers, the Earl and Baron of Danvers repeated in astonishment to each other, without knowing it, Braddock's dying words: "Who would have thought of it?" Publicly, no one questioned Braddock's generalship, even though, privately, some politicians and military men reflected that with a little imaginative daring—an asset not possessed by the late Edward Braddock—perhaps with a massed bayonet charge supported by merciless artillery, the French and Indians could have been swept from the woods, Fort Duquesne captured, the French evicted from the Ohio Valley, and, for all practical purposes, that theater of the Seven Years' War closed. Publicly, no one questioned Braddock's personal selection for the task by the Duke of Cumberland; privately, many who knew Cumberland said that he had picked his "peer in wit," and so no better outcome could have been expected.

In ominous irony, two men associated with the debacle were colonials: Benjamin Franklin and George Washington. Franklin, ever the entrepreneur, had supplied Braddock with his wagons and horses; most of these were lost in the disaster, together with all the artillery, the commander's papers, and £25,000 in specie. Franklin had, the previous spring, orchestrated the Albany Congress, sponsored by the Board of Trade in London, first to woo the Iroquois from the French—unsuccessfully, as it turned out—and then to study the feasibility of a union of the colonies as an official body that would complement Parliament and work with it for the good of all concerned. Many of the colonial legislatures vetoed the idea or would not even debate it. Franklin's own Pennsylvania rejected the notion. The idea came to naught. It was considered much too radical a solution to the incipient friction between the colonies and the home government. But the conduct of the war, and the bill ultimately presented to the colonies by the

Crown in the form of new taxes and regulations for its successful conclusion, would later precipitate congresses far less benign than the Albany, for many of the more astute colonials would begin to wonder for whose sake and benefit the war was being fought.

Colonel Washington, as a volunteer on Braddock's staff, did his best to rally those regulars and colonials who did not panic. He rode from company to company, swearing as heartily as a drill sergeant over the din of volleys, his coat plucked to pieces by musket balls and two mounts shot from beneath him. Brave but foolhardy British officers and stalwart rank and file fell like ninepins around him during the two-hour fight. Washington was largely responsible for extracting the survivors—stalwart and scurrying alike—from the deadly ambuscade. He buried Braddock's body in an unmarked grave to prevent its abuse by the Indians. Following his earlier surrender at Fort Necessity, it was his second humiliating defeat in a year. He did not know it, but the tonic of these bone-chilling experiences would serve to make him a wise and patient general in the decades to come.

*   *   *

The gravity of these events was lost on Hugh Kenrick. 1755 was an uneventful year for him, until his father called him into his study one late summer afternoon to inform him that he was to attend Dr. James Comyn's School for Gentlemen, in London, near Westminster. Hugh was now fourteen.

Garnet Kenrick decided to entrust his son's further education to this reputable academy for two reasons: to subject Hugh to a stricter regimen of study than the Tallmadge tutors could impose, with special emphasis on commerce, law, accounts, and mathematics; and to remove the boy from his uncle's glowering displeasure. Whole seasons, he reasoned, would pass before Hugh returned home for the holidays, and the passage of time would serve to ameliorate his brother's fuming hostility. Also, he wished to see Hugh avail himself of the freedom of a cosmopolitan city; he was curious to see what effect exposure to more demanding tutors and to life in London would have on his son's burgeoning mind.

He grinned wryly when, after he broke the news, Hugh's eyes lit up in excitement. "Dr. Comyn was a classmate of mine at Oxford," he explained. "I have seen him recently and exchanged several letters with him about you. He is much impressed with your abilities, and is eager to make your acquaintance." The Baron paused. "You must promise me that you will do nothing that would bring disgrace to this family. The city is rich in temptations and distractions."

"I promise," replied Hugh.

"Your mother and I will accompany you and see that you are installed in our house. We will travel early in September and partake of the fall society for a week or so. When we leave, Mr. Worley will be responsible for you. Hulton will valet for you. You will spend time at Mr. Worley's business, working with his clerks and, well, as you once desired, getting your hands dirty in all sorts of chores. And you will breakfast and dine with him and his family more often than you will at our house there."

"What subjects will I encounter?" asked Hugh.

"More Latin and Greek, of course. Fencing—you are adept at the art, so Mr. Tallmadge's master tells me, but Dr. Comyn has the instructor in his employ who taught that same tutor. Dancing—you are deficient in that art, but, again, Dr. Comyn has an excellent master at hand. French—that will cost me extra, but I believe you will profit from strict lessons. Drawing, merchants accounts, mathematics, Euclid, algebra, Roman and Greek history, modern history, Milton, Pope, geography, an introduction to navigation—well, quite a busy curriculum, Hugh. You will be occupied." The Baron paused. "The school is within walking distance of the house. About fifty other boys—mostly sons of gentry—also attend." The Baron paused. "It is not Eton, nor Harrow. It is a school, I believe, that will be more to your liking."

*   *   *

To Roger Tallmadge, during a noon-time break from instruction, Hugh said, "I am going to London, to attend an academy."

Roger looked dismayed, almost desolate. "What good luck!" he said instead. "When do you leave?"

"Next month. I shall come home for Christmas and Twelfth Night."

"It must be very expensive."

"My father says almost twenty guineas a year. It would be more if I boarded at the school itself."

"We went to London once, but it was mostly to see father's associates."

"I'll write you about the things I do and see."

"Yes! Tell me about the menagerie at the Tower. I've heard it has an elephant and a tiger. And then there's London Bridge! And the king!"

"And Westminster Bridge. I've heard it is a beautiful thing to see. And the Observatory."

The boys walked silently for a while. Then Roger said, "Father says there is to be another war with the French and the Prussians. My brother Francis wants Father to get him into the army."

Hugh chuckled. "That would be a good place for Francis. He is not a diligent student. Perhaps the army will instill a quantum of wisdom in him."

"You would make a wonderful officer, Hugh."

Hugh laughed. "I don't think the army would welcome me, no matter how much my father paid for a commission."

"I would like to try the army, just to see what it's like. Did you know that the Duke of Cumberland had his own company of boys to command when he was only ten? And he's an authority on all the armies' uniforms and customs and battles."

To this, Hugh had nothing to say. He was deep in thought.

They stopped by a birch tree on the outskirts of the landscaped grounds. Beyond were the green, hedged planes of the Tallmadge pastures. Roger looked at the ground. "I will miss you, Hugh."

"And I, you. You are my only friend."

"And you, mine."

They shook hands.

The next day, to Reverdy Brune, after dancing class, Hugh said, "I am going to London, to attend an academy." They walked alone on a path between some hedges in the Brunes' landscaped grounds. The girl was wearing a white cotton dress, and a straw hat tied to her raven-black hair with a red ribbon.

The regret in his words did not escape the girl's notice. "I am very happy for you," she said with feigned indifference.

"I will miss you," he said.

Reverdy Brune did not reply, but his words momentarily disturbed the composure of her face.

This did not escape Hugh. He grinned. "And you will miss me. I know that you will not permit yourself to say it, because so young a lady may not confess such thoughts."

"I am not a lady," she protested. "I am the daughter of a mere squire."

"You are a lady," said Hugh. "Here. I shall prove it." He took one of her gloved hands, raised it to his lips, and kissed it.

Reverdy jerked her hand away. "You are very presumptuous, Hugh Kenrick. Everyone says so."

"It is no vice to be presumptuous," replied Hugh gaily. "It is a foundation of civil society."

"You are mocking me."

"I like to see you frown."

"A frown is a sign of agitation."

Hugh shrugged. "Or of thought, or of anger, or of purpose…or of character." Hugh smiled and studied the girl's face in detail. The girl blushed under his scrutiny. "I am picturing you as you will be the next I see you, Reverdy. You will be a little taller, and your features a little sharper."

The girl turned away. "You needn't boast just because a famous artist has done you a picture. Father is hiring another artist to do ours."

"Will he do one of you alone?"

"Yes," she said proudly.

"I should like to have a picture of you."

"Father would not approve of that—and he certainly would not pay for it."

Hugh reached into his coat pocket and took out a golden guinea. He handed it to the girl. "Here. Give this secretly to your artist. Tell him that you wish to make a surprise present of a miniature to your father. Swear him to secrecy. I shall expect to see you in a fine locket when I return for the holidays."

Reverdy Brune smiled with delight at the intrigue, then took the coin and slipped it into her other gloved hand. They sat down on a stone bench in a bower. She said, "You would think we were going to be married, Hugh Kenrick, the way you carry on."

It was a superfluous comment. It was known by both of them that their parents desired such a marriage. The Brunes wished to marry into nobility, and the Kenricks wished to acquire some interest in the Brunes' lands. More words had been exchanged between the sets of parents on the subject than by the subjects of the arrangement.

Reverdy abruptly looked straight at Hugh. She said, with some concern in her words, "Father says at the table that there may be a war."

"That is the talk in our house, too."

"Do you think your father will purchase you a commission in the army, or get you a place as a midshipman in the navy?"

Hugh shook his head. "No. He says I would do better reading the French, instead of fighting them. I agree with him."

"Father says that General Braddock's death should be avenged, and our country's honor restored." The girl paused. "It would be marvelous if you had a part in those things."

Hugh shook his head. "My father says Braddock was a martinet and a fool who would not listen to the colonials about how to fight the French there. Our country's honor?" He looked pensive for a moment, then shrugged. "I must first establish my own honor, before I devote concern to my country's."

"How selfish of you, Hugh Kenrick!" exclaimed the girl.

"I do not deny it," he replied.

"You are shameless!"

"I have nothing to be ashamed of, least of all my honor."

Reverdy Brune tapped one of her shoes in impatience.

Hugh grinned. "Have you any other sins to accuse me of, Reverdy? I shall admit to those, too."

"You are mocking me again."

"I believe that you enjoy being mocked—by me."

Reverdy turned to face him, and she blinked at the laughter in his eyes. "And now you are showing conceit," she said.

"Is it conceit that you mean, or self-assurance? If it is conceit, then you underestimate me, Reverdy, and I will be disappointed. If you mean self-assurance, then that is something you should cherish in a man, as a man should cherish it in a woman." He reached over and took one of her hands from her lap. "I know that you feign humility to hide your own self-assurance. You will tell me some day, when you are able to, why you should wish to mask so alluring a virtue." Then he raised her hand and kissed it again.

Reverdy Brune smiled in wonder at this observation, and forgot to withdraw her hand.

Chapter 11: The City

I N THE FIRST WEEK OF SEPTEMBER, THE KENRICKS BOARDED A CHARTERED
packet at Swanage, sailed to Dover, and there hired a coach to London.
The coach reached the city two days later, crossed Westminster Bridge,
and deposited them at Windridge Court, the name of the Earl's wall-
enclosed, terraced residence on the Thames near the York Stairs, only a few
doors downriver from the palatial residence of the Duke of Richmond.

The London that Hugh Kenrick saw every day from the carriage that
he shared with his father, mother, sister, and uncle on its way to and from
concerts, outings, and social engagements in the following three weeks was
not his London. His London did not include the mountainous heaps of
rubbish sitting in the streets, nor the streets obstructed by vendors' sheds
and stalls and the crowds drawn to them. It did not include the invasion of
the thoroughfares by new houses, whose broad stone steps jutted abruptly
into the course of wheeled traffic, often causing congestion and public dis-
order. It did not count the shells of ruined houses and sagging, windowless
tenements in the worst districts, nor the mobs of ragged citizenry outside
of them, and who called the shells and tenements home. It did not subsume
the broken pavements and the small lakes of sewage that gathered in their
depressions, nor the rotting hulks of expired horses, fed on by packs of wild
dogs. It discounted the cacophony of street vendors hawking their wares
and services, and shut its ears to the horns, drums, and calls of tradesmen
and the general deluge of profanity. It did not countenance the teams of
alert, feral thieves, pickpockets, and cutpurses, who would strike at the
unwary or the careless propertied man or woman and vanish into the
crowds with their booty: wigs, swords, purses, watches, lace cuffs, bonnets,
silver buttons. It did not take cognizance of the innumerable, anonymous
figures of men—and some women—propped up against or lying alongside
the grimy brick and stone walls of dark alleys, some of them groggy with
gin or opium, some unconscious and bleeding from a brutal robbery or
assault, and some dead from starvation, bad liquor, exhaustion, or murder.
It was not the London of the countless pairs of eyes that followed the rumbling passage of liveried carriages through disreputable neighborhoods with
envy, hatred, larcenous intent, or, occasionally, with innocent wonder or

wistful hope.

These phenomena comprised the norm for that aspect of London, and were mostly noted, ignored, or forgotten by those for whom they were not the norm. From Hugh's perspective, that London was the "is"; his London was the "ought."

Hugh's London was a fastidious milieu of fine proportions and elegant craftsmanship; of large, spacious, and airy rooms with carpeted floors, ample candlelight, and gay Chinese wallpaper. Of fireplaces designed by Robert Adam, laden with bronze neoclassical Greek and Roman statuary and flanked by framed botanical prints by Furber and Ehret and theatrical prints by Hayman. Of wide, linen-clad tables set with brilliantly painted Staffordshire porcelain and delicate chinaware from Chelsea, Derby, and Bow. Of stately grand balls and masquerades in the homes of the mighty and powerful. Of leisurely dinners and tea parties with neighbors and acquaintances, serenaded by hired musicians. Of afternoon salons with fellow aristocrats, and often with well-read merchants, manufacturers, and men of commerce and their wives, who, though drawn largely from the ranks of Dissenters and Nonconformists, were beginning to be recognized and granted grudging though civil entrée into polite, refined society by the upper classes, literati, and intelligentsia. It was the laughter, easy conversation, and sophisticated rapport that sparkled in these gatherings which became for Hugh the norm in relations between adults.

Hugh's London included many circulating libraries, such as Fancourts, with its forty thousand volumes, and browsing in the second-hand bookstalls in St. Paul's Churchyard and the Law Courts. It was pristine shops with bow windows that artfully displayed countless novelties and goods. It was family games on rainy afternoons, and, on "glorious days," excursions up the Thames on private yachts with liveried watermen to row and lunch far upriver at a fashionable inn. In the evenings, it was family theatrics, the putting on of scenes from famous and obscure plays; Hugh himself had played Hamlet at the age of eleven, to the acclaim of his parents and their aristocratic friends. It was trips to the Tower to see exotic animals, and to Vauxhall, Ranelagh Gardens, or the Pantheon to socialize, to listen to orchestras play compositions by Rameau, Vivaldi, and Boyce, to view the work of new artists, to gather gossip or political news, to see and be seen.

It was the theater, to see *The Beggar's Opera*, or *The English Dancing Master*, or some light farce at the King's Theatre, and concerts by the Academy of Ancient Music and ballets by Gluck at the Haymarket Theatre.

It was Italian opera, some authentically Italian, the rest by Handel. It was attending services at St. Paul's Cathedral and listening to a heavenly choir. It was the London of scores of clubs, some, like Samuel Johnson's, built on dominating personalities and composed of men of like mind and scope of wit, and which usually met in taverns to talk about anything that struck the fancy: politics, mathematics, astronomy, America, women, literature, drink. Others, open to anyone who was a devotee to or dilettante in some field of knowledge, art, or science, no matter how general, eclectic, or arcane, usually met in drawing rooms or private libraries.

Hugh's London left him little time to himself—to read, to think, to enjoy his own company. He did not much mind his London, but it left him tired and secretly anxious for the day when his parents and uncle would depart for the journey back to Danvers—and he would be left alone, with only a deferential valet and the obliging Mr. Worley to oversee his daily life. But his parents, usually content with rural Danvers, on this occasion could not be sated by all that London had to offer, and so extended their stay by almost three weeks.

Hugh was taken by his parents to the School for Gentlemen and introduced to Dr. Comyn and his staff of instructors. There Dr. Comyn submitted him to a brief oral examination, audited by his parents and his future mentors. Hugh stood before a massive desk and answered questions put to him by the berobed scholar.

"What is a serpent, and who invented it?" asked Dr. Comyn.

"It is a wind instrument, sir," Hugh answered, "eight feet long when unraveled, and encased in leather. It was invented by Guillaume of Auxerre, in 1590."

"Name the 'good' emperors of ancient Rome."

"There were five, sir: Nerva, Trajan, Hadrian, Antoninus Pius, and Marcus Aurelius."

"What is pi?"

"A letter, the sixteenth, in the Greek alphabet. It also serves as a symbol for the ratio of the circumference of a circle to its diameter, whose value is three-point-fourteen."

Dr. Comyn grinned. "Who was Theophilus?" This was a favorite trick question of his. No prospective pupil had ever correctly answered it.

"Which one, sir?" asked Hugh.

Dr. Comyn grunted surprise, while one of his instructors muttered, "Bravo!"

"Any or all, milord."

"Theophilus the Presbyter in the eleventh century set down the rules for the building of cathedrals and the design of stained glass. Theophilus, emperor of Byzantium in the ninth century, persecuted thousands of idolaters. He was somewhat mad, sir."

Dr. Comyn bestowed a benevolent smile on the boy. "Well, one last test, milord. A mundane one, I fear. Describe the earldom of Danvers."

Hugh glanced at his parents, startled by the request. He recited, "The earldom of Danvers consists of the parishes of Danvers, Todd Matravers, Onyxcombe, Cryden Abbas, and Chalkbourne. The first three parishes lie in the heath land, Onyxcombe and Chalkbourne on the chalk downs. They were originally Saxon estates that pledged fealty to William the Norman; each parish sustains a market town of the same name. The earldom is rent roughly in half by the Onyx River, which is formed by the confluence of numerous brooks and streams, which themselves emanate from underground springs in the heights beyond the chalk downs. It is so named because at certain points, and in a particular light, its waters appear black. The Onyx joins the River Piddle some miles west of Poole. Agriculture is the earldom's chief occupation. Quarrying and fishing are its other chief sources of revenue."

Dr. Comyn nodded, smiled, and addressed a beaming Garnet Kenrick. "You would be surprised, your lordship, at how many young gentlemen do not know their own homes." He extended a hand to Hugh. "You have displayed an admiral stock of knowledge, milord. Welcome to the school."

*   *   *

From all this whirl of social and familial activity, one incident fixed itself in Hugh's memory. It occurred at a concert given by a neighboring family of the Kenricks, the Pumphretts, who owned Bucklad House next door to Windridge Court.

Bucklad House had undergone lengthy renovations, and the Pumphretts wished to mark their completion with a concert, to which were invited a list of London worthies. Lady Chloe, wife of Sir Henoch Pannell—who was Baronet of Marsden in Essex, Surveyor-General of Harwich in Suffolk, Gentleman of the King's Bedchamber, and member for the pocket borough of Canovan in the Commons—was the mover behind this event. A donation of five guineas per person was levied, the receipts to be given to

Lady Chloe's own organization, the Westminster Charity for London Waifs. "She's doing her penance early," confided Sir Henoch with sly derision to friends in the Commons who had been invited to the concert, "so that she may enjoy the rest of the season without the encumbrance of conscience. She is essentially a *moral* woman."

The Pumphretts, into whose family Pannell had married shortly after his triumphant return to London following his erasure of the Skelly gang in Cornwall, were the owners of Bucklad House, and had underwritten almost the entire cost of its renovations. Gervase Pumphrett, Lady Chloe's father, had insisted on this arrangement to ensure that the Pumphretts retained some property in the family's name and thus prevent Sir Henoch from claiming that his money kept up the place. Sir Henoch had contributed some funds to the rebuilding of its stables. He stayed at Bucklad House when he attended sessions of the Commons or saw to his other official business in the city.

He and Lady Chloe resided at Pannell Hall in Suffolk, but Sir Henoch had his own modest lodgings in London, in Canovan itself; he was, in fact, that borough's sole enfranchised resident. Here he rendezvoused with fellow gamblers, wenches from the street, and courtesans from the best parlors, with smugglers and other figures of the netherworld, and with other members of Parliament to plot strategy. This was the norm for many members of Parliament, to have a refuge from public dignity. His faction in the Commons was ultra-conservative; he was its "whip." He was Whiggish when it was expedient, Toryish when it suited his purpose, even though the defining line between the two parties was growing more blurred as parliamentary Whiggism absorbed tradition-bound Toryism.

Baron Garnet Kenrick and his wife had been reluctant to accept Lady Chloe's invitation; she bored them, and her husband was a coarse, indelicate, and rude man. And they had wanted to rest a full day before beginning the arduous journey back to Danvers. But the Earl wished to cement a subtle if unacknowledged political alliance between his Tory colleagues in Lords and their counterparts in the Commons. "There are moves in the lower House to raise the land tax and lower the gin excise," he explained to his brother. "There are bills being talked about that would also lower the customs on Irish lace, Dutch tile, and Spanish oranges. Sir Henoch's party can defeat them, or at least see that the sting is taken out of them. We must show our good faith to him. All of us, even Hugh. He is a caitiff and a rake, but in his plebeian realm he wields an effective mitre."

And so the Kenricks, dressed in their best finery, early that evening trooped next door to Bucklad House to join a throng of other guests, few of whom attended because they relished the program of music or pitied waifs.

The group of musicians who comprised Lady Chloe's little orchestra was as fine as could be hired and assembled. Besides a tenor and a soprano to sing the arias and duets, it even counted moonlighting members of the Royal Band, the king's own orchestra. "His Majesty would not call them an orchestra," whispered Lady Chloe to Effney Kenrick before the performance, "even though the Band features players of strings. I fear that the strings are not often called on to help serenade the royal ear at the Queen's Palace."

Effney Kenrick nodded sagely, and stifled a yawn.

The orchestra played little-heard compositions by Corelli, Torelli, selections from Gluck's operas, and a single opus of Scarlatti's. Sixty-two guests crowded into the new dining hall, which could also double as a ballroom. The chairs were comfortable, the servants attentive, and the room made warmer by the diverting French and Italian tapestries on the walls. The odors wafting from the buffet in an adjoining room were torturously enticing and were responsible for an impatient and unabated rustle in the audience.

It was during the merciful "intermission" that Garnet Kenrick and Hugh chanced to join a circle of guests gathered around Sir Henoch in an anteroom. Sir Henoch, who had once lived an austere, almost monkish life, this evening sported a burgundy velvet suit, three diamond rings on his fingers, and, next to the medallion of his baronetcy on his frock coat, another scintillating ribbon and orb which looked like a royal decoration, but which was actually a gold De Charmes pocket watch set with diamonds in the face, one for each hour. His powdered wig, by the fashionable French wigmaker de Gonville, had cost seven guineas, his gold-edged tricorn fifteen. He was determined to make an impression.

An exchange of remarks on Braddock's defeat in Pennsylvania and the looming tasks of financing and planning the impending war with France led to other matters. "Marsden? It was a pitiful collection of superannuated huts, inhabited mostly by lazy cottars, when I was raised. But these have lately been converted into cloth factories, in which I have a not insignificant interest." Sir Henoch smiled, then managed to swallow a burp. He had been drinking, and stood with a glass of claret in hand. "I am the first baronet of the place since Bowler Ricks, my most immediate predecessor, expired in the third year of Charles the Second's reign," he boasted without prompting.

"Was he also a made baron, Sir Henoch?" asked the Marquis of Colewort with a muted but superior sneer.

Sir Henoch appraised his frank guest before he answered. "Made? Yes, he was made. He did Charles a service or two before Charles ascended the throne. As did I, your lordship, for our own gracious and grateful sovereign." After a short pause, he asked, "And you?"

The circle of listeners stood wide-eyed at this reckless insinuation.

The Marquis of Colewort, a tall, pale man with pretensions to French radical thought and an uncritical convert to Bolingbroke's *The Idea of a Patriot King*, replied grandly, "My family claims its heritage to Edward the First, Sir Henoch." He paused a measured beat, and added, "And you?"

"Mine, your lordship? Woolgatherers. A long line of woolgatherers. And before the invention of that worthy occupation, scratchers of the soil for roots, bulbs, and grubs. You see, your lordship?" chuckled Sir Henoch. "We are both made. All the peerage is made."

The Marquis stiffened, and a hand moved to rest on the silver-inlaid pommel of his sword. "Civility, Sir Henoch, and the highest regard for your wife and her noble purpose, dictate that I do not pursue this intercourse. I take my leave." The Marquis touched his hat, bowed to the women in the circle, turned, and left the room.

"And thank you for the five guineas, your lordship," said Sir Henoch to the retreating back.

"You have invited reprisal, Sir Henoch," remarked the Baron of Grenody, his occasional card game partner at Canovan.

Sir Henoch shook his head. "Nonsense, sir! That one has no bottom. He is a mere fopdoodle, and, I hear on good authority that his ancient heritage is nigh to Queer Street. Besides, His Majesty favored me once with an audience—to hear first-hand my account of the noosing of the notorious Skelly—and at one point in it confided that he dislikes Colewort. Colewort, you see, pleaded on several occasions for Prince Frederick. He is persona non grata at the court."

Garnet Kenrick asked, "And what story did you tell His Majesty?"

"About Skelly?"

"Yes."

"No, no," protested Sir Henoch. "I am tired of telling that story."

Other guests seconded the Baron's request. Sir Henoch chuckled and adamantly shook his head.

Garnet Kenrick said, "Perhaps, then, you would favor us with an account of what actually did happen, Sir Henoch?"

Again the circle of listeners gaped discreetly into space. This was graver than an insinuation. The notes of a Gluck concerto grosso ticked away the long seconds.

But before Sir Henoch could rally a response, Garnet Kenrick said, "I have myself exaggerated my own accomplishments while professing the wildest humility, Sir Henoch. Such is the *ton* of our age. And the public reports of the Marvel affair and the Falmouth trial were so diverse in their claims that one could not know what to believe."

Sir Henoch's eyes narrowed in appreciation and relief for the Baron's shrewdness. He smiled pleasantly at the Baron, and at his son, whose attentive green eyes also made him uncomfortable. Without knowing why, for drink had dulled some of his mind, he ran a finger along the length of a scar on his cheek. "Well," he said, "it was simply a matter of outfoxing the fellow, and trapping him in his lair, in those damned caves near Marvel. When I think of a hundred desperate men against our brave troops—well, I needn't have worried. Our fellows made short work of 'em!"

Lady Ornsby, Baroness of Tiverton, one of the circle, frowned. "I'd heard that there were hardly more than a dozen of them," she remarked, moved by nothing more than a desire to reconcile contradictory but authoritative hearsay.

Sir Henoch frowned, but dared not rebuke her, for she was a friend of his wife's, and also of the Earl of Danvers. "Oh," he replied, "so many of Skelly's batmen deserted him when they saw the army arrayed before them, that the commanding officer was never quite certain, until it was over, what he was faced with."

"I've heard that you were familiar with Skelly and his lieutenant," said the Baron. "What kind of men were they?"

Sir Henoch shook his head. "Peculiar, eccentric, and quite foolish. I did not get to know them so well, your lordship, other than to observe that about them."

"Skelly, I know, once owned an emporium here in London. Near your borough, I recall. I purchased a gewgaw there once, when I was my son's age. And his lieutenant was a man of numerous accomplishments—poet, playwright, and author of that engaging novel, *Hyperborea*."

Sir Henoch raised his brow in astonishment. "Engaging, your lordship?

I would not say so. It was found by finer minds than my own to be seditious claptrap. So it was stigmatized and burned right under the author's
nose, before he danced for Jack Ketch. And did you know this? That a copy
of it—the second volume, I believe—was found on Skelly's person at
Marvel. It had stopped a bullet, but saved him for the rope. Had the same
in his pocket when he died. One of the sheriff's men filched it, I believe."
Then Sir Henoch's brow knitted in distaste and he shook his head. "No,
your lordship. Do not waste any sympathy on those men. They were smugglers, your lordship—and murderers."

"They were never tried for murder, Sir Henoch."

"No matter, your lordship. There is not a gang in existence that has not
committed the crime. It matters not what a murderer owned or accomplished before he condemned himself."

"I agree with that sentiment, Sir Henoch. But the fact remains that
they were not tried for murder. A trial might have revealed that the fault
lay with the deceased, and not with the dock."

"Perhaps, your lordship," replied Sir Henoch. "But this is a moot point.
They were hanged, and the justice of that provable murder was collateral
with that required for their other proven smuggling offenses."

Garnet Kenrick cocked his head thoughtfully. "A somewhat dangerous
notion, Sir Henoch—'collateral' justice. It is the genesis of all sorts of government mischief; general warrants and writs of assistance, for instance."

Sir Henoch hummed in apparent cogitation, then sighed and said, "To
tell the truth, your lordship, this is a subject on which I plan to write a book
someday. And, at the present, I reserve my energies for this tenure of talk
for the benches of the Commons. You will forgive my reticence." He smiled
blandly, then put his glass on the sideboard behind him and clapped his
hands once. "But—while his lordship's mind grumbles in curiosity, my ear
discerns the rumblings of bellies for sustenance of a more temporal fare!
Please! All of you! Avail yourselves of the bounteous kickshaw which my
lady has had prepared for the affair. And you will discover that the
Pumphrett hospitality does not attempt to palm off slipslop on its guests.
Our cellar's stocks have been called nearly as superb as Robert Walpole's!"
He glanced once at his dazzling watch, and made his way through the
circle.

As they moved away, the Baron asked his son, "What do you think of
him, Hugh?"

"Sir Henoch is a sophist," remarked Hugh.

"And a very crude one, at that," chuckled the Baron. "An ostentatious, unsavory, rotund boor. If you called him a sophist to his face, in all likelihood, he would feel paid a compliment, knowing full well the meaning of the word."

"If I were to write a satire, I would cast him as a simurg. You know, that Persian beast that can speak and seem to reason," Hugh said. "Did you expect him to tell the truth about the Marvel fight and the trial?"

"No."

"Then why did you bother to ask him for it?"

"Because a man of his stamp and manner often tells the truth with a lie. In this instance, he implied that the truth has been buried, and that he was one of the chief gravediggers."

"Yes. He wriggled out of having to tell the story of how he caught Skelly."

"He has had much practice in that art. He is in the Commons."

"Are all the men who sit in the Commons of his stamp?"

"Not all, but too many. Some are less accomplished sophists, others more. While you are here, Hugh, take advantage of your privilege and observe Lords and the Commons in session."

"I shall."

The Baron put a hand on his son's shoulder. "Well, let us concede that Sir Henoch heard our own rumblings, and have a bite to eat." He glanced across the dining hall, and over the heads of the throng espied his wife. In another corner of the room, he noticed Sir Henoch talking with Basil Kenrick who looked as though he were stoically enduring torture. Sir Henoch Pannell, after all, was a mere raised commoner. Garnet Kenrick smiled. "Ah, but there's your mother, besieged by Lady Chloe and her clique. Shall we rescue her first?"

But Hugh stopped to ask, "Father, is it true?"

"What?"

"That Romney Marsh, an executed criminal, wrote *Hyperborea*?"

"Yes, Hugh. It's true."

"Did you know it when you gave me his book?"

"Yes."

"Why didn't you tell me?"

"I wanted you to form your own estimate of the work, without prejudice toward the author."

"I suspected, in time, that it could not have been penned at Strawberry

Hill."

Garnet Kenrick laughed again, this time at Hugh's allusion to Horace Walpole, the literary son of another late prime minister, who had built himself a "Gothick" palace in Twickenham. "Then, by whom?"

"By someone toward whom Sir Henoch and his ilk were mortal enemies."

"As, indeed, Sir Henoch was."

Hugh looked troubled. "It explains the tone of the novel—a story written from the perspective of a man utterly outside the pale of society. Yet, it is a joyful novel, an exciting story. It is, somehow, the most moral story I have ever read. It could not have been written by a criminal." He shook his head. "I am surprised that it was not suppressed."

"But it was. When we went to St. Paul's Churchyard and Duck Lane, did you notice any second-hand copies of *Hyperborea* there waiting to be perused?"

"No."

"That is because the surviving copies are in hiding, waiting to emerge from their own caves. Someday, Hugh, our country will be of a mind to allow you to flaunt your own copy."

Hugh did not pursue the subject. As he and his father crossed the room they encountered the Baron and Baroness of Marrable and their retinue. Garnet Kenrick was obliged to introduce his son and allow himself to be drawn into a discussion of the "pistole fee" affair between Lieutenant Governor Robert Dinwiddie and the Virginia House of Burgesses.

Later that evening, Garnet Kenrick paid Lady Chloe another five guineas to have her orchestra play Vivaldi's "Echo" Concerto. He told himself that he wished to see the delight on his son's face when the piece was played; but he admitted to himself, in the course of the performance, that he had wished to hear it, too.

"Why did you annoy Sir Henoch?" asked Basil Kenrick when he, his brother, and Effney Kenrick were alone in the orangery of Windridge Court. "He said that you as much as called him a liar, and in front of witnesses."

"Because he is an objectionable, slithery snake, Basil, and he needs regular whacking. Also, I wanted the truth about the Skelly gang. He knows that truth."

"But the truth is known, dear brother. Why would you presume that it was not?"

The Baron shrugged. "Look at Sir Henoch, Basil. Can you imagine him serving as a model for a painting entitled *Allegory on Truth*?"

The Earl dismissed the subject. "Pshaw! I don't care what his character is or is not, dear brother. All he need do is take his cues from Hillier come the voting, and that is the limit of my interest in him and the Skelly gang and the rest of it." He paused to glare at his brother. "And another thing, Garnet. Please don't advertise the fact that you esteem *Hyperborea* and its author. Sir Henoch mentioned what you said to him, and he was quite amused. Why on earth would you own to such a thing?"

The Baron looked thoughtful for a moment, then answered, "Justice, dear brother."

When he was alone in his room that night, Hugh took out his copy of *Hyperborea* and reread large sections of it and tried to accept that this greatness was authored by a criminal. He could not reconcile the two things; which led him, because he would not question the greatness of the novel, to question the notion of criminality. He fell asleep in his bed, a volume open on his chest, and the candles in the sconces above him sputtered out.

Chapter 12: The Apprentice

"THE CITY IS RICH IN TEMPTATIONS AND DISTRACTIONS."
Garnet Kenrick had no specific temptation or distraction in mind when he cautioned his son about London. He was, however, certain that Hugh would not succumb to the vices that usually lured aristocratic boys from their duties and obligations: whoring, drinking, gambling, and a multitude of other reckless, inane, or expensive diversions. He did not expect to receive a single letter from his son begging for money, nor from shopkeepers dunning him to pay the boy's debts. Neither he nor his wife could even imagine what would be tempting to Hugh.

"If he would not bow to dissipation and frippery in the person of His Grace the Duke," explained the Baron to his wife a few evenings before they left London and their son behind for the journey back to Danvers, "it seems hardly likely that he would be seduced by the middling sorts of the same things. He has set his own course." He paused in thought, then looked at his wife in mild astonishment. "He is somehow dumb to the things that most of us must invent rules for or against."

Effney Kenrick nodded in agreement. "It's not that possibility which worries me," she replied. "It is that London will not be seduced by Hugh…"

"What an extraordinary notion, my dear!" exclaimed her husband. "Why should London be seduced by Hugh?"

The Baroness watched the lanterns of a waterman's boat drift by on the black Thames beyond the window of their bedroom, and composed her thoughts. "There are times, Garnet, when I have glimpses of a vision of Hugh as a full man, and then he becomes a measure of what all men should aspire to be. I can't say why I think of him that way; it somehow seems logical, and inevitable. And I know that most men either will be blind to him, or fearful of him. Or both."

The Baron grunted. "They are that now. Except for his friend, Roger."

"I am afraid that Hugh will be solitary all his life. Surrounded by people, but essentially alone. And unhappy."

"I fear it, too, Effney. But if he becomes such a man as you envision, then solitude could not crush him." The Baron shrugged. "Else, he could not become such a man." He rose from his chair and joined his wife at the window. From behind her he put his hands on her bare shoulders. "And—there is Reverdy. A sweet girl with will and gumption. She should provide him with solace in his solitude." He kissed his wife's neck. "As you do me, my dear."

"That is my earnest hope, Garnet," said the Baroness with wistful conviction.

*   *   *

In the third week of September, Hugh's new life began. His mother bade him a tearful farewell, his father a comradely one. His uncle warned him to mind his manners and read his Bible, while his sister, Alice, asked only if she could ride his pony. And then the carriage was gone. It was a Monday morning. Hugh's valet escorted him to Dr. Comyn's School for Gentlemen.

His life for the next two years was almost evenly divided between Whitehall and the Lawful Keys in the Pool of London. That is, between the sedate, civil, and orderly routine of his home on Windridge Court and the academy, and the maelstrom of mercantile commerce below London Bridge far down the river.

Each morning, a little after sunrise and after breakfast, Hugh walked with his valet, Hulton, to the school, which occupied a three-story building on nearby Chapel Mews. The valet's escort was necessary to discourage footpads, thieves, and rogues who might recognize in Hugh's finery the material for kidnapping and ransom. The valet carried a cudgel and two pocket pistols, and Hugh his own sword.

The school, staffed largely with Dissenters, Quakers, and other non-conventional academics and instructors, encouraged free thought. Pupils were prompted to do their own original thinking above and beyond the wisdom they received. Almost anything was tolerated, so long as it could be founded on cool reason. Ironically, it was a past mathematics instructor who gave Dr. Comyn's school its unofficial motto: Question your time, take a foothold outside of it, and acquire a perspective. This was advice Hugh could heed, and he took it seriously.

In the school he sat at his own desk with other young gentlemen in a single room, auditing the lectures of a succession of instructors, breaking for tea, dinner, and exercise in a gymnasium. He dutifully construed Latin, annotated Milton and Pope, struggled with French and German, and mastered algebra and geometry. He wrote a brilliant essay on modern European history in the style of Polybius's "The Constitution of the Greek City States," comparing France, Prussia, the Netherlands, and England with Athens, Sparta, Thebes and Crete. In another paper he paraphrased Isocrates, and was asked by his pleased instructor to read it to his fellow pupils.

"England has so far out-coursed her companion nations in thought and deed," he wrote, "that her champions are masters of all. Because of her universal repute, 'English' is not so much a term of birth as it is one of attitude and mental comportment, and is the stamp of a universal culture rather than a term of descent." He had added, "Diderot and d'Alembert and their fellow Encyclopedists could be called 'English.'"

"But we are at war with the French," protested one of his fellow students.

"But not with the Encyclopedists," replied Hugh. "This should comprise a portion of our pride."

"This is true," remarked the instructor. "Diderot does not bear arms. His own king is a greater enemy to him than we could ever be."

Another assignment, however, left this same instructor curious. He had given his pupils the task of translating the Magna Carta from the Latin, and of appending to the translation a précis of its history. Each pupil was asked to recite his précis in class. In the course of his recitation, Hugh said, "The Great Charter was invoked by Simon de Monfret in 1265 to call a parley of the barons. It was subsequently confirmed by Edward the First in 1297." Then he paused and looked thoughtful. "The best that can be said about this period of our nation's history is that the numerous depredations were committed by Normans and Angevins, who were the descendants of the invaders. But their system of rule was taken into the bosoms of Englishmen, and this system was not rejected in any principal sense. When the barons obliged King John to sign the Great Charter, they were and remained barons, and a baron was a rank foreign to this island until the Conquest."

Some of the pupils who were baronets themselves gasped. The instructor cleared his throat. "You question your own heritage, milord. Do you not find that an unseemly notion?"

Hugh shrugged. "I have made a pertinent observation, sir," he replied. "I cannot answer for my heritage or my lineage. Only for myself."

"That is a leveling notion!" accused one young baronet.

"A republican notion!" chimed another.

"But a true observation nonetheless," answered Hugh.

The instructor quelled the uprising by rapping his pointer once on the floor of the dais. "Those who dispute the truth of milord Kenrick's observations may procure for themselves copies of Henry Care's *English Liberties*, Rapin-Thoyras's *History of England*—the Tindal translation—or Nathaniel Bacon's *Historical Discourse of the Uniformity of the Government of England*. These are but three of a shelf of works that make the same assertion. Copies are likely to be found in the inventory of any reputable bookseller in this city."

On another occasion, Hugh wrote an essay on the career of King John, to which he appended an aside on the distinct differences in meaning between the terms "King of the English" and "Rex Angliæ."

"The first term means 'king of the conquered.' The second term means 'English king.' King John signed the Great Charter 'Rex Angliæ.' There is, therefore, some credence in modern historians' arguments that the use of the second term marked the true beginning of our nation."

Later in the aside, he commented: "I cite Edward the First, who, in issuing a writ for parliament, employed a phrase whose literal meaning must have eluded him, in regard to Philip, King of France, who was threatening to invade this island: 'If his power is equal to his malice, he would destroy the English tongue from the earth.' If his power is equal to his malice: What an odd thought for a sovereign to have, especially this one who is also called Longshanks, who was constantly at war with the barons, who persecuted Jews and goldsmiths, who killed Llywelyn, the Prince of Wales, and had his brother David executed by all the means it is possible to kill a man, and who executed William Wallace, the Scottish patriot. Why, here was a king moved by malice! His power might have been equal to it, had the barons submitted to him." Hugh ended the aside with another observation: "I think it ought to be the goal of Parliament to disempower the malice which can rule and ruin the nation, or even a single man, or group of men, such as the Jews, Catholics, and other Nonconformists. Yet, what I note in my readings is an unending struggle between members of that august body to apply their malice by wresting power from the King, so that they themselves may exercise it, and those who seek, too often vainly, to stem that malice by checking that power."

His modern history instructor said to Hugh in private: "I shall not require you to read this work to your fellow pupils, milord. It would...well...cause a stir. It is, however, worthy of Addison, or Sidney, or

Locke. But, pray, milord, do not voice these sentiments until you speak in Lords, or in a pamphlet."

Hugh was a competent fencer before he left Danvers. Under the tutelage of the school's fencing master, he became an excellent foilsman. He applied himself in this art as earnestly and eagerly as he did in his other studies. Once, during a session with the master, Hugh startled the man by asking him, "Is it not true that the skills I learn here will help sharpen my thoughts?"

The fencing master, an Italian who fashioned his own foils and supplemented his school income by teaching French and Continental manners to other aristocrats' children, drove Hugh back across the polished floor of the gymnasium with a series of savage thrusts and counter-parries. "Not without your conscious design, sire. There exist connections and applications between the art of the rapier and the art of the mind that you must forge with your own head."

"Cicero!" exclaimed Hugh as he parried a thrust aimed at his heart.

The Italian responded with a half-circle feint of his foil that sent Hugh's foil flying through the air to clatter on the floor. "I recommend Cicero, sire," he said, planting the tip of his foil over Hugh's heart. "I am master of the blade; he, of rhetoric."

Hugh smiled. "Then I must learn to wed you and Cicero."

This remark brought an unwilling grin to the Italian's expression. He was a proud man who spoke to his students, not with them. He stepped back and stood to his full, imposing height. "Why that pleasant visage, sire? I have just gored you."

"You have taught me that the true wisdom of a foilsman lies not in his wrist, but here." Hugh tapped his own forehead twice.

The Italian drew himself together and turned his back on Hugh. "Do not patronize me, sire. I know my own value." He began to walk away.

Hugh bowed slightly to the retreating figure. "I do not patronize my peers, Signor Albertoli."

The fencing master stopped, stood for a moment, then turned and acknowledged Hugh with his own bow. Then he said, "Pick up your weapon, sire, and let us resume the lesson."

The next week, after the lesson, the fencing master bowed again and held out a book. Hugh took it. It was a copy of George Silver's *The Paradoxes of Defence*, published in London in 1599. "A volume of wisdom, sire," said Albertoli. "May you profit from its connections and applications."

That night Hugh read the book and was surprised by the amount of wisdom he did find in it. "Truly," he said to himself, "this is reason wedded to action." And a week later, he delivered an essay on Aristotle's argumentative fallacies to his instructor in rhetoric. "Milton wrote in the *Areopagitica* that the strength of Truth should never be doubted. 'Let her and falsehood grapple: who ever knew truth put to the worse in a free and open encounter?' To which one could add the caution: 'To seek a true defence in an untrue weapon, is to angle the earth for fish, and to hunt in the sea for hare. Truth is ancient, though it seems an upstart.' Briefly put, truth shines best when allied with reason: it is compromised when wielded by fallacy."

The rhetoric instructor looked up at Hugh and bid him to rise from his desk. "This last quotation, milord," he asked with a quizzical frown. "Ben Jonson?"

Hugh shook his head. "No, sir. A contemporary of his, Mr. George Silver, a fencing master."

The instructor's brow furled. "But what have his words to do with the subject?"

"One should not choose a dagger to slay a wyvern, sir, when one needs a broadsword."

The instructor cocked his head in appreciation. "Excellent point, milord," he said, "but most attorneys would not subscribe to the notion. They thrive on the daggers of particulars."

"Particulars should be governed—nay, subsumed—by general principles, sir. Like the craters one can see on the moon through a telescope, they would not—cannot—exist apart from the body. Particulars can be derived only from the general. A particular existing alone is an absurdity."

"What gives you leave to express your certainty in those statements?"

"Aristotle—and nature, sir."

In his art lessons, Hugh exhibited fine draughtsmanship. His renderings of the nearby Abbey, of Westminster Bridge, and of St. Paul's Cathedral were the delight of his drawing master. He also did sketches and studies of the Chelsea Waterworks and the London Bridge Waterworks, the most elaborate mechanical "engines" of the time; of inanimate, man-made objects such as staircases, water towers, steeples, the piazzas of the Royal Exchange and Covent Garden, of the tripod scales in the Steelyard, of the nine-story Dye House near Blackboy Alley, of the timber and coal wharves across the Thames; of wherries, arches, and pocket watches. Of his brass top. His instructor collected these drawings and sent them with his report to Dr. Comyn and the boy's father. "Master Kenrick's drawings conceive of accurate and often thrilling perspectives. Some are worthy of Canaletto, others of illustrations for the *Encyclopedia*, and still others of the best pattern books. Together, they would make a pretty book of engraved prints, ready for framing, and could grace the walls of the most prosperous households. Were he to enter an allied trade, Master Kenrick would become accomplished and quite popular, quite as much as Mr. Hogarth."

One day, three of his fellow pupils decided that it was time he was humbled and made one of their own. They cornered him one day in the cobblestone yard behind the school. They were the sons of other barons. The oldest boy challenged Hugh to a duel.

"To the death?" inquired Hugh.

"No!" laughed the boy, glancing at his friends. "Only so far as to cause injury and require a surgeon's ministrations."

Hugh frowned. "If it's not worth a fight to the death, sir, then it's not worth a fight." He paused. "What is your grievance with me?"

"We hear," said one boy, "that you did not pay the Butcher his due respect."

"It is said that you ruined the hands of the Marquis of Bilbury, at Eton."

"You voice sentiments that are alien and unnatural."

"And dangerous."

"True on all accounts," replied Hugh. "But injuring me will neither erase nor even balance those facts. What is your solution?"

There was no answer, except for a trio of smirks on his tormentors' faces.

"You have heard those stories, sir," said Hugh. "I must remind you that my skills have improved since then. If you wish to reduce this conflict to a test of physical prowess, a fight to the death is the only condition on which I will condescend to it."

"You deserve punishment, sir, the tonic of a good drubbing," said the oldest boy, who moved toward Hugh, his hand lazily reaching down for the pommel of his sword.

Hugh whipped out his own sword and in a blink cut a gash on his attacker's left cheek. The boy jumped back with a cry. The other boys reached for their swords. Hugh's blade flicked across the nose of one and ripped the sword hand of the other. "I told you—to the death!" cried Hugh. "Shall we pursue this?"

The three boys staggered away sobbing. "You are mad!" yelled the assailant with the injured hand. "Mad! Mad!"

"If you have disfigured me, your father shall pay!" shouted the boy with the injured nose.

"To the death!" answered Hugh. "Those are my only terms! Those or nothing! Spare me your society! Get you to a surgeon!"

And the three boys disappeared into the school. Hugh glanced at the tip of his sword. It glistened with blood. He found a rag on the ground nearby and wiped the tip clean. Twenty other pupils had gathered around to watch the fight that did not happen. They moved out of his way when he passed. There were no more attempts to initiate him, or to humble him. To make him bend.

*   *   *

East of London Bridge on the Thames were the Lawful Keys, or wharves, twenty of them, near which all merchantmen bringing goods into the country were obliged to anchor to have their cargoes unloaded by lighters and deposited on the wharves for inspection and distribution. Custom House sat conveniently in the middle of these keys, with its own wharf and stairs. This was the most congested part of the Thames on any given day; not infrequently, a thousand ships of all sail were anchored below the Bridge, each waiting its turn to be unshipped and "customed." Until later in the century there were no other "lawful" keys; the twenty that Hugh became familiar with comprised a monopoly, protected by statute. The port duties, warehousing charges, and other miscellaneous expenses paid to the keys' proprietors by ship captains and merchants were not regulated. Bribes in money or in kind were necessary to unload cargo into the warehouses, or onto barges that would take the goods upriver under the Bridge to stairs, private wharves, and landing places beyond.

Benjamin Worley, the senior of Worley and Sons, was a partner with the other owner of Lion Key, John Biddle, whose sister he had married. Lion Key sat west of the Billingsgate docks, in between Somerset and Botolph Keys. Worley acted as agent not only for the Earl and Baron of Danvers, but for other prominent men of means as well. By himself, he owned another warehouse behind Lion Key, on Thames Street. This was Number 66; warehouses were the first buildings in London to employ numbers. He was also a partner in two merchantmen with their captain-owners. One, the *Nimble*, traded along the coast of Europe and in the

Mediterranean; the other, the *Busy*, in North America and the Caribbean.
Worley and his family lived in a modest mansion on Mincing Lane, complete with a staff of servants, a stable for his post-chaise and team of horses,
and quarters for all his staff.

Worley, of course, got preference for his merchantmen when they came
up the Thames, as did merchantmen belonging to captains and syndicates
with whom he did the most business. His only extraordinary expense was
to provide the customs man assigned to Lion Key a modest "subsidy" in
order to clear his own and other vessels' cargoes with the least amount of
duty and with the best dispatch. Through Lion Key passed grain, resins,
timber, whale oil, Lettish deerskins, and other imports from the Baltic;
wines, olive oil, spices, medicinal herbs, silks, and edibles from the Levant
and southern Europe; tea, fine woods, opium, china, and other exotic goods
on consignment from the occasional East Indiaman; and tobacco, cotton,
hemp, sugar, beaver pelts, and rum from North America and the Caribbean.
These goods were carted directly to No. 66 Thames Street, to be collected
and paid for by merchants who had contracted for it, or sold to bidders on
site.

Here at the Keys were also unloaded holds of corn at the Great Bear
wharf, to be bought and sold in the coffeehouses of the Corn Factors'
Exchange, most of it reloaded onto barges and taken upriver to the Queen-
hithe wharf. And at Billingsgate were unloaded holds of coal from Newcastle and Europe, bought and sold by dealers at the Coal Exchange nearby,
and also barged upriver to private depots.

Here teams of Merchants Constables, a private police force paid by a
combine of merchants, warfingers, and lightermen, patrolled the alleys,
depots, and byways of the Keys and Custom House, watching for solo pil-
ferers and gangs of thieves. Here customs officials with their ledger books
and tax tomes haggled with ship captains and merchants over the value or
legality of goods, some intent on guaranteeing the Crown its due income,
others open to entering less than what was due for a negligible fee. Always
in the background was the thunder of the drays, lorries, and barrel wagons,
the tumultuous hustle, jostle, and shouts of porters, laborers, and
lightermen. Now and then men would pause to watch a wall of London
Bridge plummet into the river, for at this time the houses on it were being
demolished so that its piers could be reinforced.

It was into this maelstrom of commerce that Hugh was taken by post-
chaise every Friday and Saturday morning.

His first task was to follow a clerk through a section of Worley's own warehouse to recount barrels of Havana snuff recently brought in on the Caribbean vessel, the *Busy*, and then to observe a pair of factotums measure out the snuff into teakwood casks for a Strand shopkeeper. "Sixteen barrels, and one hundred casks to a barrel," explained the clerk. "Goodly, though, has supplied us with only fourteen hundred casks. He must remove the two extra barrels or pay rent on 'em here."

The clerk paused to look at Hugh, expecting to see incomprehension, or boredom. Hugh, though, was studying him intently. The clerk said, "And we're already chargin' him half a penny to fill the damned things. And then, we can't guarantee that the barrels won't be tampered with." The clerk smiled weakly; his charge seemed to understand everything. He turned to one of the factotums. "Mr. Peters, run along to Goodly's and tell 'im he's short, and he'd better send a wagon." The factotum obeyed, rushing down the aisle out of sight. The clerk picked up the man's wooden scoop and handed it to Hugh. "Pardon me, milord, but Mr. Worley said you told him you wanted to get your hands into it."

To the clerk's surprise, Hugh took the scoop, smiled at it, and walked to a snuff barrel and a pile of teakwood casks. He opened the lid of one and began to work. The remaining factotum sneezed into his, sending up a cloud of snuff. The clerk laughed, and so did Hugh. The clerk was unsure of Hugh's status; he was the son of a real baron, the nephew of an earl, and his own employer was more or less beholden to that family. He did not understand the arrangement. Caution got the better of him, and he found a scoop and began measuring out casks himself.

By noontime, all the teakwood casks had been filled. The clerk and the two factotums regarded Hugh with amazement. He had measured out the greater number of casks, and stood with his hands on his hips, hatless, coatless, and swordless in the sweltering warehouse, sweat dripping from his forehead, beaming with pride. "What is next?" he inquired.

Later, the clerk gained admittance to Worley's sanctum-like office. "He works!" he exclaimed to his employer. "He's as filthy as a coalheaver, and he...enjoys it!"

This did not surprise Benjamin Worley. He had been warned by the boy's father. But he had already believed it. He had been spying on the snuff-cask crew throughout the morning and early afternoon, in order to accustom his mind to the sight of a laboring aristocrat.

Still, Benjamin Worley struggled to understand his new "employee."

He had been instructed by the boy's father to drill him in the fundamental operations of his business. With that mandate, he allowed himself a certain degree of familiarity with the boy, and ordered him about without fear of reprimand. He subsequently put him to work at a tall desk with other clerks to enter numbers into the great account books, and after two weeks, Hugh had answers to questions that Worley did not have time to ask. Much to the merchant's surprise—and much to his scandal—Hugh also showed a flair for physical work, and seemed to delight in exercising his body in the most degrading labor, moving easily with the pence-a-day laborers and porters, who could do nothing but move physical objects, unloading drays and wagons. He noted that the sight of crates and bales and ships at anchor on the Thames seemed to animate the boy's face, and for a reason he could not fathom sensed a kinship with him. His own sons, Josiah and Lemuel, who also worked in the office, exuded more airs than did Hugh Kenrick.

When it was safe—for he did not know how much the boy knew about the sub rosa end of the business—he allowed Hugh to audit the clearance of cargo by the customs man when no extraordinary "fees" were expected. He instructed him in the art of double-entry bookkeeping, the fundamentals of drawbacks, and the mechanics of tariffs, excises, and customs. He took him on a tour of the Keys, introduced him to other merchants and wharfingers, and pointed out the specialty of each Key.

"Of course, milord, as it may have occurred to you, the Keys do not confine themselves to receiving merely. There, you see," he said, gesturing with his cane to a Key that was piled high with crates and barrels, "there go nails, and hats, and shoes, and farm implements. Not to mention books and fine furniture, and tools of all types. Which ship is she? Ah, yes, the *Dolphin,* bound for Boston and New York. Owned by Captain St. John. Nothing dutiable on board her, of course. Except for wool. The colonials make much of their own, you see. Shouldn't, but they do. Well, it does commerce good to neglect some law. But the *Dolphin* here, she'll pick up a good wind at Sheerness, round the thumb at Margate, and skirt the coast past Ramsgate. Probably stop at Brighton, and Portsmouth, and Weymouth to take on more cargo—perhaps passengers and indentures—if there's still room for them. Then she'll stop at Falmouth to pick up mail for the colonies, and hope to join a convoy at Penzance. Damned convoys! We're back to that again! 'Pon my word, milord, you can't age five years peacefully these times without a damned war! Ah! Here's the Angry Angel!" exclaimed Worley, looking up at the signboard of a coffeehouse. "Run by a man who was once a priest, but he had an eye for well-turned ankles, and…well, why don't we stop in and see if we can pick up some news?"

Worley wrote a report for Hugh's father: "He takes pride in having performed the most menial tasks. My clerks and apprentices are flummoxed by his behavior. He is, however, excellent in the account books, but he also seems to take irregular pleasure in acquiring grime and calluses. He has no difficulty in grasping the mechanics of any aspect of this trade. The ship captains seem to like him, as he exhibits an inordinate interest in their vessels and trades. He walks and talks among them and tradesmen and such as an equal, neither humbly nor condescending. I would swear he was raised in America, but for my certainty that he has never been there…"

*   *   *

Hugh was indeed dumb to the city's conventional temptations and distractions, insensible to the things others found interesting or amusing. One afternoon, he accompanied Worley, his sons, and some of the senior clerks to Billingsgate to witness and wager on an illegal boxing match between two of the fishwives. The two ugly women pummeled each other's faces, using the coins clutched in their palms (there to prevent them from pulling each other's hair) as cutting weapons. The crowd shouted profane encouragement to one or the other of the combatants. Worley and his sons joined in with practiced zeal. When the fight ended in a draw, Worley remarked to Hugh: "Disreputable market here, milord. Noted for its language, you see. Could pick up quite a vocabulary, if you'd a mind to—and a few skirts, too, if you don't mind the smell."

The experience left Hugh bored, indifferent, and with his first taste of a jadedness that had an odd gleam of dignity. His life was a jeweled vessel, and he meant to fill it with the best wine.

Hugh was unaware of the pang of solitude. The city was open to him. Ideas kept him company. He was too engrossed in the excitement of being alone. There is, in any great city, enough to occupy any mind that is vigorous enough to see it. "My city" was the unspoken premise that powered his actions and thoughts. Alone, he approached the city as a prospective conqueror.

He performed his chores at Worley's with excruciating carefulness, growing confidence, and quiet delight. He felt a surge of pride for having performed them, menial though they might have been. With each task he completed, his observers noted an odd combination of grimness and joy on his face, and could not fathom the incongruity, except to conclude that it was evidence of some form of madness. They could not know that with each completed task—when he finished an inventory, or balanced the double-entry account ledgers, or helped watermen unload their lighters of cargo unshipped from a merchantman riding at anchor below London Bridge—Hugh felt that he owned the city, that he had contributed to its life, and that he could stake a claim to its existence, that the city was then more rightfully his than those who commanded it, more than the dukes, more than the Lord Mayor, more than any guild. "Something has gone out into the world," he would think, "something done right, something of value, and my hand was in it."

Hugh remembered a time long ago—remembered the music, the fire-works, the city revealed by flashes of light—and he was prepared to do splendid things. This was a proper place for him. He was moved by some wordless anthem that had no melody, an anthem that only he could hear.

This was a fever that strikes most men in their youth, but which they are cured of when they encounter the world and the demands of others. Hugh developed immunity to the cure, because he preferred the fever to what he saw passed for healthy men. Benjamin Worley was not the worst instance. To Hugh, the cure left most men sickly, weak, and robbed of their vitality and power to live. They reminded him neither of Drury Trantham, nor of himself.

Chapter 13: The Cosmopolitan

T O HIS FRIEND ROGER TALLMADGE, HE WROTE: "I SHALL NOT KNOW WHAT to do with myself when I come home for school recess. I have been somehow electrified by the school, by my responsibilities at Mr. Worley's business, and by the city itself. I will be afraid to shake your hand, next I see you, lest I cause you harm of some sort."

Reverdy Brune kept her promise, and sent Hugh a locket containing her miniature portrait. It showed a haughty profile of her, imperiously self-assured, her black hair tied back with a green ribbon, her black eyes turned to the viewer with a touch of condescension. Hugh sent her a locket miniature of himself with his next letter, a self-portrait in crayon. "I have bought a chain and attached it to your locket, and now you hang on the wall above my cluttered desk, to remind me of my future with you."

When he reread the last line, it occurred to him that it should have read, "to remind me of our future together." But he decided to leave the clause as he had written it. His marriage to Reverdy was, after all, tentative, a mere understanding, a verbal pledge, as remote in his coming life as his majority. She was a thing to prize, a joy to anticipate. He did not fully understand why he preferred to leave the clause unchanged, except that it seemed to reflect his own terms.

Hugh absorbed the details of Benjamin Worley's business without judgment, hesitation, or reservation. There was a curious aspect to it that gnawed at his sense of right, but he did not know enough about the enterprise to identify it. It was his introduction to commerce, to industry, to trade. Through Lion Key, No. 66 Thames Street, and Worley's office, he could touch the rest of the world. This made him happy.

The city was an insistent distraction. In his free time, Hugh roamed it, sometimes with his valet, Hulton, sometimes by himself, to Hulton's consternation. He had asked the valet to purchase him some ordinary city clothes, so that he could walk the less prosperous streets and neighborhoods without attracting the attention of criminals or prompting tradesmen to raise the prices of their wares. "A brownish ensemble," he said to Hulton, "tattered or repaired, threadbare though not transparent, wooden buttons on a commodious frock, ripped hose, square-toed shoes, evil-looking shirt with no frills, and a hat that looks as though it had been fetched up from the Fleet Ditch. And a frayed pigtail bow. All washed and rid of vermin, of course. I wish to move freely among the populace, not feel their afflictions moving freely about me."

Hulton looked scandalized by the assignment—and worried. "Milord, may I point out that your father the Baron has charged me with your safety and comfort, and should anything wicked or untoward happen to you, he has assured me of the direst consequences for me." He paused. "I might also add that my colleague, Mr. Runcorn, has also promised me bodily harm should you encounter a misfortune that can be ascribed to my oversight or negligence."

Hugh laughed, and then and there composed a document that exonerated and absolved the valet of all responsibility in the event that Hugh met with harm. He signed the note, dated it, then folded it neatly and sealed it with wax. He rose from his desk and handed it to Hulton. "There you are, Hulton. It may not stand up in a court of law, but it will count for much in the court of my father's justice—should it ever be needed." He paused to grin. "Mr. Runcorn must be satisfied with the same."

"Thank you, milord." Hulton fingered the rectangle of paper as though it were a purse of gold, and bowed slightly.

Hugh studied the valet for a moment, then resumed his seat. "Hulton, I know that you have been perusing my books when I am away at school or Mr. Worley's. The composition and grammar books here on my desk and on the shelves were left askew, that is, not as I left them. Do you confess?"

Hulton blushed. "Yes, milord," he answered, almost in a whisper.

"Feel guilt no more, Hulton," chuckled Hugh. "Such curiosity is not to be punished or discouraged. Your speech and expression have improved much over these months. I shall write my father and recommend that he raise you to butler. You have managed the house here admirably. Where did you learn to read?"

"In a charity school, milord, in Wapping. Then I was bound over to a parish apprenticeship. Dreadful experience, that. I was taught to fashion shoe buttons, but my master was indifferent to my skills, and sold my apprenticeship to a gentleman, for whom I worked as a cook and server. Your father some years ago had supper with this gentleman, and hired me away from him. I have been here at Windridge Court ever since."

"Do you wish to remain a servant always?"

The valet frowned. "I do not know what else there is to be, milord."

Hugh did not pursue the subject, for the valet's answer was too incredible and deserved further examination. He dismissed the man so that he could go on his unusual shopping errand, giving him some crowns for the purchases.

Together they went on outings to see and study things that interested Hugh: to printing and bookbinding shops, to naileries and silversmiths, to the engine house of the Chelsea Waterworks, to gunsmiths, to the Battersea enamel works and factory in York House, far upriver, and far downriver, to the Deptford and the East India shipyards at Blackwall. "Truly magnificent," he remarked to Hulton, gesturing with his disreputable hat to the forests of masts and docks as a ferryman rowed them across the Thames. "The sight of it makes one want to be a part of it all!" He paused. "I am a part of it, now." Hugh slapped Hulton on the back with his hat with exuberance.

Hulton did not understand his master's enthusiasm. "Yes, milord," he replied. The ferryman, pipe in mouth and pulling doggedly on his oars, regarded his fares with amused curiosity. Hulton felt uncomfortable with Hugh's familiarity. In a sense, he resented it. In another sense, it pleased him; he had been treated like a man, almost as an equal. He could not grasp why. Then he felt so severe and sharp an emotion well up in him that he could not contain it. His hands shot up to cover his face and he sobbed.

Hugh turned to him in surprise. "Hulton, is something the matter?"

The valet turned away and wiped his eyes with the sleeve of his coat. "Nothing, milord. It is being on such rough waters. They make me dizzy." When he thought it was safe, he faced his master again. Hugh Kenrick was studying him with a puzzled frown that grew less and less puzzled. The green eyes seemed to see through him. Hugh smiled. It was the most benevolent, welcoming smile Hulton had ever seen on a man's face. It was a smile of congratulation. "You are not a thing," it seemed to say, "a thing that I and my father can order about. You are a man on hire, in service, and a great many wonderful things are possible to you still."

Hulton glanced away, then reached into the leather bag he toted. He took out a large bottle and a metal cup. "Would you like some ale, milord? The salt air here makes one thirsty." Hugh nodded and the valet poured a cup.

Hugh took the cup. Hulton knew that they would never speak of the moment.

Hugh said, "Hulton, do you recall, when we toured the farms beyond

Westminster, that the wagons we met taking fruit and vegetables into the city were the same wagons we met bringing night soil and manure from the city, to be sold to the farmers as fertilizer? It is an efficient way of doing trade, I am sure, and it is done on a vast scale. But—but I doubt that those wagons are ever cleaned and scoured."

"Yes, milord. I recall."

"It accounts for the odd smell of our vegetables and fruit. Washing the produce ought to diminish the odor borne by it, and whatever else lingers on the outside. Ought to rid it of the sea coal odor, too. See that the scullery boy washes all edibles brought into our house henceforth. Meat, poultry, and fish, too."

"Yes, milord."

At day's end, both Hugh and Hulton retired early to their separate quarters, for it had been a long, tiring excursion. Church bells rang eleven o'clock, muffling the sounds of carriages crossing Westminster Bridge on their way to the Saturday night concert at Vauxhall Gardens.

The valet lay in his bed, but was afraid to go to sleep; he might forget the glimpse of what he had not even known was nearly snuffed out of him so many years ago. All it had taken was a boy's impromptu joy; not a great speech or a soul-riveting sermon. Merely a slap on the back. A tear rolled down Hulton's cheek. He thought: It is a terrible thing, joy...the joy of being alive. And dangerous. But I want it. His fists clenched beneath the covers. I want to feel as Master Hugh felt; I want to be what he thought I was. And I can be that, for I have seen it inside myself... I am not a thing, I am a man...

Hugh Kenrick lay in his bed, happy that he had jarred something loose in the valet, happy that he had seen it revived. He had not planned the incident; he was as much surprised by the incident as had been the valet. But what made him even happier was that the incident had proven the power of something, the efficacy of a notion which he could not yet name.

Some weeks after the event, at the end of a letter to his parents, he made these observations:

"I attended a concert at Montagu House on Great Russell Street the evening last. The house is owned by the widow of the Duke of Montagu, the Duchess of Marlborough, a near neighbor. I met some acquaintances of our family and had a pleasant exchange with them. It was mostly Italian music that was played—Torelli, Scarlatti, and Vivaldi, and one piece by an Austrian, Leopold Mozart (this latter artist's work was played during the buffet intermission, so I could not hear it well). I believe that Italian music is so popular here because it expresses emotions and feelings that Englishmen would not otherwise permit themselves to express or contemplate. We are capable of stirring music, and pretty music, but very little that evokes care about something close and personal and grand...

"Thank you for raising Hulton to the rung of butler. He is quite happy with his new livery and recompense, though I believe he will grow out of these things in the future, for I have encouraged him to peruse our library when he is not engaged in his duties. You know—and this is probably not an original descant—that people hate those who make them feel their own inferiority. Without any conscious ruse on my part, I have that effect on many of my fellow pupils at the school, and on Mr. Worley's sons, who seem to go out of their way to make things dull and miserable for me at the warehouse (though they daren't go too far; I have not spoken to their father yet about the matter, for that would be on a level of their pettiness).

"At supper at Mr. Worley's one evening, I told the company what books I had purchased on Duck Lane that day, viz., Moleworth's *Account of Denmark*, Montesquieu's *Works*, Harrington's *Oceana*, Sidney's *Discourses*, and both Locke's and Hume's *Essays*, but no one evinced interest. Instead, Mrs. Worley merely blinked, and asked me with the same eagerness I had shown if I had seen any good books on tarot cards and ghosts (she patronizes a multitude of fortune-tellers, and believes her house is haunted)!

"I believe it is because I somehow—and I know not how—make them see how shallow, or hollow, or tinseled are the things that animate their lives or command their devotion. I believe that my rank in society has very little to do with their hatred of me; that is, they would behave in the same manner were I a commoner but similarly disposed in character. However, I am glad to say, Hulton is an exception to this rule, as he is very much like Mr. Runcorn (please, give him my fondest regards!) and other men of mahogany or oaken character."

Chapter 14: The Mohocks

EARLY IN NOVEMBER, ON GUY FAWKES NIGHT, TWO MISFORTUNES OCCURRED. The sign of the Three Quills tavern on Burleigh Street, near Covent Garden, gave a warning groan, then fell to the street, taking with it the entire front of the four-story brick building. It was a large sign, its four oak frames encasing a lead signboard on which had been painted in white three writing quills, crossed at the nibs. Like many London business signs, it had hung from a horizontal timber pole over the tavern entrance, supported by thick ropes anchored to moorings on both sides of the roof above. Neither the ropes nor the sign gave way; the building could no longer tolerate the weight of the sign and the impossible stress it caused, and it shed its burden. Four tenants whose beds were on that side of the building fell with the wall; three perished, as did a passing horse and wagon and their owner, who were buried under the rubble. Fifty tavern patrons, who had been noisily engrossed by a cockfight, were trapped in the basement.

There were lampposts on Burleigh Street, and these soon lit scores of people drawn out by the thunder of the collapse. They rushed from dwellings, shops, coffeehouses, and other taverns. Burleigh connected the Strand with Exeter Street, and the rubble blocked it from the Exeter end. The street came alive with screams, shouts, oaths, and the usual commotion of confusion.

Hugh Kenrick the day before had noted an advertisement in a newspaper for a staging this night of Henry Fielding's *Jonathan Wild* at the Theatre Royal in Covent Garden, and decided to attend. But the dramatization of the life of the notorious criminal mastermind bored him, and, giving up hope of seeing some redeeming aspect in the production, he rose during the third act and left. He had anticipated some insight into the motivation of such a man, but the play was a mere anecdotal chronology, highlighted by grisly murder scenes and pious moralizing by the characters in long, windy speeches. This was the second misfortune.

There were no hackneys outside when Hugh emerged from the theater, so he drew his plain cape around himself against the chill evening air and braved a walk back to Whitehall. He wore his sword and carried a pocket pistol. He made his way across Covent Garden past its empty vendors' stalls to Tavistock Street, then through an alley to Exeter, and then another to Burleigh, which led to the Strand. This was the route taken by his hackneys in the past. The Strand would lead to Charing Cross and finally to the Banqueting House and Whitehall Courtyard. It was a mere fifteen-minute walk.

But when he turned into Burleigh, he found chaos. Under lamplight and flambeaux, scores of men were toiling atop a mound of rubble to reach people trapped beneath it and inside the building. Some tenants holding candles stood on the edges of their exposed rooms, watching the turmoil below.

Hugh continued down Exeter and left the commotion behind. He came upon Rooker Alley, which had but one lamppost, but the alley led to the Strand and he was eager to get home. There seemed to be some well-dressed men near the single lamppost, and he did not see any vagrants or idlers lurking in the doorways. He turned into the alley and walked quickly. All his senses were alert. One of his hands rested on the pommel of his sword, the other gripped the tiny pistol in his cape pocket.

"Evenin', luv," said a soft woman's voice from one of the dark doorways. "What say we burn Mr. Fawkes together, in me own room? Only a shillin', luv."

Hugh glanced at the woman who stepped into the faint light. She wore a battered straw hat and a dress of some faded color. The neckline revealed too much of her bosom and the sores on it. The face was heavily rouged, the eyes black holes of feral intelligence. She raised her skirt to show her bruised and discolored thighs.

Hugh shivered once, shook his head, and went on, ignoring the prostitute's shrill curse.

The men beneath the lamppost ahead had moved beyond its light, but Hugh could see them moving about strangely. Voices rose in drunken altercation. "Shine my boots, and pay me a pound for the privilege!" demanded one voice.

"And if you lack a pound, your wardrobe will do!" said another with a laugh.

"My nails need trimmin'," said a third voice. "Your choppers look sharp enough. If I'm not satisfied, we'll knock out your present teeth and let you grow new ones, and hang you by your feet from yonder lamppost until you do."

The fourth man said nothing. Swords slithered out of their scabbards.

One of the menacing figures struck the fourth man with a fist. The victim fell to his knees. "Don't speak unless spoken to!" said one of the voices. "That's manners!"

Hugh's steps had slowed until he found he had stopped to watch the drama with fascination. Mohocks! Macaronis! Idlers from the aristocracy who roamed the city's streets terrorizing neighborhoods.

"Cut 'im!" yelled one of the voices. "Show 'im we mean to have our boots cleaned!" A figure moved, and Hugh heard the fourth man yelp in pain.

Hugh's eyes narrowed in anger and his face tightened for action. He knew what it was like to be the subject of viciousness. What would Drury Trantham do? He would quietly draw his sword and attack the criminals without warning!

But a split-second of doubt about the bravery or foolhardiness of his contemplated action stayed Hugh's hand. He thought: These are real, dangerous, and possibly murderous men, not villains who can be disposed of in a story, on paper, and I may regret interfering in this crime.

But this thought was pursued by two more: That the man who created Drury Trantham was some extraordinary kind of criminal who had paid with his life for what undoubtedly was his honor; and that it was his spirit and sense of right that propelled Trantham into a fray. Could he, Hugh Kenrick, do no less?

The three Mohocks were beating the fourth man with the flats of their swords now, laughing, jeering, and cursing. Their victim lay on his side, helpless, unable to rise.

Hugh drew his own sword and charged. He could see neither the faces of the four men, nor the details of their clothes. They were all mere dark gray silhouettes against a black background.

The first man's back was turned to him. Hugh did not subscribe to the code of fair play when dealing with his mortal enemies. The tip of his sword swept passed his shoulder and then back in an arc to cut the hind of the back-stretched leg, on the white hose beneath the end of the man's breeches, and then into the skin and sinews beneath the hose. The man squeaked in surprise, then howled in pain as he turned to see the cause of it. But he collapsed in the turn because the hamstring of his left leg had been severed.

Hugh did not give the second assailant a chance to grasp the new situation. That man crouched, his blade ready, and squinted his eyes to better see his assailant. But before he could reach a conclusion, Hugh leaped over the figure of the victim, lunged with his sword, and pierced the wrist of the man's weapon hand. Then his blade flashed up and down and sliced off a portion of the Mohock's left ear.

This man merely gasped in the knowledge of what had been done to him, and his sword dropped to the ground. Then he, too, howled in pain and, one hand pressed to his gushing ear and the other to his stomach, he turned and ran into the darkness in the direction of the Strand.

Hugh whirled around to find the third Mohock ready for him. A kernel of Signor Albertoli's lessons seized his mind: "In a tight circumstance, do not pause to appraise your opponent, for you will only give him time to appraise you. Beat, attack on the blade, and feint, and judge his quality by how he replies"—and this advice Hugh heeded. His purpose had been to eliminate as many opponents as possible in the shortest time, aware of the odds that at least one of these men would put up some kind of fight.

This the third Mohock did. He was the biggest of the three assailants, and skillful enough to parry Hugh's feint in answer. Hugh did not give him enough time to recover, but attacked and lunged repeatedly, driving the man back in the direction of the lamppost, allowing the man no time or opportunity to develop a counterattack. And as they moved closer to the light, Hugh could see the man's frightened but angry face and the teeth clenched in desperation. The man had not assumed the fencing position that Hugh had—torso angled to the side to present a difficult target, free hand in the air at arm's length behind him for balance and torque—and Hugh reminded him of these things with a quick twist of his wrist to flick the man's free hand that was clawing the air almost parallel with his sword hand. His blade did not touch skin, but brushed over a silken glove. The man grunted once, and removed the hand from danger.

And then there was enough light from the lamppost to see the Mohock's face. Hugh recognized the Marquis of Bilbury, his tormentor from Eton years ago.

The shock caused him to pause in surprise, and gave the Mohock a chance to counterattack. Hugh parried every ruse the Marquis tried, and refused to be driven back into the darkness. He did not think that the Marquis recognized him; the man continued to duel from pride, or simply to teach the intruder a lesson.

Hugh kept up his defense with a series of croises, derobements, and counter-parries. He knew that the Marquis was exhausting his knowledge of ruses, and was waiting for the moment when the Marquis left him an opening. The stalemate began to enrage the man, who tried to circle Hugh to throw him off balance. Hugh answered each movement to his right or left with an advance of his forward foot and a lunge that made the Marquis stop to parry. During one of these lunges, he allowed himself to glance at the Marquis's weapon hand; it, too, was encased in silk, the better to hide the palms and fingers disfigured by the hot poker.

The Marquis's lips pursed in concentration, and Hugh recognized the sign that his opponent was growing weary in mind and body. The man was nearing the limit of his skill and endurance.

"Damn you to hell!" shouted the Marquis, who launched a brutal but sloppy attack. He tried to maintain his composure, but his emotions were guiding his actions now. Hugh almost expected the man to toss his sword aside and rush him with his open hands or even try to tackle him.

The Marquis grimly began a badly executed compound attack. Hugh answered it with a deft riposte, a glide along the length of the man's sword, then with a liément that connected with the guard on the opposing sword and yanked the weapon from the Marquis's hand.

As the man's sword flew through the air to fall to the ground, Hugh placed the tip of his sword over the Marquis's heart. "You are beaten," he said. "Now—go!"

The Marquis's chest heaved in anger and exhaustion. "Who are you?" he snarled.

Hugh smiled, more to himself than to the Marquis. He felt that now he had a right to feel as he did. He said, "Drury Trantham, champion of these parts and of any others which you may pollute with your presence!" he pointed his sword in the direction of Exeter Street. "Now—be gone!"

"You're but a younker!" sneered the Marquis. "A barber has yet to scrape your phiz! Yet you beat me! Who was your blade master?"

"A famous Gascon swordsman!" answered Hugh, pressing the tip of his sword harder against the man's waistcoat. "And you are dawdling!"

The Marquis nodded to the gleaming shaft that lay in the mud a few feet away. "And my sword?"

"You have forfeited it," said Hugh. "Collect your injured friend, who may need you as a crutch, and make haste." He nodded once to a dark mass of spectators who had gathered in the alley to watch the fight. "Make haste, sir, because I believe many of those gentlemen put their money on the wrong sword. They may want to take their losses from your own pockets."

The Marquis glanced warily around him at the crowd, then with a last sneer at Hugh scrambled over to help his moaning companion stand on his one good leg. This man also left his sword behind on the ground. The pair hobbled away. The Marquis threw one last look at Hugh over his shoulder, then with a curse urged his companion to move more quickly, and they vanished into the darkness.

Hugh picked up the Marquis's sword. It was a beautifully made weapon, of Spanish steel, light yet strong, unlike so many English swords. The pommel was inlaid with fine silver wire filigree, together with the Bilbury coat of arms, which was also of silver. He would keep this sword as a memento of this night—this night in his city. He sheathed his own sword, then looked for the fourth man. The man had risen, and stood watching him from the shadows.

Hugh strode over to him and stopped. "Will you share an ale with me, sir?" he asked. "I believe we have both earned a gill each."

"More than a gill, good sir!" answered the man. "And the invitation should be mine! Will be mine, and I will brook no argument from you, sir!"

Hugh smiled and picked up the weapons abandoned by the fleeing Mohocks. He stood in the near darkness opposite the man. He could perceive only that the stranger was tall and thin. He offered the figure a choice of the swords.

The stranger shook his head. "No, thank you, sir. I have no talent for them, and no patience."

"Are you injured?"

"Not fatally," chuckled the stranger. "Merely a cut here, a welt there, and bruises everywhere. In a week, they will be gone."

"Are you certain?" insisted Hugh. "I can take you to a surgeon."

"Thank you, sir—but, no."

"And your pride, sir: Is it not injured?"

"It has never known a wound, sir, and I have been intimate with more humiliating situations than the one from which you have just rescued me."

"They might have killed you."

"True," said the stranger thoughtfully. "And I believe they planned to. There is a method to that kind of hectoring."

"Do you live here?" asked Hugh, indicating their surroundings with one of the swords.

"No, sir. I was on my way to an appointment, and Burleigh Street, my usual detour, was blocked. Otherwise, I would not have ventured down this lane. And you?"

"No, sir. I had gone to the theater, and was making my way home."

Then both Hugh and the stranger noticed that some of this alley's denizens were standing a few steps away, listening to their conversation. Hugh planted the abandoned swords upright in the ground. "These I do not want," he said. He gestured with an arm to the Strand. "Let us have that ale, sir. Do you know of a congenial place?"

The pair turned and strode away from the scene. "My own destination, sir. The Fruit Wench, on the boulevard ahead, near where Villiers Street meets it."

"I've seen the sign. Is it a good tavern?"

"Good enough that tradesmen frequent it. And in the rear, a comfortable coffeehouse. The proprietress likes to see half her patrons sober." The stranger paused. "I have been rude, sir. May I congratulate you on your superb knifery? It was almost worth being ambuscaded by those ruffians to see such a display of skill."

"Thank you, sir. But it has left me tired."

"You did not fight tiredly."

"No. I was fighting for my life. I had committed myself, and if I had slipped, I might have shared your likely fate."

"You might have suffered more, for having interfered," remarked the stranger.

They were nearing the Strand, and walked quietly in lockstep. Then the stranger asked, "May I know the true name of my savior, sir?"

Hugh laughed. "You don't believe it is Drury Trantham?"

The stranger grunted once in humor. "Forgive me the doubt, sir, but I am acquainted with that man's marvelous adventures. I did not believe he came to life and jumped from his pages to rescue me."

Hugh almost gasped with delight. Never before had he met another person who had read *Hyperborea*. He glanced at the indistinct face of his companion and offered his hand. "Hugh Kenrick, of Danvers and Windridge Court."

"Ah!" exclaimed the stranger, shaking Hugh's hand, and as though some question had been answered in his mind.

"And yours?" asked Hugh, eager to know the identity of someone whom he was certain to be a friend.

They had entered the Strand. The light from a lamppost bathed them in a flickering glow. The stranger stopped resolutely beneath the lamppost.

"I am Glorious Swain," said the stranger.

Hugh could see the man's face now, and gazed up at a countenance as black as the alley from which they had just emerged.

Chapter 15: The Fruit Wench

GLORIOUS SWAIN WAS A LANKY BUT ELEGANT MAN, A HEAD AND A HALF taller than Hugh. He was dressed in a neat blue frock coat and waistcoat, from which he had already brushed the mud and dirt it had acquired from his encounter with the Mohocks. He sported a fine brown tricorn and a combed and powdered peruke. His face was severe, reflective, sedate. It had the flat, angular contours of a lump of coal.

Hugh was stunned. He had never before spoken with a black man; had never even met one. He had only seen black men from a distance, working as porters, or carpenters, or liveried servants. The neighboring Pumphretts had one. He had seen one or two black women near the Lawful Keys, acting as laundresses, and one or two who were maidservants of fashionable women shopping on the Strand. Black people were exotic human beings to Hugh, as exotic as kilted Scotsmen. He knew that most were slaves, but that some were freemen. He brazenly studied the face of Glorious Swain, noting with fascination all the hues and valleys of black and how they worked together to form a sum of character and intelligence. The frank brown eyes returned this survey with patience and humor.

"What a name!" exclaimed Hugh at length. "'Glorious!' How did you come by it? Did you adopt it, or were you baptized with it?"

Glorious Swain did not answer these questions. Instead, he asked, "You are not disappointed with my ebon hue, sir?"

Hugh frowned. "No, sir."

"You do not regret having risked your life to save mere me from those rogues?"

"No! Especially not now!"

"And—why not?"

"You look like an interesting man. And you have read *Hyperborea*."

"Is there something…special about my color that piques your curiosity?"

Hugh shrugged. "I am sure that your pallor is but a superficial aspect of your character, sir."

Swain barked once in irony. "Hardly superficial, sir! But you are right. It is not integral to my manliness." He paused. "Would you regard me, sir, as an exceptional exemplar of my race?"

"I believe you would be exceptional in any society."

"That is begging the question."

Hugh shrugged again. "I have not met others of your race, sir, so I cannot honestly answer your question."

"That is a better answer," said Swain. "But it is true: I would be exceptional in any society." He smiled at the look of disappointment on Hugh's face. "And as I am certain that we both believe that boasting is a sign of vanity, I will add that my self-estimate is merely an honest but dispassionate conclusion, drawn from a lifetime of encounters with a numberless multitude of incogitant yahoos."

Hugh grinned. He liked this man. "Let us repair to the Fruit Wench. We have much to talk about."

"I agree, sir," replied Swain. "We may talk for a while, until my friends arrive."

The pair strode along the Strand on the footpath that was separated from the street by lampposts and stone stanchions. A light fog had descended over the city, blurring passing figures and carriages and helping the man and boy focus on the discovery of each other.

"Now, sir, to your name," said Hugh. "It is not a Christian name."

Swain laughed. "Indeed, it is not. But the simple explanation for it is that I was born on a 'glorious' day. And on London Bridge, in fact, on the Surrey side, to the roar of the tide-drawn rapids below."

"Explain that, please."

"My parents, you see, were owned by a Mr. Swain, a pin maker, who lived above his shop on the Bridge. He dubbed my parents Timothy and Dimity. How he came to own them, I never learned. My parents helped him make pins. My mother also took in sewing, and was allowed to earn money that way. My father worked occasionally in a ropeworks near Chamberlain's Wharf. When I was christened 'Glorious' the ritual should have made me a freeman, but that matter has never been resolved. I am not certain of my legal status, whether I am a slave at large or a freeman at liberty, for the courts do not know how to rule in principle on the issue. But I regard myself as an Englishman, and go where I please and do what I do. My only true nemesis is a press gang—and Mohocks, of course."

"Did those men know you were black?"

"I do not know. I don't think it mattered to them what my color was. No doubt, like other of their victims, I was a lone man, defenseless, ready to be ruffled and plucked."

"Where are your parents now?"

"In heaven, I suppose," answered Swain. "They and Mr. Swain died of a pox when I was three or four, all within a week. I was subsequently adopted—or possessed—by a fashionable courtesan who had been a regular customer of my mother's. For her, I acted as pageboy until I was six or seven. She died of the malady usually associated with her trade—blind, covered with sores, and not very fashionable to look at. One of her gentleman friends took me in as his own page, but not for long, for soon I was the page for another courtesan, I believe as part payment for a night of extraordinary licentiousness. She, one night, drank herself into an unconscious state, and never awoke from it. Her parish advertised and sold my status. By this time, I was twelve."

"What an adventure!" laughed Hugh.

"An adventure? Not quite, my young friend." Swain sighed. "Another gentleman indentured me to work as his cook and servant. He even paid me a pittance, until he gambled away his means, including an annuity left him by an uncle, for which he had signed a promissory note at the faro table. From Queer Street he went to a sponger, and I with him. He was sentenced in turn as an indenture and sent to the colonies. I was sent to Bridewell to learn another trade. I have had brief careers as a wainwright, a draper's assistant, and a glove maker's assistant. Drapery and gloves are still my trades, though I have resorted to duffing, a more lucrative trade."

"Duffing?" asked Hugh.

"Donning four or five stone of untaxed Dutch tea beneath a greatcoat and selling it to hawkers in this great metropolis. It sells especially well in the plumb neighborhoods." Swain paused to sigh again. "And I also work at a charity school, run by Quakers, teaching poor children how to read and cipher. It is on Rope Street. That is not so lucrative a pastime, but I do enjoy it and the company of the gentle and pacific Quakers."

Hugh glanced up at his companion. "Such a life! Yet you have fashioned a pride impervious to pain!"

Swain shook his head. "It was not without effort, sir. And error."

"I believe you. But it is no mystery to me why you feel kin to Drury Trantham."

"Do I, sir?"

"How could you not?"

Swain laughed and put a hand on Hugh's shoulder. "You are a warmly presumptuous young hellion, sir, and I think we will become fast friends! Ah, here we are!"

They had stopped beneath the sign of the Fruit Wench. A lamppost and links on either side of the sign lit the face of a smiling, comely young woman, her hand balancing a basket of grapes, lemons, oranges, and pippins on her head. "That is Mabel Petty," said Swain, "nominal owner of this establishment. She once worked as a fruit wench out of Covent Garden. She married the former (and late) owner of this place. Then it was called The Tattered Wig. He lived long enough to sire four children by Mabel, of whom only one, a daughter, survived to lend a hand. Agnes Petty, whom that phiz more closely resembles than it does Mabel, had trod the boards here since the age of five as a serving wench. I do believe the sign painter has emulated the style of Mr. Hogarth's worthier portraits."

"I've seen some of his work, and I concur," said Hugh.

The tavern inside was a large room, smoky from innumerable pipes and churchwardens, crowded with tradesmen, watermen, sailors, and their women, raucous from dozens of conversations, and melodic from contesting choruses of "Marlborough Goes to War" and "The Anacreontic Song." Many freshly commissioned army officers were also present, sitting in groups of bright scarlet coats, boasting of the various ways they meant to deal with the French and Indians in North America.

Swain exchanged nods with a florid-faced woman behind an elevated bar. "Your friends ain't showed up yet, luv. Find a table and I'll send Tim over with a tankard. One for your friend, too?"

Swain nodded again. "Thank you, Mabel." He handed her a couple of coins. They found a small table in a far corner. A boy in an apron followed them shortly with two tankards of ale. As he sipped his drink, Hugh surveyed the lively, noisy scene with wonder.

"First time in a tavern?" asked Swain.

"Yes. It is quite a riot of life, isn't it?"

"Too much so, at times," remarked Swain. He gestured to the scabbardless sword Hugh had carried under his arm from Rooker Alley. "I perceive a coat-of-arms there, sir. Do you know whose it is?"

Hugh glanced once at the sword, which he had propped up against the wall. "It is the Bilbury arms, sir. You were assaulted by the Marquis."

"How do you know that the weapon was not stolen by that Mohock?"

"I did not recognize the coat-of-arms, sir. I recognized the man. I have trafficked with him in the past. He is older, but no wiser."

Swain took a swig from his tankard, then said with hesitation, "Sir, I am familiar with the name of Kenrick. Are you a relation of the Earl of Danvers? I must confess that your Whitehall address caused me to suspect the possibility."

"I am his nephew, and the son of the Baron of same."

"I see," replied Swain. "Which would make you..." The man sat up stiffly, and pushed his tankard away. "Milord, forgive me if I spoke out of turn, and—"

Hugh rushed to protest. "No, no! I beg you to speak on the same terms, sir! Spare me the delicate addresses! Speak to me as from man to man! Think of me in those terms! I will be offended if you do not! I wish to be regarded in that manner, as a commoner, valued for his virtues, despised for his vices!"

Swain sat back, startled by the outburst. "If that is your wish...sir," he said, "I will comply with it. However, I will point out that, even though you may eschew your rank, or even renounce it for all time, you will never be a commoner. Your virtues are not common, and your honor and pride, I am certain, are the sibling offspring of uncommon effort. You have my esteem, for all that, sir."

"And you, mine," answered Hugh. He raised his tankard. "A toast to ourselves and our friendship, in keeping with the spirit of this place!"

Swain smiled and raised his tankard to touch Hugh's, and they each drank a draught.

A moment of silence passed. Then Hugh asked, "How did you discover *Hyperborea*?"

Swain chuckled. "When it appeared years ago, foul reviews of it ran in many newspapers here, including the *Evening Post*, the *Daily Auditor,* and the *Register*. No one seemed to like it, but there was a universal, peculiarly dehortative ring in all the commentaries. This was a natural invitation to me to purchase a copy of that book. So disliked a novel deserved a fair reading." Swain paused. "But before we discuss that work, sir, tell me which play I owe my health to."

"*Jonathan Wild*," answered Hugh. He waved a hand in dismissal. "But I do not recommend it. It is a mere patchwork of incidents, loosely sewn together. It would have been dull even had it been well done, which it was not."

Swain grinned. "I must confess that I have seen it, too, and concur with your estimate of it."

The two then began an animated discussion of *Hyperborea*, exchanging with excitement descriptions of their favorite characters, scenes, and passages. The glow of a shared, vital concern dulled their awareness of the tavern and its intrusive hubbub. They had reentered the world of Drury Trantham, a starkly clean literary sanctuary uncomplicated by the mundane, the sordid, and the contemptible. At one point, Hugh remarked, "The first time I read it, I became so fond of Trantham, I was angry with Mr. Marsh, the author. How could he send his hero to the bottom like that, and end all possibility of further adventures!"

"That was my foremost reaction, too," said Swain. "For a while, I could not forgive Mr. Marsh."

"And then I thought: It doesn't matter. He died as he had lived. He died for something of his own, just as he had lived for something of his own. There was just enough incident in the novel to make him unforgettable. More would have been superfluous."

"That was my conclusion, too!" chuckled Swain. The man was almost beside himself with joy. "And your anger with the author in time grew to be love of the work?"

"And the highest esteem for the author," concurred Hugh. "Yes. Perhaps what he was saying was, 'Here is my hero; he lives, he conquers, he dies. He is mine to give to you, and mine to take away. As you cherish him, so cherish yourself, and he will never pass from your life...'"

"Oh, what a thought to cling to!" cried Swain. "I wish I had said it!"

But Hugh did not hear Swain's exclamation. He was lost in the corona of ineluctable truth of his own statement, and struck by the fact that he was its origin. He was unable to distinguish between the truth and the fact. He looked dumbly at Swain across the table, newly aware of facets of himself he had never before had reason to contemplate. He felt weightless.

Glorious Swain knew, at that moment, that he was no longer enjoying the company of a precocious adolescent. He knew that he was looking at the frown of a man in the efflorescent throes of discovering himself. He had personal knowledge of the phenomenon. Until now, he had not witnessed it in anyone else.

Hugh noted that his silent companion was staring at him with an odd intensity, and that he was smiling. At this moment, their friendship was sealed.

"Ti neon ep'astu, Muir?" inquired a voice.

Hugh and Swain glanced up at a figure that loomed above their heads.

It was a tall, scholarly looking man who, however, wore a suit of clothes almost as ostentatious as those sported by the Mohocks. He carried a lacquered rosewood cane with a silver knob. Hugh was intrigued by the stranger's question, which was ancient Greek for "What's new in the city?" It also intrigued him that he had clearly addressed Swain, and called him "Muir." The stranger nodded to Hugh in silent but suspicious greeting.

"My new friend here, Mathius," answered Swain. "He rescued me from a gang of Mohocks. Good evening."

Mathius turned again and bestowed a smile on Hugh. Then he said to Swain, "We are ready, Muir. The meeting awaits your arrival to convene. You are this evening's chairman." He held out the cane, and Swain took it. "Give me a moment to bid a civil farewell to my friend," he said. "I will join you and the others shortly."

The stranger nodded, turned, and made his way through the crowd to the rear of the tavern.

Hugh thought it curious that the man had not introduced himself, and that Swain had not attempted to make introductions.

Swain saw the confusion on Hugh's face. He asked, "Have you ever heard of the Society of the Pippin?"

"No," replied Hugh. "It is something 'new in the city'—at least it is for me."

"Good. That means that our secret is still a secret." Swain paused. "It is a club of intellects, of eccentrics, of men of letters. We meet twice a month to talk, to debate, to discuss, to enlighten each other. There are many such clubs in the city, as you may well know, but our society is unique. None of us knows the others' true names or professions. We are the second generation of the Pippin. The tradition of anonymity is useful; it protects us from betrayal or discovery. In the Society, I am Muir, brother of Maia."

"May I join?" asked Hugh eagerly. "What must I do?"

"The membership is limited to seven," said Swain, shaking his head. "Each of us has adopted the name of one of the seven brothers of the seven daughters of Atlas. However—I shall broach the subject of your membership with the others. I believe you would be a worthy addition. But I cannot guarantee admission." Swain rose and offered his hand.

Hugh rose also and shook it. "But—how shall we meet again?" he asked.

"I will leave a message at your residence," said Swain. "You see, many times I have sold a stone of tea to your house, and miscellaneous wares to your servants." He bowed gravely. "Until next time, my friend." Swain turned and hurried from the table.

As Hugh watched him disappear into the crowd and smoke and turn to ascend some bannistered stairs to the floor above, it occurred to him that Atlas did not have seven sons.

*   *   *

It was only when he was sitting at the window of his room that night, lost in thought, watching the moving light of a waterman's boat glide down the Thames, that Hugh felt his hands shaking. He held them up and studied them, as though they did not belong to him. It must be *bellator tremens*, he mused, the force of yesterday's Latin lesson surfacing in his mind: warrior's fear. *Postmodum quod eventus*, he thought with a smile at the irony. It had waited until long after his encounter with Glorious Swain. He had not felt this reaction at all after facing and routing the bullies at school. Then, he had insisted on a duel to the death. Yet, tonight, he had put himself in mortal danger, fighting a man to a probable death—but had spared his opponent's life. And he was not certain that if he had had to fight the bullies, he would have killed at least one of them.

What had been the difference? he asked himself. Was it the physical peril? Fighting the Marquis was an act of mere bravery. The bullies' purpose, however, had been to subdue him, body and soul. To make his entire being submit to the fact of their wishes, to place themselves in the scheme of his concerns, like a team of runaway lorry horses that could turn in his direction at any moment and trample him to death.

Yes, thought Hugh: I would have fought them to the death. I may sometime meet a brute more skilled with the sword than I, and he may conquer my body. But the bullies' purpose was more insidious than that of any Mohock or highwayman, and if I am to remain the man I am, I shall never allow that purpose to be accomplished.

Chapter 16: The Member for Canovan

"IT HAS BEEN HEARD IN THIS ASSEMBLY ON A NUMBER OF OCCASIONS that the colonials are unhappy with the means with which this coming war is to be paid for and prosecuted. Oh, how they grumble, those rustical Harries! The means, as we all know, and as they rightly fear, must in the end come out of their own rough, bucolic purses. To my mind, that is but a logical expectation. Yet you would think, to judge by some of the protestations that have reached our ears, that the Crown was proposing to engage the French over Madagascar for possession of that pirates' nest, and obliging them to pay the costs of an adventure far removed from their concerns. But—the threat is to their own lives, their own homes and families, their fields, their shops, their seaports, their own livelihoods, and they higgle and haggle over the burden of expense! A very strange state of mind indeed!" The speaker looked around him at his listeners, and smiled. He had their attention. His subject was novel. He turned and again addressed the Speaker of the House, as the rules required him to do. "I am merely a messenger, sirs. Do not entertain thoughts of murdering me for what I have said, or am about to say."

The colonials were, in fact, on the minds of many of his listeners, though not in the manner that was being presented to them. The rapid train of events concerning France threatened a new war. Because of a flurry of diplomatic moves, some believed there would be no war. Others were disquieted; they were afraid that the Newcastle government was not moving quickly enough to prepare for one. The speaker was certain of war—which would not be declared until the following May—but was concerned with aspects of it which he believed were being overlooked by all.

"And, no doubt, many of these same said colonials will pay with their own skins, too. However, if the reports of officers in His Majesty's service in the colonies in the past are to be warranted—and I don't for a minute doubt the substance of their complaints or the truth of their anecdotes—not many colonial skins will be cut by French bayonet or bruised by Indian war club. The colonials, it is commonly said, are uniformly lazy, undisciplined, contentious, quarrelsome, niggardly, presumptuous, and cowardly, among themselves as well as among our brave officers and troops! It is thought by many in high and middling places that if the colonial auxiliaries under General Braddock's command had been more forthright and daring with their musketry in that fatal wood near the Ohio, that brave and enterprising officer would be sitting in this very chamber today to receive our thanks, and not buried in some ignominious patch of mud in the wilderness. But—the colonial temperament is a matter of record. Our colonials! Scullions all, the sons of convicts, whores, and malcontents! From the greedy gentry of the northern parts, to the posturing macaronis of the southern, every man Jack of them unmindful of the fact that he is a colonial, a mere plant nurtured in exotic soil for the benefit of this nation! Oh! How ungrateful, our Britannic flora!"

Many of the listeners cheered or stamped their feet in agreement. The speaker seemed to pace up and down before them, his stocky frame swaggering a little, as though he were a popular pugilist basking in the acclaim of spectators before the match had even begun.

The hall, only a little larger than a ballroom, was packed with hundreds of cramped, restless men seated on long benches. It was on the second floor of a drab, mongrel-looking building which, but for the two turrets over its roof, could have been taken for one of the warehouses directly across the Thames from it. It was known as St. Stephen's Chapel. The hall was a stark cavern, with oak wainscoting darkened by generations of candle soot, lit by a handful of inadequate windows, several dozen sconces, and a great chandelier. There were no paintings, tapestries, or banners to mark the hall's importance, only an ornate, elevated chair in the aisle that divided the rows of benches, on which sat a man in a black cloak, a great white whig, and a black tricorn, and a raised, covered table before him, at which sat two black-cloaked clerks and other functionaries. On the table lay a mass of paperwork. A great gilt scepter, or ceremonial mace, usually rested on that table, too, but the House had been resolved into a Committee of the Whole House; the rules required that the mace be placed under the table when the House was not sitting in a formal session.

This was the House of Commons. The man on the throne was Arthur Onslow, Speaker since 1728 and for another six years, and also member for Guildford. The orator was Sir Henoch Pannell, Baronet of Marsden, and member for the borough of Canovan.

The opposing rows of benches were of four tiers each, and above them were long balconies supported by iron Corinthian pillars. These were the public galleries, and both were today packed with spectators. Not only was the new war to be discussed, but this was one of the first sessions of a Parliament that, thanks to the Septennial Act of 1716, would sit for the next seven years.

Among the spectators was Hugh Kenrick, who had a front-row seat. He was leaned forward, arms crossed over the wooden railing, listening intently to the speaker. Today was a school holiday, and he had decided, out of sheer curiosity, to come here to audit the event. A week had passed, and he had received no word from Glorious Swain.

Sir Henoch waited for the commotion to subside, then went on. "Yes! Ungrateful, their noggins emboldened by a few leagues of water!" He placed his arms akimbo and looked thoughtful. "Now, it is thought here in this hall, and in London, and in all of England, and even in Wales and Scotland, that His Majesty's government—we here, within these ancient walls, and they across the way, in Lords"—with these words, he raised a finger and vaguely indicated another building just south of the Chapel, pronouncing the words in a slyly mocking tone—"are the corporate lawgiver and defender of our excellent constitution. Why, the most ignoble knife-grinder and blasphemous fishwife would be able to tell you that! Yet " here Sir Henoch raised the same finger in the air—"proposals for new laws, or for the repeal of old ones, or for changes in existing statutes from colonial legislatures—those self-important congresses of coggers, costermongers, and cork farmers—arrive by the bulging barrelful on nearly every merchant vessel that drops anchor at Custom House. These proposals are dutifully conveyed by liveried but sweaty porters to the Privy Council and the Board of Trade, to the Admiralty and the Surveyor-General and the Commissioner of Customs."

Sir Henoch placed a hand over his heart. "I am not friend to many members of those august bodies, but they truly have my sympathies, for they have the thankless task of sorting through those mountains of malign missives to segregate the specious from the serious. Many of these pleadings and addresses are shot through with a constant harping on the rights of the colonials as Englishmen, and so on with that kind of blather, like a one-tune hurdy-gurdy, a tiresome thing to endure, as many of you can attest. Virginia and Massachusetts are particularly monotonous and noisome in this respect. The planters would like to sell their weed directly to Spain or Holland, without the benefit of our lawful brokerage, while the Boston felt factors wish to fashion their own hats for sale there—or here!— without the material ever crossing the sea to be knocked together by our own artists. Well, sirs! We must needs remind our distant brethren that we are busy bees, too, and that the rights of Englishmen are only as good as the laws we enact allow—here, as well as there!"

These last words were accompanied by emphatic stabbings of his finger at the floor, and then vaguely at the west. Again the House exploded with cheering and stamping. Sir Henoch's eyes swept the length of both benches, then he let his sight rise to the galleries to gauge the response from that quarter. There were no hatters in Canovan, but allies of his on the benches had arranged for several dozen of them from other parts of London to come today to hear his speechmaking. He saw many men up there shaking their fists and shouting things he could not hear for all the din. Several of the men, he presumed, must also represent the tobacco trades, and the pin-makers, and the cobblers, and other trades dependent on colonial material. Hirelings, he thought with contempt. Bought for a shilling, sold for a pound!

His sight stopped, though, on the grave face of Hugh Kenrick, who seemed to regard him as though he were some kind of unnatural phenom-enon. He smiled and nodded once to the unexpected visitor. No doubt the boy would write home, and the Earl of Danvers would know that he had kept his promise to argue for more stringent trade restrictions, especially as they concerned colonial trade. He doffed his hat once, then turned to con-tinue his harangue.

"Gentlemen," he began, pivoting around with both hands extended in dramatic helplessness, "must I ask these questions? Does the beadle instruct the university? Does the postilion choose his employer's destina-tion? Does the bailiff counsel the magistrate?" He paused. "No!" he exclaimed with vehemence. "Should the colonials be permitted to advise us of our business? No! This is a custom unwisely indulged and which must be corrected! They must be reminded as civilly but as strenuously as pos-sible that they are residents of that far land at this nation's leisure, pleasure, expense, and tolerance! This nation's, and His Majesty's! They wish us to respect their rights. Well, and why not? We would not deny them those rights. But, if they wish a greater role in the public affairs of this empire, let them repatriate themselves to this fair island, and queue up at the polling places—here!—where they may exercise those native rights on the soil from which they and those rights have sprung!"

Again the benches cheered, but Sir Henoch waved his hands to silence his supporters. "Yes! For that is the nub of the matter! Here—" again the finger stabbed downward—"they will find no special circumstances, no calculated abridgment of their rights! There—" again the finger stabbed west—"in New York, and in Boston, in Philadelphia, and Williamsburg, and Charleston, they find themselves in special circumstances that necessitate abridgment, and like it not! But—they elect to be there, and not here! And if they cannot purchase this simple reasoning, if they persist in pelting us with petitions, memorials, and remonstrances, I say it must be the time to forget civility, and chastise the colonials as good parents would wisely chastise wayward and misbehaved children!"

In the midst of another round of cheering, one man rose in the benches opposite Sir Henoch. The Speaker, from his raised throne over the busy clerks, noticed him and nodded to him. He recognized the individual as Mr. Herbert, member for Ruxton.

Mr. Herbert waited until all eyes were on him, then said, addressing the Speaker, "May I remind the gentleman over there that we are here to debate, I hope in time in this committee, what portion of the likely war debt we may decently assign the North American colonies, and how this House may help them assume that responsibility? The gentleman's sulfurous outrage seems out of proportion to the modest proposal to which he replies. We are, after all, at war with the French—or will be—and not with the colonies! Or has Sir Henoch been privileged to see an Admiralty plan for the blockading of Boston and New York harbors?"

The House laughed, and Sir Henoch's laugh was the heartiest. In a gesture of exaggerated humility, he bowed to Mr. Herbert and doffed his hat. "You are so right, sir! Will the House please forgive me my enthusiasm, my passion, and my misfired patriotism? I leave the floor so that the debate on the particulars of finance may continue." He then bowed in thanks to the Speaker.

Sir Henoch plumped down on his seat. He had accomplished his purpose, which was to put many members of the Commons in a certain rigid frame of mind in regard to the colonies; the particulars, for the moment, did not interest him. He leaned closer to Mr. Kemp, the member for Harbin, another pocket borough, and muttered, "Not yet, I don't doubt!"

Mr. Kemp frowned and shook his head. "Not yet? What don't you doubt, sir?"

Sir Henoch managed to look sagely melancholy. "Someday," he answered, gesturing to the austere hall at large, "this great wapentake may need to sanction an extended bit of westering to prune and trim our Britannic flora."

Kemp scowled with impatience. "Oh? So we're scratching our backs on that post again, are we?" He sighed. "You make too much of the matter, sir. I'll hear no more of it, thank you. 'Tis but idle card game chatter."

Sir Henoch shrugged, and turned to listen to the next speaker. "For the nonce, sir," he said to himself. "For the nonce."

*   *   *

The debates droned on past noon. Sir Henoch's calculated outburst, which was in answer to another member's proposed bill for relaxing restrictions on some imported manufactured items of colonial origin— among them, hats—was followed by verbal exchanges on a series of minor bills. These ranged in subject from an increase in the number of officers in the Scottish customs machinery, to an extraordinary levy on imported peacock feathers, to the appointment of a committee to study whether or not the ground powder of Abyssinian oryx horns, said by many physicians to possess remarkable purgative qualities, ought to be admitted duty-free. The Commons wished to dispose of these petit matters before turning in earnest to the subject of William Pitt's speech of the day before attacking Newcastle's proposed Hessian treaty.

Many of the nearly six hundred members took an impromptu recess from the proceedings and from the airless hall to repair to nearby taverns for tea, ale, and dinner. Others milled about outside in the Palace Yard. The day was gray and damp, and the House's servants had set up burning barrels in the Yard for members to warm themselves over.

Sir Henoch Pannell and Mr. Kemp emerged from St. Stephen's Chapel and took a turn around the Yard to warm their limbs. "I'll say it again," said the member for Harbin, "you make too much of it. And at a bad time. They're all still dazzled by Mr. Pitt's declaiming against those subsidies. Your words were forceful, though not, I'm afraid, as memorable as his will be. I must agree with Mr. Herbert that your ardor was disproportionate. The subject was a mole, and you advocated eliminating it with a howitzer!"

Sir Henoch finished lighting his pipe, then said, "True, sir. But my words were forceful enough. Did you not observe our brothers? There's the memory I care about! You know that the ember of a notion can sit for a long time in the ashes of a mind, and then, with the right draft, burst into a sudden flame that can set that mind on fire!"

Kemp wrinkled his face. "What a pretty sentiment, Sir Henoch! Have you been having tea and talk at Twickenham with our brother Mr. Walpole?"

"'Twas my own thought, Mr. Kemp," growled Pannell, "and you'd do well to mark its truth." He saw someone watching them, and nudged his companion with an elbow. "Ah! Here's a notable-to-be!"

Hugh Kenrick had also left the hall for fresh air, and had been wandering around the Yard studying the men who governed the country. He stopped when he saw Pannell and Mr. Kemp approach. The member for Canovan bowed and made the introductions. "Well, milord," he asked, "how did you find my speech?"

"I found it interesting, sir," replied Hugh.

"Interesting? Thank you, milord."

Hugh frowned. "But strangely off the mark. It is my understanding that the colonies were not settled by any policy of government, at any time, but chiefly by men wanting to put some distance between themselves and the Crown and its policies. Your speech created an impression contrary to the recorded facts. I am not widely read in the subject, but I believe that what I have so far encountered in my limited exposure to it gives me leave to conclude that your analogy of 'Britannic flora' has no, well, roots."

Kemp chuckled, and rolled his eyes. "Well, my botanist friend," he said to his companion, "how will you answer that charge?"

Sir Henoch gave the member for Harbin an evil look, then looked blameless as he addressed Hugh Kenrick. "I'm sorry if I left you with that impression, milord. I don't deny the facts. However, these long-late expatriates of whom you speak adopted English law to order their lives—and what better polity could they have adopted? How would they have fared if they had borrowed the French, or the Spanish, or the German modes—and in time accepted English customs and ways, and, I might add, English protection—at their invitation, permit me to remind you, milord—and their lands and destinies became, in effect, virtual English colonies and concerns." He shook his head. "But, lack-a-day, milord! The facts and circumstances are now immaterial, as ghostly as the claims of the Jacobites!"

Hugh's brow knitted in thought. "We may adopt French fashions, Sir Henoch, and French art, and French food, and French social graces, but our doing so would not constitute an invitation to the French to invade England, or to punish it, or to chastise it, or to otherwise treat this nation as its colony."

Sir Henoch hummed. "It's a very inexoteric subject, milord. We could stand here all day, tossing this ball back and forth. Forgive me for saying so, but I am more widely read in the subject, and I don't believe a single history writer I have encountered has got it all right."

"I do agree with you that English law was the best polity to adopt, even though I think there are dubious aspects to it. And I agree with you that the writers have not yet found the correct prism of interpretation."

"You are gracious for saying so, milord."

Hugh studied the member for Canovan for a moment, then asked, "You are the one who hanged Romney Marsh, are you not?"

A moment passed before Sir Henoch could reply. An unsavory feeling curdled his nerves. "I did not hang that criminal, milord," he said. "That was the lawful duty of the sheriff of Falmouth, in obedience to a court's instructions. I merely caught him and handed him over for justice." He collected some courage, and asked, "Why do you ask, milord?"

"Romney Marsh is a ghost I would like to have conjured up this morning. It would have been most interesting to hear what reply he would have made to your speech."

Sir Henoch permitted himself a mocking smile. "Am I to take it, milord, that, like your father, you have read that scurrilous fiction of his?"

"*Hyperborea*? Yes, sir, I have. Many times."

"And also found it engaging?"

"Engaging? No, sir. Enthralling, yes." The city's church bells marked one o'clock. Hugh checked his pocket watch, then said, "I must go now, Sir Henoch. I shall try to attend more of the sessions, my schedule permitting. I look forward to hearing you speak again." He nodded to both men, turned, and walked away.

The men bowed to the retreating figure. Sir Henoch's eyes narrowed into slits. "There goes a republican puppy!" he remarked, some anger in his words.

"So to speak," replied Kemp, not understanding the anger.

The pair moved to join a group of other members hovering around one of the burning barrels. The member for Norwich commented with gentle unkindness on Sir Henoch's speech. "A fiery piece of hack-work, Sir Henoch, worthy of the ravings of an inmate of Bedlam—but," he added, "very keen in its construction!"

The member for Bristol seconded those remarks, and added, "We ought to be discreet in what we say about the colonials, Sir Henoch. Mr. Herbert is not only a friend of the member who proposed the bill you questioned, but he acts as agent for some of the larger purses in New York and Philadelphia. Your sentiments are likely to be conveyed to those parties on the next mail packet."

The member for Nottingham ventured, "And—we may need to approve a credit of perhaps a million to the government, Sir Henoch, and that may be barely enough to raise a proper army and outfit the navy. The colonials, whatever their shortcomings, may be obliged to make up the difference in the ranks, and in the accounts."

"What is wanted, sir," volunteered a member for Oxford University, "is a dollop or two of commiseration, not a brace of cudgels!"

Sir Henoch snorted violently. "The colonies ought to be lunged like any Arabian mount, sirs!" he roared. "Kept at a distance in politics, and exercised vigorously, until they learn who is the master, so that they may be led and ridden more easily!"

This explosion of emotion startled the men around the barrel. They all knew that the man was not playing theatrics now, as he had for the benches.

Sir Henoch went on, waving his pipe in the air. "No, sirs! The colonies have not been lunged vigorously enough! They have been allowed to acquire an elevated sense of themselves!" He snorted again. "Yes, sirs! The day will come, I fear, when we will too late realize that their impudence has been spawned by our neglect and indulgence!"

A moment passed. The other men glanced at each other. Their colleague's fit seemed to have passed, and it was safe enough to speak. "'An elevated sense of themselves,'" mused the member for Norwich. "A quillety way of putting the matter, Sir Henoch. My compliments." He saw the stolid features of his adversary soften a little. "Why, it could become the theme for a great speech!"

"As indeed it will become, some day, sir!" answered Sir Henoch. "And I'll be the one to deliver that oration! No cribbing from any of you now, or I'll defame you!" he added, half in jest, half in warning.

Kemp said, rubbing his hands together over the barrel's flames, "There's no chance of that, sir. Only you seem to know the lay of the notion."

Chapter 17: The Sparrowhawk

W HEN HUGH RETURNED TO WINDRIDGE COURT, HULTON HANDED HIM two letters. The butler said, "The envelope in your father's hand was delivered by a boy from Mr. Worley's establishment, milord, about an hour after you left for the Commons. The second came not half an hour ago, and was delivered by a Negro gentleman." Hugh thanked Hulton and took the letters to his room. The second envelope read, "Hon. Hugh Kenrick, Bart., Windridge Court." He opened it first. It was from Glorious Swain.

"Sir: Greetings! Good news, and bad. The members of the Society will not alter the rule of seven. They will, however, consider admitting you as an auditor of our meetings, with no privileges of participation. You would be but an honorary member, with no right to vote and no voice in Society affairs. They argue that I know your identity (which I did not divulge), and you, mine, and so this fact violates a cardinal rule of membership, which is mutual anonymity. However, I have given you my highest recommendation. They have asked that you submit an essay to them, on any subject matter, advocating some novel or unconventional notion, so that we may together judge the quality of your cogitations. Meet me tonight at eight of the clock at Ranelagh, if you can. I have an occasional position there as waiter. If this is not convenient, leave a message with Mabel Petty at the Fruit Wench fixing another time and place. Your grateful servant, Glorious Swain."

This letter left Hugh grinning. His father's, though, put him in a more somber mood. It was dated four days earlier.

"My dear son, Hugh: This letter may reach you before or after the fact. The expected hostilities with France (and perhaps even with Frederick of Prussia, if he combines with France—what inconstant enemies!) have moved your uncle to decide to attend Lords for an indefinite length of time. He is preparing for the journey even as I pen this caution. He feels it necessary to commune with his fellow ermines and comites to form a better opinion of the state of affairs and perhaps convene with them to weave a policy more to his liking. Please, I beg of you, do not provoke him on any matter. This will prove, I am certain, a difficult task for you, and if you accomplish it, I shall be both proud of you, and relieved.

"I would come up to London myself, as I would like to, but I have deferred for too long my turn as justice of the peace in these parts and must fulfill that obligation. There is also urgent business to see to in Weymouth and Poole. Moreover, I have decided to set aside fallow parts of the estate for the cultivation of conies, and have been busy planning and supervising the digging of warrens and hutches for them. I anticipate an interruption (or, at least, a reduction) in the importation of American pelts and furs, and as the tailors and clothiers here will be wanting substitutes for their trade, the revenue to us from the hair of these prolific rabbits may prove lucrative. The meat also can fetch a nice price in the markets. A hundred gross of coney skins, at current prices, can net in excess of £30, and some forty thousand or so of them could keep us in silver for the duration of the war, which I fear will be a long and dreadful contest, if Newcastle retains the seals. Neither your uncle nor I expect him to; however, no matter when he resigns, his successor will need to sweep the stables clean of his blunders.

"In any event, you and your uncle need only tolerate each other for two weeks. Though your uncle is in a foul temper, he has given me his promise not to bait you. I have said to him, and I say to you, that I wish sincerely that you and he could establish some form of amity. And, I say to you, in strictest confidence, that such an amity can only be of your design. Your uncle is, after all, an earl, and he subscribes to the idea that earls vanish in a puff of phlogiston if they practice the witchcraft of reasonableness, never to be seen again (except by God and his bailiffs). In two weeks, though, you will be coming down for the holidays. I have had nothing but glowing reports about you from Dr. Comyn and Mr. Worley, and I trust that you harbor no apprehension about your welcome. Your mother and I miss you sorely. We are planning some festivity in your honor (on top of the usual Epiphanic folderol!), and we will invite some neighbors here whom your uncle would otherwise scare off or rather not see. You can regale the company with your adventures in that great rabbit warren known as London.

"Please have Mr. Hulton make preparations for your uncle's arrival. The kitchen there has a list of his favorite fare and beverages, and these must be restocked. Your uncle is bringing his own major-domo, Alden Curle. You should warn Mr. Hulton that he may need to defer to Mr. Curle for the length of your uncle's stay..."

Hugh finished the letter, thought for a moment, then rang for Hulton with the bell-cord by his bed. The butler knocked on the door a few minutes later. Hugh said, "My uncle is coming to attend Lords, Hulton. My father instructs you to make preparations for his stay."

"Yes, milord," said the butler brightly. "I shall have his room tidied up and shop for his table myself. There is a list in the kitchen."

"And the coach and four need sprucing. Tell the stable and footmen to see to that, too. The front court needs to be swept of leaves and muck. I know that he will be traveling the city on visits, and receiving visitors here."

Hulton smiled. "All the silver will be polished, milord."

"Uncle will be accompanied by Mr. Curle."

Hulton's eager expression soured. "Oh…"

"I know that you and he can't abide each other, Hulton. Father recommends that you defer to Mr. Curle, even though you are both now of equal rank."

The butler sighed in concession. "He is senior, milord."

"And, in two weeks, I will leave for the holidays. Don't let Curle needle you. I know that he is wont to play crass tricks on you and tries to get you into trouble. My uncle would discharge you without so much as a hearing, and he would have the right. This is his house. Neither I nor my father would be able to intercede, once he's done the deed."

"I shall endeavor to be a paragon of patience, milord."

Hugh smiled. "Would you bring me a plate of something? And some coffee? I have some work to do here before I go to Mr. Worley's."

"Immediately, milord," said Hulton.

When he returned a while later with a tray of food and the coffee, Hulton found Hugh at his desk, hard at work copying a sheaf of papers. When he had finished laying out the food on a small side table, he asked, "May I ask, milord, how was the session?"

"Interesting, Hulton," said Hugh, putting aside his quill. "It is a great machine, Parliament. For good, or for ill, I have not yet decided." He turned in his chair and studied Hulton, although the butler was not the subject of his thoughts. "I heard a man there make a speech, and this speech, I believe, was calculated to become a model for artificial divisiveness within the empire. He is a man angling for importance, for he has nothing else to do. He is like a jealous, spinsterish aunt, who, in her incessant, peevish remarks and querulous behavior, aims to stir up animosities within a large and otherwise contented family, so that she may patch together a compact more to her liking."

"How was his speech received, milord?"

"With revolting felicity by many on the benches," said Hugh. "And I swear that most of the gallery had been hired to add their own thunder to the din."

"Which members of our contented family did he rail against, milord?"

"The colonies."

"Oh, yes. The colonies," said Hulton. "There is a great deal of talk on that subject. I hear it noised in the taverns and other public places."

"What are your sentiments, Hulton?" asked Hugh, taking a sip of his coffee.

"Mine, milord? I have none. I boast the virtue of refraining from expression of an ignorant opinion, when I lack the prerequisite knowledge of a subject. I know little about the colonies, and so I have little to say about them."

"A fine rule, Hulton," said Hugh. "You have a respect for knowledge that the speaker lacked. He has much knowledge of the colonies, yet I believe he lied about them."

"Lied, milord?"

"Yes. Yet, at the same time, while I believe he lied, I believe he is right to worry about them."

"Who was the speaker, milord?"

"Our neighbor at Bucklad House, Sir Henoch."

"I see." Hulton reached down and poured more coffee from a silver pot into Hugh's cup, and added a spoonful of demerara sugar from a pewter bowl. He handed the cup and saucer to his master. "What do you think Sir Henoch had to gain by such a speech, milord?" he asked.

Hugh sipped on the coffee. "Nothing for the present," he said. "He is a shrewd man. To look at him, though, you would not think he could project any affair beyond next day's breakfast."

"Slippery creatures, these politicians, milord," remarked Hulton. "I am old enough to remember what many were wont to say about the late Earl of Orford, Robert Walpole, that he was a hick and a fribblous noddy. Yet, he commanded for twenty years."

Hugh sighed. "Well, I must do some work here, Hulton. Please have a hackney waiting for me in the yard after an hour."

"Yes, milord." Hulton left the room.

Hugh hurriedly copied the essay he had not been required to present to his fellow pupils by his modern history instructor, and refined some of his remarks on King John and the role of malice in political power. He re-read it quickly, decided that it was novel and unconventional enough for Glorious Swain, then tied the nine pages together between two blank sheets with a red ribbon, and wrote on the top sheet "G. Swain." He finished the plate of food Hulton had brought him, and left his room to take the waiting hackney to Worley's office and Lion Key.

Until eight that evening he inventoried and prepared the cockets and other papers for cargoes to be loaded the next day onto three merchantmen anchored in the Pool of London: hats, muskets, watches, beer, upholstery, and cider for the *Busy,* bound for Boston; candles, clocks, mirrors, bolts of cloth and silk, millinery, and pickles for the *Ariadne*, his family's own schooner, bound for Philadelphia; and paper, carriage wheels, glass, ink, farming tools, furniture, and tallow for the *Sparrowhawk*, bound for Yorktown.

For this last vessel, there were some extraordinary items to clear: a printing press, spare parts for it, and several cases of Caslon Type in various sizes. It was not merchandise bought on colonial credit, as was the usual transaction at Worley's, but goods paid for in specie and cash, including the duties, by a printer in Caxton, Queen Anne County, Virginia. Hugh had counted out the money days before, and entered it into a special account book. Worley sent Hugh this evening with a lighterman to the *Sparrowhawk* to arrange the shipping with the captain, John Ramshaw, as the captain had expressed a desire to be present when the press was transferred from the wharf to the ship's hold.

A swarm of lanterns on the deck of the *Sparrowhawk* lit the bustle and clutter of an enterprise that spent little time at rest. The crew was busy painting, repairing sails, polishing brass, replacing rotted timber, measuring rope. Hugh was not surprised by the number of cannon or guns he saw. Several of them had been removed from their carriages, and carpenter's mates were intent on fitting new iron to the carriage joints and fixing new sets of tackle to the sides.

He saw that many merchantmen in the anchorage were similarly occupied. He smiled at the sight, as the lighterman rowed him out to the *Sparrowhawk*. There were more burning lights in the Pool of London than on either side of the city.

The captain's steward appeared with another lantern and escorted Hugh down the main hatch to the cabin. Here John Ramshaw sat at a desk. Present also were two other men, seated in chairs to the side.

Ramshaw, a man with a wide, hard face and black hair streaked with shots of silver, put his mug of punch aside and scrutinized Hugh through puffs of pipe smoke.

"Mr. Worley's man, sir," said the steward, who then left the cabin.

"Mr. Worley was too busy to come himself, I presume?" said Ramshaw.

"Yes, sir," said Hugh.

"And you are…?"

"Hugh Kenrick, sir. I've come to set a time for the loading of the press, and to return these." Hugh opened a leather portfolio and laid before Ramshaw a bundle of papers, which included a special cocket for the press and its accessories, clearance papers for Yorktown, and copies of the Caxton printer's license and the royal governor's permission to own and operate a press in the colony of Virginia. The captain examined the papers closely. The cabin was silent, except for the sputtering of its lanterns and the hammering, footfalls, and voices on the deck above. The vessel creaked now and then as she played with her anchor and rode the tide of the Thames.

Hugh glanced at the two seated men, and saw that they were studying him. He looked around and noted the contents of the cabin. On Ramshaw's desk were account books, a quadrant, some papers, the remains of a meal on a plate, an inkstand with quills, and a desk lamp. The lid of a huge chest nearby held an astrolabe, an octant, sandglasses—all new, they seemed to Hugh—and rolled bundles of maps and charts. There were more chests on the other side of the cabin, and a small bookcase. In one tightly packed shelf of books, Hugh espied a copy of *Hyperborea*.

Ramshaw finished the last document, put it aside, then reached for a quill and signed the two itemized receipts that had accompanied the papers. He handed one back to Hugh. "What time does Worley's rouse itself, Mr. Kenrick?"

"Sun-up, sir," answered Hugh, putting the receipt into the portfolio.

"Can he have a lighter ready by seven?"

"Yes, sir."

"Good. We'll be taking on some extra ball and powder about noon, finishing up our repairs by evening, and seeing to some other business. I hope to push off by mid-morning the next day." He turned and addressed one of his companions. "You'll stop at the Turk's Head tomorrow and pick up newspapers that Mr. Stook has been saving for me these past months, won't you? They should be the *Gazette*, the *Craftsman*, and anything else he's remembered to set aside. Pay him a pound or two for his trouble, and ask him to do the same favor, as we'll be back in March or April. Take Flit-cross with you."

"Are they for you or Mr. Barret, sir?" asked the man.

"Mr. Barret—when I'm through with them." Ramshaw looked up at Hugh with a caustic smile. "We'll be bringing those papers aboard without customs clearance, Mr. Kenrick," he said. "Or has the Customs Board decided to tax hand-me-down news?"

"Not that I'm aware of, sir," answered Hugh. He wondered why he was the object of the captain's bitter sarcasm.

"I ask that because Mr. Wendel Barret, publisher of the *Caxton Courier*, will reprint much of that news on his press. I wouldn't want to see him incur the wrath of the Crown by cheating it of so much lawful revenue."

Hugh did not reply.

Ramshaw said, "Mr. Kenrick, these are my surgeon and bursar, Mr. Iverson and Mr. Haynie."

The two men nodded to Hugh, who nodded back.

"Mr. Kenrick," said Ramshaw, "how much is Mr. Worley paying his clerks these days?"

Hugh frowned, startled at the question. "The senior ones, between ten and fifteen pounds per annum, I believe."

"You are wearing twenty, at least," observed Ramshaw, "not including your fine sword." He paused. "You are a clerk, are you not?"

"Yes, sir."

"Are you a relative of Mr. Worley's?"

"No, sir."

"Ah! Then you must have a position at the Admiralty, or the Treasury, or some other such bloodsucking bureau, and your duties collect dust because you are never there to perform them, but for which you are paid nonetheless." Ramshaw turned to the bursar. "Mr. Haynie, how much does a copying clerk make in government service?"

The bursar shrugged. "Oh, between fifty and a hundred and fifty a year, I should say, depending on the department and on his sponsor's con-nections and his letters of reference. That is in salary only, of course, exclu-sive of the fees a clerk may charge merchants for doing what he is paid to do." The bursar looked thoughtful. "Then a clerk could collect somewhere between five hundred and a thousand a year."

"That would account for our visitor's wardrobe," said Ramshaw. He smiled wickedly at Hugh. "Are you larking at Mr. Worley's, Mr. Kenrick?

Moonlighting for an expensive mistress? Paying off a debt? Subsidizing some amusing vice?"

"My father paid for my wardrobe, sir," said Hugh, offended by the man's insolent taunts, but somehow pleased with the frankness of the interrogation.

"Oh? And who is your father? The Duke of Richmond?"

Hugh did not want to answer, for he knew what effect his words would have on the three men. He answered reluctantly, "No, sir. My father is Garnet Kenrick, Baron of Danvers, and brother to the Earl of Danvers. Mr. Worley is his commercial agent."

The bursar and surgeon shifted nervously in their chairs. Ramshaw did not move, but simply stared at him. "That would explain the sheen and cut of your cloth, sir," he said. "Still, you must have a sumptuous salary."

"Or at least a custom commissioner's clerk's," mused the surgeon.

"No, sir," said Hugh. "I work gratis for Mr. Worley, when I am not in school. I am learning the family business, so that someday I may manage my family's affairs as well as does my father now."

"And your father does know his business," remarked Ramshaw. He gave Hugh a curious, almost shrewd look, then addressed the bursar. "It would account for our never having traded in a single Dorset lobster pot, would it not, Mr. Haynie?"

"It would, sir," replied the bursar after some hesitation.

Hugh did not grasp the meaning of the cryptic exchange. Ramshaw saw the blank look on his face. "Please forgive my ribaldry, Mr. Kenrick—Oh, how would you prefer to be addressed?"

Hugh smiled for the first time. "Mr. Kenrick is quite satisfactory, Mr. Ramshaw," he answered.

Ramshaw's eyebrows went up and he grunted once in surprise. "Mr. Kenrick, then. You see, Mr. Kenrick, when I bring the *Sparrowhawk* up to the Keys, half my time is wasted on wrangling with customs men and other pompous supernumeraries, jockeying for the favors of the lightermen, and paying everyone to waste my time, to boot. This wastage leaves me in an immoderate temper."

"Your temper is shared by many other captains, Mr. Ramshaw," said Hugh. "It is an aspect of commerce with which I have become well acquainted."

"And the abuse?"

"No other captain has equaled the tartness of your tongue, sir."

The bursar and surgeon laughed. Ramshaw simply smiled. "I'm sure I've never been blessed with such a compliment." He turned and said to his companions, "Will one of you offer Mr. Kenrick a chair?"

Iverson and Haynie began to rise, but Hugh waved them down with a hand. "Thank you, but, no. I must be getting back to the Key."

Ramshaw gestured to a small cask on a stand near his desk. "Will you at least have a draught of punch, then? It will warm your insides for the ferry back."

Hugh nodded. "Thank you, sir."

Ramshaw found another mug, filled it from the spigot himself, and presented it to Hugh. He picked up his own mug and touched it to his visitor's. "To your health, sir."

"And to yours, sir," replied Hugh. They tilted their mugs and drank.

Ramshaw returned to his desk. "Before you go, Mr. Kenrick, I've heard talk in town of a new dictionary of the language that has come out. Put together by a Doctor Johnson, working alone. A singular accomplishment, if you'll pardon the pun. Could you tell me where I might find some copies? I'd like to take a few with me to hawk in Virginia for my own pocket."

"I believe it was published by Mr. Strahan, the principal book printer. I have seen it in some bookshops, and plan to purchase a copy of it myself. Grove's on the Strand, near St. Martin's Lane, carries it, as does Bigelow's at Charing Cross, on Cockspur near the Mews Coffeehouse."

"How much is being asked for it?"

"In guineas or in pounds, sir? It is more than the appraised value of my wardrobe, including my sword."

Ramshaw grinned. "That's Attic salt I deserved to have flung into my eyes. Thank you for the information on the dictionary, sir. Will you be attending the loading of the press on the morrow?"

Hugh set his mug down on the desk. "No, sir. I shall be at school."

"Which one? Westminster?"

Hugh shook his head. "Dr. Comyn's academy, in Westminster."

"Never heard of it, though I'm sure it hasn't dented your common sense." Ramshaw rose and extended his hand. "Well, Mr. Kenrick, good evening to you. Convey my regards to Mr. Worley, and tell him I'll be waiting on the Lion Key stairs at seven." He shook Hugh's hand. "Mr. Haynie, please see our visitor to the deck, would you?"

When the door closed on Hugh and the bursar, Ramshaw said to Iverson, "He doesn't know."

"About his father and the Lobster Pots?" queried the surgeon. "No, I don't think he does."

"Well, he'll learn that end of his family's affairs in time."

"There'll be nothing for him to learn, if this new war saps the smugglers."

"No, I don't think it will tame the business. Swell it, yes. Recall what we unshipped offshore to that new gang in Cornwall last week: redirected tea, tobacco, sugar, maize, and all sorts of French and Dutch spirits. When the French make it riskier to bring those things in regular-like, the prices will go up, and the taxes, too. But there won't be any drop in want for those things. No, this war will fatten many a smuggler's goose. Including mine."

"That Trott chap in Gwynnford doesn't need fattening," chuckled the surgeon as he helped himself at the cask to another mug of punch. "He must be the largest gang leader I've laid eyes on, ever. I fully expected his galley to capsize when he stood up in it—or this ship to list when he stepped aboard."

Ramshaw laughed. "True, sir. But he's a good man, leading a gang of good men. Skelly's successors. He was so overjoyed to hear that Jack had come out of that Braddock business near Duquesne alive that he gave me twenty pounds to buy him a gift. 'He reads,' he said to me. 'Get him something to read.' He couldn't think what. So I've decided that Jack will acquaint himself with Dr. Johnson. I'll make up the difference in price, if there is any. After you've picked up the newspapers, go around to those shops on the Strand and purchase that dictionary, three or four of them. I'll give you the money tomorrow. Hire a ferryman to bring you back here, and we'll fetch them up on the other side, out of sight of Customs. Damned if I'll pay any more taxes on knowledge."

The surgeon lit a pipe and settled back in his chair. "That Kenrick chap has a bit of Jack in him, don't you think?"

"A bit," agreed Ramshaw.

*   *   *

Hugh had wanted very much to ask Ramshaw about his copy of *Hyperborea*, but no opportunity had presented itself. So he had to satisfy himself with the thought that it was somehow right for Ramshaw to have it. He liked the man, and would have even had he not noticed the novel in the bookcase. He wondered for a moment about the mysterious exchange about "lobster pots" and his father, but this was a fleeting thought and he forgot it as he climbed down the rope ladder to the waiting lighterman.

After Hugh was seated in the wherry, the lighterman maneuvered alongside and out of the way of a succession of ferries and barges wending their way through the still hulks of the merchantmen. The wherry tread water beneath the bowsprit and figurehead of the *Sparrowhawk*. Both Hugh and the lighterman looked up. A platform had been rigged under the figurehead, and was lit by several lanterns; two crewmen were renewing the blue, red, and yellow colors of the wooden bird, a stylized and very regal sparrowhawk. Its menacing yellow beak was less foreboding than the baleful, intent eyes. The head stared west, pointing to the future.

Hugh reported to Mr. Worley, then took a hackney back to Whitehall to pick up the essay he had copied for the Society of the Pippin, and rode the same hackney to Ranelagh Gardens. He paid the admission and hunted through the vast pleasure palace for Glorious Swain. Half an hour later he spotted him in a group of other liveried waiters, carrying a tray of steaming hot dishes. Swain broke off from the group. "No time to talk, my friend!" he said. "We've been assigned to some important guests. Is that your essay?" he asked, nodding to what Hugh held in his hands.

"Yes." Hugh tucked the rolled sheaf beneath one of Swain's arms.

"It's the Duke of Cumberland and his party we're serving. If you want to see him, there are vacant tables opposite his box."

Hugh shook his head. "We met, many years ago." He paused. "I'll be going home for the holidays in two weeks, Mr. Swain. I hope to hear from you before then."

"You will, sir." Swain bowed slightly, and turned to catch up with the other waiters.

Hugh purchased a glass of claret from another waiter and wandered around the Rotunda, not wanting to leave so soon for the chilly hackney ride back to Windridge Court. He stood at the main entrance and observed the crowds. The orchestra was playing a lively Rameau rondeau, and some guests were actually dancing to it in front of the stand. The great cylindrical fireplace in the center blazed away, warming the whole vast space. A pleasant memory came to him when he noticed the table near it at which he and his family had suppered many years ago, and he had clutched the top in his pocket following his battle for it with John Hamlyn.

The Duke of Cumberland and his party occupied some boxes across from it. He could see the man, who seemed to have grown more portly. And he remembered the Duke's visit to Danvers, and the dull eyes, and the whipping, and that whole day.

But instead of a bitter memory, a realization dawned on him, like a theater curtain drawn open to reveal a magnificent opera setting. How far I
have traveled! he thought to himself. The man caused me pain, and dissension in my family—but I was right! Right to fight for my top…right not
to apologize…right to do everything that I have done… And that day in
Danvers, and so many like it before and since, were recast in his mind to
become the consecutive scenes of a great tapestry, and it seemed that he
was an observer in some quiet chapel, strolling leisurely along its length,
recounting the epic of his own life. I shall do splendid things, great things,
he thought, and the fireworks of celebration beyond the chapel exploded
and flashed through its windows and lit up each episode. Splendid and
great—but to whom? he asked himself. To me, in my capacity as a man. I
have been true to that day in the park… And Hugh, unconscious of the act,
because his mind and body were electrified by this personal vision, smiled
with contented pride and joy.

He saw the Duke lift a fork and wag it in the air to say something, then
rise from his table and laugh merrily, and glance around with jerky nods to
his companions, who in turn laughed as if on cue. The Duke sat down
again, and plunged his fork into a golden partridge on the plate before him.

And who is the happiest man in this place—in this city? Hugh thought to
himself. I am. For I have a self—or is it a soul?—and it is of my own making.

Two men, one slim, almost effeminate, and fashionably dressed, the
other stocky, plainly dressed, and with a twitch in his hands and a tic in
one eye, came from behind Hugh and stood beside him, waiting to be seated
inside the Rotunda. "I don't see why we should be subsidizing German
princes and kissing Elizabeth's ample Russian prat," whined the slim gentleman in a high voice, "when we could be spending the money on shoring
up the colonies, or relieving the poor, or improving our awful turnpikes!"

"Well, if you approve of thievery, sir," said the older, plainly dressed
man in a deeper, boisterous voice, "there's little point to moralizing about
what the rogues purchase with their plunder! Your outrage is misapplied!"

Galvanized by some law of fastidiousness that impatiently rejected the
intrusion, Hugh abruptly turned to the older gentleman. "True enough,
sir!" he said to the startled man, and handed him his claret glass, then
turned and left. The exchange between the two men did nothing to
diminish the glow he felt inside himself. He simply did not want anyone or
anything else near it.

Chapter 18: The Member for Onyxcombe

THIS VISION IS SELFISH, EXCLUSIVE, AN ISLAND UNTO ITSELF. ONCE REALIZED, it cannot be regulated, debased, or mitigated to accommodate the churlish, the banal, or the commonplace. It occurs on but one scale—the magnificent—and is proof against all schemes to amend it or render it palatable to the mundane. No median is possible to it; it exists in its natural state, encompassing one's whole being, or it does not exist. The light that illumines it, and reveals to a man the cathedral of his soul, can be of many strengths—from a candle to a sun—but it burns on one fuel only: his integrity. The vision contains an element of eternity that has nothing to do with time, but everything to do with the width and breadth of his life. It is measurable, but indivisible.

Betrayed, it will avenge itself. The action would contradict both it and a man's ineradicable knowledge of it, leaving him, should he survive the cataclysm, a mechanical, insensate manqué, drained of all future capacity for sublime and earthly joy. Betrayed, it will become his worst nemesis, and he the impotent enemy of the implacable justice of its memory.

Animate, it can make him maddeningly intolerant and insufferably imperial, together contemptuous of lesser souls and indifferent to them. It could cause him to say to others, should he be provoked to speak to them in his thoughts: You think in terms of nooks and crannies, of niches and pigeonholes, of ruffles and fringes; I think in terms of vistas and frescoes, of oceans and continents, peopled by gods, heroes, and myself.

This vision is unassailable by others, whether they be foul-mouthed fishwives, glib-tongued wits, or icy earls; impregnable to blasts of malice, disdainful of attempts by humor to demean it, deaf to the silent salvos of others in whom the light does not burn or has been extinguished, one of ostensible boredom or regal ennui. They see in his features either a stressed courtesy, or a reproachful innocence of their own corruption or vices, and a knowledge of them.

Such a man is newly struck by the meanness of most men he encounters, and tired of it at the same time. Such a man is usually startled by evidence that others do not know him, or are wary of him, or are meekly tentative in their dealings with him. He is quietly astonished that they do not

cherish things as passionately as he cherishes things—or even themselves—or are ignorant of the fundamental laws of life he takes as given or
self-evident. Such a man cannot be merely dismissed with a pat on the
back. He can only be loved or hated: the love requiring a courage to know
him by accepting the flashes of the vision that arc from him to other men
and their affairs; the hatred requiring a rejection of that vision and a fear
of him, a fear difficult to disguise. Such a man has for society few or no
friends, an array of dedicated enemies, amidst an army of insensible
strangers.

This vision is the most private possession a man can claim, not to be
flaunted, or traded on, or spoken of lightly—and woe to the careless casuist
who ascribes to this reticence the absurd orthodox virtue of modesty or
humility! For then, in some hard, memorable way, he will learn never to
accuse a hero of cowardice. This vision is the foundation of a man's pride.
It allows him to live and think and act in a universe wider and greater than
the dim, minikin one of the solely scrupulous man; in one denied by, and
so denied to, the man who permits the vision to sputter out; and in a universe invisible to the man in whom the vision had never dawned.

Hugh Kenrick could not now imagine living apart from it; indeed,
could not imagine a life worth living if it were a mere disembodied abstraction. That unexpected, though inevitable moment in Ranelagh Gardens had
revealed to him that, rather than being a pawn of fate, or a vessel of destiny,
or a product of chance, his soul—or was it his self? He would never distinguish between the two—was the sum of all his own evaluations, decisions,
and actions, and that the sum was ineluctably and inexorably noble.

Hugh Kenrick was learned enough to understand that the vision had
another name—honor—and wise enough to know that it was both a cause
and a consequence.

He also knew that the preservation of his honor was a sacred responsibility. It was one he gladly assumed, for among many less important reasons, it helped to make living among other men bearable.

*   *   *

When Hugh returned to Windridge Court after school the next day, he
found an inn coach sitting in the courtyard and footmen and servants
unloading trunks and other baggage. His uncle had arrived. He had
resigned himself to his uncle's stay, but dreaded it all the same.

The first person he met inside the house was Alden Curle, his uncle's butler and major domo of the Earl's half of the mansion in Danvers. Hugh had always disliked Curle, who was obsequious and servile to a fault, so much so that some species of arrogance and presumptuousness would bubble to the surface of his manners. Curle, tall, thin, impeccable in his livery, stopped in his hurry down a hallway when he saw Hugh. In both hands he gingerly held the Earl's crimson velvet mantle with its miniver of ermine. He bowed. "Good afternoon, milord," he said. "It is a pleasure to see you again."

Hugh sighed. "Good afternoon, Curle."

"We arrived not thirty minutes ago," Curle rushed to say. "His lordship is preparing to nap after the journey, but asked me to instruct you, when you came in, to sup with him at nine of the clock."

"Yes, of course. Where is Hulton? He was to escort me from the school."

"I sent him out for some fresh fish and vegetables."

Hugh studied the waiting butler. "I hope you thought to compliment him on the state of the house and the grounds," he said.

Curle shrugged. "I haven't seen enough of the house yet to compliment him, milord, but be assured that I will do so when I have taken stock."

"How is my uncle, and how was the journey?"

"His lordship is fine, but tired, milord," replied Curle gaily. "The journey was without incident, except at Portsmouth, where a press gang almost made off with poor Claybourne whilst he was on an errand! But his lordship intervened with the captain of the vessel Claybourne was taken to, and secured his release, and with a choice of words I did not know he could make, and which was as impressive as the captain's! His lordship is especially attached to Claybourne, as you know. And, on the Dover Road from Canterbury, our coach was ambushed by highwaymen, but we were being followed by a troop of dragoons scouring the area of smugglers, and the ambush was foiled. We were treated to a fine chase over a neighboring field, and the dragoons shot two of the rogues on the gallop! His lordship, out of gratitude, presented their captain with five guineas! How generous of him!"

"Yes, he is capable of that, on occasion," remarked Hugh. "How long does my uncle expect to stay?"

Curle's face went blank and he shrugged lightly again. "As long as he may, milord," he answered. "Why do you ask?"

Hugh frowned. "I ask such questions, Curle."

The butler's face shot red at the rebuke in a mixture of embarrassment and anger. "I beg your pardon, milord," he said, moving back a step and bowing.

"What are you doing with that?" asked Hugh, nodding to the robe draped over the man's hands.

"It needs brushing, and some repair to the lining, milord," said Curle. "It is some time since his lordship has donned it." He added, in a hushed tone, "His lordship will sit with his peers tomorrow, or the day after, milord."

"All right," said Hugh. "Get on with it." He turned and mounted the great staircase to his room, two steps at a time.

The butler watched him ascend. Wrestling for control of his expression were surprise at his master's words, regret for his own, and the sting of the curt dismissal.

Curle duly reported the essence of this exchange four hours later to Basil Kenrick, when the Earl had arisen from his nap, and as Claybourne and another valet flitted about the room dressing him. Curle did not actually report it, but slipped it into his chatter about the state of the house and grounds, without, however, allowing it to sound like a complaint.

But the Earl knew it was one, and his glance, with languid contempt, shifted to Curle, whom he could see standing behind him through the full-length mirror. Claybourne had been about to fit an immaculate white wig atop the sparse gray-brown hair on the Earl's head, but stopped when the Earl held up a hand. "Is that what he said, Curle?" he asked. "'I ask the questions'? Those were his exact words?"

"'I ask such questions,' your lordship," said Curle, apology for the correction in his reply.

With some disappointment to Curle, Basil Kenrick's eyes lit up in amusement and his mouth bent in what the butler knew was a smile. The Earl said nothing for a moment. He was pleasantly surprised. That was the proper response to a servant's effrontery. Perhaps there was hope for his nephew after all. He wondered what accounted for the change. "What else did he say, Curle?"

"He enquired about your robe, your lordship," said Curle with reluctance. "I happened to have it in hand, and was taking it to the tailor to be brushed and repaired. Then he bade me to continue on my errand, and went up to his room."

"What did he say exactly?" demanded the Earl. He sensed that his nephew's words had grated against the butler's pride and would be humiliating for him to repeat, especially in front of other servants. And he knew that Curle would be truthful, because the man would be afraid that his employer could easily ask the nephew for the truth.

Curle knew the purpose, but managed to swallow a gulp, and said, "'All right, get on with it,' your lordship." Too late, he threw a warning look at Claybourne and the other valet; they had already traded muted grins over his discomfiture.

The Earl gestured for Claybourne to continue. As the valet adjusted the wig on his master's head, the Earl asked, "And the robe? It will be ready by tomorrow?"

"This evening, your lordship. I shall fetch it myself."

"How are the house and grounds?"

"In a proper state, your lordship. The grounds have been swept clean, the coach has been dusted, and the coachman and footmen are this very moment making their livery presentable. The stablemaster reports that one of the team is sickly and has bare spots, and it happens to be the postilion's mount. He does not think it is fit enough for duty, and requests that you view it yourself to decide whether or not to replace it."

"I'll see it before supper," said the Earl. "And the house?"

"Again, your lordship, in a proper state. I could find nothing amiss—or missing."

"Hulton is major domo here in your absence, is he not?"

"Yes, your lordship, ever since your brother the Baron raised him up."

"A conscientious, honest chap, Hulton," remarked the Earl. "My brother acquired him ages ago. Against my advice, as you know, but I suppose he was a good choice. My brother occasionally exhibits good judgment." He snapped his fingers. "A guinea, Claybourne."

The valet hurried to the dressing table and took a gold coin from a satin purse that bore the Kenrick coat-of-arms in silver thread. He came back and handed it to his master.

The Earl smiled and held it up. "Give this to Hulton, Curle, and also my thanks. My brother would approve."

Curle stepped forward and took the coin. But the Earl's eyes held his in the mirror, and he realized that the guinea was not to be given to Hulton, but was his own reward for his obedience.

And the Earl, aware that Curle detested Hulton, knew that Hulton would never see the guinea, that all the other butler would receive was Curle's condescending thanks, and that neither he nor Curle nor the valets would break the code of silence and ever mention the guinea again.

The Earl disliked Hulton because his brother had employed the man; the valets disliked him because the Earl did, that is, because they valued their positions more than they did justice; and Curle because Hulton was a reproach and a threat. It was a cabal of malice the four men established, into which they would draw others, and enjoyed by each according to his rank and sense of power. Each party to the cabal was a rock-solid Christian.

As Curle slipped the guinea into his pocket, there was a knock on the Earl's chamber door, and another servant entered. "Your lordship," said the man, "there are gentlemen downstairs come to see you, among them Mr. Hillier, who comes direct from the Commons in answer to your summons to see him most urgently, he says."

As Claybourne helped Basil Kenrick into his frock coat, the Earl said, "I'll see Hillier first. Put him in my study, and prepare a service of tea."

"Yes, your lordship," said the servant. "And the others?"

"They may wait, if they wish. Ascertain their business."

"Yes, your lordship." The servant bowed and left the room.

*　　*　　*

The first act Basil Kenrick performed, soon after he alighted from the inn coach, was to send a servant out to find Crispin Hillier and deliver to him a written summons for his presence. The Earl wanted fresh news of Parliament. He had returned to London for one of his infrequent immersions into politics, and wanted to waste no time. He disliked London, and wished he could exercise his influence from Danvers. London overawed him, and he derived no sense of importance in it or over it. His only power lay in the few alliances he made with other peers and commoners, men he otherwise did not like and preferred not to deal with.

He made Hillier wait another twenty minutes, until he was absolutely satisfied with his appearance, and then descended to his study.

Crispin Hillier, his man in the Commons, was registered as the member for Onyxcombe, Dorset, but it was understood by all in the Commons that he represented Danvers, a much larger and more prosperous town, though it had never been granted a seat in the assembly. Hillier was one of the few commoners with whom the Earl would actually speak on more or less equal terms, sans ritual and distinction. He was older than the Earl, and in some ways wiser. It was the Earl's father who had selected him for the seat decades ago, which seat he had retained without interval ever since. He owed his political career and affluence to the Earl, who guaranteed his return to the Commons every election year with a sack of shillings liberally distributed to his constituency. This was a common practice in those times, though not every member of the Commons had as a patron a member of Lords. There were worse inequities at large in the Commons than the custom of purchasing a yard or so of green cloth on the benches of St. Stephen's Chapel. Hillier was spared the task of having to campaign for the seat, of having to advocate, oppose, or stand for anything; of having to make merry with those whose votes had been bought, and acting the buffoon to entertain men he despised; of having to answer to charges of venality by an opponent, for the Earl saw to it that he was spared the bother and worry of an opponent.

Crispin Hillier was a short, compact man, tending to the rotund, though he was lively and active enough for a wit and fellow member of the Commons to dub him the "Moloch of Mitigation." He was a Londoner by birth and preference, though this did not stop him from representing a rural constituency he visited only from necessity, perhaps once a year, and during election weeks, and knew less about than did a native of Calais. He was a lawyer, and maintained a practice that often took him to the Law Courts in nearby Westminster Hall to represent clients ranging from bankrupt gentlemen and jilted brides to notorious felons and unlucky pickpockets. He carried a silver-topped cane, dressed in the dark hues of a Quaker, and wore reading glasses. He was painfully respectable.

Now, the House of Lords, though not an elective body, acted as a kind of senate for the country, as a check on the power of the Commons. Though it could not originate "money bills," that is, bills that had to do with raising revenue by taxes or means of any kind, it had the power to veto or amend any that came from the Commons. The Commons jealously guarded its privilege of originating money bills; if any were submitted or amended by the Lords, these bills, before discussion or recognition, were in the Commons literally and contemptuously tossed to the floor by the Speaker or his clerk. But if amendments to a Commons money bill were by consensus viewed as practical, the bill was redrafted to incorporate the Lords' changes, and usually passed by the Commons and then sent to the king for his assent. Nor could the Lords change any fundamental feature of a money bill, such as the rates of taxation, the method or agency of collection, or the estimated revenue from the new charge; it could only attach amendments that would mollify or increase its severity.

The House of Lords, to which the Earl belonged as a peer, was powerless over the nation's purse; this was a consequence of the Commonwealth and Protectorate of nearly a century before. The Commons reserved the right, won after centuries of warring with kings and lords, to judge what was good for the country and what was not. On one hand, this was a good thing, a step in the right direction; on the other, a bad thing, for the Commons, though it ostensibly represented the eligible electorate and regularly heard passionate oratory on the liberties of the Englishman, represented its members exclusively and bitterly fumed about its privileges.

The Commons' chief enemy was the Englishman and his liberties, and so far as the typical member was concerned, an Englishman's liberty was limited to the right to elect him, but did not extend to telling him what to advocate or vote for; all else was privilege. Crispin Hillier and many of his better-read colleagues on the benches agreed with parliamentarian Narcissus Luttrell's observation in 1693 that, regarding the rights of Englishmen, "their representatives are here, and their consent is sufficient." This was a presumptive power for which Parliament had beheaded a king, banished many a lord, and persecuted legions of royalist pamphleteers and essayists. The Commons had abrogated an abuse, but called it governance. It was quite constitutional.

Hillier's value to Basil Kenrick was his envied privilege to introduce private bills in the Commons, specifically money bills and bills that would allay the effect of land taxes and assessments on property. Hillier was occasionally successful in getting these passed, no mean feat even for one who had mastered the complex and byzantine rules and procedures of the Commons. Hillier also joined, and on occasion led, opposition to any ministerial proposals he construed as displeasing to the Earl, such as a reduction in import duties on certain commodities or the relaxation of criminal or revenue law, though, of course, he would never mention the Earl. His ardor in this realm had earned him the wit's nickname.

Hillier also sat on many committees that reviewed petitions against new and old taxes; petitions against new taxes were summarily rejected, for the unspoken rule of the Commons was to take no cognizance of any challenge to its power; petitions concerning the burdens of old taxes were accepted and discussed, for the members knew that a merciful recognition of one grievance could be balanced with the callous ignorance of another. "What one hand giveth back, another taketh away," Hillier had slyly remarked on numerous occasions with his fellow committeemen when they had reluctantly granted the petitioners' grievance the venue of debate from the benches of the Commons.

And so, in the quiet of the Earl's study, in comfortable chairs and with tea and brandy at their elbows, Crispin Hillier and Basil Kenrick talked. Hillier reported on many things, among them: the mood of the Commons vis-à-vis the Duke of Newcastle and the French threat; the rumor that the Speaker, Arthur Onslow, had indicated a wish to retire, perhaps before the current Parliament had adjourned; the status of various private and ministry bills before the House, and in which the Earl had an interest; the expected resignation, or even dismissal, of William Pitt as Paymaster of the Army, and possibly even that of Henry Legge, Chancellor of the Exchequer, in light of their opposition to the Hessian subsidies; and Sir Henoch Pannell's speech on the colonies.

When Hillier had finished reciting the gist of Pannell's speech, Basil Kenrick was silent for a moment, the clip-clop of hooves and the rattle of coach wheels on Whitehall Street beyond the courtyard wall seeming to mark the progress of his thoughts. Presently, he said, "Goodness, Hillier, that won't do!"

Hillier smiled. "That was the sentiment of many members, your lordship, as I learned upon canvassing the House in the lobby some hours after the event. Though, however, many others received the speech with fervent alacrity."

"Alacrity," sighed the Earl. "Such a harsh-sounding word, don't you think? Confound it, Hillier, it ought to mean the opposite of what it does! Every time I encounter it, I think of some unpleasantness, such as alum, or acid! 'Lord So-and-So punched Mr. By-and-By on the nose with alacrity for the insult,' or, 'Mr. Hillier replied with alacrity to each of Mr. Pitt's points, and made the former cornet of horse choke on his own confusion.' Do you see what I mean?"

Hillier chuckled in amusement. "I quite agree with you, your lordship. But that is a matter you must perhaps take up with Mr. Johnson."

"If Mr. Johnson is not on speaking terms with his former patron, the Earl of Chesterfield, he would hardly trade words with me." The Earl grunted once, then asked, "Do you think Sir Henoch made a permanent impression?"

"No, your lordship, I do not." Hillier put aside his cup and saucer to think for a minute. "I would express it this way: Sir Henoch waved his own ensign, to which many rallied in the heat of the moment, but it was subsequently deserted on the approach of the Hessians." Hillier cocked his head once. "It was undoubtedly a cunning speech, your lordship. I wish I'd made it myself. I told him so, too, and asked him what was his purpose. He was somewhat circumspect, though he assured me he would not raise the subject again. He was content with the results."

"But you gave me to understand there were no results."

"None that we can see, your lordship—except, perhaps, that Sir Henoch has proved to himself and to others that there exist grounds for concern—or that they will exist, once the war is finished, and it has not yet even begun. Who knows how much time will pass, and what the outcome will be?"

"Are you in agreement with him, Hillier?" asked the Earl. "I mean, ought the colonies to be chastised and brought to brook?"

Hillier shook his head. "No, your lordship, not at present. Though I must concede that sooner or later—preferably later—the issue should be faced and resolved. The colonies are growing ever so full of themselves, and if we expend men and treasure to retain them, well...they may possibly conclude that they are too valuable to remain colonies." Hillier paused to finish a thought, and added, "They may conclude that they are a cause unto themselves." He frowned. "That, I believe, was the warning contained in Sir Henoch's speech." He shook his head. "I must credit him for knowing that it was not a point to be said in so many words."

The Earl scoffed in protest. "Surely, such rifled wisdom is not possible to that...puffed-up buffoon! I have made Sir Henoch's brief acquaintance, or rather he made mine, and cannot believe that the rascal is some sort of Oracle of Albion!"

Hillier shrugged. "I'm certain that it is a wisdom, your lordship, that emanates, not from the head, but from a queasy gut. When the time comes, I believe we shall all know the sensation, and speak as Sir Henoch spoke, from the rumbling turmoil of our innermost fears."

"Hmmm...fears that we may lose the colonies, and the better part of our great fortune? Fears of other kinds of unstoppable disturbances?"

"Yes, your lordship."

A moment passed, and then the Earl sat forward and folded his hands on the desk. "Well, that won't do, either, Hillier. They oughtn't to be chastised, unless they provoke the Crown. And they needn't be chastised, if they are not given cause to complain or otherwise misbehave. And speeches like Sir Henoch's would give them cause."

"Well put, your lordship!" said Hillier. "Said with inspired alacrity! Do you plan to speak in Lords?"

"No, no," replied the Earl, waving a hand. "Not unless I am myself provoked! But—are you certain that Sir Henoch will not pursue the matter?"

"No, I'm not entirely certain of it, your lordship. I've only had his assurances. Should he speak on the subject again, it must be outside the House. Mr. Onslow would not permit it to be put in the business of the day."

"Yes, of course. But we must be certain that he does not stir up trouble in any quarter."

Hillier frowned. "Excuse me, your lordship, but we can't stop a man, or even a member, from speaking his mind outside the House, unless he means something treasonable or seditious."

Basil Kenrick smiled. "I wish to make better acquaintance with Sir Henoch, Hillier. You will invite him, on my behalf, to sup with me and you tomorrow evening. Here, of course, as we wouldn't want to be seen together in public. There may be other guests, including my nephew."

Hillier was dumbfounded. Never before, in his long association with the Earl, had he ever been invited to sit at table with him. Not even in Danvers. He had made plans, barring a long session of the House, to go to Vauxhall Gardens tomorrow evening, but that was now impossible. And he was certain that Sir Henoch Pannell would also cancel his own plans, once he had received such an invitation.

"Yes, your lordship," said the member for Onyxcombe, with a bow of his head.

Chapter 19: The Supper Room

T
HE SUPPER ROOM OF WINDRIDGE COURT WAS A RECTANGULAR SPACE twice as long as its banquet-sized table, with cream-colored papered walls punctuated by silver sconces, gold neoclassical statues on marble pedestals in blue niches, and portraits of ancestors of the Kenrick family.

There were eight of the latter, though not all were of earls. Two represented barons, younger brothers of their primogeniture-favored siblings. One was of Sir Bowler Kenrick, member for Onyxcombe under Elizabeth I, gentleman usher to that queen, author of two published treatises on mathematics, and the family's only dabbler in physics, for which he was very nearly charged with witchcraft. The other was of Sir Stanier Kenrick, also member for Onyxcombe—the last Kenrick to sit in the Commons on behalf of the dynasty—adventurer, traveler, renowned minor poet, unrepentant rake, planner of the grounds of the Danvers estate, and captain of a troop of cavalry that participated in the decisive charge at Blenheim in 1704 and captured three French colors; Sir Stanier personally presented those colors to his commander, the Duke of Marlborough, and they now hung with all the other Duke's captured banners in the vast arcade of Westminster Hall. Neither brother outlived his elder one to inherit the earldom. Both had had their likenesses recorded at their own expense: Sir Bowler with his trimmed beard, ruffled collar, and a twinkle in his eyes, holding in his arms a great tome whose Latin title was obscure and illegible; Sir Stanier with his shoulder-length locks, feathered tricorn, and filigreed breastplate, which bore the indentations of several French musket balls and the crisscrossing scars of innumerable sword-hits, standing with a sword in one hand and a captured banner in another.

There was not a single smile, however, on any of the portraits, earl or baron. They glared at each other from across the room, or down at the occupants of the banquet table.

Hugh Kenrick appeared promptly at nine in this room, and crossed it to the table, whose far end had been laid for two settings.

Basil Kenrick, fifteenth Earl of Danvers, stiffened as a servant closed the door behind his nephew and as he watched the boy approach. A boy?

No, thought the Earl. And not quite a man. He could not fathom the change in Hugh, but it was a change nonetheless. He was seated at the head of the table, but in an instant Hugh was standing before him, almost like a soldier at attention braced for a dressing-down. Yet, there was an aloof, almost menacing quality to his person, and in his movements and carriage. The phenomenon put the Earl on his guard. He had the unshakable feeling that he himself was the object, not of deference or respect, but of toleration, and that in this toleration was an element of indifference. For a moment, he experienced the humbled insignificance of a servant in the presence of a true aristocrat. He fought a compulsion to rise and bow to Hugh in greeting.

Basil Kenrick had never before addressed his nephew by name. He had always resorted to "sir," or "young sir," or "you." But as a concession to his brother, he had secretly practiced pronouncing "Hugh" in the privacy of his chambers and study. And now he could not utter the simple syllable; some unsavory emotion choked it in his throat. He started to say "sir," but decided on "nephew." It seemed easier. He tried to imbue the word with a quantum of affection; he was not certain he succeeded. Worse still, he had the absurd notion, as he spoke, that the eyes of all his ancestors were upon him, witnessing his predicament with the silent jeering capable only to an aristocrat.

None of these things endeared his nephew to Basil Kenrick.

After what seemed like an eternity, he said, "Good evening, nephew. You are looking well."

Hugh, with a nod of his head, replied, "Good evening, sire. As are you."

The Earl gestured to the setting near him. "Please, nephew, sit." With another hand he signaled to two waiting servants, who stood by a long table that held the supper on trays covered with copper and silver domes.

As he took his seat, Hugh realized that this was the first time he had ever been alone with his uncle. He was not aware of any tension between himself and the man, only of the strain within himself to be civil, and the effort to keep from exhibiting his boredom and indifference. He sensed that his uncle was uncomfortable, too, and decided to put him at his ease. And so he tactfully remarked on the precedent.

"Yes," replied the Earl, astonished both by the fact and the gentleness with which Hugh made the observation. "It is the first time, is it not? Well, it is my earnest hope that this repast augurs the foundation of a mutual confelicity between us." A servant approached and put a plate of food before him.

The reply, "Pompous ass," flashed through Hugh's mind. He hoped it did not show in his expression. Another servant placed a plate of food in front of him. Hugh began to ask his uncle what he had been doing, but stopped, because it struck him that his uncle did nothing, and would not be able to reply. It was inconceivable that he would be doing anything. Instead, he asked his uncle why he had decided to attend Lords.

"To know what is the mood of Parliament, and to block any actions that would imperil this nation," said the Earl. "Newcastle must be prodded into taking stronger actions to prepare for this conflict with France, or into stepping down and letting someone who will take those measures steer our policy."

"The French seem to be after our colonies," said Hugh. "One can only wonder how the colonists would fare under the French Crown. There is France, with twenty millions of people, and an estimated revenue of twenty millions of pounds per annum, and it is all at the uncontested disposal of the Crown. I believe that if the French tore the colonies from us, the colonists would revolt against France."

The Earl blinked at this statement. "Why do you think that, nephew?"

Hugh shrugged. "I do not believe the colonists would tolerate the terms of conquest which the French ministry would likely impose, nor long put up with being treated like cattle, as much of the French populace are."

The Earl did not wish to pursue this line of conversation. He himself believed that the colonists ought to be at the absolute disposal of his own Crown, and that they were merely extraordinary servants of it. However, he did not want to seem reluctant to discuss the subject. "Yes, of course," he said. "So we must establish a policy that will retain the colonies, and see to it that the French are removed from Canada, and from the Indies. Then we shall enjoy peace again." He paused. "Your father reports that you are excelling in your studies here," he broached.

Hugh knew that his uncle had changed the subject, but did not understand why. "It is a good school," he replied. "The instructors are sound. One is left alone to master the subjects, and not much required to engage in social distractions or sports, as pupils are at other schools."

The Earl, so adept at conversation with his peers, and with men like Crispin Hillier, found himself helpless from that point on to raise any subject that would elicit the interest of his nephew. Secretly he hoped to incite Hugh to make some outrageous, offensive statement that would give him an excuse to punish him or exert some kind of control over him. Checking this wish was a curiosity about the boy's new manner. As they ate, their conversation continued in fits and starts, the Earl introducing mundane subjects, and Hugh responding with frigid courtesy.

The Earl, after one long silence, raised the subject of his brother's new project. "The Earl of Uxbridge, as you know, has had some troubles with the villagers and cottars around his park who wish to destroy his rabbits. That is because he regularly prosecutes poachers of them, and will not allow free ingress on his lands for any reason. Your father does not antici-pate such trouble."

On this subject, Hugh agreed. The villagers and tenants in and around Danvers had a certain affection for his father, who treated them fairly and generously. This affection, he knew, did not extend to his uncle. "Yes," he replied. "Father wrote to me about the conies. He expects them to be a prof-itable venture." He changed the subject. "Do you expect to attend any con-certs or plays while you are here, sire?"

The Earl almost smiled, so pleased was he with this diplomatic tack, and grateful, for he knew what his nephew, brother, and the villagers thought of him. "Perhaps," he said, "if time allows, and if it is not tiring." He paused to take a sip of wine. "Have you been to Lords?" he asked.

Hugh shook his head. "No, but I have been to the Commons, and heard speeches made. Our neighbor, Sir Henoch, gave one on the colonies that roused the benches and the galleries."

The Earl regarded his nephew with new interest. "Oh? Mr. Hillier was here earlier, and told me about it. What did you think of it?"

"It was a heartfelt address, moved by a curious enmity toward the colonies." Hugh paused in what his uncle sensed was the first instance this evening of genuine interest. "I would say that he cozened the House into sharing this enmity, except that I do not believe that the House was entirely a dupe of his artifice."

"Perhaps it was not," remarked the Earl. "But...you were not per-suaded by his artifice?"

"No, sire. It seemed to be a speech without purpose, as another member rose and pointed out, but there is always a purpose to such well-laid ranting. I have learned that in my rhetoric lessons." Hugh sighed and pushed his half-finished plate away, and a servant whisked it from the table. "And then the House debated some election grievances, which were postponed, and turned to some minor, silly-sounding bills. I did not hear what was said about Mr. Pitt's cause, or whether the Crown's war chest was deep enough to oppose the French, because I had promised Mr. Worley I would assist him in the afternoon and left before anything else was said. But I met Sir Henoch in the Yard, and had a cordial exchange with him."

The Earl made up his mind. "I am pleased to hear this, nephew. I am having him and Hillier here tomorrow evening for supper. You will have occasion to exchange pleasantries with Sir Henoch again, as I wish you to attend, also. As a kind of ally, you see. Then you will witness some true politicking."

"We did not exchange pleasantries, begging your pardon, sire," said Hugh. "I scored him on his artifice, but he is quite a resilient sophist."

"So much the better," said the Earl. He paused. "A word of caution, though. At tomorrow evening's table, speak from true motives, but never talk sententiously. Keep your wisdom with your pocket watch, and produce it only when you think it necessary."

The request was a demand, Hugh realized, and could not be refused. "Yes, sire," he replied without enthusiasm.

A servant set a large glass of syllabub topped with strawberries in front of him. It was a favorite of his, but now he had lost what little appetite he had. The supper and conversation droned on, and an hour later his uncle dismissed him. Hugh went to his room and fell upon his bed, drained of energy. He had not known, until now, how exhausting self-control could be.

*   *   *

"What is the nature of your borough, Sir Henoch?" asked the Earl the next evening.

There were five settings now at the richly appointed table. Crispin Hillier and Sir Henoch sat across from each other along a length of it; the positions of their chairs had been minutely adjusted so that they sat at a subtle distance from the Earl at the head of the table.

At the Earl's right sat Hugh, who had resumed his rigid formality. To the Earl's left sat an elderly man who did not seem to know why he was here. This was Andrew, Viscount of Wilbourne, another close neighbor of the Kenricks. He was an amateur botanist who grew flowers in his small garden that overlooked the Thames. He also bred racing dogs. He had once served as proxy Lord Chancellor in Lords—a position analogous to that of Speaker in the Commons—three long Parliaments ago, standing in briefly for a peer who had taken ill. It was the only time he had ever spoken in that House; he had not missed a single session there in thirty years. Wilbourne wavered between lucidity and absent-mindedness. He could be convinced of opposing views on any subject within the space of a minute, and some peers practiced this cruelty on him for their own amusement. He was small, thin, and fragile-looking. When he entered Lords his colleagues often wondered if his robes weighed more than did he, and if they were too much of a burden for him to wear. He listened to this evening's talk with an expression that may have been either cool comprehension or utter bafflement. Basil Kenrick had invited him to the supper "for balance," as he had explained to Hugh, and not because he expected the Viscount to contribute much to the conversation.

"Well, your lordship," answered Sir Henoch with a marked jauntiness, "in truth, it is a mongrel franchise. I own Canovan and all the property in it, and as I am the sole householder and payer of the poor rate and other assessments, the place is a burgage. And, as I am its only legal inhabitant, and its only enfranchised voter, it is also a scot and lot borough." He laughed once. "I nominate myself, entertain myself, vote for myself, elect myself, and represent myself in the Commons." He laughed again, hoping that the Earl would see the humor in the irony, too.

"A very salubrious arrangement, Sir Henoch," remarked the Earl, refusing to smile. "May you always have such a faithful and captive constituency."

"Thank you, your lordship. It compensates in no little way for the fact that neither Marsden nor my country estate has representation."

"And many happy returns, Sir Henoch," interjected Crispin Hillier.

Sir Henoch beamed at him. "Thank you, Mr. Hillier."

Hillier had not warned his fellow member of the purpose of this supper. He had simply delivered the Earl's summons, confessing to Sir Henoch only that he had reported his speech. Sir Henoch knew that Hillier was the Earl's voice in the Commons, and Hillier presumed that Sir Henoch had offered to speak at some time on the Earl's behalf against the relaxation of the duties on finished hats of French, Dutch, or colonial origin, by way of another thread of connection between the two Houses. He knew that the two had met before, but did not know the nature or depth of their former association. Hillier had come this evening in a state of dour, morbid expectancy; he could have been attending a hanging at Tyburn Tree.

Sir Henoch was in a buoyant mood; he had never imagined that the
Earl would thank him in this manner. He had even cleaned his teeth for a
second time this day, and doused himself with rose water for the occasion,
as he had for his interview with the king many years ago.

After a spate of small talk, and when the party had nearly finished the
main course, the Earl addressed the member for Canovan. "Mr. Hillier
informs me that the Speaker allowed you to speak at length on an irrelevant
subject the other day. Is this true?"

"It is, your lordship," replied Sir Henoch, almost shrugging. "I believe
that Mr. Onslow had had some extra helpings from his chocolate pot that
morning, and so was in a sweeter mood to accommodate me. I don't say
much in the House, your lordship, but when I speak, I tend to speak in volumes." He paused, sensing that the Earl's question was merely an overture
to another matter, which he could not guess at. "He did, afterward, take me
aside to remind me to limit my remarks in future to the day's business, and
not again tumble a slumbering House from the wrong side of the bed."

"I would agree with him on that matter, Sir Henoch."

"Your lordship?"

"The colonies are an important appendage to this nation. It would not
do to antagonize them at this particular moment."

"The business of the day," said Hillier, "indeed, of the war, is not yet
the arrogance of the colonies, Sir Henoch, nor their miseries, concerns, or
feelings of neglect."

Sir Henoch seemed to realize then the reason he was here. For a
moment, he said nothing. He was, however, wise enough to concede the
Earl's point, yet practical enough not to appear too conciliatory. "True
enough," he said. "But I am sure that treacly oration will not do the trick,
nor will the malady of colonial discontent be corrected by a dose of extract
of peppermint. I fully expect the matter, once the peace has been restored,
to be a subject of the committee of the whole House."

"I fear that, too, Sir Henoch," said the Earl. "I share your sentiments,
but believe that your remarks were ill-timed." He paused. "I trust that you
do not construe my words here as an attempt to breach the privilege of your
House. But there are prior issues at hand. Everything in time, Sir Henoch.
You will have your day again, I am sure. Please, stay your oratory on that
subject. One enemy at a time. There are other things you and Mr. Hillier
can work together on in the Commons."

"Yes, your lordship."

"You know, of course," continued the Earl, "that Mr. Hillier here sits on a committee that is considering a petition from some colonial merchants to reduce the duty on hats from their quarter."

"And I on a committee that is considering a petition from city shop-keepers to reduce the duty on Spanish oranges, your lordship. I can say with confidence that the notion will never be debated in the House."

The Earl hummed in approval, but said, "When, at your house some time back, you offered to speak against the reduction of duties on other commodities, you did not include hats. Is there a reason why you assumed I might be interested in those articles?"

Sir Henoch was at a loss for words. He could not openly confess that he was certain that the Earl and his brother were closely connected with the smuggling into the country of hats and other commodities along the Dorset coast, and that his certainty was bolstered by intelligence gathered through informal conversations he had had with contacts within the Customs Board bureaucracy. He could no more admit this certainty than he could propose blackmail. Of course, Sir Henoch knew that Hillier's committee was considering hats, and that other committees were considering petitions of a similar nature. He had merely mentioned hats in his speech; he could just as well have mentioned Irish lace or French shoes. It was immaterial. So he concluded that the Earl was probing him for the depth of his knowledge of the Earl's culpability.

After these ruminations, Sir Henoch replied, "Nothing in particular, your lordship. Only that you, together with so many others charged with the dignity of England, would consider such a reduction a threat to the Crown's solvency, and a blow against the nation's interest." He spoke these words facing the Earl in the most self-righteous manner he was capable of.

The Earl seemed satisfied with this answer, and, letting the matter rest, became intent on finishing his plate. Hillier smiled approvingly at his colleague, and did the same. Viscount Wilbourne blinked at him. And the nephew, who had not said a word all evening, looked perplexed. Sir Henoch was certain, judging by the look on the boy's expression, that he was as mystified by the exchange as was the Viscount. The young baronet looked like the perfect scion of aristocracy: he wore a spotless white wig with a green ribbon on the tail, and a pearl gray suit that was as lustrous as his uncle's. There was a fastidious air about him that seemed directed at the company, not the table. Too much of a prig for politics, mused Sir Henoch. He decided to test the mettle of the boy, and perhaps pay him back for the encounter in the Palace Yard. He wondered if the Earl was aware of his nephew's "republican" leanings.

"May I compliment his lordship on the excellence of his port?" he said after taking a long swallow of it. A servant immediately appeared and refilled his glass.

The Earl seemed to smile, and nodded acknowledgment.

Sir Henoch addressed Hugh. "Milord seems to be in a state of mental percolation. Have you anything to say on the subject of our Britannic flora?"

Hugh had been content to endure the conversation in silence, for it either did not interest him, or concerned matters he did not fully understand. But now he had been invited to speak his mind. "Only that I was prompted, by the talk, and also by your speech in the House, Sir Henoch, to recall an episode from my Roman studies."

"Oh? Which episode, milord?"

"The fate of Cremona."

"Cremona?"

Viscount Wilbourne spoke. "It is famous for its violins," he announced.

"I was reminded," continued Hugh, "of what happened to the citizens of that fortress town when they surrendered to Antoninus Primus's legions."

"Nothing disreputable, I trust," remarked Sir Henoch, fearing that it was.

Hugh shook his head. "They were plundered and butchered. Their houses were burned, their temples razed, and their riches carted away. No man, woman, or child was spared the sword, outrage, or the fetters. The survivors were made slaves, to be sold to the highest bidders. And when the citizens of Rome heard what had happened, their probity compelled them to resolve not to purchase the new slaves. Out of spite, the captives were put to death by their captors."

"Well," sniffed Sir Henoch, "Roman history is quite gory. To my recollection, the reduction of the intrusive barbarians was never the stuff of bedtime stories or children's tales."

"Cremona was a Roman colony, sir, populated by Romans, and one of Rome's most prosperous."

Sir Henoch's ignorance was not feigned. "Forgive me, milord, but I don't see the relevance."

Hugh asked rhetorically, "Will the scarlet of our martial tunics some day share the shame of the praetorians' scarlet cloaks?"

Sir Henoch fell back in his chair, unable to answer. Hillier watched the Earl's face grow pink. And Hugh held Sir Henoch's glance, waiting for an answer.

Hillier said, "What gives you leave, milord, to construct such a dire analogy?"

Hugh answered as though it were obvious. "Sir Henoch's patriotism, Mr. Hillier, together with a wealth of sorry precedents in Roman history for his proposed lex Britannica."

"And the violins?" asked Viscount Wilbourne, looking around desperately. "What happened to them?"

The Earl threw the Viscount a sharp look, then addressed Sir Henoch. "Rome was in the midst of a civil war," he said, blandly changing the subject of the conversation, "over who would be emperor, Vettilius or Vespasian." He paused, then waved a hand in dismissal of the subject. "Civil wars are notoriously fratricidal, Sir Henoch, and sufficiently lurid enough in their episodes to seduce the attentions of someone the age and experience of my nephew. And, anyway, my nephew's analogy is quite erroneous."

"And, who became emperor?" asked Viscount Wilbourne.

"Vespasian," answered Hugh, ignoring his uncle's slight, "the son of a tax collector. He began construction of the Coliseum for the entertainment of the masses, and banished the philosophers because their teachings caused men to think and contemplate disloyalty."

"Very interesting pastime, the study of history," remarked Hillier, attempting to lessen the sudden tension. "It has many uses, I am sure, but as a repository of moral guidance, I'm afraid it has nothing to offer us moderns."

"Quite true, Mr. Hillier," replied Hugh. "Roman history especially is a nonpareil chronicle of the absence of reason in men's affairs. It is my earnest hope that we do not emulate the Romans in that respect. That we speak a different language, wear different clothes, and eat different foods, will not guarantee that we will not. The consequences must be the same, if we do emulate them."

Sir Henoch sat forward and took another swift draught of port. He was angry. The insult the boy had offered him could not be repaired, and he knew that he could not ask for an apology. He said, not looking at anyone in particular, "I've found that reason, which ought to direct men's affairs, seldom does. That is not my doing. When I speak, it is not men's reason that I address to the exclusion of their passions. It is, after all is said, the passions that govern their reasoning. I believe I am correct in thinking that some very prominent philosophers have averred this precise position. This Scottish scrivener, Hume, I heard even approves of it." Then he dared himself to face Hugh. "Milord, reason is but the application of caution in men's affairs, once a sentiment has been decided. That is all reason is, or should be."

"I will be found dead in my bed," stated Viscount Wilbourne, "before I am ever caught agreeing with a Scot!"

Both Hillier and Sir Henoch laughed in relief for the diversion. Hillier exclaimed, "Your lordship, you're a poet!"

Viscount Wilbourne glanced around the table with imbecilic delight. The Earl, though grateful for the diversion, too, began to wonder just how much the Viscount's mind had decayed.

Hugh turned to his uncle. "Sire, may I be excused before dessert?"

This, too, caused the Earl to feel relief. His nephew's request would save him the bother of sending him away. "You may, nephew."

"We shall only be discussing imaginary revenues calculated on imperative expenditures, milord," said Hillier. "Dull matters, no doubt, for one so lively as yourself." He paused. "Or perhaps some other excitable subject."

"Say, rather," chimed Sir Henoch, "imperative revenues based on imaginary expenditures, sir. I confess I don't see the distinction." He turned to Hugh and smiled broadly. "Good night, milord."

Hugh nodded. "Good night, gentlemen." He bowed slightly to the pathetic form of Viscount Wilbourne. "Good night, your lordship." And with a final bow to his uncle, he turned and left the supper room.

When the doors on the far side of the room closed behind Hugh, Sir Henoch turned and addressed the Earl. "Your lordship, you have a nonpareil relation in that boy. I don't recall ever having observed so much bottom in one so young."

"He has been a pain to me, at times, Sir Henoch," replied the Earl, a subtle menace in his words, "but he is blood, and quite above judgment by all but his father and me."

Sir Henoch shook his head. "No aspersions intended, your lordship," he replied. "And forgive me the presumption, but I do believe he reads things less innocuous than Tacitus and Plutarch. Why, just the other day, he admitted to me that he bosoms that stigmatized work, *Hyperborea*, and even speculated on what its villainous author might have said in answer to my speech! What an obsession! What an imagination!" He shook his head again. "I could not believe that his lordship allowed such trash in his house, so I did not credit it. Though if his father your brother approves of it, as he intimated to me at my house some time ago, well," concluded Sir Henoch with an expression of pouting incredulity, "one can't know what to think."

The Earl studied his guest with a mixture of admiration and contempt. "You hanged the author, did you not, Sir Henoch?" he asked.

Sir Henoch frowned. That question again! "No, your lordship, I did not. I merely saw to it that he was."

"I would not allow it, Sir Henoch," said the Earl after a short moment, "and you were wise not to believe that I would."

Sir Henoch rushed to say, "I sincerely hope that his lordship does not contemplate punishment for the lad's words to and about me. I cannot be insulted! I have been called worse things than a patriot—much worse—and been the subject of inelegant hilarity."

"I have not yet decided, Sir Henoch," replied the Earl with a finality that closed the subject of his nephew.

A moment of silence passed. The Earl signaled the servants to begin serving dessert.

"Speaking of boots, your lordship," said Sir Henoch, reaching inside his coat and bringing out some neatly folded sheets of paper, "I dictated my speech to my secretary, and now take the liberty of presenting you with a copy of it, so that you may better judge its force and wisdom, word for word. I have received many compliments on it, and some criticism. Why, some spy in the galleries took it all down, and I'm told it will appear in *Gentleman's Magazine* or some other gossipy rag—though my name will be changed to some unflattering style." He handed the papers to the Earl.

"Thank you, Sir Henoch, for your thoughtfulness." The Earl took the papers and put them to the side. "I shall read it tonight, before I retire."

Viscount Wilbourne abruptly grinned. "Have any of you heard the latest gossip about Bute and the Prince of Wales? The daft Prince dotes on the Earl, and the Earl dotes on the lad's mother, the Dowager. An unnatural ménage, that!"

The members for Onyxcombe and Canovan were startled by the Viscount's outburst and the relative sanity of his subject, and the Earl was embarrassed. But even though the topic had been raised by a man whom they by now had concluded should be mourning the loss of most of his faculties, the career of John Stuart, third Earl of Bute, Groom of the Stole, and advisor and confidant of both the Dowager Princess of Wales and her son, George, absorbed their attention for the remainder of the evening.

But not entirely the Earl's. A number of things seethed beneath his awareness of the social gossip and political speculation. One was the oily guile of Sir Henoch Pannell, who was, he was forced to admit, what his brother had called him, "an objectionable, slithery snake who needed regular whacking." The man could be useful, but only with careful handling. Another was the embittering presence of Viscount Wilbourne. It served him right for having absented himself from Lords for so long—two years, he recalled—for otherwise he would have known of the man's pronounced senility and never chosen him for table ballast. The Viscount had been quite sane this morning in Lords, and had even given him a warm welcome, which fact alone should have alerted him to the man's condition, for in the past he and the Viscount had exchanged barely twenty words.

And, finally, there was his nephew, a model of decorum all evening, until he rose to Sir Henoch's bait and all but bit off the hand of that angler. Basil Kenrick did not know whether to be pleased that Hugh had put the man in his place, or to be angry with Hugh's pointed and contemptuous treatment of a man who could be an important political ally. Well, he would not make the mistake of inviting Hugh again to another of these conferences. The Earl resolved to reprove his nephew on the matter, but not harshly.

There were, after all, other kinds of punishment.

Chapter 20: The Society of the Pippin

Hugh's exit from the supper room was more an escape for him than a polite withdrawal. He had tried to abide by his father's request not to provoke his uncle. But he could stand it no longer. His uncle's advice, in fact, was in part more practical than his father's; he had spoken from true motives, though sententiously, for there was no avoiding that if he was to say anything at all. His uncle had only himself to blame. If he had pursued the exchange with Sir Henoch—if he had said, "By your own argument, sir, the Romans were largely incautious, if caution is to be taken as the sole measure of reason"—he would have only invited more of the man's sophistry, and there would have been no end to it. So he had let the man have the last word.

There was a strange irony, he thought. If it had been a private exchange between himself and Sir Henoch, he would have driven the man to the precipice. But it had taken place in front of witnesses who, like Sir Henoch, did not seem to mind the man's error or his interest in that error. They, in fact, approved of it. Sir Henoch was determined, for his own reasons, to have the last word, as though having it demonstrated the efficacy of something more than the man's sophistry. Hugh could not imagine what that might be. No, thought Hugh, as he walked to his room: If he had had the freedom to debate Sir Henoch, the man's last word would have not been a word, but a howl. It would have been deserved justice for such a shifty, slap-dash soul.

Hugh's frustration was tempered by the disturbing revelation of the extent to which his uncle was enmeshed in the country's politics. And if his uncle was an active agent in those matters, then his father must also be somehow involved. Hugh had not devoted much thought to politics—it was a realm as distant from his consciousness as were the politics of Egypt and Persia—that is, politics as it was actually practiced. The secretive nature of the supper, together with the tone of conversation, repelled him. If that was the essence of what his uncle had called "true politicking," then he wanted nothing to do with it.

Before he reached his room, he was intercepted by Hulton, who proffered a salver that held a sealed note. "It came about an hour ago, milord," said the butler, "and I would have asked one of the attending servants to hand it to you, but his lordship instructed us that there were to be no interruptions." He paused. "A young boy delivered it."

Hugh eagerly snatched the note and tore it open. It read: "Greetings, sir. If it is convenient to you, please meet me and my friends at the Fruit Wench this evening at eleven of the clock. You have been adjudged worthy of our company. We will be sitting in the rear of the place, behind the last partition of curtains, which are green. Ask Mrs. Petty for a pippin and she will admit you. Do not introduce yourself, and greet me by no name but Muir. Your grateful servant, G. Swain."

With a triumphant bark of a laugh, Hugh rushed into his room, threw off his wig, and began to change into a suit that was less lustrous and more practical. Hulton followed him in and attempted to perform his duty as valet, but Hugh was too much of a whirl of movement for him to keep up. "Are you going out, milord?" he asked.

"For a while, Hulton."

"Is it advisable, at this hour of night? It is nearly eleven."

Hugh grinned. "You may accompany me, if that will put your mind at ease," he said. "But you will need to sit in a tavern for a while. The Fruit Wench. Do you know it?"

"Yes, milord. It is a reputable establishment, though it has had some moments of commotion."

"I am meeting some new friends there. A club of thinkers, I believe."

"I see, milord." Hulton frowned. "Is his lordship's supper finished?"

"No. I asked to be excused from it, and Uncle allowed me to go. I got into a scrape with Sir Henoch."

"A scrape?"

Hugh shrugged. "An argument, which he thinks he's won." He paused to reflect, then said, in an exaggerated, theatrical tone, "'He daubed his vice with a show of virtue.' *Richard the Third.* Richard, vilifying one of his victims, at the same time construing the method of his own villainy." He laughed. "And Shakespeare never even met a Whig!"

"That is a nice observation, milord," said Hulton after some hesitation. "It could have been made about my colleague, Mr. Curle. But I am not acquainted with either of the gentlemen you cited."

Hugh paused to stare at the man with astonishment. Then he grinned, went to his bookcase, and took out a volume of Shakespeare's *Histories,* and handed it to Hulton. "For you to peruse in the Fruit Wench. I am surprised and disappointed that you have not availed yourself of these plays."

Hulton smiled in self-mockery. "I glanced through them, milord, but they looked longish and forbidding in their language and complexity."

Hugh shook his head. "That is not the way to wisdom, Hulton," he said. "Although you are better read than you let on." He continued as he retrieved his greatcoat, "The portrayal of Richard the Third may or may not be a fair one, but I believe his creator was speaking to the ages about the requisites of power. His observations on that subject can be applied to worms like Mr. Curle, and Sir Henoch...and my uncle." Hugh put on his hat. "Well, let us get you into your own coat, and pick up a lantern and a pistol, and be off."

As they made their way through the chill air and darkness out of Whitehall to Charing Cross and the Strand, Hugh asked his companion, "If you had the liberty to choose, Hulton, and could get out of service, what would you like to do, or be?"

After a moment, the butler replied, "A tobacconist, milord. I enjoy a pipe now and then, and am at my most thoughtful when I have one and am at my ease."

They walked on, and after a moment, Hugh said, "I shall speak with my father about setting you up somewhere, Hulton, and giving you generous terms for repayment, if you are willing to risk it."

Hulton was speechless for a moment, then asked, "Why would you do such a thing, milord?"

"I would like to see you independent, Hulton. It would give me great pleasure. I could say to myself, as I passed your shop, 'I know that man.' And it would get you away from mere service, and away from Mr. Curle's machinations, and my uncle, who I know does not like you, either." Hugh paused, then reached into his coat and took out some coins. "Here is some money to slake your other thirst, while you wait for me in the tavern."

Hulton took the coins. "Thank you, milord."

*   *   *

London was large enough a metropolis that the Society's members rarely risked encountering each other in public or in private. Yet, while they lived and worked in widely separated parts of the city and in disparate professions, and were habitués of various strata of London society, the club had a rule that governed even this happenstance: should one of them recognize a brother Pippin in the street, or in a tavern or other public venue, he would not enquire after the other's identity, and each would greet the other as strangers; and should he inadvertently learn the other's identity, he would keep the knowledge to himself.

It was a spacious private room that Hugh was escorted into by the proprietress of the Fruit Wench, with its own fireplace and chandelier. A large table held the remains of a supper. Seven men sat around it in armchairs, each with a tall glass of port, ale, or brandy before him. Some smoked pipes or long churchwardens, and the thick smoke in the air seemed to have been generated by the combustive energy of their conversation. The room was the last compartment of three in the tavern, separated from another private room and the main room beyond by a neck-high curtain on a brass bar above a paneled partition. The middle compartment, also occupied by a private party, served to diminish the raucous hubbub of the business in front.

"'Ere's your gentleman you was waitin' for, you scoundrels," said Mabel Petty with mock contempt. "Looks too fine a gent for the likes of you."

"None of your sass, Mrs. Petty," said one of the men. "And bring us another round of port, if you please—and none of that lymphate brew you serve sailors and soldiers. We want something that bites back!"

"I oughta bite your nose off for such lyin' slander!" replied Mrs. Petty, who exited with a peal of laughter.

All the men turned to look at Hugh, who stood waiting at the entrance. Glorious Swain grinned and nodded in greeting.

"Forgive me for being tardy," said Hugh to the company, "but I was detained and got your invitation only a short while ago."

"No matter," said one of the men. "One or another of us is usually past the appointed time of sitting."

"Approach, young sir," said the oldest of the men.

Hugh stepped closer to the table.

"You are truly the author of the interesting tract on King John?" asked the same man.

"I am, sir," said Hugh, "if the tract is the one I gave to this gentleman some time ago." He nodded to Glorious Swain, who was sitting placidly back in his chair with a pipe.

"A very diverting argument you make," said another man, "about malice. It is a subject the Society has never before thought to discuss."

"It was an ingenious, entertaining read," said another.

The oldest man said, "Only one of us had reservations on the subject, but our agreement was unanimous that you should be permitted to attend our synods."

"Your sponsor here was quite enthusiastic about your character and mental ambition, sir," said another man, "and championed your candidacy with sometimes frightening fervor."

Hugh smiled, and bowed slightly. "You honor both him and me with the wisdom of your decision, sirs."

One of the men laughed. "No false modesty! There's a Pippinish qualification, brothers! A fellow who knows what he's all about!"

"Hear, hear!" agreed several of the men together.

The oldest man rose from his chair. Leaning against it was the rosewood cane Hugh remembered was handed to Glorious Swain in the tavern by one of the members. Its silver knob was in the shape of a pippin resting on a bed of ornate leaves. "Your sponsor states that he has explained our rules to you, sir. Do you agree to observe them?"

"I do."

"Your demi-membership," continued the man, "was the subject of some vigorous and often bitter debate among us, at an extraordinary meeting called for that very purpose. Muir's proposal was, at first, quite upsetting to us all. It entailed the relaxation of a strictly enforced rule."

"The rule of seven," said one of the men.

"I still say that our subject was, more properly speaking, a proposed quasi-membership," speculated another.

"But Muir was equal to the hustings, and defended your nomination with brilliant reasoning."

"We hope, therefore," said the oldest man, "that you appreciate the exception we are making for your and our brother's sake."

Hugh nodded. "I do, sir, and promise to observe your rules as intimately as I maintain my honor."

One of the men idly addressed Hugh. "It's going to be a novel distraction, being audited by one so young—by a mere boy, in fact."

The man's words contained a challenge. Hugh knew this, and so did the other men. They waited for a reply. Hugh drew himself up and said, "I will not mind your many years, sir, if you will not mind my few. I am not aware of a Newtonian law that proclaims that sagacity is the exclusive preserve of the aged."

The men exploded in laughter. "Well said!" proclaimed one of them.

The man who had tried to nettle Hugh nodded in concession. "What you hear, sir," he said, waving a hand to indicate his friends, "is the beating of a chamade for my surrender. But, I parley no more with you. You are right. Here is my sword." He raised his glass of port in salute.

The oldest man, who was serving as chairman, waited until the laughter had died down, then said, "Sir, our talk is finished for the evening—the subject being how to best keep up correspondence with our peers in France, in lieu of the coming hostilities, without inviting charges of treason—and our only remaining business is your matriculation."

"One question more," interrupted Glorious Swain, who had a mischievous look on his face, "before that business, chairman, if you will indulge me."

The chairman asked, "And that is…?" Swain's companions looked at him expectantly.

"What risky thing has my candidate ever done to merit our select company?"

Hugh held Swain's glance and grinned. "I have read *Hyperborea*, and wish I could thank the author for having so enriched English letters with that work."

"Auctoris damnati!" gasped one of the men. "There's a brassy fellow!"

The chairman shrugged. "I believe that answer sanctions our decision, gentlemen. Let us proceed. Mathius, a chair, please."

One of the men rose and took a chair from by the fireplace and placed it at the table. The chairman gestured to Hugh. "Sit, sir, if you please."

Hugh obeyed, removing his hat and adjusting his sword.

The chairman said, "It is necessary to assign you a name that will both conform to the Greek motif of our society, and recognize the valor which brought you to your sponsor's and our attention. Muir, I believe, has chosen a very appropriate alias."

Swain rose and faced Hugh. "Miltiades," he said solemnly, "after the commander who led the Athenians to victory at Marathon over the Persians."

"Will you accept Miltiades as your sole name in our company?" asked the chairman.

"In all modesty, yes, I accept it," said Hugh.

"Spoken like a true Pippin!" laughed one of the men.

Another retrieved something from a vacant chair across the room. It was a wreath of apple leaves, preserved in thin wax, though many of the leaves were brown and brittle with age. The man fitted it over Hugh's head. "The corona of a scholar!" he said. "Now, for a pippin!"

The chairman handed Hugh the rosewood cane. "This is our Bible, sir," he said. "Swear on it that you will tell no lies, practice no deceit, and never let slacken your lust for Eve and her wares!"

"I swear," replied Hugh, amused by the men's behavior.

"It's the fruit of knowledge, lad," said another member. "Ignorance cannot be bliss, for there is nothing in it to digest. Knowledge sates the appetites of noble minds!"

"The crown," said the chairman, "was last worn by your sponsor, some years ago. A former member, who got into a chance conversation with him, had decided to remove to the colonies. But before he left, he sponsored Muir in much the same manner as Muir has sponsored you."

Another member abruptly rose, went to the entrance to the room, and called out, "Agnes, we need you to seal a covenant! And where's that port?" He returned and grinned at Hugh. "Eve must be the last component of your tripos, Miltiades."

One of the men noticed an odd look on Hugh's face. "Sir: do you detect a strain of blasphemy in our rhetoric?"

"It would be called that in regular society, sir," answered Hugh.

"Ah! But we are not regular society, sir," said another member. "We are worse than the Hellfire Club and the Medmendham Club put together! Members of those societies pursue mere sensual objects and ends—though we are not above that ourselves, on occasion. No! We pursue that which allows such men to waste their time and money, and others to accomplish great things and the wonders of the ages! What do we advocate?" The man pounded a fist on the table. "La raison humaine! That is what we esteem here in Angleterre! We recognize no other Eves!"

Agnes, Mabel Petty's daughter, rushed through the entrance with a tray of bottles. "Here's your port, sirs, and what else did you be wantin'?" She was a pretty girl of eighteen, with black hair under a mobcap, and frank gray eyes. She put the bottles on the table and laid the tray aside.

"We would be wantin' a wanton, deary," said the man who had challenged Hugh, "to buss yonder youth and so complete our ceremony."

"Hey! Who's sayin' I'm a wanton?" protested Agnes, her chin thrust out and hands on her hips. "I don't go round peckin' every man who begs for the favor, and I'll smack the one what thinks I does!" She held out a palm and snapped her fingers. "Pay for the port, and I'll be on my way! Ten and five, please!"

The chairman approached her and dropped some coins into her palm, but then clasped her wrist so that she could not leave. "Not even for a crown, my dear?"

Agnes's brow furled in thought. "You're askin' for a smackin', sir," she replied in warning. "I means it! And my mum'll give you all the royal boot, to boot!"

"I am not the man who requires your favor, my dear." The chairman gestured toward Hugh. "There is your Adonis, waiting the lips that will admit him past the gates of our society." He turned to Hugh. "Have you a crown, Miltiades?"

Glorious Swain chuckled. "I have the dues," he said, taking out his purse and giving Hugh a coin.

Agnes Petty hesitated. None of the men could tell whether it was the crown that made her reconsider the request, or Hugh himself, whom she noticed for the first time. She looked suspiciously at the chairman. "You're not askin' for nothin' but a sisterly kind of peck, are you? Won't be no harm in that, I'd say."

"Just sit on his lap for a moment, and deliver your blessing, my dear. That's all we ask."

Agnes grimaced, yanked her hand from the chairman's grasp, and dropped the coins into her apron pocket. She briskly walked around the table and plopped down on Hugh's lap, snatched the crown from his fingers, then rested her arms on his shoulders. "A young one, for once!" she exclaimed. "What an armful you're goin' to be for some lucky girl!" She paused to scowl and ask, "What d'you want to hang about with these gouty codgers for, anyway?"

"For their wisdom, Miss Petty," replied Hugh tentatively, for he was uncomfortable with this situation. The only other women who had been this close to him were his mother, his governess, Bridget, and Reverdy Brune, but not in this manner, nor for this reason.

"Well, all right, then," sighed Agnes. "Here's some wisdom you won't ever get from them and won't be forgettin' from me!" She kissed him roundly on the lips. She seemed to linger against her will, then disengaged and jumped up from Hugh's lap. There was a blush on her face. Without another word, she handed him back the crown, then swept past the men, picked up her tray, and was gone.

All the men regarded Hugh with amusement. Hugh, a little disconcerted by the experience, but not displeased, removed the wreath from his head and laid it on the table. He handed back Swain's crown.

"I do believe," remarked Swain, "that you sparked a flame in that girl, Miltiades."

"Well," said the chairman, coming back to the table, "it is time we introduced ourselves. The scepter, please, Miltiades."

Hugh handed the walking stick to the chairman.

All the men rose from the table. The chairman laid the cane on it in front of him. "But, first a preface concerning our purpose and spirit. Collectively, if you please, gentlemen. As Muir has no doubt informed you, we comprise a Pleiad of wisdom. We represent the seven twin brothers of the seven daughters of Atlas and Pleione."

"We, too, are hunted by Orion," said another member.

"We are the second generation of this Society, which was founded in the last year of the reign of Queen Anne."

"We are not Whigs."

"Nor are we Tories."

"We are outlaws of the intellect!"

"Unlicensed, unregulated, and unguilded!"

"We commune freely and daily with Clio."

"We are the acolytes of Calliope!"

"And the slaves of liberty! Adamites all! We sing Lady Liberty's virtues! She is Eve in disguise! She hands us the forbidden fruit of knowledge, from which we take manly bites!"

"We are mancipated to her apron strings, and are happy men!"

"Thus the name of our club, sir: The Society of the Pippin!"

"Among ourselves, we speak without fear of censure or reprimand by the watchmen of church and state. This is more liberty than that enjoyed by anyone in Parliament!"

"And when we die, Hell will not be the terminus of our departing souls."

"We are destined for Helicon, home of Apollo and the Muses!"

The chairman bowed to Hugh. "I am Tobius, twin brother of Taygete, a daughter of Atlas." Outside the Fruit Wench, he was actually Robert Meservey, physician, occasional lecturer at the College of Surgeons, essayist, and contributor to many of the city's numerous periodicals.

"I am Abraham, twin brother of Alcyone," said Jacob Mendoza, the second oldest member. He was a watchmaker and clocksmith by trade, and a Jew. Under still another name he was the author of many irreligious, satirical letters he sent to the city's newspapers; some of these letters were actually printed. He was known to the Society as a secular adherent of Sadoc, who in the second century before Christ founded a sect of skeptics, which maintained that the soul was mortal, that heaven and hell did not exist, nor angels or spirits, and denied the resurrection of the soul from the dead. "Abraham" did not object to the Greek mythology of the Society; it was much pleasanter lore than any he had ever encountered. He cherished it, his own conviction notwithstanding, because it was deliciously pagan. He attended neither synagogue nor church.

"I am Mathius, twin brother of Merope," said William Horlick, a part-time Grub Street hack who produced fables, gossip, and advice for chap-books and almanacs, and part-time clerk for a wine merchant. He had written several novels in the style of Samuel Richardson, and a volume of poetry and musings in the style of Samuel Johnson, but had not been successful in persuading a patron or a publisher to promote his work.

"I am Claude, twin brother of Celæno," announced Daniel Sweeney in a muted brogue. He was a cabinetmaker, a locksmith, and an Irishman. He was an Anglican by default, and an indifferent one at that, for he owned a prospering business in a parish where church attendance was closely scrutinized by pastor, vestryman, and neighbor. He hailed from Dublin, where he once published a series of violently anti-Catholic tracts, which earned him death threats. He disowned most of the Irish who lived in the Wapping and St. Giles sections of London; he called them "beggarly beasts, who would make a foul pigsty of heaven, if they could suborn St. Peter to allow them into it." He disowned Ireland. "It will never become a fit, cosmopolitan place to live, until it abandons Popery and the English abandon it."

"I am Elspeth, twin brother of Electra," said Beverly Brashears, a bookseller and, in his own circles, a noted antiquary and advisor to those rich enough to collect and maintain private libraries. His obsession was to someday be able to publish the journals of Parliament—both houses—and to that end constantly instigated petitions for a bill that would allow the public reporting of sessions and debates. He bribed his borough's member in the Commons to submit his petitions, even though they were repeatedly rejected without a reading. He continued to author, under another name, a series of pamphlets calling for the accountability of representatives, of Parliament, and even of the king for their actions and policies. "The king his majesty can do as much wrong as his minister, a member of the Commons, or a scheming link boy."

"I am Muir, twin brother of Maia," said Glorious Swain.

"I am Steven, twin brother of Sterope," said Peter Brompton, a musician and music tutor to the children of many of the city's most prosperous families. He was adept on many wind and string instruments, and played often with orchestras at Ranelagh and Vauxhall Gardens.

The men sat again, and poured themselves glasses of port from the new bottles. A glass was offered to Hugh. The members toasted him. He toasted them, and marveled at the difference between this gathering and his uncle's supper. There was no coyness here, no pretence, no undercurrent of deceit, no evidence of ulterior purpose. These men were open, honest, and frank. Still, the custom of the names bothered him.

"Tobius" saw the question in Hugh's expression, and asked, "What confuses you, Miltiades?"

Hugh replied, " Muir explained the reason why you employ aliases—

"I am the third member to bear the name Steven," said Peter Brompton. "Muir there is the fourth member to carry his. It's only Tobius who is a mere second owner of his name. He is very ancient, you see. He knew some of the original members, when he was your years."

Hugh smiled in answer to the distraction, then continued, "I still don't see the necessity for it."

Tobius leaned closer to him, and said in a near-whisper, "Intra muros, sir." He gestured with a circling finger at the walls of the room. "Then, inter nos. I cannot overly stress this caution. The cider of nomic wisdom is not the staple of our mental compotations. It is not imbibed here."

"What we discuss here," said Swain, who sat next to Hugh, "could be judged seditious or treasonable—"

"Or even heretical," interjected Abraham, "if the subject turns to religion."

"—and that could lead to arrest and certain conviction."

"Our Pippin names," said Claude, "protect us from a Judas."

"Thirty pieces of silver can purchase a man a full life in London," remarked Elspeth. "At least for a year."

"It's an awful temptation," added Mathius.

"Dr. Johnson may say what he wishes," said Tobius, "and the king's men may dismiss his logodaedaly as despient. And should he ever offend some ensconced half-wit, he has many friends who would rush to pay his bail. We, however, are not so famous, nor so notorious. We are mere clerisy. We have not earned universal precony. We would be punished, bankrupted, hanged, or transported, and no one would wink or mourn."

"Just as it is ironic that knowledge of anatomy and progress in medicine should depend almost wholly on the blossoming of Tyburn Tree and the depredations of grave-robbers," said Claude, "so it is that advances in moral theories, and ethics, and politics are born in nocturnal covens such as ours."

"Dr. Johnson once ventured in here one bilious evening," recalled Mathius, "seeking refuge from the rain. He heard us talking and sampled our company."

"Half an hour later, though," said Swain, "he rose, begged our pardon, and fled!"

"The diet of discourse here was apparently indigestible!" laughed Tobius.

"The food for thought too exotic to his palate."

"He is a hard-working man, and I should have been proud to be one of his *Dictionary* clerks, but he is a devoted Tory."

Hugh thought for a moment, then said, "What you are saying, then, is this: If I told a magistrate, 'The king is not a god, and Parliament is not a convocation of infallible Olympians,' he could have me seized and punished?"

"As a modern Anaxagoras, sir," answered Abraham. "And, if you had communicated that notion to the populace, you would be hanged once for treason, once for sedition, and once for heresy."

"Nevertheless," said Hugh, "I think it most ironic—even cruel—that, while you are all dedicated to the pursuit of knowledge, you fear to know each other."

"That irony gnaws at us every meeting," said Mathius.

"But it does not prevent us from enjoying one another's company," added Claude.

"We are freethinkers, Miltiades," said Elspeth, "living in a free nation. Yet, even here, we are obliged to maintain the wise tradition of signing our various manifestos 'Anonymous.'"

"Half the letters one sees in the newspapers are signed with false names," remarked Abraham. "Most of them Roman."

"Would a normal man," asked Tobius, "resort to such a ruse if he did not fear brute reprisal or subtle persecution by those in a position to harness the engine of coercion?"

Swain put a hand on Hugh's shoulder. "That is why we were so happily startled by the contents of your essay, Miltiades. It was a fresh perspective on an old problem."

"We have decided to discuss malice at our next meeting," said Tobius, "and hope you will attend to audit our thoughts on the subject. In a fortnight."

Hugh looked crestfallen. "I may be away…with my parents," he said.

"No matter. I am sure that Muir will apprise you of our deliberations." Tobius rose and tapped the tip of the walking stick on the floor twice. "Gentlemen, let us adjourn this meeting." He picked up his glass of port.

All the members stood with their glasses. Hugh followed suit.

"Long live Lady Liberty!" said Tobius.

"Long live Lady Liberty!" repeated the members in unison. As Hugh said the words with them, a thrill shot through his being. He tilted his glass up to drink along with the others, and like them tossed his glass into the fireplace.

Chapter 21: The Toast

HUGH'S INITIATION INTO THE SOCIETY OF THE PIPPIN WAS AS RIOTOUS as its members would permit its meetings to become. In an age noted for the excess of its pleasures and vices, the Society was more sedate than most of the clubs that met in London's innumerable taverns, coffeehouses, ale-houses, and private billets. Its members did not drink themselves under the table, nor gorge themselves to groaning immobility from a table indiscriminately piled with steaming cookery. Its custom was to have a light meal with some moderate drink, and to debate politics, government, foreign affairs, art, literature, agriculture, business, and anything else deemed by the members worthy of sober discussion and sharp thought.

The ending toast was not sedate. It was radical, and risky. "Long live Lady Liberty" was not the same as "Long live the king" or "Long live His Majesty." The average magistrate, or high court justice, or army officer, had he overheard the toast unaccompanied by a toast to the king, would have instantly concluded that here was a conspiracy to overthrow the government and evict the throne. A toast that consciously omitted esteem for the sovereign was a toast uttered by men who did not esteem him, by men moved by another, insubordinate allegiance. To not wish the sovereign well, even as an afterthought or by rote, was to wish him ill. To neglect wishing liberty and the king well in the same breath was to sire a schism.

To the vessels of the "nomic" wisdom of the time, such a schism was imaginable only in terms of chaos, anarchy, civil war, unchecked rioting, universal destruction, and the reign of Satan. All good things, even liberty, emanated from the sovereign, with Parliament serving as a grand ombudsman. The sovereign was the lynchpin of existence, balancing church and state in both his hands; remove him, and society would crumble. The fate of the Commonwealth in the last century had proven that; was not Oliver Cromwell merely a king without a crown? The average Englishman, regardless of the power of his mind, could no more imagine a polity without a sovereign than he could a world without a God. A sovereign—whether he was elected, an heir, or a conqueror—was both a metaphysical and psychological necessity to him, the head of the body politic that ensured order and tranquility, even though, more often than not, the literal head was a criminal, wastrel, or functioning idiot. A sovereign was the keystone of society, an icon bathed in an aurora of sanctity and near-divinity, unapproachable except by his leave, even though he might be a dullard who despised Englishmen, as George II at this time was. The king could do no wrong; he was above judgment and prosecution, and so were his emissaries and any institution officially connected with his name. Parliament could do wrong, but was immune from criticism and accountability by all but its members for its multitude of wrongs. Virtually the only redress acknowledged by Parliament was a riot.

It was only the non-royal, non-elected, unenfranchised, unconnected, non-patronage-seeking Englishman who could do wrong and be punished, and there was an abundance of opportunity for him in this respect; the more than one hundred and fifty hanging offences and the swelling number of regulatory, commercial, and tax laws were designed with him in mind, not the sovereign or Parliament. For all that, however, his battle cry, his slogan, his chant, when he took to the streets in riot or immersed himself in a campaign against a new tax or law, remained "Life, Liberty, and Property."

The omission of a toast to the king, therefore, was not lost on Hugh. Up until then, though he was fascinated with the Society's members, except for Glorious Swain, he could not say whether or not he liked any of the men. But that omission, the ritual of words that were not said, was more impressive, and carried more weight, than anything else the men had said that evening. He felt a profound admiration for them. They could live for their own purposes, their own reasons, their own ends, without their heads needing to be anointed by the oily fingers of royalty. He shook hands with these men, and watched them leave the room, one by one, his eyes wide with happy esteem for them.

Hugh shook Swain's hand last. They were alone in the room. "You dared me to mention *Hyperborea*," said Hugh.

"It was a test," acknowledged Swain.

"Have they all read it?"

"Yes. Though not all own a copy, and not all prize it to the same degree."

Hugh sat down in a chair and gazed into the fireplace, lost in thought. The sounds of the tavern were as loud as ever, though still far in the background of his consciousness. He said, "I would say that your ritual—the aliases, the initiation, the secrecy, and all that—is an exercise in vanity, busy silliness meant to fabricate for yourselves some measure of importance, but I know that they are all men of strong convictions."

Swain found an extra glass and poured himself another draught of port, then sat down near Hugh. "The dangers are real enough, Mr. Kenrick. Men who risk such dangers are, I believe, entitled to some ritual, silly or no."

"Yes. I realize that now." Hugh looked at the pensive countenance of his friend. "Please don't take offence at what I am about to tell you."

Swain frowned. "I can't take offence at what I have not heard."

"Soon after we met, I wrote my father and asked him if our family owned shares in the Royal African Company, or the South Sea Company."

"Oh? Why?"

"Because I had learned some time ago that these enterprises are intimately engaged in the slave trade." Hugh paused. "I did not want our friendship to accommodate or overlook a wrong."

Swain let a moment pass before he asked, "And what was your father's answer?"

Hugh shook his head. "The family does not own such shares."

"And now your conscience is eased?"

Hugh looked perplexed. "I do not believe in a conscience, Mr. Swain. It's just that...I don't wish you to think that I am making an exception for you." He paused again, and struggled to find the words. "I no more patronize you, than you me."

Swain looked away from Hugh, then faced him again. His eyes were hard with anger, and the anger tinged his words. "You ought to some time journey to Bristol, young sir, or Liverpool, and contemplate the cargo ships sitting at anchor in their harbors, and listen for the wails and moans and cries coming from below their stinking decks, and then question your rejection of conscience. I have, many times, and asked myself what great power is required to eradicate the evil. They are kin, in a manner of speaking, suffering and dying on those ships, as fully capable of being what I am, yet so distant in everything that matters to me. Although they are strangers in my realm, I know that should I raise a finger in protest, I should soon join them, and I would shortly perish, if not from the misery, then by my own hand, like the Jews of York on the occasion of Richard the First's coronation." Swain paused and shook his head. "Do not think that because I am virtually free, the matter does not roast on the turning spit of my mind. But—I have yet no answer, no solution, no argument that would make the blind see. If I were to sacrifice myself by protesting on their behalf, I would sacrifice a reproach to the institution. 'The Scotsman, the Jew, the Irishman, the Spaniard, the Frenchman, and even the Chinaman, have all exploded our venomous presumptions about them,' the defenders of slavery could say. 'But where is the Negro who contradicts our belief that his race is a base, witless, soulless breed?'" Swain slapped a hand over his heart. "Well, here he is, sirs, and I am he." Swain sighed. "Beyond that, well, it is the only matter in which I confess helplessness."

"Can nothing be done for those people?" asked Hugh.

Swain shrugged. "No. Not until all England becomes a chapter of our Society. And that would leave Spain and France." He shook his head again, and smiled a little. "How can anything be done for them, sir, when we Englishmen are 'rudely stamped, unfinished, and scarce half made up,' in regard to our own liberty? We are a nation of piecemeal bondsmen, who have not yet espied perfect freedom." He noticed a fleeting grin on Hugh's face. "What amuses you?"

Hugh briefly explained his own quotation from *Richard the Third* to Hulton. Swain's dour expression made room for a chuckle. "We have much in common, my friend, even in the style of our thinking."

After a moment, Hugh asked, "And if my family had shares...would you still speak to me?"

Swain shook his head. "As you do not believe in a conscience, I do not charge sons with the sins of their fathers. I know that your family would not own those shares for long, once you had a say in the matter." He paused. "Thank you for being honest with me, Mr. Kenrick." He gestured to the table. "I will tell you what decided me to accept the invitation of the Society—more than their esteem for me, more than the prospect of enjoying the company of my equals."

"What?"

"Rum."

"Rum?"

"The Society has, from its earliest days, abstained from it. Rum, whether of English or French origin, comes from the sugar islands of the Indies, whose plantations employ slaves almost exclusively, except for convicts sentenced there for servitude, which they usually do not survive. Jamaica and Barbados are our courts' first choice of slow execution. The places have such a bad reputation that prisoners are known to have begged to be hanged instead, or have killed themselves, rather than be transported to the Indies. The slaves do not fare much better. The weather and the work consume them like a glutton eating fistfuls of black currants. Of course, there are many other things of slave origin that the Society could abstain from—sugar itself, and tobacco, coffee, the meanest cloths, and perhaps even tea—but then we should starve ourselves. So the symbol of protest became rum, the warmest, sweetest beverage we know."

"I have finished the play, milord."

Hugh and Glorious Swain turned in their chairs to see Hulton standing at the entrance to the room. Hugh rose. "I must go now, Mr. Swain. But we should meet again, before I leave for the holidays."

Swain stood up. "Yes, my friend. Leave word with Mrs. Petty, and we can arrange a rendezvous. I stop by here several times a week."

"Good night, my friend," said Hugh, shaking Swain's hand again. "And thank you for your sponsorship." He paused to grin at the man. "When you were admitted, surely it could not have been Agnes Petty who completed your tripos!"

"No," laughed Swain, "it was Mrs. Petty herself. She was pried from my lap only with great difficulty by my brothers! Never again!"

And they parted.

On their way back to Windridge Court, Hugh and Hulton were silent for a while. The light of Hulton's lantern revealed some solitary snowflakes whirling in the air before them. Then Hugh said, "It's a wonderful thing, Hulton, to feel this way about some fellow men. It allows one to move ahead with one's life without the brake of a cloying, melancholy disgust for the others."

"Yes, milord," replied Hulton. "I saw your friends leave by way of the tavern. They seemed like thoughtful gentlemen."

"They are. How did you find the play?"

"Illuminating, milord. Richard the Third was a right bastard, and seemed to have the best lines, which were instructive. I would not have wanted to be in service in his household. I might not have survived the employment."

Hugh laughed, and slapped the butler on the back.

Hulton seemed to remember what he had said, and added, in a near-whisper, "Is it permitted to refer to a late king as a bastard, milord?"

"Hulton, it is right to call a late or living king anything—or nothing at all!"

"Yes, milord," replied Hulton, who felt the tingling, dangerous thrill of being willing to lie for his master at any time, for any reason.

Chapter 22: The Peerage

HUGH REPEATED THE LIE IN ANSWER TO HIS UNCLE'S CASUAL QUERY over breakfast the next morning. His personal affairs, he reasoned, should be of no concern to his uncle, especially if they concerned the Society of the Pippin; he knew that his honesty would be used by his uncle as a weapon against him. He did not feel morally bound to tell the Earl that particular truth. So he lied as casually as his uncle had pried, and listened with indifference to the mild rebuke the Earl had voiced over the insult to Sir Henoch Pannell.

His indifference to his uncle's concern allowed him to reply: "I don't think that anyone raised to the petit peerage—such as Sir Henoch—ought to be permitted to sit in the Commons. He ought to be made to sit with his alleged peers, or with the non-voting peers, and to endure their solicitous sneers and cold courtesy."

Basil Kenrick blinked in surprise at the reply. He could not decide whether it was Sir Henoch who was the object of his nephew's contempt, or Lords, or him. He found himself in the paradoxical position of agreeing with the boy. The little twinge of hope he felt in his breast that he was winning Hugh over to his perspective vied with the sharp dread that the boy actually despised the very notion of the peerage. He recovered enough, after that moment, to say, "He is a man of parts, nephew, and deserves some respect. He is chief of a party of members in his House that can greatly assist Lords in preserving the strength of this country and advancing its interests. I have convinced him that he should divert his warlike oratory from inveighing against the colonies to chastising Newcastle, so that this likely war can be speedily prosecuted and brought to a quick end."

"So, he has been allied with Mr. Hillier in the Commons?"

"That is true. And it is no impropriety. There are peers who control a dozen or more seats in the Commons. Our family is fortunate to have controlled merely one all these years. The squires of Dorset are quite independent, and will not be encroached upon, or bought. Likewise, we resist their encroachments."

Hugh merely frowned at this remark.

The Earl felt obliged to add, "The politics of the Crown is rich in inconsistencies and anomalies, nephew. Intrigue is the spice of a life of political action. You should not begrudge Sir Henoch's political fortune. He was made a baronet at the king's pleasure and by his assent, and there is no arguing against that, once the deed is done. It is exempt from examination." The Earl seemed to smile. He was feeling wise and superior. He was reciting facts that he knew his nephew could not alter with his Whiggish sentiments. "And—it is not strictly a peerage, petit or grand," he continued. "Someday, Sir Henoch may even be rewarded with a life peerage—a baronage, earldom, what have you—for whatever other services he may render to win the esteem of a ministry and the king. You should know that it is not uncommon for a mere member of the Commons to desert that House for Lords, though the late Earl of Orford, Mr. Walpole, early in his career, declined a title so that he might retain his influence in the Commons."

The Earl droned on about the power of the House of Lords, repeating facts already known to Hugh, and would have for the rest of the morning, but for Hugh's reminder that he must leave for Dr. Comyn's school. But his uncle had the last word.

"Both Houses have been sitting to late hours. You will come to Lords directly afterward, and observe how natural gentlemen comport themselves and mediate the Crown's and the nation's affairs."

Hugh dutifully complied. After classes later that afternoon, he deposited his books at Windridge Court, had a bite to eat, then walked reluctantly to the House of Lords. He was admitted to the Peers' Chamber without trouble by the attendant at the doors, once he had identified himself. As there was no gallery for spectators here, he stood below the bar with other spectators, many of whom were members of the Commons, and observed with little interest a sitting of his uncle's peers.

The Peers' Chamber was measurably more impressive than was the Commons, longer by about thirty feet, and more spacious for its more than two hundred legal occupants. There was more light here from great windows that curved with the ceiling thirty feet above, and more warmth coming from an ornate fireplace on the side. Rows of benches for the peers rested below long tapestries on the walls on both sides, depicting the defeat of the Spanish Armada. A magnificent gilded throne, and the canopy of state raised above it, looked to Hugh to be in a decrepit condition; this was the seat of the king, when he deigned to make an appearance. To the throne's right were seats for the archbishops of York and Canterbury, and further on, beyond the fireplace, seats for the lesser bishops—all peers, the Lords Spiritual.

Facing them from the other side of the chamber were the benches of the Lords Temporal above the rank of baron, for dukes royal and dukes raised, for earls, marquesses, and viscounts. On cross-benches separating the Lords Spiritual and Temporal sat the barons. There had always been more earls than barons, more barons than viscounts, and one or two lonely marquesses. In between the barons and the throne were the tables and woolsacks (cushioned chairs) of the Lord Chancellor or Speaker and his clerks, and places for the Lords Chief Justice of the King's Bench and Common Pleas, the Master of the Rolls, miscellaneous judges, and the Masters in Chancery.

The House of Lords acted, without ever having admitted it, as a senate, and viewed itself as a select body charged with the duty of checking the power of the Commons, though it was a standing question whether it acted on behalf of its members or for the nation. It often exceeded this implicit mandate, as when, in 1747, it reprimanded the editors of *London Magazine* and its rival *Gentleman's Magazine* for having breached the privilege and secrecy of both Houses for publishing accounts of the trial of the Jacobite Simon Fraser, Lord Lovat, and of other debates and occasions. Its members could be tried, but never punished, and were exempt from all corporal penalties but execution for a capital crime. A peer could only be judged by his literal peers; like the king, he was considered above the judgment of commoners; this was a political rationale, as well as an aristocratic one. It had been the privilege of Lord Lovat, though his hanging for treason was a public event that brought the city to a halt. The dignity of a peer was otherwise not to be subjected to whippings, brandings of the hand, the pillory, penal servitude, or other standard punishments.

The House of Lords debated the same matters as did the Commons, and its veto and amendment powers could steer the Commons in a direction more favorable to the peers' sentiments and interests. If the two Houses could not reconcile by established procedures their differences on a resolution or bill, managers of the Houses would arrange a conference between them in the adjoining Painted Chamber, so-called because of the classical themed frescoes on its walls, the appointed lords seated at a long table, the appointed Commons men standing in deference, hats in hand. More private bills were debated in Lords than public; these naturally concerned land and property. Lords was also the "supreme" court of the land, having final authority on cases that had exhausted the wisdom and purview of the law courts. Civil and criminal appeals from England, Ireland, and Scotland were the House's chief business after the hearing and debating of public and private bills, in addition to adjudicating writs of error involving constitutional issues, impeachments of peers, and the swelling number of divorce cases.

The House of Lords considered itself, after the Privy Council, the exclusive and privileged advisor to the king, and any member, or group of members, or even the House as a whole, reserved the right to call personally on the sovereign to offer direction on policy, strategy, or controversy.

The Commons was especially jealous of Lords for its judicial prerogative, and resentful of the fact that Lords could foil its best constructed or most well-intentioned bills, for endorsement by both Houses was necessary for a bill to become law—after the king's signature. Lords viewed the Commons as little better than an elected rabble and mouthpiece for the mob, and resented that House's power over money and supply bills, not to mention the necessity of having to expend precious time and money every election to guarantee friendly blocs of seats in St. Stephen's Chapel.

Hugh was aware of these facts, though the corrupt—and corrupting— link between the two Houses was not quite real to him. Parliament was an idealized abstraction, flawed in his mind only by a few technical blemishes, and by the fact that men like his uncle and Sir Henoch Pannell could have a role in it. Parliament the ideal and Parliament the fact sat in his mind in much the same manner as did his knowledge of the solar system: There was his conception of the sun and its six planets and their satellites, derived from charts and descriptions in books; and there was the orrery, that imperfect but still marvelous, whirling representation of it. As Hugh did not have a mathematician's knowledge of the solar system, he did not have a solution to Parliament's blemishes. He was certain, however, that there was something wrong with the institution, and this certainty stemmed not exclusively from a knowledge of politics or political history—which was growing formidable—but from the unflawed knowledge of his own existence, coupled with an implicit resolve that neither the solar system nor Parliament ought to be an impediment to his life.

Hugh stood for an hour below the bar, straining his hearing to listen to exchanges between some of the peers on some private enclosure bill. The spectators around him whispered or talked among themselves. His uncle sat in a row of other berobed and beribboned peers, and nodded to him with cold approval. The earls on either side of him seemed to be asleep. The peers looked like guardians of some sacred responsibility. He knew that, in fact, it was less than what it ought to be. The scene before him was his future, or rather what his father and uncle insisted would be his future. He felt a terrific headache intrude upon his thoughts. The whispers and talk of the spectators and the speeches of the peers became painful. He turned and left for Windridge Court.

After that day, Hugh did not pursue any serious matter with his uncle. He listened to him, mentally shrugged, and escaped his uncle's company when he could. His task was to endure the time with his uncle, and then depart for Danvers for the holidays. The Earl of Danvers simply wanted to make his nephew tolerable.

Hugh was obliged to spend almost every evening in the Earl's company, sometimes alone with him, at other times at dinner with the Earl's guests. Glorious Swain left a note with Hulton inviting him to an evening at a nearby coffeehouse; Hugh wrote a letter of apology to his friend, explaining his predicament, and left it at the Fruit Wench with Mrs. Petty.

The single Sunday with his uncle began with services at St. Paul's Cathedral, where he and the Earl sat in a borrowed pew near other families of aristocrats. The minister on that day, in unctuous tones magnified by his canopied pulpit, weaved his sermon around certain passages from Richard Allestree's *The Whole Duty of Man*, a popular devotional· manual that preached against resistance against authority, and advocated passive obedience of a sovereign's laws, regardless of the consequences. "For what matters it to our mere fleshly existence," he spoke to the congregation, most of whose members were wealthier than he could ever dream to be, even for all his connections within the Anglican Church, "that it may be made miserable by the whims of a king, nay!—even by a king's ministers? A king and his satraps will answer to God as surely as will their subjects! And who is to say that a king's devilment is not a test by God of his children? A king is anointed, regardless of his character or personal construction, and to obey him is to obey God. His character, his vices, his weaknesses are all God's concern, not ours. And so, I ask anyone, who can stretch his hand against the Lord's anointed, and be guiltless?"

"I can," replied Hugh, his lips moving in silence. His glance was raised to study the great dome above him when the minister's words reached his ears, and he did not fully grasp the import of his reply until a moment later. He had been imagining the great feats of engineering required to erect the

dome and ensure that its walls and sides held it in place. It was a superb
edifice, he thought, and ought to serve some better purpose than as a place
for ministers to mouth platitudes and homilies for the instruction of posturing congregations. The place demanded reverence, he thought, for
heroes of some kind, for greatness in some form; for the adoration of something other than an elusive, allegedly all-knowing and all-powerful ghost.
The notion of God had always been superfluous to what drove Hugh to
think and act as he did. God was irrelevant to all his purposes, great and
small, absent from all his thoughts.

These thoughts stunned Hugh, but did not shake him. He had not committed apostasy, or deserted the faith; the faith had never found a comfortable home in his mind. It was the faith that deserted him, after a contentious and unprofitable tenancy.

Hours later, in the sanctum of his room, Hugh wrote these and companion thoughts in his notebook. He was pleased and proud for having had
them.

*   *   *

The two weeks passed for Hugh Kenrick with excruciating slowness,
gauged, it seemed to him, to the fall of stubborn, damp grains of sand in
some malign hourglass. He found relief from his uncle and his awareness
of time in his studies, at Dr. Comyn's school, at Mr. Worley's office, and in
Hyperborea. As the day of his departure for Danvers drew nearer, he began
to relax and congratulate himself for having endured his uncle's presence
and demands. He even generously credited his uncle for not being as auto-
cratic as he knew the man could be.

Another respite from Windridge Court was an evening with Glorious
Swain over supper at Shakespeare's Head tavern in Covent Garden, where
they lost themselves in talk about Romney Marsh's novel and the virtues
and vices of modern English literature.

Hugh felt reckless and invincible, enough so that he gladly accompanied his uncle to a rout at the Pantheon Pleasure Gardens on Oxford Street,
two evenings before his departure for Danvers. The Pantheon was a
smaller, more intimate version of Ranelagh, with a great brick stove in the
center of its circular promenade. It had been hired for the evening by
Guthlac Blissom, eighteenth Marquis of Bilbury. The Blissoms were an
ancient family, as old as the Kenricks. The Marquis and the Earl were once

schoolmates at Eton and Cambridge, and the Marquis now controlled eleven seats in the Commons. Unlike the Earl, however, he professed a sincere though unreasoning belief in the country's mercantilist laws and statutes, and would have been shocked to learn of his colleague's arm's-length connection to smuggling. Had he learned, he would have ventured to Lords and delivered an attack on the Earl of Danvers and on such law-breaking.

The rout offered a bounteous fare, an orchestra, and a dazzling array of the crème of London society, and was a gay, brilliant affair. The Marquis regarded himself as a connoisseur of the arts and letters, granting small pensions to painters, poets, and composers whose work he helped to exhibit, publish, or have performed. On this occasion he had had two rooms of the Pantheon turned into galleries for the work of several of his painters, while the orchestra would introduce two new country-dances by one of his composers.

The Marquis contrasted violently with both the affair and his artistic pastime. He was a tall, waxen-faced, cadaverous man who, even in his finery, looked as though he had just risen from a coffin. His wife, the Marchioness of Bilbury, was a squat, rotund, ugly woman whom no amount of finery or cosmetics could prettify. The jaded, the debauched, and even the most civil of their guests avoided protracted conversation with the pair and spoke with them only when absolutely necessary.

The eighteenth Marquis of Bilbury was the father of Brice Blissom, now merely Baron Ainslie, but heir-apparent to his father's title. He was their only son. He was not at his parents' side to receive guests when the servant announced the entrance of "The Right Honorable Lord Kenrick, Earl of Danvers, and his nephew, the Honorable Hugh Kenrick, Baron of Danvers." Brice Blissom was on the other side of the hall, entertaining other young, aristocratic bucks with a lewd story. He heard the announcement, though, excused himself from his friends, and rushed across the circle. His father had expressed a wish that he meet the Earl, an important political ally. But he had not expected to hear the name of the person who had disfigured his hands at Eton years ago. It was with an admixture of curiosity, anger, and obedience that he shot across the floor through the knots of guests.

He nearly stopped in his tracks when he saw Hugh Kenrick, the boy who had bested him in Rooker Alley. He continued on, biting his lip and feeling his face turn crimson. His father made the introductions, and the young men behaved as though they had never encountered each other before now. Their elders watched them closely for any signs of lingering animosity, but all they detected was an apparent mutual indifference in the young men to each other's presence.

The Marquis dismissed his son, instructing him to introduce Hugh to some of the more important guests.

As they walked together around the promenade, the young Marquis asked, "Have you told anyone?"

"No," replied Hugh. "The incident was not important enough to relate to anyone."

"Will you?"

"No, not unless someone asks me why I possess a sword bearing your coat-of-arms. Then I shall say I found it in a gutter, which would be near the truth."

The young Marquis did not wish to introduce Hugh to anyone, much less his friends, who would subject him, and not Hugh, to their acid mockery and make jokes about his gloved hands. So he stopped near a group of guests he was certain did not know the story. "So...you are a patron of blackamoors?"

Hugh shrugged. "I am the friend of a man, who calls me friend."

"You took up a sword in defense of that?" scoffed the Marquis. "At the risk of your own life?"

"And would again, sir. At times, one acquires friends in the most unusual circumstances. These friends make living with the rest of humanity tolerable."

"Blackamoors cannot be said to be wholly human, younker."

"Good only for service in the king's navy, or for porters' work?"

"Or worse."

Hugh shook his head. "Sir, have you not read your Aristotle? You were merely born, but allowed your rank to fashion your character and concerns. My friend also was born, but fashioned himself and his concerns with his own hands. Ergo, he is your moral and intellectual superior. He is a duke in his realm. You? You are a lackey in the realm of others."

The Marquis's features twisted in pure hatred. He hissed, "That is...unchristian, blasphemous filth you utter!"

"Call it what you will," replied Hugh, "but it was no insult, neither to you nor to my friend. It was merely a fact I wished to point out for your edification."

The Marquis stopped to face Hugh, and leaned his face closer to his nemesis's. "I will have satisfaction against you someday," he warned, "and the world will owe me a favor!"

Hugh smiled. "That is not a very Christian purpose, sir," he replied. After a pause, he said, "I knew you would be here this evening, sir, and in the coach on our way here, composed a doggerel in your honor. I had not planned to recite it to you, unless I received an invitation to. May I?"

"Go ahead!" dared the Marquis. "Add ridicule to your offenses!"

"'Blink, blink! I splashed my eyes with ink! Blink, blink! It's such a chore to think!'" Hugh grinned. "The first line can accommodate a thousand variations, as long as it rhymes with the second and agrees with its subject. The second line is immutable, though its noun can accommodate a thousand synonyms. To wit—'Blink, blink! I wish not to see the link! Blink, blink! It's such a task to think!' I shall call it 'The Bilbury Lament.'"

The Marquis's face had grown crimson again. He narrowed his eyes and stepped back. "Stay away from me, younker!" he warned.

Hugh bowed slightly. "As easily done as said, your lordship."

The Marquis turned sharply and retreated into the crowd.

The evening passed for Hugh without further incident. He could be charming and gracious in polite society when he had a reason to be, which tonight was some kind of satisfaction with himself. He inspected the paintings, mostly portraits and pastorals, in the galleries, and exchanged intelligent comments on them with other guests. He engaged in civil but inconsequential conversation on politics and the royal family with others without provoking them. He surrendered to a contagious benevolence and complimented several of the young ladies present—most of them daughters of aristocracy, some of them courtesans—on their beauty, and a few of them wondered why the handsome young man was blind to the inviting flutters of their fans. He even felt bold enough to essay a minuet, a courant, and a gavotte. At the end of the gavotte, he found left in his hand a lady's scented lace handkerchief; he smiled in bemusement and wondered which of the now-dispersed half dozen elegant women he had partnered with had put it there.

It was while he watched the orchestra perform a country-dance that he was startled to recognize a Pippin among the players. It was Steven—twin brother of Sterope—or Peter Brompton. The musician happened to glance up from his sheet music and missed a note on his violin when he in turn recognized the young aristocrat staring at him from the promenade. The youth he knew only as Miltiades inclined his head with a wink and a restrained grin. "Steven" returned the wink with a smile.

The young Marquis of Bilbury, who had surreptitiously watched Hugh Kenrick's course over the hours with seething anger, observed the silent greeting between Hugh and the musician with special curiosity. The Earl, who was too far away to note it, however, had observed his nephew's conduct throughout the evening with grudging approval.

Those who knew him well, knew that the best praise one could expect from the Earl was his silence. This was how he complimented his nephew. Other than desultory remarks on the health and fortunes of the elder Marquis and some of his guests, he said nothing in the coach that took them back to Windridge Court. Hugh volunteered an appraisal of two of the portraits he saw in the exhibit, and briefly commented on the quality of the orchestra. When they arrived at Windridge Court, Hugh and the Earl went to their separate chambers without further word, Hugh to begin packing for his journey home, the Earl to prepare to retire.

Two mornings later Hugh's baggage was loaded onto the Earl's coach, which would take him to Canterbury, where he would board an inn coach for Dover. There he would take a packet to Portsmouth and Poole. In his baggage were presents for his family, Roger Tallmadge, and Reverdy Brune, and also his notebook, which he called his "diary of ideas." He had begun making notes for an essay on the differences in the eudæmonist systems of the ancient world, part assignment by his instructor in moral philosophy, part private project. He hoped to have time to work on the essay during his holiday.

He gave Hulton two guineas as a present, and promised the butler-valet that he would return with an answer from his father about starting the man in his own tobacconist's shop. "And take care not to give my uncle cause to dismiss you, Hulton." Snowflakes began to fall and gather on the ground.

"I shall bury myself in Mr. Shakespeare's *Histories*, milord," replied Hulton, "and never frown when his lordship interrupts my leisure." He paused. "Are your pistols handy?"

"And primed," said Hugh, patting the pockets of his greatcoat. The blue coach bore the Kenrick coat-of-arms on its doors, and so stood a very good chance of being stopped by highwaymen. A loaded musket with double ball lay hidden beneath one of the interior seats. Hugh was determined not to be robbed.

The Earl had gone to Lords earlier in the morning, and Hugh had already bid him farewell. Hugh stepped into the coach, Hulton closed the door behind him, and they exchanged waves before the butler signaled the coachman to go.

*   *   *

That evening, before supper was served, Basil Kenrick came into Hugh's room and took stock of its contents, paying particular attention to the bookshelves and the desk. He returned to his own study, took out a sheet of paper, and made out a list of items. Then he rang for Alden Curle. When the major domo appeared, he asked, "Curle, where is Mr. Hulton?"

"He has retired, your lordship."

"Has he seen to my nephew's room?"

"He has cleaned and prepared Master Hugh's room, your lordship, and locked the door to await his return."

"Give Mr. Hulton the day free tomorrow, Curle."

"Yes, your lordship."

"Curle, there is something I want you to do tomorrow, while Mr. Hulton is out. Remove these things from my nephew's room, and bring them here." He held out the list.

Curle took it, glanced over it, and bowed. "Yes, your lordship."

Chapter 23: The Theft

Hugh Kenrick returned to Windridge Court in the middle of January, his mind still aglow with pleasant memories of his holiday at home in Danvers.

His parents, as he and they learned, could no longer regard him as just a child. Now he was a man, an independent force who moved for his own purposes and by his own power. This they all acknowledged the moment he alighted from the coach that brought him from Poole Harbor to the broad steps of the great house. His parents welcomed him as an intimate, were pleased with the adult stranger who embraced them, and accepted him as both a son, a man, and a special friend. They were pleased with their son, and pleased with themselves.

Hugh spent endless hours with his father, in his study, on horseback traversing the snow-dusted estate, hiking in the hills around the house, talking about school, politics, Mr. Worley's business, London, and the Earl. He was home two days before either his father or mother thought to ask him about the Earl's health and business. He told his father about his encounters with Sir Henoch Pannell, and his conversations with his uncle. He did not tell anyone about his latest clashes with the Marquis of Bilbury, or about the Society of the Pippin.

With his mother he took long walks arm-in-arm through the estate grounds, the cold winter air somehow accentuating their closeness. He read to her some of his school essays, sang songs with her as she played the forte-piano, and taught her the movements and steps of a new gavotte. He joined the family and invited neighbors in parlor games, in the staging of nonsense plays, and even in snowball fights with townsmen on the great lawn. It was an interlude of gaiety, laughter, good fellowship—and rest.

Hugh's parents were happy for him, and relieved for him, for it was apparent that he was forcing himself to endure the close proximity of his uncle. They were certain that an explosion would come someday, and that their son's practiced reticence would have dire consequences for him and the family.

"I'm glad that Basil hasn't much baited him," said Garnet Kenrick to his wife one evening, "and that Hugh hasn't taken what little bait Basil has tossed his way. But I'm still afraid that Hugh is merely a cask of gunpowder, and that every time Basil bids him 'good morning, nephew,' another pinch of the black stuff is added to it. And I cannot imagine what the spark could be that would touch it off."

"Would you have him behave any differently?" asked Effney Kenrick.

Her husband smiled, and in his smile was a mixture of fondness for his son and mischief for his brother. He shook his head once. "No."

Roger Tallmadge looked at Hugh with a benevolent envy, as he would an older brother who was brimming with tales and adventure stories from the great city of London. Hugh did not disappoint him. Hugh looked at Roger in the same way he looked at Hulton, as a friend who had the potential to become an even closer friend, on a par with Glorious Swain. Their reunion was exuberant, though Roger sensed that something was different about Hugh. He could not fathom the difference, and did not much bother to. He admired his friend, and could not even entertain the possibility that something could ever drive them apart.

Reverdy Brune could not stop looking at Hugh; that is, she caught herself looking at him, almost against her will, when she knew it was inappropriate to stare directly at a man. She, too, sensed something different in him, was fearful of it, and thrilled by it. Here, she thought, was a man who was going to be something, or someone. For the first time in their relationship, she was reluctant to speak. She did not wish to mock him, tease him, or practice on him her increasingly potent art of coy coquetry. Of all the people who spoke to Hugh during his stay, she said the least—less than even a servant—and she had every reason to say the most. She was unnaturally taciturn when they were together, whether alone or with others. She knew that little needed to be said to him, or by them to each other. She felt happy and fortunate that she was fated to a union with Hugh Kenrick.

Hugh reciprocated, and said little to her. He saw the woman who was to be his wife when the time came. She walked and moved with a sense of her own worth, with a pride that she was to be a part of his life. She saw him, he thought. This was all he required of her, for him to want her; to be seen and wanted by her, was enough.

Any doubts their parents might have had about the success of a marriage of Reverdy and Hugh were dispelled one evening when the couple danced a minuet. There was, especially during the dance, an extra element of solemnity in their movements, and how they held each other's eyes with a happy absorption that made them conscious of nothing but each other and the music that harmonized their motions. Reverdy's mother leaned closer to Effney Kenrick as they watched the pair, and from behind her fan, remarked, "It's difficult to tell, my dear, whether the music lends grace to them, or they to the music." Hugh's mother could only nod in agreement.

Two days after Twelfth Night, Hugh left Danvers for the return journey to London. He was aware of the fact that his uncle would be there, but the man's presence now loomed no larger in his mind than the ubiquitous presence of beggars on the city's streets. His father received a letter from the Earl not long after Christmas, in which he reported that his business in London was nearly concluded and that he would return to Danvers in a month when Parliament neared its recess. Hugh remained in high spirits even though his coast-skirting packet was nearly driven against some rocks by the sail-ripping winds of a winter storm, and when the inn coach from Canterbury was delayed in its departure for London by snow. From the London coach inn a hackney took him to Windridge Court through a freezing rain. He greeted with a grin the servant who rushed from the house to open the hackney door.

Once he was inside, he told a servant, "Please ask Hulton to come to my room."

The servant blinked and gulped once. "He is not here, milord."

"Where is he? On an errand?"

Again the servant blinked. "He was…dismissed, milord."

Hugh frowned and asked sharply, "Dismissed? Why?"

The servant paused to draw a breath. "I have been instructed by his lordship, milord, to request that you direct any inquiries to him that you might have about Mr. Hulton. We staff were all so instructed."

"Then get me Mr. Curle."

"This is his day off, milord. He went out, I know not where."

"Then I'll speak with my uncle."

"His lordship has gone to a concert at the Opera House, milord, and is not expected back until very late this evening." The servant lowered his eyes. "I am very sorry I cannot accommodate you, milord."

Hugh slapped his gloves against his leg once. "All right. Take my things to my room. Then bring me some tea and bread."

"Yes, milord." The servant rang for another man and together they carried Hugh's trunks and baggage up to his room.

Hugh had raised the idea with his father of establishing Hulton in a tobacconist's shop in the city, and his father had regarded the idea as both novel and agreeable. "And what would you do then for a valet? I could send you Mr. Runcorn, but he is nearly the major domo of our household, and it would be difficult to replace him. Besides, he and Mr. Curle are near trading blows on the Danvers commons. Well, I'm thinking ahead of myself."

Hugh had shrugged. "I'll find someone to replace Hulton on recommendation. I don't require much, and Windridge Court will not be as busy once Uncle has returned home. I'll raise one of the servants."

It was then that Garnet Kenrick revealed to his son that he was toying with the idea of venturing into a banking partnership with other men of means. "Not as greatly capitalized as, say, Vere's and Glyn's, but large enough to meddle in the trades. There is money to be made on commissions on bills of exchange and credit, even during a war. We could collect a percentage of Mr. Hulton's revenue until he paid back the original costs of setting him up... He would need to be introduced to the essentials of trade, of course." He smiled at his son. "I like this idea, Hugh. There is some risk in it, of course, but it appeals to me. It would be a small venture, perhaps just one of many small ventures that could grow to greater things, and our bank would be sending woolens to Portugal and manufactured goods to Holland and Russia and so on...but there is potential in this modest idea..."

He had wanted to share this news with Hulton. But now the man was gone. Hugh's eyes narrowed in a suspicion he did not want to credit until he learned the truth behind Hulton's dismissal.

It was while he was shelving some books he had brought back from Danvers that he became aware of things that were missing from his room: a pair of shoes with silver buckles; a suit of clothes; several pair of silk hose; some shirts; a porcelain statuette of a Greek goddess disrobing for a bath; the Marquis of Bilbury's sword, which he had left propped next to his desk. Some candles. And some books—including *Hyperborea*.

He checked his desk last. Nothing seemed to have been disturbed. There was his brass top, sitting next to a silver bowl of gold guineas and silver crowns. The topmost of the coins had collected some dust. From a sconce over the desk was suspended Reverdy's miniature portrait in its silver locket. He finished shelving his books, knowing that he must control his shaking hands.

When the servant appeared again with the tea and biscuits, Hugh waited until the man had laid out the things on a little table before he asked, "What has happened here?"

"Milord?" replied the servant anxiously.

"Things of mine have been removed from this room. Why?"

The servant gulped. "It must have to do with Mr. Hulton, milord. He was caught stealing, you see, and his lordship dismissed him—Oh, milord! I have told you too much! You are to ask his lordship for the particulars...!"

"You may go," said Hugh abruptly. His suspicion was now half confirmed.

The servant bowed out of the room, glad to escape the murderous fury he saw in Hugh's face.

It did not matter to Hugh who removed or stole his things. The fact was that they were gone. They were extensions of his body, of his life. He felt the same about their absence as if he had been physically assaulted. They were his things, as much his as his arms and legs. But he would not yet allow himself to draw a conclusion about who was responsible for the violation, not until he he had all the elements before him.

He had finished, in Danvers, his paper on ancient eudæmonist systems. He reread it while he waited for his uncle to return.

Near one o'clock in the morning he heard voices downstairs. Hugh rose and left his room. He heard his uncle instruct a servant to prepare his room for retirement while he saw to some business in his study.

*   *   *

After a cordial, though strained exchange of pleasantries about the holidays with the Earl in his study, Hugh bluntly asked, "Why was Hulton dismissed?"

The Earl had expected this curtness, but still did not like it. "He was a thief, nephew. I discharged him when his thefts were discovered. There was not a single thing that is either recovered or still missing that could not have earned him a hanging, had I elected to bring charges. But, it was the season of benevolence, and so I granted him mercy. I warned him that if he was ever seen near this house again, he would be arrested, and the devil may take him."

"Who discovered these thefts?"

"Mr. Curle. He noticed some things poking out from beneath the villain's cot downstairs. He brought the matter to my attention, as was his duty."

"And did you not suspect that Mr. Curle could have engineered these 'thefts'? He has never liked Mr. Hulton."

The Earl's face flushed red. "That is a slanderous insinuation about a man who has been in honest and loyal service here for years! If Mr. Curle had been here to hear it, I would expect you to apologize to him."

"Mr. Curle knows what I think of him, sire, and he's never expected an apology. And if I once refused to apologize to a duke, I would hardly stoop to apologizing to that chap."

"I would demand one, sir," replied the Earl.

Hugh changed the subject. "What else was taken? From the house, that is?"

The Earl poured himself some brandy before answering. "Some plate, a tea chest, a pair of silver candleholders your grandfather had made as a present to Queen Anne—she died before he could make the gift, you know. A quarter gross of candles that cannot be accounted for. Odds and ends, bric-a-brac, some table service." The Earl knew that his nephew did not believe him but could not prove any suspicions he might have. Everything that was still "missing" had been taken by Curle and dumped into the Thames the day after Hugh had departed for Danvers.

Except for the books. These had been burned in the study's fireplace, the flames tended by the Earl himself before he departed that evening for the opera.

Hugh asked, "Why would he steal a book? Specifically, *Hyperborea*? It has no pictures or engravings in it, and he would not know its value. It is the only book of value missing from my collection."

The Earl shrugged. "There is a market for filth, nephew. For all kinds of it. Pictures, objects, and even books. These things, I hear, fetch fabulous prices, and change many leprous hands. That must have been the fate of your precious books. Especially this libelous fiction you refer to. Your father should never have given it to you, in any event."

"Then why would such a well-read, observant thief not help himself to the bowl of money on my desk? There are twenty-six pounds in it, all told."

"I do not know, nephew."

"And the Marquis of Bilbury's sword? It was a beautifully made sword, and would have fetched a handsome price in the thieves' market."

The Earl sniffed at his nephew's audacity. He had inspected the sword, and wondered why his nephew had it. "I know nothing about that, nephew. If it was taken by Hulton from your room, well, what were you doing with it?"

"I caught the young Marquis and his friends taunting a man one night. I bested him in a fight and took his sword as a prize. He did not know who I was then, but he knows it now."

The Earl frowned. "Is that what you do here, nephew? Get into fights and behave like a rascal or a drunken apprentice?"

"That is a question you should put to the Marquis, sire," replied Hugh, not caring what his uncle thought now. "When were these 'thefts' discovered?"

"A few days after you took our coach to Canterbury," answered the Earl, staring with undisguised malice at his relation.

Hugh rose from his chair before he lost control of his anger and contempt and blurted out an accusation of complicity of his uncle in a conspiracy not only to remove Hulton from the household, but to punish him. Hulton, he realized, had merely been the means to a larger end. He did not believe in Hulton's guilt; it was a certainty that went beyond the fact that the valet had had numerous opportunities to steal. "Good night, sire." He turned without further word and left the room. He had seen the look of interest in his uncle's eyes when he mentioned the Bilbury sword, a look of foreknowledge, of eager curiosity—but not of surprise.

The Earl chuckled at his nephew's exit. He was content that Hugh could prove nothing, though the suspicion would fester in his mind. That was punishment enough! He turned and rang for Claybourne, and left his study to retire for the night.

Hours later, Hugh came downstairs and through the darkened house went to his uncle's study. He approached the fireplace, and used a poker to stir the ashes beneath the dying fire. He soon came upon a charred but recognizable corner of a cover of one of the volumes of *Hyperborea*, and then the half-consumed fragment of a spine. There was even a whole page, from the center of one of the volumes, scorched brown but still readable. With the poker he moved them out of the ashes and embers to a spot just behind the firedog to let them cool off. Then he picked up the page and dropped it into his dressing gown. The other fragments he let lie, so that they would be discovered. His uncle should have had the fireplace cleaned out after committing the crime.

That morning he had breakfast in his room; he did not wish to see his uncle. He walked alone to Dr. Comyn's School to report his return and to learn what his schedule of instruction would be for the months ahead. Then he took a hackney to Benjamin Worley's office on Lion Key. Once they were past the mutual greetings, he made an unusual request. It startled the merchant, but he complied. "Does your father know, milord?" he asked.

"No. I shall write him at the first chance."

"Well…let me think for a moment. There are so many places…Ah, yes! I know just the place! And not far from Windridge Court. On Cutter Lane. There's a solicitor there I use now and then, Nathan Rickerby. Owns the premises, and shares the ground flat with other legal types. Lives with his family on the second flat, and rents furnished lodgings on the third. Board, of course, is included. No drinking allowed, and no table on Saturdays and Sundays. I'll draft a letter of introduction for you immediately, milord."

"Without it mentioning my association with my uncle," said Hugh.

"Yes…of course. But, milord, how will you explain yourself?"

"Oh, I'll make something up. I'll say that I'm the son of a merchant who's taking his family to India, or America, and that they're enroute."

"Yes…I'm sure you'll be able to invent some plausible background."

"And I'll pay the month's rate with ready money. That should quench his inquisitiveness."

"It will, no doubt about that, milord," said Worley. "And, as you're the epitome of a gentleman, he won't risk probing you too far. Well, let me get on with this letter…" He paused, though, because curiosity got the better of him. "May I ask what is the nature of the dispute between you and your…his lordship?"

Hugh did not mind telling him. "He's a liar, and a thief, and he destroyed some of my property while I was away. Or had it stolen. It is his house—and my father's—but I will not stay in it while he is there. He is returning to Danvers in a month."

"I see…" Worley drafted a letter of introduction, then handed it to the clerk whose impeccable handwriting had won him the position of chief correspondence clerk at the firm. He worried, though, that his action might embroil him in a family affair.

Hugh presented the letter to Mr. Rickerby later that morning. The solicitor was sufficiently convinced by Hugh's changed story that he was the son of a Devonshire squire whose family was preparing for a Grand Tour on the Continent, and that he, Hugh Kenrick, had been sent ahead to acquire a knowledge of Holland, Prussia, Spain, and Italy at Dr. Comyn's before the family came to London to collect him and embark on the two-year excursion. He showed Hugh the single room in the rear of the third floor. Hugh approved of it, and handed him a month's rent, one pound.

In the afternoon, Hugh hired some porters to transfer his books, clothing, and other personal possessions to Cutter Lane. His uncle was at Lords. Alden Curle looked disapprovingly at the parade of porters coming and going on the main staircase. "What means this, milord?"

"What it means, Mr. Curle," replied Hugh, "is good riddance to you."

"But...what shall I tell his lordship?"

"That he offended me, more than you are wont to do, when you ask me questions I have not given you leave to ask."

Curle stepped back, opened his mouth to speak, then closed it and turned to retreat down a passageway.

When he was settled in his crowded lodgings on Cutter Lane, Hugh walked to the Fruit Wench. Mrs. Petty greeted him and gave him two sealed letters. One was from Glorious Swain, advising him of a Pippin meeting to be held in a week. The other was from Hulton, dated a week and a half ago. Hugh went to a table and read it:

"Most Honorable Sir:

While you was away, the most evil thing happened to me. I have been discharged by his lordship for theft of objects from the household. These objects were found, it was said, under my humble bed in the servants' quarters, by Mr. Curle, who reported this to his lordship, who came to see for himself.—The day after you departed, I was given a day free, and the next day I had been sent out with Cook to the market. When I returned, I was taken to his lordship's study and shown these objects, that had been put there, and told to account for where they were found. I could not do this, for these objects were in their proper places when I last saw them. His lordship also asked me about things that were nowhere to be found. I could only say that I don't know, your lordship. Forthwith, his lordship told me that, as it was the season, he would discharge me that moment, instead of calling the watch to take me to gaol and bringing charges. I was turned out with my bag, hurriedly packed, and escorted out of the courtyard, and told never to come near the Court again. I will say here, swearing on a bible if I had one, and upon my honor, as a lord would swear at a Parliament trial, I am not guilty of these actions. I am not a thief. I will confess I carried the book of Shakespeare histories you lent me in the back of my breeches, and forgot it was there until hours after I was turned out, so much was I dismayed. I will keep it, and return it if we meet some day. Many of your possessions was on the table in his lordship's study, even your favorite book, and a fine sword, and the clothes you had me purchase for your larks about the city. I cannot think how all these things I saw and then the objects that were said missing could fit beneath my mattress. Your possessions were in their proper places only the day before when I dusted your room and made it tidy. I do not know who on the staff would hate me so that he would so trouble himself, except Mr. Curle, but I would not credit him with the cunning. I have sought employment in service, as I know no other trade, but his lordship has put out the bad word on me, and I have been rudely treated wherever I have applied. So I have taken the King's shilling, for patriotism in the war, and for lack of chance in private service, for otherwise I must beg in the streets. It is a new regiment raised here in London, and the sergeant says I will rise in it for I can write decently. He lent me the pencil and paper on which I write this. I will now shoulder a musket, and maybe someday command men as I have been commanded. The officer who inspected me is not much older than yourself, milord. I bid your good self farewell, and thank you for all the kindnesses and considerations you have shown me. I am afraid of this new business, but a turn in the world might make me the man you think I ought to be.—Your most grateful and appreciative servant, Hulton."

The letter was written in a labored, mongrel style, half print and half script. There was a blot close to the crude signature, noted Hugh. Was it his imagination, or was it a tearstain? He rose, went to the serving bar, and waved for Mrs. Petty. He asked her, "The man who left this with you: Was he alone?"

Mrs. Petty shook her head. "No, dearie. He was in the company of a recruitin' sergeant, who stood over him like a hawk whiles he scratched out that note."

"What regiment?"

"I don't rightly recall, sir. Never saw the uniform in here before. New piping on the cuffs I don't recollect seein' anywhere."

Hugh sighed. He wished Hulton had been more specific about the regiment he had joined. He gave Mrs. Petty a shilling for her trouble, and left the Fruit Wench.

Chapter 24: The Letters

U NAWARE OF THE EVENTS AT WINDRIDGE COURT, GARNET KENRICK wrote to his brother, the Earl:

"Brother Dear: Although the details may cause you to nod off, I have entered into a banking partnership, as I had warned you I might before you left for London, and I owe you at least a brief sketch of the enterprise. I have been in correspondence with the three other principals for about a year. I will bring the largest amount of money to it—£10,000— while the others will pledge £5,000 each. Here is the roster: George Formby, a Lancashire mercer extraordinary, who also owns an ore smeltery which regularly pigs Swedish iron; John Swire, of Stafford, who has turned his late father's pottery into a bustling capital of crockery; and James Purse-house, who with his late father built up a prosperous grocer's or whole-saler's trade in London (and who comes to our project with a most felici-tous name!). These men are also active in insurance, and to my knowledge have suffered no untoward losses in that realm, which points to a valued keenness for success or failure. Pursehouse owns shares in two mer-chantmen, and Formby and Swire own shares in the East India Company and are husbands of the Indiamen *Regale* and *Cronus*, respectively.

"Now, although I have provided the largest bloc of capital, and will direct some old but mainly new business to this fresh combination, I chose to insist that our family name be omitted from the public name of this enterprise. I wish this venture to sail on its own wind, and not because our family are known to be connected with it. Mr. Worley will continue to deal principally with the bank of Grimme, Holtby & Brizard on Lombard, so far as our present business is concerned, and the *Ariadne's* balances will also continue there. Our personal accounts will be maintained at Martin's Bank. Before you leave London, I invite you to call on the new bank's premises, which is on Lombard, closer to Blakely Court than the Change Alley, and directly across the way from the Catherine Wheel Coffeehouse. Mr. Pursehouse owns this three-story building, and resides on the second floor with his family. The street floor will be converted into the banking office proper. The clerks will billet on the third. Mr. Pursehouse will manage our own accounts. It would be a nice thing if you expressed an interest in pledging some capital, though neither he nor I will press you on the matter..."

Basil Kenrick read the balance of the letter, and sniffed at the invitation and the comments that preceded it, and set the letter aside, though he was tempted to treat it as he had his nephew's note of two mornings ago. Hugh's note had been much shorter, and less welcome:

"Sire: It is obvious that my person and presence excite no love, nor even the slightest benign feelings in you for me, just as, admittedly, your person and presence excite no fondness in me for you. The reasons for this mutual animosity need not be gone into here, as they are too well known to both of us. I enclose with this note evidence of your duplicity, as proof that I know you are the author of a grave falsehood and offense, and the perpetrator of an injustice that may cost Mr. Hulton his life. He was a better friend to me than you could ever be. Should you wish to communicate with me, please do so through Mr. Worley, or my father. Hugh."

Hugh's note, and the page from *Hyperborea* that had been pinned to it, were now ashes in the fireplace. No, thought the Earl, he would not be communicating with Worley or Pursehouse or Hugh. He merely despised Worley and Pursehouse for being simple commercial men. He hated Hugh for the act of daring to suspect him of the theft ruse, for having rooted through the fireplace for evidence of it, for having thrown that evidence back in his face. How dare he, a scion of the aristocracy, think that prerogatives exercised by a peer could be judged by the standards of the *mobile vulgus*? There was evidence of the corruption of the nobility! Damn them all, thought the Earl, including his brother and his presumptuous son! Damn them all! A lord can commit no definable wrong!

Secretly—secret even to himself—he damned anyone who could make him feel guilt for what he was, for what it was in his power to do, as he knew they could do, and had done. The guilt fought a nocturnal battle in his mind with what he wished the world to be, and though vanquished, remained at large on the periphery of his consciousness, stinging him with its muted taunts. What a mean, vicious creature was guilt! He would have nothing to do with it! Let it camp in the wastes of his soul, starved of recognition, and hurl its poisonous pebbles at the sturdy stockade of his concerns! Let anyone see if it bothered him!

Upon reading Hugh's note, and the page from the unmentionable book that had accompanied it, the Earl had calmly set them aside, but then rose and flung them into the fireplace as though they were vipers. He angrily rang for Mr. Curle and demanded the name of the servant responsible for emptying the ashes and cleaning the fireplace. When he learned the name, he gave the butler an order to dismiss the man, and reprimanded Mr. Curle for not having seen to it that the staff more thoroughly performed their duties.

This morning, he glanced once again, with amusement, at his brother's letter, then rang for Claybourne to help him dress for this afternoon's session at Lords. He would reply to his brother at his leisure, he thought. And as Claybourne carefully shaved him, and as the assistant adjusted the garters of his hose, Basil Kenrick wondered where his nephew was, and what reduced circumstances he must be enduring. He chuckled once at some dark thought, and Claybourne's razor slipped with a sting and drew blood from a small cut. The Earl jumped out of his chair and slapped the valet. "Be careful, you damned fool!"

"You...laughed, your lordship," said Claybourne, astounded by that, and stunned by the only physical violence the Earl had ever subjected him to.

"I'll laugh when and as I please, you ninny, and you'll learn to shave around it, or you'll follow Hulton!"

Claybourne bowed and stammered, "Yes, your lordship."

*   *   *

Hugh wrote to his father and apprised him of the incident, attaching to his letter Hulton's farewell missive. "It is a breach between me and Uncle that can never be mended. He is moved by a malice I cannot comprehend, though I believe that he would bear less malice toward me were I his fawning sycophant. But then I should earn—and rightfully deserve—his contempt. And, perhaps, yours. Father, I am wounded beyond care, even should he attempt restitution. I do not wish to have a reason ever to speak with him again."

Hugh moved back into Windridge Court after his uncle departed for Danvers, and only because, now that trustworthy Hulton was gone, he was nominally responsible for the place and its contents. He searched the city's bookshops and managed to replace all his missing books but *Hyperborea*.

Garnet Kenrick read his son's letter and Hulton's over breakfast one morning, pursed his lips in anger, and handed the letters to his wife. "What are we to do with him?" he asked, referring to his brother, not his son.

When Effney Kenrick finished reading the letters, she replied, quietly but with finality, "Bear him as we would a cross, until he is gone from our lives."

Her husband stared at her in amazement. These were the first rancorous words he had ever heard her speak about anyone. She looked at him and made no effort to hide the meaning and emotion he saw in her eyes. He thought he should feel offended by her words, but instead reached over and grasped the wrist of the hand that held Hugh's letter. "Until then," he said softly, "we shall bear it together."

The next day brought a perfunctory note from his brother, advising him of his pending return, and mentioning Hulton's dismissal only in passing. In light of his son's letter, Garnet Kenrick knew that his brother's assertions were lies. He implicitly trusted his son's veracity, and implicitly trusted his brother's deceitfulness. The Baron's eyes narrowed in contempt, and he was tempted to crumple his brother's letter into a ball and hurl it across the room. But he controlled himself, and showed it to his wife.

When the Earl arrived three weeks later, the Baron confronted him with the letters, Hugh's and Hulton's. He waited calmly until his brother had read them. The Earl finished them and tossed them to the floor. "Whose word do you trust, dear brother: mine, or your son's and some menial's?"

"My son's and the menial's, Basil."

The Earl turned away in his chair, and said, with bitter peevishness, "You are no brother of mine, Garnet."

"That, too, is untrue," replied the Baron. "You see, dear brother: It is not merely a matter of it being your word against his and Hulton's. All the tangible evidence has been destroyed, or disposed of. The evidence, for my belief in the statements of one or the other, lies within your character, and Hugh's. You are wont to be vindictive; he truthful, and valorous." He sighed. "In truth, Basil, I wish I could say that we were not brothers."

Basil Kenrick shot from his chair and waved a fist in the air. "I would prefer that he got drunk and spent himself into debt than he behave as he does!" he shouted. "That is normal behavior for one his age! He doesn't honor me! He abides me! I could see through his insolence the whole time!"

Garnet Kenrick shrugged. "In light of your past treatment of him, I rather think that that is a just attitude for him to adopt."

"He is a nemesis!"

"How?"

"I don't know! He...frightens me! That is all I can say!"

The Baron picked up the two letters from the floor. "Hear this, dear brother: I will neither punish him for his actions, nor check his path. He is bringing honor to this family, something absent from it for some genera-tions, as we both know." He frowned. "You are a peer of the realm, Basil, yet you dishonor us with your childish foolery."

"Do you hate me, too?"

The Baron shook his head. "Why, no, Basil, I don't hate you. But more and more, it is only when I see you that I dislike you to distraction." He paused. "Effney and I will ensure that the two of you are kept separated, when you and he are in the same vicinity. We will do this more for his sake, than yours." He waited for a reply, and when none came, said, "Tomorrow, after you've rested from the journey, you may tell me what you have accom-plished in Lords." He turned to go, but stopped to add, "And be assured of this, dear brother: I shall find another copy of that novel you burnt, and make a gift of it to Hugh again. Do me the honor of not assuming the power of the French Parlement or the Congregation of the Index."

"What are you talking about?" demanded the Earl.

"Surely you remember, Basil," said the Baron with mock gaiety. "Some years ago Montesquieu's *The Spirit of the Laws* roused the indignation of the Papist establishment in Paris, and was put on the Prohibited list by the Papal Court. It is one of the books that Hugh writes is missing from his shelf. I find it odd that you should frown upon it, for it pays us Englishmen numerous compliments."

The Earl snorted at the observation. "Why do you defend him?" he asked. "He is nothing like you, either!"

The Baron cocked his head in thought, then said, "He is imbued with a species of vitality which neither of us possesses, Basil, but which it would be a crime and a sin to suffocate. I do not know what is its cause, but it is no nemesis to me, and I am frightened less by it than by the punishment with which some men are driven to reward it."

Chapter 25: The Thinkers

IN MARCH OF THE NEW YEAR THE HOUSE OF LORDS PASSED A BILL ENTITLED "An Act for the bettering of the Militia Forces in the Several Counties of that Part of Great Britain, called England." In April, French forces invaded the Mediterranean island of Minorca, a British possession. In May, Admiral John Byng, sent by George II to relieve the island, failed to, and for this almost a year later was court-martialed and subsequently executed by firing squad on the quarterdeck of the *Monarch*, a third-rate warship captured from the French ten years before.

On May 27, the king, through the Lord Chancellor, formally advised both Houses of Parliament of his declaration of war against France. Siraj-ud-Daula, nawab of Bengal, captured Calcutta in June after fierce fighting and a loss of seven thousand Indian troops. One hundred and forty-six Englishmen and other Europeans were afterwards confined by him in a 14-by-18-foot jail, already known as the "Black Hole" by drunken sailors who had been detained in it, and overnight all but twenty-two suffocated to death in the 100-degree heat. Louis Joseph Montcalm de Saint-Veran, French commander in North America, captured British Forts Oswego and George in August, and began construction of Fort Ticonderoga.

In Virginia, the tobacco harvest was jeopardized by the absence of small planters and field-hands, who, being in the militia, had been sent to the frontier to quell French-incited Indian raids. Frederick the Great of Prussia, also in August, invaded Saxony with 67,000 men. Russia, stung by a treaty of neutrality between Frederick and England, sided with France and Austria. History's first world war, variously called the Seven Years' War, the Third Silesian War, and the French and Indian War, had begun in earnest.

In England itself, the pin-making industry of Lancashire continued to supply the nation with pins and provide employment for hundreds of children who otherwise would have perished or had to endure near-slavery in parish workhouses. Liverpool was beginning to rival Bristol as a port and commercial center, and a canal begun the year before to connect it with the coal-mining region would eventually reduce the cost of carrying coal to the Irish Sea and cause the auctioning of all the packhorses it replaced. The woolen weavers of Gloucester succeeded in having passed an Act of Parliament that allowed justices to fix their piece rates. Surgeons, who studied anatomy, were still regarded as "inferior tradesmen" by physicians, who practiced blood-letting as a standard panacea, prescribed potions composed of herbs, saltpeter, and birds' beaks, and strived to preserve and codify the often deadly admixture of medieval lore, primitive notions of cause and effect, and wishful thinking concerning the relief of human ailments. Joseph Black, a British chemist, discovered carbon dioxide in this year, though oxygen itself would remain hidden behind that elusive, contradictory, and perplexing relic of ancient Greek science, phlogiston, an element thought to be produced by fire and human respiration.

Concurrent with the escalation of hostilities among the European powers, the intellectual realm advanced haltingly. Old ideas, beliefs, and customs fought a desperate and often vicious rearguard action against ineluctable refutation and the phenomenon of man being recast as a Lockean individual capable of acting on his own power for his own ends.

The phenomenon was not welcome in all quarters: there were those in this realm who wished men to remain a deferential subject of the church and state, to labor under those institutions' rules and conditions to produce the glories and wonders of the age, tithed by one hand and taxed by the other. The French were the most enthusiastic exponents of the phenomenon, but could not practice it openly under an absolute monarchy allied with a powerful church. The English, by grace of a monarchy limited by a jealous legislature, indulged it by default. In France, Diderot was imprisoned in the Château de Vincennes for offending a Court lady with his method of arguing in favor of Locke's thesis on the evidence of the senses. In England, while a man could be tried in the Old Bailey for publicly libeling the sovereign or slandering the Virgin Mary, virtually anything else could be said in private or in print about the state and church without fear of official or ecclesiastic retribution. Virtually anything could be said, but little done; it was an actionable offense to assault the Crown or Church with more than words. In England, a treatise on atheism could be bought for three shillings in any bookseller's shop, though its author was likely either a High Churchman such as Swift or a Dissenter who had submitted to the test oath; in France, an author could argue his atheism only in elegant, hyperbolic prose in a manuscript circulated privately among friends and colleagues. In England, the treatise would be signed by "Anonymous" or "A Concerned Gentleman" or a Roman-style pseudonym; in France, under the author's true signature.

It was not long before Hugh Kenrick realized that the Society of the Pippin consciously confined itself to words, and that even in this realm there existed risk, for many of the things asserted and debated among its members could be construed by the authorities as conspiracy to sedition. The risk was rarely discussed; prudence and discretion kept it at bay.

Hugh attended several meetings of the Society as a silent observer and occasional recorder of the club's minutes. Soon the rule was suspended, and he was permitted to join in the discussions. Only Mathius objected to the suspension. His protests were congenially countered by the other members, though no one could determine whether his strenuous arguments against allowing Hugh to speak were based exclusively on tradition, superstition, envy of Hugh's erudition and acumen, or jealousy when the members paid Hugh more attention than he thought was due. Mathius was as wily in argumentation as any of his colleagues, but he had never introduced an original subject for discussion. Hugh not only raised novel ideas, but could examine and argue them in depth. This virtue fascinated all the members, including Mathius. His objections were overruled, and Mathius managed to cloak his bruised pride behind a convincing mien of good fellowship and savoir-vivre. Thus, his colleagues discounted their unspoken suspicions of envy or jealousy, and ascribed to his dissensions mere inordinate worry and, as one of the members humorously put it, "a brief interval of Tory gout."

*   *   *

"Ego humilibus devitare, superbis autem tribuere aestimatum meus."

This radical inversion of a common Christian homily—"God resisteth the proud, and giveth grace to the humble"—was the opening statement of Hugh's first "paper" to the Society, and it took the members by surprise.

"Sublime!" exclaimed Elspeth

"Wickedly delicious!" laughed Claude.

"It borders on the blasphemous!" remarked Mathius.

Muir frowned and turned to Tobius. "I have not been schooled in Latin, my friend. What has he said?"

Tobius leaned over and said, "'I shun the humble, but reward the proud my esteem.'"

Muir grinned at Hugh. "A wonderful ethic!"

Hugh chuckled. "I would have translated it in due course, had you but given me the time," he said. He then gave a half-hour discourse on the importance of pride in man's life, and made sharp distinctions between it and vanity. He ended with the statement: "For the man of spirit, there is no serenity in servitude, nor peace in passivity, when his liberty is under assault, when his life and field of action have been abbreviated by the vanity of power. For the man of spirit, servitude gnaws at his pride, and consumes his time, while in the lesser man passivity may cripple his soul, and inculcate in him an unreasoning malice toward those who are neither servile nor passive."

"What are the alternatives, then?" asked Abraham.

"None, sir. Just...liberty."

"Have you finished, Miltiades?" asked Tobius, the chairman.

Hugh bowed in answer, and took his seat. His doing so touched off an explosion of speculation. Hugh finished his dessert and listened to the excited exchanges between the other members, and waited for them to come to the inevitable conclusions. When they had, he deftly fielded a barrage of questions.

"Is your discourse a direct answer to Mr. Pope's *Essay on Man*?" asked Claude. "It is a work, may I remind you, revered both here and on the Continent."

"In part, sir," answered Hugh. "My answer is in reply to many standard works. Pope, for example, attempts to exalt man and humble him, too. He lauds self-interest, but avers it should stem from a concern for others."

Steven asked, "Are you a deist?"

"When I think of God, perhaps I am. But the notion grows fainter each time I address the subject with my reason."

"Are you, then, an...atheist?" asked Mathius.

"Very likely," said Hugh. "I have not given the matter much thought."

"You have twisted a truism," said Tobius, "and created a tenet of a novel ethic. Have you given any thought to the consequences, were it ever to be propagated, on modern morality? The results could not be but revolutionary!"

Hugh frowned in thought. "It is not wholly a tenet, sir, but the consequence of a new morality. It is but a clue to it. The system in which my statement would be a mere facet awaits the mind and hand of a great philosophical engineer."

"It is Aristotelian in color," remarked Muir.

"That is true," said Hugh.

"The term 'meus' or 'my' seems to be superfluous," said Steven. "It is the only flaw in your opening statement."

Hugh shook his head. "No, sir. The term specifies the personal action of a particular kind of man, one who does not dispense freely his respect for others in society. Thus the statement is rendered compatible neither with the poor rate, nor with the peerage."

The members laughed in unison. Abraham waited until they had finished, then said, "You are critical of the work of one of our sages, sir. Would you not call that an act of vanity?"

Hugh shrugged. "No, sir. Mr. Pope addressed the subject of man according to his lights, and tried to mate our new vision of man with the old. I take pride in having stated that the union he proposes cannot produce anything but more misery and confusion. The esteem Mr. Pope pays man and reason is leavened by Christian precepts. His work is a beginning, but it is sour to my taste."

"It is more than vanity that would prompt one to substitute God with oneself," said Mathius, "and then utter what could be called a heresy. Satan did so, and look at the world."

"Satan must share credit for the world with God, sir, if what occurs in the world is by God's will." Hugh smiled. "That is what I would say, if the subject concerned me. My utterance, were it, and not its antipode, a common truism, would contribute to a happier world, and oblige men to regard each other with more honesty than they do now."

Mathius asked no more questions.

"Just think of it," mused Elspeth. "A new ethic unhobbled by hypocrisy, an ennobling ethic that did not need the angel-water of any church to give it sanctity. It staggers the mind."

"It is invigorating!" echoed Muir. "Just to begin imagining the consequences makes me heady!"

Tobius smiled at Hugh, then addressed his colleagues. "Sirs: When the old peerage is deceased, a new peerage shall take its place—the peerage of the intellect!" He gestured with the ornamented cane to Hugh. "And here will be its first marquis!"

"Hear! Hear!" exclaimed the members, who slapped the tabletop with their open palms. Abraham rose and said, "I propose a toast to a youth who has not only justified his presence in our company, but justified the purpose and character of our society!"

"But the French philosophes have not even gone that far," protested Mathius. "Why should we toast such a…dangerous idea?"

"What?" laughed Claude. "And let the French have all the fun?"

"For once, an Englishman has had an original idea!" seconded Steven. "Let the French be on the receiving end this time!"

"I am in correspondence with Helvétius," said Tobius, "and I shall write him about this on the morrow."

"And I with Dumarsais," said Abraham. "I shall add a postscript to a letter to him I have finished."

"You must admit," said Muir to Mathius, "that the idea proffered by Miltiades is in the spirit of our Society."

"Yes," sighed Mathius. "It is."

"Well, then!" exclaimed Abraham. "Here's to Miltiades!"

The other men also rose and finished their glasses of port.

"Your address was a bracing gust of cold air," said Glorious Swain to Hugh after the meeting had adjourned and the others had dispersed. They sat together in the front of the tavern over glasses of port. "I cannot remember last being so excited by an idea, and I have never seen the others so roused."

"Mathius opposes me," said Hugh. "The tone of his questioning was not one of dispassionate inquiry."

"True. I do not know what his profession is, but any subject beyond the realm of poetry and prose is difficult for him to grasp."

"He was not merely shocked by my address," observed Hugh. "He was hostile to it."

Swain puffed thoughtfully on his pipe, then smiled. "I have heard the others say of Mathius that his mind resembles a fragrant flower garden, nurtured by a rich but thin soil, in which an oak could never take root."

At the next meeting, it was Mathius's turn to present an idea. He argued, with more emotion than reason, that "man and nature are inseparably intertwined, and that man's salvation and happiness depend on his eschewing the refinements and pretensions of society, on leading a simpler and blameless life, and on not offending nature. Man would then be in harmony with nature, which would spare him the tribulations of catastrophe, pestilence, and sorrow. Nature is not to be commanded," he ended. "It is to be obeyed."

Mathius bowed, sat down, and waited for a response. After a long silence, Elspeth blurted out, "Gadso, sir! That sentiment would clinch our own demise!"

"I'm rather fond of society's refinements," remarked Claude.

"What do you mean by its 'pretensions,' sir?" asked Muir.

"In a word," replied Mathius, "that we can improve on nature. Show me the ship that can't sink, or the house that won't fall, or the clock that won't stop. All that we do, all that we create, is as mortal as we are, and will be conquered by nature."

Tobius shook his head. "We command nature by obeying her laws," he said. "And when we discover the rules of her laws, we arrest her progress."

Hugh remarked, "We do not so much 'obey' nature's laws, sirs, but observe them."

"It is a unique thesis you present, sir," said Abraham, raising his hands to indicate the city beyond the tavern, "here, in the middle of London, as unnatural a phenomenon as one could imagine, one which gives life to so many. London has checkmated nature."

"Look at Rome," insisted Mathius. "And Greece! Both, in the end, humbled and consumed by nature!"

Elspeth shook his head. "The facts contradict you, sir. They point to those societies having done themselves in, not nature, which merely dispatched her weeds and vines to grow over abandoned temples and market squares."

"Liberty was their breakwater against nature, sir," added Steven. "And when they allowed their liberties to crumble away, so went their societies."

"Admit it, Mathius!" laughed Claude. "You had some wrong beef before you composed your thesis, and it has compelled you to bolk such shameless flummery!"

The members laughed. Mathius retorted, "That was unkind of you, Claude. I have devoted at least as much thought to my thesis as you have to your morning tea!"

"Nevertheless," replied Claude, "we forgive you."

Again the members laughed, but stopped when Hugh sat forward to speak. Everyone turned to him. "You pose an inanalogous thesis, sir," he said. "Nature is never so cruel and aggressive as are men. Nature has no intention, no purpose, no goal, no…state of grace to grant, nor one for men to perceive and betray. It does not plot, connive, or single any man out for reward or punishment. It has no soul, no consciousness, and so cannot contrive harmony. It is simply…there. It is merely mechanical, and not sentient."

Mathius sniffed. "You are indeed not a deist," he said.

"I never claimed to be one," replied Hugh. "On the other hand, man acts. Nature is governed by her own laws. These laws are impersonal, and if we master them, they can help us live and act. It is an error to personify nature beyond the requirements of humor. I once contemplated penning a moral satire which employed sheep, but abandoned the idea, because it seemed to be a cheap and cowardly way of saying what I wanted to say."

The members waited for Mathius to reply. The man wanted to, but could not. His face registered various distortions of speechlessness, and at last settled on an expression of bitterness. This was the only instance in the Society's annals when a member's idea had been so thoroughly and unanimously opposed. Mathius fell back in his chair and threw up his hands in concession.

The Society's meetings presented Hugh with the opportunity to speak as he could not even at Dr. Comyn's School for Gentlemen. It was a far more satisfying venue than was the school, for now he had an audience of seasoned, mature minds. At the meetings he could dare to give expression to his most deeply felt and hard-thought ideas. He could hear the other members propose provocative ideas he encountered nowhere else. Glorious Swain—Muir—delivered a provocative address on the notion of conscience, a notion Hugh had never seen defined or challenged anywhere in his wide reading, even though he and Swain had once discussed it.

"The trouble with the notion of conscience," said Muir, "is two-fold. I mention only the first, and dwell on the second. The first trouble is its connection with the notion of original sin. Here conscience is viewed as a kind of molasses of guilt applied to all who were, all who are, and all who will be. This connection I hope to address at another time. It is the secular notion of conscience that has troubled me and whetted my curiosity. It suggests a moral knowledge independent of one's actual character and actions and knowledge. The Bard made an observation on this very phenomenon: 'Policy sits above conscience.' Now, I do not think a conscience is a legitimate measure of one's moral character." He ended his address with, "A truly moral man has no need of a conscience. All his actions are moral, and are one with his character. His actions are not apart from his conscious morality, and his morality is not an extraneous body of knowledge, sitting in the back of his head, waiting to rebuke him or pounce upon him were he to commit a wrong action. This man's self is in accord with his virtue. His day-to-day policy and his life-long policy are complementary, in perfect, seamless, indistinguishable harmony…"

Mathius asked, "But you do not deny the existence of conscience?"

"No," answered Muir. "The sad truth is that most men are plagued by one. Conscience makes criminals of men, causing them only to regret their actions, without telling them anything useful, and whether or not they ever commit a crime. How else to explain the numerous, sincere gallows confessions at Tyburn Tree? No, I merely say that conscience is impractical. A truly moral man could not regret or rue his actions." Muir paused in thought. "Something both practical and moral is wanted, and remains to be discovered."

"Presuming that morality is spiritual," broached Claude, "how could it be practical?"

"If it is practical, then how could it be spiritual?" asked Tobius.

Muir said, "In the course of preparing my address to you, I had glimpses of the possibility of such a union. Breathless as these were, I was unable to magnify them for closer scrutiny, nor put them on paper. I no sooner imagined them, then they slipped away back into the fog of my confusion."

The members were quiet. It was a disturbing idea that Muir had introduced to them, so disturbing that it caused each of them to think of himself, of his profession, of how he had conducted his own life up to this moment. And in this unsettling but edifying moment, each saw a glimpse of what Muir had glimpsed, and understood the enormity of the obstacles to an answer each sensed was ecstatically right, but knew not why.

At length, Tobius said, "You have revealed to us a new Olympus, Muir. It is distant, and its peak is shrouded in clouds. How long would it take us to reach it, and how should we scale it?"

Muir looked around at his companions, and smiled. "You are my closest friends, and one of you will solve the problem some day, and tell me the answers." His glance swept the gathering, and stopped on Hugh's attentive face, but did not linger on it.

*   *   *

. "You are capable of fresh breezes yourself," said Hugh later. "I cannot recall a meeting when so few questions were asked of the speaker."

They were strolling together along the lamp-lit Strand. Music, singing, and laughter came from the numerous taverns and coffeehouses they passed on this spring night. Watchmen cried out the hour—eleven of the clock—and coaches and gentlemen on horseback paraded up and down the street.

Glorious Swain chuckled. "Thank you, sir." He paused. "I did not wish to call attention to it at the meeting, but I believe that you will be the one to give me and the others maps to Olympus." Hugh turned to face him, but Swain held up a hand. "No protestations, sir! You have two advantages over the rest of us: your youth, and my certainty that you alone among us are not burdened with a conscience, and never will be."

Hugh said, "Thank you, Mr. Swain." But then he shook his head. "What you say is true, but it is not my ambition to become a philosopher."

"Perhaps not. But you will become one. I believe it is the only matter in your life in which you have never had a choice."

Again Hugh shook his head. "I choose to think, sir. There is nothing mechanical or predestined in that."

"That is why I say what I say."

They walked in silence until they came to Charing Cross, the Y-shaped junction of the Strand, Whitehall, and Cockspur Street. In its center, facing Whitehall beyond, was the bronze equestrian statue of Charles I by Hubert le Sueur, poised atop a tall, narrow, rococo-ornamented stone pedestal enclosed by a circular iron railing. The steed seemed to have more majesty than its rider, for while Charles's left hand suggested tightly held reins, his right hand was raised as though he were holding a sword, or more likely a baton of state. But, whether sword or baton, that hand was significantly empty. The statue had been saved and hidden by Royalists during the Commonwealth, and restored to Charing Cross after the fall of its successor, the Protectorate. A symbol of the country's more recent history, it would survive into the next century. Charles was beheaded in 1649 by ancestors of the Whigs and Tories, and when kings were welcomed back, they came without the baton of absolute power. That had been appropriated by Parliament.

Around powerless Charles jostled the nightlife of London: coaches, sedan chairs, carriages, strollers, and parties of revelers. On this crossroads were taverns and coffeehouses that exhibited freaks and "oddities" such as centaurs and mermaids for a price of a few shillings; respectable establishments hosted by well-bred ladies and gracious gentlemen, such as the Red Lion Tavern and the British Coffee House; night-cellars, or brothels, and private gaming clubs of all kinds; several coach inns for travelers from beyond London; linen drapers' and lacemen's shops; silversmiths, saddlers, victuallers, hosiers, and haberdashers. Pickpockets and confidence tricksters preyed on country folk and foreigners. Beggars plied their trade, prostitutes accosted passing men, and ladies of rank and their escorts slummed behind domino masks.

In front of the statue was an elevated pillory, where convicted felons were put on display for public view and public punishment. Besides being pelted with stones and dung by the crowds, prisoners were often subjected to the branding of their hands for theft—depending on the assessed value of the stolen objects—or to the removal of their ears or the slitting of their noses, if they had been found guilty of forgery. Other prisoners, men and women, charged with crimes such as perjury and extortion, would be chained to the tail of a cart and publicly whipped on their bare backs as they were led past or around the statue. No criminals were ever hanged at Charing Cross; but, like Tyburn Tree, and later Newgate, the place became the venue for a circus-like exhibition of what passed for justice.

There were other pillories in the city—in Southwark, at the Haymarket, outside of Westminster Hall, or wherever great throngs of Londoners passed through in the course of their business—but none was so appropriate as Charing Cross. Here many terrible crimes were committed, and here many awful punishments were carried out, presided over by a great criminal. No one could say whether the statue honored Charles, or served as an example of what lay in store for living a life of crime. The solemn, dignified face of Charles gazed above and beyond this "full tide of human existence"—as Samuel Johnson years later was to characterize Charing Cross—his lofty countenance insensible to the ironies of his own effigy and of the justice exacted beneath the hooves of his steed.

As they threaded their way through the crowds and dodged carriages and sedan chairs, Swain glanced up at the statue, which was silhouetted against the night sky and barely visible in the light of the street lamps, flambeaux, and torches of the linkboys. He asked, without immediately knowing the reason, "Can you ever forgive your uncle?"

Hugh's father had asked him the same question. Hugh repeated his answer. "No. There can be no reprieve for his crime. He assaulted my mind."

Hugh had since made inquiries, but could not locate Hulton or even learn which army regiment he had enlisted in. He continued to scour bookshops and second-hand stalls throughout the city, but could not find another copy of *Hyperborea*. Swain had offered to loan him his copy, but Hugh cordially refused. "I could not guarantee its safety." He had reached an agreement with Nathan Rickerby—to whom he had revealed his true identity, but made take an oath of secrecy—and could rent the room on Cutter Lane for a year. With his father and Benjamin Worley he had attended the opening for business of a new bank, Formby, Swire and Purse-house; his father surprised him and made an interest-bearing deposit in his name. "Why?" he had asked. Garnet Kenrick merely answered: "Every man of good character should have an account." But his father's eyes had said: "For having had the courage to call my brother a liar." Hugh continued to excel in his studies at Dr. Comyn's School; he had reached a point where he brought more to his studies than his instructors gave him.

Swain smiled, and said, "My friend, when I am with the Pippins, I am among my preferred company. When I am in your company alone, I feel that I am near a new Olympus."

"I had thought you disapproved of my not forgiving my uncle."

"I did, at first. Perhaps it was because I was jealous of you. I have no family to forgive for anything. But the logic of your justice is not to be impeached. It takes time to accustom oneself to Olympus."

They stood at the side of the pillory for a while to watch the parade of nightlife and make their observations on it. Then they shook hands and parted, Hugh back to Windridge Court, and Swain to his room in a house that stood in an unlit alley deep in the bowels of London.

Chapter 26: The Critics

I N EARLY APRIL, HUGH RECEIVED AN EXCITED LETTER FROM REVERDY BRUNE announcing her planned visit to London in July with her mother and older brother, James. It was the wrong season to visit the city; the warm weather, together with the odors subdued in the cold months but released by the heat, drove much of London's wealthy society to country homes.

But James Brune had business to conduct. He was acting for his father, Squire Robert Brune, now infirm and unable to travel, who wanted to establish an arrangement with McLeod & McDougal, a firm of Scottish agents and traders. The firm had branches in Bristol and Glasgow, correspondents in St. Petersburg and Copenhagen, and partners in New York and Jamaica. McLeod & McDougal had a warehouse near the Lawful Keys, but did most of its business in the Virginia and Maryland Coffeehouse in Cornhill. The Brunes had wool to export and have factored, mutton to sell, and money to invest. Insurance looked attractive to both father and son, despite the war, as did consols, or consolidated annuities. The elder Brune had had his eye on McLeod & McDougal for a long while, as well as on other trading firms, and the firm's cautious approach and constant solvency finally moved him to make an overture. McLeod & McDougal expected James Brune, and would welcome him; it had markets for wool, Scotland to feed, and opportunities to exploit.

Hugh glowed with happiness that he would see Reverdy again, and her anticipated visit caused his mind to buzz with plans. She had been to London only one other time in her life, when she was five. He thought of her visit in terms of displaying his domain to a future queen. Glorious Swain noticed the special exhilaration in his manner over supper in a tavern one evening, and asked him about it. Hugh confided in him. "Where are you staying now?" asked Swain.

"Windridge Court," answered Hugh. "My uncle won't return until perhaps September next. He had planned to lease the house for the summer to another country earl, but my father talked him out of it. But I often stay overnight in my room on Cutter Lane. It's closer to the school, and to so many bookshops. I saw Dr. Johnson in one of them last week, browsing through titles. I wouldn't have known it if the proprietor hadn't greeted him. He's a very strange-looking person. I seem to recall encountering him somewhere, even speaking to him."

Swain nodded. "I've seen him. His household has bought tea from under my coat on numerous occasions. Well, St. Peter may guard the gates to heaven, but Dr. Johnson seems to be now the sentry at Helicon's propylaeum."

"He would like that compliment," remarked Hugh, who had read some of Johnson's essays and reviews in the *Literary Magazine*, "but I'm reluctant to second it. I do believe that, if he ever came to know the Society better, he might try to have us prosecuted. He is a spokesman for everything that is Tory."

Swain shook his head. "I don't agree, my friend. He is a brilliant man, and I don't believe he would punish rival brilliance, even if he disagreed with it."

In May, a new book of poetry appeared and enjoyed a brief sensation, *Twenty Moral Fables in Rhyme, concerning Good Men and Bad Manners, with a short dissertation on the Art of Fables*, by W. Horlick, printed by Taller and Wyshe for a patron and sold for ten shillings. The work was dedicated to that patron, the Marquis of Bilbury. It was favorably mentioned in many periodicals, among them the *London Literary Register*, which hailed the collection as "worthy of the affection of the most discriminating gourmand of verse."

So endorsed, sales of the book grew brisk, and soon it went into a second printing. *Twenty Fables* became a topic of conversation over tea and supper in the best homes; between ladies and their guests during morning levees. Mothers read some of the fables to their children for their moral instruction. Some ministers even adapted the fables and preached them as sermons. One bookshop sold several copies to officers preparing to depart with their regiments for North America. Many gentlemen, who did not usually read verse, purchased copies for their wives or mistresses, and sometimes for both. For a while, *Twenty Fables* was the bon livre of London.

Elspeth was to have given a lecture to the Society on the premises underlying an older book, John Mason's *An Essay on the Power of Numbers, and the Principles of Harmony in Poetical Composition*, coupled with an encomium on Mason's book distilled from another, shorter book written by Elspeth himself under the non de plume of Sawny Driscoll, though none of his colleagues knew it. But one of the members, before the lecture began after supper in the Fruit Wench, made some derisive comments on *Twenty Fables*, and noted what he thought was its undeserved popularity. "It's all I hear now!" bellowed Claude. "I'm either asked if I've read it, or assaulted with gentle quotations from it. It grew so tiresome that I bought a copy of it, and found that it is the uninspired ejecta of a mere poetaster!" *Twenty Fables*, which all the members but Hugh now confessed to have read, became the subject of a lively exchange for the rest of the evening.

"It is but the *Decalogue* chopped up into twenty dollops of duty, and acted out in masquerade by the most unlikely and inappropriate animals."

"The 'Dialogue between Two Diverting Dogs,' on adultery, was especially egregious."

"Aesop would not have composed a single one of these fables, even in his most fuddled state!"

"Oh, no, sir. He might have, but we would never have known it, for when he became sober, he would have disowned them, and used the fables for kindling."

"On the whole, 'tis merely a dog-cart passing for a phaeton."

"And if you rummage certain of these tales, you may see some snitched Steele and poached Addison!"

"And Cowley, and even Pope!"

"Swift is firmly represented in the fables presented by the cats and mice."

"I cannot forgive him for his presumption! He pens bad verse, then, in his dissertation, presumes to initiate his reader in the art of emulating it!"

"His muse must have been Morpheus."

"And your remarks seem to have been inspired by Momus," ventured Mathius, who was not an active participant in the conversation, and who labored to keep the hurt and acid from his words. He had made some objections to the criticisms that flew back and forth over the table, careful not to reveal his authorship of *Twenty Fables*. These were ignored. But now he had had enough. "You are being too severe, sirs! The work is not without some merit, surely!"

Tobius said, "Oh, I grant you that, sir. It has the merit of complete sentences, of an occasional amusing though I suspect accidental rhyme, and some fervor in its exposition—though the image of a furabund rabbit orating like Hamlet on the virtues of conjugal moderation was more than I could tolerate. A compulsion to load my fowling piece and blast the creature was fortunately checked by the fear that I should need to explain to my neighbors why I was potting a book!"

Elspeth said, "My dear Mathius, think what you may, but the rest of us must agree that these fables could have easily been composed by the Prince of Wales, and patiently emended by Lord Bute!"

"Who would have been obliged to begin by inserting points throughout, in order to knacker a seventy-five-page sentence," observed Abraham.

Again the table burst out in rollicking laughter. It was no use. Mathius leaned back in his chair and endured it.

"I don't quite understand the reason why that trash is the *ton*," remarked Muir. "So much that is worthy of praise, goes unnoticed."

"Oh, it's merely some form of contagion, or a flash of distemper, such as afflicted our cattle a few years ago," said Steven, shrugging his shoulders. "People will recover their senses by September, and we'll hear no more of it."

"The Marquis of Bilbury at times subsidizes the queerest projects," commented Claude. "I wonder if some contagion possessed him when he put guineas behind this one."

"Lords are grateful for the slightest gratitude paid them," observed Tobius, "and often have less practical sense than do their dependents. Look at Lord Chesterfield. If he'd donated even a tenth of Dr. Johnson's lexico-graphic expenses, he would have immortalized himself."

The meeting adjourned without the members ever suspecting that the author of *Twenty Fables* sat in their midst. Mathius did not know the purpose behind his good fortune, when one day two months ago the son of the Marquis of Bilbury called on him in his room near Fleet Street and claimed to have heard of his talents, and asserted that his father might be willing to underwrite publication of some of his work, if he could see a sample of it. William Horlick did not pause to question the father's or son's motives. Horlick had spent wasted days in the anterooms of many prospective patrons, only to be snubbed or turned out without seeing anyone but insouciant servants. He was so desperate for a patron—and for the fame and security one could grant him—that he did not even question the anomaly of a lord deigning to seek him out.

The elder Marquis of Bilbury did not know the motive behind his son's surprising request that he underwrite the publication of what he frankly considered some indifferent and oft times juvenile verse. But it was the first evidence of his son taking his station in life seriously, and he would not discourage that development.

William Horlick did not know that the younger Marquis had paid one of his footmen to spy on Peter Brompton, the musician who seemed to know Hugh Kenrick, and report on the nature of his association between the commoner and the aristocrat, and that eventually the Marquis had learned of the Society of the Pippin. Brice Blissom had then begun to frequent the Fruit Wench, eavesdropping on the Society's meetings from the next compartment. He soon grasped the character of the club, and was offended. One evening, after watching the members disperse from the tavern, he had decided on who among them seemed to be the weakest and most open to influence. He had also noticed that the members had secret names, and that minutes of all that they discussed were kept in a great ledger book, which they took turns in maintaining.

That was when the young Marquis had hit upon a way of avenging himself on Hugh Kenrick.

And so it was a wounded, disconsolate Mathius who bid his companions good night and left the Fruit Wench that evening. Brice Blissom, had he chosen to eavesdrop on the Society tonight, would have laughed and counted his blessings, for neither he nor his cat's paw had ever expected *Twenty Fables* to be discussed by the club, much less be excoriated by it.

*   *   *

By July, *Twenty Fables* had been discarded and nearly forgotten by the literati and reading public, forgotten by the Society of the Pippin, forgotten by Hugh, who had not read it. Out of a sense of fairness, he glanced through a copy of the work in a bookshop a day or two after the Society had trounced it, and understood then why the members had laughed at it. It was truly awful, on a par with the intellectual and literary essays of many of his schoolmates. If the book had been justly ignored, it would never have been praised by the press, and never have caused the satirical guffaws of the Society. He sensed the hand of influence in the book's brief life: a patron wealthy enough to pay for the work's production, wealthy enough to purchase the endorsement of a few publications, wealthy enough to get the book talked about in the right social circles. For a reason he could not immediately explain, he recalled something he had read in a second-hand copy of Dr. Johnson's *Rambler* he had bought: "All industry must be excited by hope; and as the student often proposes no other reward to himself than praise, he is easily discouraged by contempt and insult." Contempt and insult, concluded Hugh, were the only rewards that *Twenty Fables* deserved.

And then he remembered two things: that the name of the essay by Johnson was "The Advantages of Living in a Garret," and that the odd-looking man he had seen in Cottle's Bookshop on Cockspur Street, and the man to whom he had absently handed his unfinished glass of claret in Ranelagh Gardens and said "True enough!" were one and the same man.

And Glorious Swain lived in a garret. It was on the fifth floor of a house in Quiller Alley, in the shadow of St. Paul's Cathedral, in between Little Carter Lane and Nightrider Street. He had spent many evenings there, on Swain's invitation, to talk, to read, to browse through his friend's collection of books and especially his copy of *Hyperborea*. He missed having his own copy of it at hand; he was as attached to the work as others were to their bibles, and for the same reasons: it was a source of hope, of consolation, of inspiration, of proof. It was a quiet street, in whose houses lived mostly Quakers. Swain taught children to read, write, and cipher in the little Friends' chapel on the corner. When Hugh visited and in time reached for a volume of *Hyperborea*, Swain, understanding, would retire to another corner of the room to read, or go out on errands, leaving Hugh alone.

Today, a Sunday, Swain sat at his cramped desk in a corner of his room to work on the Society's minutes. He had chaired the last meeting, and was responsible for fleshing out the topic of the speaker and the main points of the ensuing discussion. Yesterday, Tobius had given the address, "An Analogy on the Window Tax and the Newspaper Stamp Tax, or Knowledge Penalized." This task Swain could do from memory, as any member could, for the talks and discussions were memorable and aided by each recording member's personal shorthand. There were ten volumes of the club's minutes, spanning almost forty years. These were kept on a secret bookshelf in Elspeth's—Beverly Brashears'—bookshop on the Strand. Elspeth merely took possession of them, without any of the members knowing where they were kept.

Hugh received a letter from his father informing him, among other things, that the Brunes would be staying at Windridge Court,

"...As our guests, nearly, for a fraction of what they would pay at the Bear Inn or other hostelry. I know you will be an irreproachable host. I have sent instructions to the steward, Mr. Dolman, who I suppose must now be raised to major domo, to prepare for the Brunes' arrival and stay...Now that Dr. Comyn's has recessed for the season, you should plan on a stay in Danvers for a while. We must discuss sending you to Oxford (or even to Cambridge, if you've a mind to) in a year or so. And I should like you to spend some time with me on this end of the business. We might even embark on a short tour of the Continent to see some of France, Prussia, and Holland, before hostilities grow nasty and render those places inhospitable...

"I have before me Dr. Comyn's report on you, and those of the several instructors. They all exude the odor of laurels, except for Mr. Cavie's, your composition tutor, who does not fault your skills but claims that you engaged him in a terrific trading of broadsides in class over some novel moral point. He claims that he was obliged to force you to strike your colors, lest you utter some treasonous sentiment. You must tell me what were the circumstances that would cause Mr. Cavie to make such a grave charge, for he does not relate them in his report, nor does he elucidate the point which has so upset him, other than to refer to your utterances as those of a Pelagian recidivist. Perhaps he is afraid that he could be accused of treason, too. I'm sure that your explanation will be quite amusing..."

Chapter 27: The Lovers

THE AIR WAS FILLED WITH THE SHRIEK OF MASSED FIFES, THE THUDDING of a dozen drums, and the shrill, banshee-like commands of sergeant-majors. The sky was unusually blue and cloudless, and the sun flashed from fixed bayonets, polished cap plates and gorgets, and clean white cross belts. A gentle but constant breeze stirred the pristine colors of the assembled regiments. Proud colonels sat stiffly in their saddles, each confident that the king would pay him and his regiment a compliment.

On the green Parade Grounds beyond Whitehall stood the broad matte of scarlet, drawn up in silent ranks at hair-trigger attention: regulars, grenadiers, fusiliers, and mounted dragoons. In the center of this crimson rectangle were poised six artillery pieces and their gun crews. Their rear was guarded by newly raised regiments from the various counties, including London or Middlesex. To one side of them stood a battalion of Highlanders in kilts and bonnets. Largely commanded by untried English officers, many of the Scots' claymore-wielding sergeants and corporals, veterans of the Jacobite Rebellion, would later discreetly advise their superiors in the art of war. Only two units knew their destinations and dates of embarkation; one regiment of regulars was to be sent to reinforce the garrison at Gibraltar, while the Highlanders were to fight the French in North America.

Facing this invincible-looking army was a cluster of men astride magnificently appointed mounts: a small man with protruding eyes and a recessed forehead, His Royal Highness, King George II; a stout man on his left, with a deceptively lazy glance and a permanent pout, who was his son, the Duke of Cumberland; to the king's right, a young man, George William, Prince of Wales, and grandson of the king; another young man, Edward, George William's brother; John Stuart, third Earl of Bute, future Groom of the Stole, the young princes' tutor, and, some said, the Princess of Wales' secret paramour; Thomas Pelham-Holles, the Duke of Newcastle, formerly Secretary of State and now First Lord of the Treasury. Madame Walmoden, or Lady Yarmouth, the king's German mistress, watched it all from the privacy of a splendid coach-and-six, for she was stouter than even the Duke of Cumberland and did not sit well on a horse. Waiting on this galaxy of notables was a multitude of royal and ministerial functionaries.

The latest number of the *London Gazette*, the government's official news-paper—never confused by its readers with any of a handful of other news-papers subsidized by a secret service fund—carried this announcement:

A grand review of new and old regiments of foot and horse, and of artillery, will commence at two o'clock next Tuesday on the Parade Grounds near Whitehall, attended by His Most Gracious Majesty, and his son, the Duke of Cumberland, and the Royal Family, with maneuvers and a demonstration of fire-arms to display the efficacy of our forces now valorously engaging the enemy in many quarters of the globe.

On the edge of the field, behind a cordon of grenadiers, milled a large crowd of spectators, drawn there by the announcement. Many came from patriotism, others from a desire to catch a glimpse of the king and other persons whose names figured so prominently in the newspapers and gossip.

Reverdy Brune was there for both reasons.

"What do you wish to do?" Hugh Kenrick had asked her that morning, a day after she, her mother, and her brother arrived at Windridge Court. The four sat together at the breakfast table. One of the Earl's Parliamentary privileges was the free delivery of the *London Gazette* to his residence, whether or not he was in London. The latest edition of it lay on the damask before Reverdy. She pointed to the announcement. "That!" she said, her eyes wide with excitement. "I have never seen His Majesty, only that fat son of his that time you riled him at Danvers, and this may be my only chance!" She glanced once at her mother, who nodded approval, and at her brother, who added, "Yes. It would be a grand way to begin our visit."

Mrs. Brune and her son, James, both understood that Reverdy would be the chief object of their host's hospitality. Mrs. Brune, who did not like London, came as a chaperone, but did not mind the inconvenience if it helped to cement the bond between her daughter and Hugh Kenrick, and so guarantee the union of the Brunes and the Kenricks. James Brune, who had visited the city many times before, had come on business, and was not so much interested in sightseeing as guaranteeing his family's solvency and future prosperity.

Hugh took the paper and read the announcement. The *Gazette* was not a paper he read regularly; it was usually full of addresses to the king, admonishments, blandishments, and bankruptcies. He smiled. "Of course," he answered. "But we should be there early enough to guarantee ourselves a view unobstructed by hats and perukes. Shall we make a picnic of it?"

Reverdy grinned and clapped her hands in delight. "Oh, yes!"

Hugh had another reason for the caution and suggestion: Hulton, who he thought could very well be in one of the new regiments.

But as the regiments marched onto the field to the tunes of "Lilliburlero" and "The Bottom of the Punchbowl" to form the great square, he did not espy the face of his former valet in any of the slow-marching companies that passed directly in front of him. Hulton was not here today.

Hugh pointed out to his companions the Dragoon Guards, the Horse Grenadier Guards, and the Foot Guards. "They comprise about one-half of the only standing army in this country," he explained. "These other regiments are 'marching regiments' that can be sent anywhere—to the Mediterranean, to the Continent, to North America. Or to Ireland, where they would more or less leave the Duke's command and come under that of the Lord Lieutenant's there."

Reverdy broke her sight away from the review and studied him with a wistful smile. "Hugh," she said, "you would look so smart in scarlet, and wearing a gorget, smarter than any of these ensigns!" A gorget was an embossed, crescent-shaped metal plaque worn by line officers beneath their throats, signifying their rank. It was a remnant of the age of armored knights. An ensign was a subaltern who carried a regiment's colors.

Hugh grinned. "But I do wear one," he replied. "It is not so invisible as you might think. It is here." He pointed to his forehead. Reverdy looked doubtful. He added, "There are battles of the intellect to be fought, Reverdy, for king, country, and liberty. One day I may captain a troop of thinkers who will solve our country's most grievous problems, which are ignorance and power." He gestured to the scarlet square and the banners. "This is but one way to fight a war." He tapped his forehead again. "This is another, and the most important. A mind can accrue honor, too, and carry its own colors, and be proud of its traditions and history. So, you see, I am an ensign in our country's most important standing army—for how secure can a country be without its thinkers? No duke or king or board of generals or even Parliament can order it broken or disbanded, not without committing tyranny."

Reverdy held his glance, stunned by the music of his words and the emotion beneath his confession. This was another reason why she was drawn to him, without any seeming choice by her in the matter.

Hugh said, "I own that I am partial to the martial pageantry we see here today. I have been fighting a war all my life—you know this—and will always." He paused. "You must know that, for the future."

Reverdy, her eyes half shut as though she were looking into the sun, nodded once. She wished to say something, but could not think of anything that could match his words.

Hugh smiled. "You are one of the very few persons who has recognized the imperial crown on my own gorget, and paid it the esteem it is due. And your esteem is most especial and the closest to my heart."

Reverdy touched his hand once, and looked away. Her mother and brother were next to them, in a conversation of their own about the condition of the regiments, and could not hear what had been said. For a moment, Reverdy was deaf to the fifes and drums and commotion on the field. She closed her eyes in acknowledgment of what had been said. Then there was a flourish of drums, and the king and his retinue moved to inspect the troops. Watching the distant figures, she said, "I shall imagine that you are out there, in front of your own men, not as a captain, but as a colonel."

Regimental colors dipped in salute as the sovereign passed by each regiment, and colonels and other officers removed their hats and bowed their heads. The bandsmen struck up "Johnny Cope."

"And you would still not bow to the Duke, or even to the King?" asked Reverdy.

"Not now," replied Hugh. "Not ever." He listened to the fifes and drums. "I like that tune. I would choose it as my regiment's own."

"It's lively, and happy," agreed Reverdy. "It makes me feel like dancing." She glanced down and saw the toe of one of his shoes tapping the grass in rhythm. "And you," she added with a grin.

The first rank of soldiers moved six steps forward to make room for the king and his party to inspect the second rank. Now the band played "Westering Home."

"Oh, what a pretty tune!" exclaimed Reverdy. "It's almost a lullaby."

"A soldier's last lullaby," remarked Hugh.

There was some jostling behind them. "See the muster of whores' whelps!" said a spectator in a loud voice.

"One-parent wonders, all of them!" chimed in another.

"Gutter gleanings," agreed still another. "I'll wager old Georgie wishes he could teach them to march like Hessian geese!"

Hugh, Reverdy, and her mother and brother turned in unison to face the speakers. Hugh saw that they were idle dandies, gentlemen of no particular means and probably candidates for debtors' prison.

Before he could say anything, Reverdy accosted them angrily. "Is that anything to say about men who could die for your king, country, and liberties, sirs?"

The leader of the group blinked in surprise and touched his hat. "My apologies, milady, if we offended your sensibilities, but I do not ask them to die for me or much else, except for what may be their hearts' content."

"If they got a good look at you, sir, I believe they would have second thoughts, too! You are ignorant, and a model of dissipation and ingratitude!"

"Most assuredly, milady," replied the leader. "We answer to your description!" But he bowed slightly to Reverdy. "We shall remove ourselves to another vantage point, and hope not to encounter another Amazon." He turned and led his companions through the crowd to another place down the line of spectators.

After the intruders had lost themselves in the throng, Reverdy glanced at Hugh, who was studying her with admiration. "Why did you not speak up?"

Hugh laughed. "You spoke my mind before I could, and vanquished the rogue before I could draw my sword!"

Mrs. Brune leaned over and said to her daughter, "Reverdy, that is not the behavior of a lady!"

"No, Mother," replied Reverdy, "but it ought to be."

Mrs. Brune gasped, but said nothing else.

They turned to watch the review again. When the king had finished inspecting the Highlanders, he and his retinue trotted back to their original places. "He couldn't be too pleased to see so many Scots in one place," remarked James Brune, addressing Hugh. "And there are more Scottish officers there than I had ever imagined he would approve."

"They are mostly Lowlanders," answered Hugh, "or so I have heard, as are probably your future partners, McLeod and McDougal."

One by one, on command, the regiments aimed their muskets into the air and fired a deafening volley. Then the cannon were fired—without ball—and their smoke joined that of the muskets to drift through the crowd of spectators. Finally, the dragoons left the formation and trotted twice in close order around the square. Then trumpeters sounded the charge, and the dragoons galloped off the field to the applause and cheers of the crowd.

The king dismounted and boarded the coach-and-six, and his son and the retinue, with a troop of Horse Guards, escorted the sovereign from the field. As the regiments marched out in another direction, the crowd began to disperse. Hugh and his party were the last to leave the Parade Grounds.

*   *   *

The Brunes stayed for a month. What enabled Hugh to enjoy their visit more and act as a gracious host was a letter he received from Hulton. Hugh had written to or visited almost every justice of the peace in London, for when a man enlisted in any of the land forces he was required by law to be taken by the recruiting officer or sergeant to a magistrate to confirm or deny his enlistment. Many of the magistrates had had their clerks dig through piles of paperwork to no avail, and written Hugh letters of regret. Others simply took his fee and never bothered to either search or reply. When Hulton's letter arrived, Hugh had nearly exhausted his resources.

Hulton, he learned, had enlisted in the 71st Foot, a regiment raised with a government levy by a Colonel Beckwith. He had spent the winter and spring in camp in Devon, but his regiment was soon to depart with other units to the mustering camp on the Isle of Wight.

"I am writing this with borrowed quill and paper, for as you know when a man takes the shilling the costs of his clothes and shoes and such are deducted from his pay which is a few pence a day. These stoppages are the greatest cause of desertion. So I cannot afford to buy my own writing materials. Because I can write some officers employ me to help write their reports, so I am in less debt to the colonel than most of my mates. The colonel and captains know where we are to go soon, but do not tell us where or when. I did not say in my letter to you what regiment I enlisted in, for I did not want you or his Excellency your father to bail me out, as I knew you would try. This is my own choice...Thomas Hulton, Pvt., 71st Foot, Devon Camp."

The letter was dated a month ago. It was with some relief, and a sad smile, that Hugh read it, and filed it with his correspondence.

*   *   *

The month-long idyll was punctuated by Hugh's obligations to Benjamin Worley and Lion Key. Every other day he would leave the Brunes to entertain themselves and work in Worley's warehouse, on the account books, or to deal with ship captains and other merchants. He had taken the Brunes on a tour of the Lawful Keys and the various Exchanges, introduced them to Worley, and even had Worley and his wife to supper at Windridge Court, where the men talked thickly and eagerly of interest rates, tariffs, the war's likely effect on trade, and other business matters. Mrs. Brune was not entirely pleased with this side of her future son-in-law, and resented the familiarity with which Mr. Worley associated with Hugh. She said nothing about it, either to Reverdy or to Hugh, but made some desultory remarks in private to her son, James. She found no ally in him, either.

He said, "Hugh will be better able to maintain his family's fortunes, Mother, for all that. He will be a man of substance, much as his father is, and will always win the trust and confidence of men like Mr. Worley. That will be a nicer asset to him than his eventual title."

"I'm sure you're right," sighed Mrs. Brune. She changed the subject. "What do you think of Alex McDougal?" The Brunes had accepted an invitation to sup with the McDougal family at the merchant's home near Covent Garden. Alex McDougal was the son of Duncan McDougal, James McLeod's partner. He was a year older than Hugh, and worked closely with his father. The McDougals were an almost completely Anglicized family, and Scottish only for their refined brogue. And, she had learned, the McDougals were almost half as wealthy as the Kenricks, and owned land throughout the North of England. Alex was a handsome lad, conventional in all other respects, except on the subject of trade, and had graduated from Edinburgh University. He could play the harpsichord and violin, recite poetry, and often quoted from the Bible. At the supper he had paid Reverdy special gentlemanly attention, and this had not gone unnoticed by Mrs. Brune. Reverdy, she knew, had not placed any importance on it. Alex McDougal was a model of decorum and manners, and while Hugh was also this, he defied Mrs. Brune's best efforts to otherwise categorize him. When he was in her presence, she felt a power emanating from him that seemed to contradict his decorum and manners. Secretly, she disliked and feared Hugh Kenrick.

"Alex?" replied her son. "He's a good fellow, and a true gentleman. We shall get along most wonderfully. Why, we've even made a pact: He's to teach me this game of golf, and I'm to teach him the game of cricket!" James Brune paused, and was struck with an idea. "I wonder if we could get Hugh to join us. He wasn't much of a cricket player in Danvers. Practically had to be hog-tied and taken to a game. But he was a terrific bowler, when he got into the spirit of things. Smashed the wicket every time. No one ever scored off of him, not even Squire Tallmadge, who is no mean batsman."

Mrs. Brune hummed in doubt. "I shouldn't count on that, Jimmie. I have a notion that he thinks he's above common diversions." She paused. "I was just thinking, though. Now that I've met young Mr. McDougal, I've been wishing you had another sister to turn his head. They'd make a nice match, don't you think?"

James Brune laughed. "Now, Mother! Count your blessings, and leave well enough alone," he chided her. "If Father ever heard you say that, he'd lock you in your room until after Hugh and Reverdy were married! I know what you're thinking! Banish the thought!" He laughed again, bent to kiss her on the cheek, and left her room.

*　　*　　*

Over the next two weeks Hugh escorted the Brunes to the best London had to offer in the summer: concerts, balls, art galleries, and Vauxhall and Ranelagh Gardens. Reverdy was dazzled by the abundance of music, art, and social life. "I shan't want to return to Danvers, if this is merely the slow season," she confined to Hugh after the first week. "I am quite at home here."

"As am I," replied Hugh.

They went to the Opera House and saw a sumptuous production of one of Handel's works. They danced minuets and gavottes at Vauxhall. They visited art galleries, and Hugh bought a painting by the anonymous Dutch "Candlelight Master" of Athena gazing critically up at a statue of herself in a darkened Parthenon. They attended the theater, and saw David Garrick in one of his own plays, *Don Juan*, with an overture liberally adapted from Gluck's ballet of the same name. Hugh did not think much of the production, but Reverdy had never before seen a full stage production of a play, and he was pleased with her delight.

A merchant friend of Mr. Worley's invited Hugh and the Brunes to an evening concert on the terrace of his house that overlooked the Thames far down river from Windridge Court. They listened to a selection of Italian and French music played by a small ensemble of musicians. When the evening was over and the guests began leaving, but before the musicians could collect their instruments and charges, Hugh persuaded the ensemble to play Vivaldi's "Echo" Concerto, and paid them a crown each for the request.

One of the violins played the "echo" portion from a second-story balcony of the house, the other remained with the ensemble. The musicians performed the piece flawlessly. Hugh, Reverdy, and the remaining guests applauded the group.

Reverdy said, "That was enchanting, Hugh. What is it called?"

"The 'Echo.' It is two souls speaking to each other over a great distance—between, say, London and Danvers."

"Or...from across a room," suggested the girl.

"Or...over no distance at all."

"Yes." Reverdy fluttered her fan in thought. She asked, after a moment, "But, Hugh: Which of us is the echo?"

"Does it matter?" replied Hugh with a smile that revealed that he had not understood the import of her question.

It was then, and only just then, that Reverdy fully grasped the nature of their relationship; at least, what it was from Hugh's perspective. She could not say whether it elated her, or frightened her. "No," she answered in a near-whisper, "I don't suppose it matters."

Hugh smiled again, took her hand, and raised it to his lips.

The Brunes had planned to hire a boatman to row them upriver to see the Battersea Enamel Works and the villages of Wandsworth and Hammersmith on a day when Hugh left to work at Mr. Worley's, but a steady rain fell on London on the appointed day, and they canceled the outing.

Reverdy, bored and restless, went to Hugh's room in search of something to read. She had been in his room many occasions before, with either her mother or brother, for tea and conversation. Now, as she stole into his room and closed the door behind her, she felt a thrill of forbidden adventure; she was alone in his room. The first thing she saw was the intriguing painting of Athena fixed to the wall over Hugh's desk. Dutifully, she went to the bookcase and examined the titles. Most of the titles she saw were too serious or daunting. She selected a volume of Plutarch's *Lives*, translated by a scholar named McChesney, then roamed about the room guiltily, unable to resist her illicit curiosity.

On another table she saw sheets of drawings and went to look at them.

In the center of scattered piles of them she saw a completed sketch of a round Doric temple, such as graced the gardens and parks of many country estates. Behind the pillars and beneath the dome of this structure she saw what seemed to be a rough rendering of a statue of a goddess. At least, it struck her as a goddess. The figure was not drawn in a classical attitude or pose. It was a tall, straight figure, frozen in mid-stride, one arm at its side, the other holding up a lamp. Its shoulders and head were thrown back in pride and determination. A wind-blown chiton caressed the lines of her body.

Reverdy lifted the sketch and discovered others beneath it. These were studies of the statue from the front, back, and sides. Then her eyes widened in shock when she recognized her own face and body. Under one of the studies Hugh had written: "A study of Reverdy as Psyche, about to light the face of her lover. Temple to be commissioned and built on the family grounds at some future date, and secluded by a gate and hedgerow."

She knew the ancient legend of Psyche from Apuleius, the daughter of a Greek king, loved and possessed by Eros, but forbidden by him to see his face. On one of his nocturnal visits, she lit a lamp while he was sleeping and glimpsed his face. A drop of wax struck his face. He awoke, and angrily rejected her for having broken her promise. Eventually he relented and took her back, and obtained permission from Zeus to marry her.

Reverdy put down the book and picked up a drawing. There were two renderings of her on the sheet, in uncorrected pencil: one of her nude, and one of her in the same pose, but with the translucent chiton stressing the lines of her body. As she absorbed the renderings, her hand wandered to trace the lines of her own face, breasts, waist, and hips. How could he know her so well, she asked herself, unless he had studied her and imagined her in a way that was so...intimate? She felt violated and ecstatic at the same time. No man ever saw a woman this way, except in a bedroom...

The door to the room opened, and Reverdy, the sheet still in her hand, turned with a start. Hugh came in. He paused, then smiled at her and removed his wet greatcoat and hat. "You see there," he said, as though he had been with her all the while, "that I have revised the legend and not imposed such an unreasonable condition upon our union." He shook his head. "You will neither be punished abandonment, nor cursed by Aphrodite." He spoke without resentment for the intrusion, without even surprise at finding her here.

"Hugh, I..." began Reverdy, but she stopped. She did not know what to say.

Hugh shook his head. "I had not planned to tell you about the temple until it had been completed. But now that you know…now you know."

Trembling, Reverdy put the sheet back on the table, picked up the book, and turned to face him again. She felt naked before him now, and helpless. She wanted to escape, to flee with her new knowledge of him, and of herself, but knew that every movement she made would be observed by him, and that this would feel as intimate as his hands on her body. She felt self-conscious and transparent in a way she had never experienced before.

Hugh was studying her now. "When you are older," he said, "you will not wear that blush and look of astonishment. You will be a woman who knows that she belongs in that temple."

Reverdy pressed the book with both hands close to her breast, and braved an answer. "I'm not sorry I am here…Hugh. I'm glad that you know me…so well…" She thought that this was something the woman in the drawings would say. She thought she could feel what that woman felt, and be what he expected her to be: a mortal, who, by marrying him, would become a goddess.

Hugh shut his eyes for a moment, then turned and opened the door. He stood aside with his hand on the latch, waiting. "You must leave now, Reverdy…before we jeopardize our future, as we would surely do, if you stayed…"

Reverdy raised her head higher and swept past him without looking at him. But then she was turned violently and his lips were on hers. His arms encircled her and she felt her arms and hands pressed by the book that was between her breast and his chest. She heard him groan in hunger as he tasted her, and she answered in kind. His lips moved down her offered neck. When she stopped resisting and submitted to the fact that she would be consumed by him and crushed out of existence, he opened suddenly his arms and with the same violence held her away from him. "We have tasted our future together…Go…"

She nodded and stepped away from him, backing out of the room into the hallway, the book still pressed to her breast. When at last she tore her sight away from him, she turned and walked as though in a trance down the hall to her room. She heard his door close softly behind her.

*   *   *

It was the Brunes' last evening in London before they departed in the morning in the Kenricks' coach for Canterbury on the first leg of their journey back to Danvers. James Brune, with Hugh's leave, also invited Alex McDougal to the supper at Windridge Court. The latter brought with him another man, Bamber Faure, Vicar of St. Thraille's, in Surrey, where the McDougals maintained a residence. Faure was in the city to see the Bishop of London on church business and had naturally paid a visit on the McDougals, for Duncan McDougal was a vestryman in the Surrey parish. Hugh would not have otherwise invited a clergyman to the house, but civility obliged him to admit the man when the pair appeared and were announced by a servant. The vicar was quiet, contributing a few mundane remarks in the course of the evening's conversation. The talk turned from business, to speculation on the outcome of Admiral Byng's scheduled trial, to the foot riots in Cornwall and Manchester, and to the likelihood of more riots sparked by opposition to the new Militia Act.

At one point in the conversation, Vicar Faure abruptly claimed with icy conviction that, instead of reading the Riot Act to any mob that might assemble in Surrey, he would read it the five axioms of Alfred the Great. "And they would either disperse out of deference to a power mightier than Parliament, or they would defy God. In which case, the rogues would deserve to be cut down by the dragoons and reduced by as many volleys as soldiers could put into them."

In addition to formulating and promulgating these axioms, checking the Danish Viking invasion of England and thus saving the isle for Christianity, and translating Bede and Boethius, Alfred the Great, the ninth-century Saxon king, could also be credited with many other things, among them: making London the capital of Saxon England; founding Oxford University to produce semiliterate nobleman and court placemen; patronizing foreign scholars and welcoming learning at court; inventing the notched candle to mark the passage of time; and redesigning lanterns so that their light would not be extinguished by wind or draft.

The contradictions rife in his axioms, however, were not so obvious to this warrior king who seemed to be everything but a logician. Nor were they apparent to most of the guests seated at the supper table at Windridge Court, to whom the axioms represented the apex of their moral instruction, beyond what they absorbed in church and from the Bible.

Mrs. Brune, seated next to Reverdy, said, "My memory needs refreshment, Vicar. Please, forgive me, but what are those axioms?"

Alex McDougal, eager to display his learning, turned to the clergyman. "May I, reverend sir?" The vicar nodded with a smile.

Alex McDougal spoke. "The five axioms of Alfred the Great were that a wise God governed; that all suffering may be accounted a blessing; that God is the greatest good; that only the good are happy; and that a fore-knowledge of God does not conflict with man's free will."

Hugh Kenrick laughed. The table was startled. He assured his guests that he was not mocking Mr. McDougal, but the axioms. And because he had laughed, he felt honor-bound to explain his reaction. "In the spirit of dispassionate argument," he began, "let us examine these axioms." He smiled at his guests. It was a daring smile, a smile of warning. "If a man can be governed by an all-knowing, all-powerful being—wise or not—then he cannot have a free will, or, at least, none that mattered. Such a will would be useless, a fiction, for whatever he thought or did would be approved or opposed by this being, not to mention foreseen by it before the fellow was born. And if he has free will, then he cannot be governed by such a being, who would be peripheral to that man's existence. In which case, how could that being be a good? And—good for what?"

Mrs. Brune gasped. Vicar Faure began to reply, but changed his mind. James Brune and Alex McDougal stared at Hugh with incomprehension.

The table was quiet. Hugh waited for a reply. No one, however, not even the vicar, gave the least sign of agreement or protest. Reverdy Brune stared at Hugh with a subtle smile, and looked pleased that the force of his words had overwhelmed the others. Hugh was not certain whether he had offended the others, or lost them. He suspected the latter.

Vicar Faure at length cleared his throat and spoke, addressing the table at large, but actually Hugh, whom he had studied throughout the evening. "Logic is not to be the sole test of men's understanding, milord. God and man work hand-in-hand, and thus determine man's destiny. You impose strict reason on a subject which does not admit its unadulterated role." He paused to smile. "Why, even Mr. Locke acknowledged this point," he concluded with smugness.

Hugh shrugged. "I disagree with Mr. Locke on many points, reverend sir, and that is one of them." His grin invited the vicar to pursue the matter.

Vicar Faure's appraisal of Hugh's knowledge and powers of argumentation was more acute than that of anyone else present. He raised his eyebrows, cocked his head in careless concession, and chose not to answer.

James Brune glanced around the silent table, and changed the subject.

"Have any of you read that new book of Mr. Horlick's, *Twenty Moral Fables*? I purchased a copy yesterday, and found it not only amusing, but quite instructive, as well." The vicar, Alex McDougal, and Mrs. Brune all admitted to having read the book, and the conversation revived on that subject.

Later, when they had a private moment together, Hugh remarked to Reverdy, "Well, that was the shortest exchange on a serious subject I have ever provoked."

Reverdy stood looking up at him with undisguised adoration. "That is because Vicar Faure could not answer you so easily," she said. She clasped her hands together. "Oh, Hugh! Someday, when you chance to speak in Lords, I shall be there to see you cause the other lords to squirm, just as you caused the vicar to fidget! I'm so proud of you!"

"I was not entirely dispassionate, Reverdy, and that was no mere exercise in algebra. I meant what I said."

"How could you not mean it? So vigorous a mind as yours would not waste time on drolleries."

"Drolleries, indeed," said Hugh. "I questioned God, Reverdy, and to question Him is to question our ethic. To question that is to question the church, and to question the church is to question the state, doubt the king, and to flout everything associated with them. Vicar Faure knew that, which is why he did not pursue the matter. He is a slyly civil man, and an uninvited guest."

"He is a coward."

"He can afford to be one. The Crown stands behind him."

Reverdy glanced to either side of her, then lightly placed her palms on Hugh's chest. "Hugh," she whispered, "you are going to be a great man, and I shall be proud to stand in your temple…or lie in your bed."

Hugh took her hands and pressed their palms to his face.

They heard the swish of a gown, and turned to see Mrs. Brune standing in the hallway where they stood. They could not tell by her expression whether she was pleased or scandalized by what she had witnessed. "Milord, your guests are about to take their leave. Will you see them off?"

Hugh nodded. "Yes, of course." He paused. "Please, Mrs. Brune, favor me by calling me Hugh."

"I will so favor you, milord, when you are my son-in-law. Not until then." The woman glanced at her daughter. "I hope, milord, you were not putting wicked thoughts into my Reverdy's head."

Hugh laughed. "No, Mrs. Brune, I was not. The thoughts were already there."

Mrs. Brune blushed and her eyes grew wide. Reverdy hid a silent laugh behind her fan. Her mother turned with dignity and left the hallway.

Hugh said to Reverdy, "Good night, my wicked wife-to-be."

"Good night, Hugh." They both knew that she did not need to do it, but Reverdy solemnly bowed her head and performed a half-curtsy, then turned and followed her mother back into the supper room.

Chapter 28: The Olympian

THE NEXT MORNING HUGH ACCOMPANIED THE BRUNES AS FAR AS CANTERBURY, and stayed to see them depart in a Dover-bound inn coach. He would see Reverdy again soon, in another month, when he made the same journey back to Danvers.

On the coach ride back to London, Hugh's mind was pulled by two passions: his future with Reverdy, and answering Vicar Faure. He was intrigued by how they vied for his attention. When he arrived at Windridge Court, he ordered a light dinner to be brought to his room, and went to work on an essay he was to present to the Society of the Pippin in two evenings. Vicar Faure's pronouncements had given him a better idea for a subject, which was to discuss the link that John Milton, in many of his works, had made between tyranny and superstition. In the coach he had remembered a line from John Toland's *Christianity not Mysterious*, a book in his collection that had been overlooked by his uncle: "To believe the divinity of Scripture, or the sense of any passage thereof, without rational proofs and an evident consistency, is a blamable credulity and a temerarious opinion."

He also recalled something his father had written in one of his letters: "There are some five hundred and sixty members of the Commons, though no more than thirty understand reason, or even recognize it. The rest are cabbage heads. The thirty require only plain common sense on which to decide their actions or votes, reason clothed in good language. All the others are susceptible to flowing and harmonious rhetoric, whether it conveys any meaning or reason or not. These latter have ears to hear, but lack sense enough to judge; or, they have sense enough, but are hostile to reason because they have cut cards with the devils of complacency or vested interest. One or the other devil has claimed their souls, and has put a cork on their minds. Sir Henoch Pannell's speechmaking can thereby be grasped and explained." And this wisdom of his father's prompted him to remember another of Milton's truisms: "It is the vulgar folly of men to desert their own reason and, shutting their eyes, to think they see best with other men's..."

Hugh worked feverishly on his address for the next two days, breaking only for short naps and wolfishly consuming plates of food. He was so caught up in his task that he sent word to Benjamin Worley that he would not be able to go to Lion Key. He was determined to build his arguments, complete the thought, and finish his labor. Nothing else mattered to him. He even forgot about Reverdy, until he would occasionally notice her locket suspended above his desk.

When he finished one morning, he forced himself to take a turn around Whitehall, to pay the servants, and attend to the duties of ownership. He did this to freshen his mind. When he returned to his room, he reread his work.

It was flawless, correct, and beautiful. "This is mine," he said to himself. He felt tears well up in his eyes, tears of joy. Oh, what a blessing it was to be a man, to create, to labor and produce such a great thing—to be alive! It was a splendid thing he had done! He rose from his desk and looked down on the neat pile of paper before him with a smile and eyes narrowed in fierce, immaculate greed. He raised his arms in triumph, fists clenched, and laughed once. What a glorious thing is pride! It is almost an end in itself! No wonder churchmen preached against it! A truly proud man is not to be found in their flocks of souls humbled by the rumor of a great invisible wizard and the inexplicable! If it is a sin to feel such pride, then it is a sin to be a man!

A servant knocked on his door and announced that a "Negro gentleman" had called. Hugh had even forgotten Glorious Swain and his promise to meet him in front of a toy shop on the Strand before the Society convened tonight. Hugh threw on his coat and hat, rolled up his essay, and rushed out.

"I'll be gone for a month or so," he said to Swain as they walked up Whitehall Street to Charing Cross and the Strand. "In Danvers."

"I'll envy you for being away from London in August," said Swain.

"I must apologize for having forgotten our rendezvous."

"It must have been something important that made you forget."

"It was," sighed Hugh happily.

Swain glanced at his friend in the early evening light. He chuckled. "You are in love, my friend. Your eyes have that special set I know so well."

Hugh grinned in concession. "My betrothed was a guest for the last few weeks, together with her mother and brother. You'll meet her some day."

"She must be an exceptional woman to solicit and encourage *your* attentions."

"She is." Hugh shook his head. "But—I am in love with other things, too, Mr. Swain." He brandished the rolled-up essay. "Wait until you hear my address! I surprised even myself, this time!"

"What is the subject?"

"Milton's notion of tyranny and superstition, and how he thought they were inseparable monsters. It meant rereading *Paradise Lost, A Second Defense,* and *The Ready and Easy Way to Establish a Free Commonwealth.* It was quite a task. I have slept very little. I'm glad I had no school chores to complete. They would have suffered." Hugh asked, "Who is chairman of this meeting?"

"Steven," said Swain. "And it is Mathius's turn to be secretary."

*   *   *

"...And so, one can see the influence of Plato even on Cicero, who wrote that 'the world which we see is a simulacrum of an eternal one.' The arm of the past has not always had a benign effect on our age. No one today, not the basest criminal, nor the most enlightened lord, asks why a sovereign is credited with special sight and intelligence, and not a common man. The notion supposes that a sovereign is privy to a more perfect world and a more perfect order. The claim is unfounded, yet is asserted by any sovereign or prince or group of men who wish to rule a nation. They proclaim, 'We are the special hosts of perfect wisdom and flawless, temporal action. Question not our edicts and actions, even though they may impinge upon your life and liberty.' Is this not the argument of the Crown, whether or not divine origin or inspiration or purpose is claimed?"

Hugh paused to assess the effect of his words on his auditors. Seven intent and expectant faces waited for him to continue. The din of the Fruit Wench was a distant sound not heard by any of the men. The scratching quill of Mathius, as he took down Hugh's words in the Society ledger, was the only intrusive thing heard by the group.

Hugh continued. "Now, we are either true to the world as we find it, or we defer to the vision of one who denies that our existence is the end of all life. Milton was a great lover and advocate of liberty, but he, like his predecessors and successors, was not wholly immune from this *Corpus Mysticum*—that is my term for the phenomenon—and his wonderful works are corrupted by a belief in a temporal philosopher-king, or in a manly viceregent over the rest of his fellows. I have read nothing in the sophist whirligigs of casuists and theologians that cannot be reduced to the level of palmistry, or tarot cards, or magician's tricks. It is a great jumble of sea-devils, that whole mass of cobwebbed literature arguing for this or that God, or for this or that prince or king or protector. The tentacles of these hideous creatures are intertwined in a thousand Gordian knots! But once one has detected and exposed a single fallacy in that maleficent lore, why must one bother to master every twist and turn of those tentacles? The untying of one will unravel the others, and free one to go on and scale the heights of Olympus!"

Hugh put down his essay, bowed once to indicate that he had finished, and sat down. He tasted his tankard of ale to soothe his dry throat.

The others were quiet. Mathius, who sat at the opposite end of the table, dipped his quill into an inkpot and continued his note-taking. The sound of his quill across the ledger page seemed to drown out the voices, laughter, singing, and clatter of china, metal, and pottery in the tavern. As he dipped his quill once more, he looked up and said, "I am nearly finished here, sirs."

After a moment, Steven remarked, "Olympus—or Tyburn Tree?"

"By God, what a provocative position!" exclaimed Claude.

"It skirts the hem of perdition!" said Elspeth.

Abraham frowned. "What you posit," he said, "needs system."

"Agreed," said Hugh, knowing this was only the opening of the discussion. "What I have asserted here, is but a beginning."

Mathius glanced up from his task. "'Tis but the gurgulations of unformed and unconnected opinions," he ventured.

"I disagree," replied Muir. "I see in it the elements of an extraordinary but unassembled orrery."

Tobius looked thoughtful. "Do you presume to criticize Milton?"

Hugh said, "I cannot fault him for his imperfect knowledge. As our own knowledge of liberty and man is imperfect, his was more so. What I am saying is this: Every good point he makes on liberty, tyranny, and superstition is an echo of Aristotle, and a premonition of Locke. Every flaw, inconsistency, and concession to kings and power is an echo of Plato, and a premonition of Hobbes."

"Where would you place our own Mr. Hume?" asked Claude.

"He is an apotheosis of cynicism and skepticism. It is easier for many men to doubt than to be certain of a thing, easier to defer to authority or popular concurrence than to trouble themselves with establishing individual certitude. Mr. Hume, from what little I have read of him, seems destined to become the patron saint of the sluggish of mind and those who are dedicated to doubt and humility."

"Still, one could take exception to your remarks on Milton," said Tobius.

"I esteem him no less than do you, sir," answered Hugh. "But, in all his works, he labors to found liberty and right on Scripture. He had not the advantage of reading Locke. I say that if liberty and her sister freedoms are to be better founded and made proof against tyranny, we must avail ourselves of another catapult of reason than Scripture. That is, nature itself, and man."

"That has always been our Society's goal," said Abraham. "To divorce man and his purpose from Scripture and the prerogatives of priests and princes."

"On this point, we are all united," seconded Tobius.

"Are we?" asked Mathius. He had put down his quill, and sat forward with his hands folded before him on the ledger. He glanced from face to face. "Is there room here for dissent, or must we all submit to our own abbreviated form of 'popular concurrence'?"

Steven gestured with his hand. "What is your difference, Mathius?"

"Speak your mind," urged Tobius.

Mathius said, "Thank you, sirs." He looked at Hugh. "What, Miltiades, have you to say about our living sovereign? Not about some cold, abstract personage, as you excoriated just now, but His Majesty?"

Hugh shrugged. "Only that I have a wonderment about whether or not he is necessary. He consumes large amounts of Crown revenue, but does nothing."

"He is the symbol of our unity, sir. He is sovereign."

Hugh shook his head. "Our minds are our sovereigns, sir, and cost no man a farthing to employ or enjoy. A man's mind commands a realm greater than that ruled by any man in St. James's Palace. That is a more practical unity." Mathius looked doubtful. Hugh explained. "What else could tell you how to live? Say, to buckle your shoes? Pull up your hose? What to eat? To walk? All that we do, every day, is commanded by our minds. You could not afford the bales of paper to record every little action that is directed by your mind on a single day. His Majesty, however, commands nothing."

"These are trifles you cite, sir," scoffed Mathius.

"Then let us broaden the vista. Does a sovereign proclaim to a cobbler which leather to fashion into shoes? To a brewer, how long he should boil his hops? To a clockmaker, how to arrange his cogs and wheels? To a physician, which powders and herbs to prescribe?" Hugh gestured with his hands. "The instances are infinite in number, sir. At what point in any of them does a sovereign enter?"

Mathius narrowed his eyes, but averted Hugh's. "Are you claiming, perhaps, that we have no need of a sovereign?"

The men at the table stiffened at the question. It was a question none of them had ever dared ask or answer, except in his own mind.

Hugh held Mathius's unwavering, challenging glance. "I am saying that a king has very little to do with our lives, except to impose on us an extraordinary and burdensome cost."

Mathius shook his head. "Quite the contrary, sir. A sovereign is the keystone of any reasonable polity. Thus the extraordinary cost, which may be a burden to some."

Hugh sat back in his chair. "The evidence does not support your statement, sir."

Mathius sighed. "To a mind so young and impressionable as your own, sir, it is not evident, I concede. But while it is the purpose of education to put the evidence in it, as forcefully as possible, clearly your education has failed in this respect."

All the other men frowned. Steven said, "Mathius, that is a personal attack, and is not permitted in Society discussion." He glanced at Hugh, then back at Mathius. "You will please apologize to Miltiades."

"I will not, sir," retorted the offender. "It is one thing to meet for informative speculation on serious matters. It is another to speak blasphemy and sedition, as this young gentleman does this evening, and in doing so solicits our willing complicity."

Claude barked a laugh of contempt. "If we limited ourselves to what you misconceive as 'informative speculation,' sir, we should be no better than a chess club. I, for one, would resign."

"And I," added Abraham.

"I stand by my charge," said Mathius, looking at Hugh.

"You must present your evidence," replied Hugh.

"No, sir!" exclaimed Mathius, rising from his chair in agitation. "You must find better instruction!" His expression changed into one of barely disguised malice. "Is it merely the sovereign you question, sir, or is it the

Crown itself?"

"You needn't answer that question, Miltiades," said Steven.

"No, he need not," seconded Tobius. "The question need not be recognized." The other men nodded in agreement. Tobius rose and turned to Mathius. "Mathius, are you ill? What has taken possession of your mind?" he asked, some anger in his words. The men of the Society had had heated discussions in the past, but had never descended to personal invective. It was a serious infraction of the Society's rules. A second offense by a member resulted in automatic dismissal, and the members moved the venue of their meetings to another tavern or coffeehouse. This had happened only once before, ten years ago.

"Do you begrudge Miltiades for his ideas, or for his youth?" asked Muir.

"We are your friends, Mathius," said Elspeth. "Tell us what burr sits beneath the saddle of your senses."

"The buckram of patriotism is most unbecoming to you, sir," commented Claude. "It does not sit well on active minds."

Mathius paused before answering. He suddenly fell back in his chair, put his hands over his face, and gave a heavy sigh. He dropped his hands and looked around at his colleagues with a pained expression. "I...I am very sorry, sirs, for my outburst. I have been, these past weeks, in the grip of a fever of grief. You see, my dear, beloved wife...left this world...and it seems that a part of me has left with her...I have not been myself...not good company to anyone...I even struck a beggar who asked me for a pence this morning..." He faced Hugh. "My most humble apologies, sir, for my words to you. I fear I have insulted you beyond forgiveness."

Hugh nodded once. "I was not so much offended by your words, sir, as surprised by your manner. I accept your apology."

The men around the table sighed in relief. Steven rose and bowed to Mathius. "Our sincere condolences, Mathius. I am certain that the loss of your wife is as much a blow to you as the loss of your company would be a blow to us."

"Hear! Hear!" agreed the men.

"What did she die of?" asked Tobius.

Mathius shook his head. "Some pox or other," he said with a sigh, "one that rotted her innards and inflamed her skin. I paid three surgeons to treat her, but they could make nothing of her condition, though they charged me a small fortune for their coincidental remedies. She was in agony, and in the end, insensible to everything around her. One morning, as I was giving her water, her lips refused to part, even though a moment before she had asked me for a drink...her first words to anyone in days." Mathius seemed to be seeing the scene as he spoke of the event, then he rested his elbows on the table and buried his face in his hands again. Abruptly, he turned away.

Steven glanced around the table, then rose. "Gentlemen," he said with reluctance, "I move that we end this meeting. But, before we depart, we should settle on a date for our next supper, and also...well...help to defray our friend's expenses, for, as we all know, death is a costly affair, to the soul, and to the purse."

"I second that idea," said Muir.

All the men, including Hugh, reached into their pockets or purses and, a moment later, presented Mathius with a handful of crowns. Mathius accepted the money. He was shocked to see a golden guinea among the coins. This had been donated by Hugh, though he did not know this. "You...are the most generous friends a man could have," he said, his head bowed.

"Will you still be able to write up tonight's minutes, Mathius?" asked Steven. "One of us could volunteer to perform the task. And it is your turn to chair our next meeting."

"She is buried," replied Mathius plaintively, "and the task will help me to...rediscover my regular frame of mind. Yes, the next meeting... It will be all right. Thank you for the offer."

"Very well." After the members agreed on the date of their next meeting, Steven picked up the ornamented walking stick and struck the floor once with it. "Gentlemen of the Society, our usual concluding toast would mock the sad occasion, and we shall forgo it this one instance. We will meet again on this same date in August. Claude, it will be your turn to challenge our minds then. Steven, you will please act as recorder."

The members rose and left the room one by one.

When he left the Fruit Wench that evening, Mathius hired a hackney that took him to the home of the Marquis of Bilbury, where, from Brice Blissom, he received the gratitude of the young aristocrat, a promise, and a small sack of money, in exchange for the Society's ledger of minutes and an oral report on the meeting itself. No one suspected that William Horlick had resigned that evening from the Society of the Pippin.

*   *   *

As no member of the Society of the Pippin knew the marital status of his colleagues, nor their professions, nor their places of residence, nor even their names, no member could have known, or even suspected, that Mathius had lied—that he was married to a hectoring, "whither-go-ye?" woman who begrudged her husband his every free moment and nagged him constantly to abandon writing and find a more secure trade, that he had recently been dismissed from his part-time position with the wine merchant, and that beneath his mild, amenable, tolerant personality seethed envy for Hugh Kenrick's mind and eloquence, and jealousy for the special esteem paid him by the Society.

No member had reason to doubt Mathius. His wife's alleged illness and death could explain the man's erratic behavior over the last few months. Glorious Swain did not suspect the truth; nor did Hugh. They stayed behind in the tavern, and talked about things they had in common. At one point, Swain suggested, "You ought to think of publishing a book of some of your ideas, my friend. Under another name, of course. You have the means, and need no patron."

It was so obviously feasible an idea that Hugh was astonished that he had not had it himself. His face brightened. Then he frowned. "It would need to be published in the Netherlands," he said after a moment. "I don't believe any printer here would risk it. You heard Mathius. My theme disturbed him, and he is a friend. Think of how the clergy would sputter about it, and all the High Tories." Then he shook his head once. "No, not yet, Mr. Swain. Abraham was right, too: What I have to say, needs system. And you were right: I have tonight expressed merely the elements of a philosophy, shown you the unassembled parts of a golden orrery, and I am not certain I have them all. There are so many links and connections that must be made clearer in my own mind first, before I could put them on paper and broadcast them to the world."

Swain took his mug of ale and clicked it against Hugh's. "And a golden orrery it will be, sir, when you have completed that task, an orrery, not for comprehending the sun and its children, but for serving as a guide for men to grasp a reason and means for living. It will employ all the limbs of philosophy."

"But I don't want to be a philosopher," protested Hugh.

Glorious Swain laughed. And Hugh, realizing the irony of his own words, joined him in the laughter.

"My friend," said Swain, "these are exciting times! I feel fortunate to have witnessed them. I thank you for that."

Chapter 29: The Idyll

ON THE LAST DAY OF JULY, HUGH KENRICK STOPPED BY LION KEY TO BID Benjamin Worley farewell until September. Worley, however, boarded the family coach with him and gave Hugh some letters and business papers to deliver to his father. He left the coach on the Surrey side of London Bridge and shook Hugh's hand through the window. "Give my regards to milord and his lady, sir!" With another snap of the coachman's whip, the coach rumbled away again to begin the long leg to Canterbury.

From his window, Hugh watched the city recede. In the still summer air, a vast, unmoving lid of brown and black lay over the city, as though preparing to suffocate it. It was created by the thousands of fires in taverns, coffeehouses, the kitchens of homes, and manufacturing establishments. The mass of St. Paul's loomed beneath the lid, a dirty gray silhouette commanding the countless spikes of church steeples and columns. This was not one of London's "glorious" days. Hugh was glad to be leaving the city, if only for a while.

He had received a letter a few days before from his father, who reported that business correspondents in Sweden and France sent him news of the imminent invasion of Saxony by Frederick of Prussia, and that this had caused him to cancel plans for a short tour of the Continent.

"Our progress through the towns and countries would be impeded by military mischief and civil suspicion," he explained to Hugh. "We could even conceivably be detained as spies by one side of the hostilities or the other, and our return delayed by months. We shall, however, undertake a tour in the future, when all the grandees have tired of their destructive bravado and peace reigns again. There is so much to see and learn across the Channel in the way of libraries and art and modes of society, and I regret not having introduced you to them sooner. For example, in Germany, in the cathedral at Weltenburg, there stands at the entrance a gold equestrian of St. George slaying a serpentine dragon. It is by the Asam brothers, and faces inward, just inside the main doors, a most unusual but effective setting. I saw it once, when I was your age, and have not seen its like on our isle. I believe you would appreciate the work, for you, to judge by some of your remarks at Dr. Comyn's school, seem predisposed to slay some of the serpents at large in this nation…"

Garnet Kenrick had ended the letter with a warning. "Your uncle may precede your return to London, or follow it, in order to attend Lords and maintain his connections there…"

The warning did not concern Hugh. Justice, he was learning, demanded cold action forged by the ceaseless bellows of moral judgment. He would never speak to his uncle again.

He enjoyed his holiday at home, despite the awkward necessity of boy-cotting his uncle in the house and on the grounds of the estate. He took his meals with his parents and sister, Alice, or alone when his family could not avoid sharing a table with the Earl. But he shared with his parents the unspoken irony of imposing on his uncle the same punishment his uncle had imposed on him many years ago. Basil Kenrick dared not speak of Hugh's constant absence, even though he could see his nephew from a window coming and going around the house and grounds. It was a subject he did not wish to discuss. He himself behaved as though Hugh was nowhere near Danvers; indeed, as though he did not exist.

Only the servants talked about the alienation of affection they had observed between the Earl and his nephew, and whispered about it in hud-dled secrecy in the kitchen and their own quarters. Owen Runcorn, raised to major domo of the Baron's staff, headed the faction that sided with Hugh and his parents; Alden Curle, major domo of the Earl's staff, headed the fac-tion of servants who sided with the Earl. Curle endured Runcorn's sly insinuations and subtle taunts, for not only did he know that he was party to the commission of a wrong, but that Runcorn could lay him low in no time, if their own animosity ever erupted into physical violence.

Hugh showed his father his sketches for the "temple" to Reverdy. Garnet Kenrick approved of the project, but with the remark, "It will never become a reality so long as your uncle has title to these grounds."

Hugh had shrugged. "Then I shall wait until he is dead." He spoke with the same indifference he might have felt for an aged sheep.

His father and he discussed his future education, once he had finished another year at Dr. Comyn's. "I think," said the Baron, "you would do well at either Oxford or Cambridge. You would be admitted to either without difficulty."

Hugh sensed reticence beneath his father's confident assertion. "But— what are your fears?"

The Baron smiled, amused that his son could detect his reservations. "That you would be sent down from either school for voicing unconventional wisdom," he said. "For branding the hands of your masters there, so to speak. These are Crown schools, and no matter what wild rumors of profligacy and dissipation one may hear about the gentlemen who attend them, those boys and men emerge from them with the Tory stamp of approval deeply seared on their foreheads. You would need to hold your tongue and stay your pen. You would more likely put all those young bucks and their instructors to shame—and yourself out, in disgrace."

Hugh felt glad that his father knew him so well. "What are the alternatives?"

They were on horseback, pausing by a pond created half a century ago by Hugh's grandfather. The Baron had ridden with Hugh over the farthest reaches of the landscaped grounds of Danvers to decide what pruning and trimming tasks needed to be assigned next to the groundskeepers. Their mounts drank thirstily from the pond. Around them were stands of willow, alder, and poplar, and beyond them, on higher, drier ground, were clusters of oak, ash, and beech. Some swans marked time on the other side of the pond, waiting for the intruders to leave. Robins and nightingales flitted from tree to tree under the cloudless, warm sky.

"Edinburgh," said the Baron, "which is acquiring a reputation for its learning, and for encouraging unconventional but useful thought. I have heard smart things said about that university. And, there is the university at Leyden, in Holland. Dissenters of all suasions send their sons there, barred as they are from the universities here. You would, I think, be happier at one of those schools, and not need play the Argonaut Meleager and slay every Calydonian bore who raised his silly head or hand against you. You would not only acquire a first-rate education, but probably associate daily with persons of like temperament and mind, and, perhaps, even make some friends there. Oh! Look!"

The Baron pointed to a robin that had flown from its nest in one tree. High above it, a sparrowhawk appeared out of nowhere, circled once, then swooped down in a dead drop and captured the surprised and luckless robin in its talons. The sparrowhawk swept back up in a violent arch not ten feet from the ground, rose swiftly, then leveled off and flew back over the trees to disappear with its prey.

Hugh said, "There is a merchantman called the *Sparrowhawk*, that anchored at Mr. Worley's key. I met the captain, Mr. Ramshaw." He glanced with his own amused smile at his father. "I am not incapable of friendship, Father. I have made friends in London. Seven, to be exact."

The Baron looked penitent. "I did not think you were incapable, Hugh," he replied. "However, they must be unusual persons. I should like to meet them, someday."

"They are a society of thinkers. I chanced upon them last year. Perhaps, when you next go to London, I could introduce you to at least one of them. They are every bit as free-thinking as many on Dr. Comyn's staff."

The Baron asked, "Are they teachers, as well?"

Hugh grinned. "I do not know what are their trades or professions, and they do not know who I am. We know each other only by club names. I am treated as an equal, in mind and in spirit."

Garnet Kenrick studied his son with undisguised astonishment. "Seven, you say? And, as an equal?" He laughed. "Dear me, I shall have to revise my estimate of humanity, Hugh! Think of it! Seven men exist who practically contradict one of Mr. Newton's laws!" He reined his horse away from the pond, and smiled broadly. He was happy that his son had found friends, happy that Hugh was happy. "Of course, you know," he said as Hugh joined him on a circuit of the pond, "that if you were His Majesty, and I a mere general, I would not be allowed to turn my back on you, as I just did, not even if I were mounted, as I am. I would need to have trained my steed here to walk backwards, away from the royal presence, so that I would not impute cowardice or unworthiness to His Majesty. There is a humorous anecdote concerning Judge Charles Pratt, who rode with the king to a review, and could not get his mount to stop backing into His Majesty..."

Roger Tallmadge was excited to see his friend again, and about one other thing: His older brother, Francis, had been appointed a cornet in the Duke of Cumberland's Own Regiment of Horse. He laughed when he saw the look of shock on Hugh's face.

"How was that accomplished?" asked Hugh.

They were alone together in a field on the Tallmadge estate, hunting for partridge and grouse for the Tallmadge kitchen. Each carried a fowling piece loaded with shot, and from their shoulders were slung leather bags stuffed with game.

"Oh, it happened by chance. My father has friends in the Ordnance Office, and they have friends in court, who have friends on the Privy Council. My father wrote someone a letter, and mentioned that Francis was seeking to purchase a commission in some old regiment. And this person wrote back saying that it could be arranged, as there were vacancies. And— there is a chance that if Cumberland is sent to help King Frederick—I guess you know how much Mr. Pitt is opposed to merely fighting the French on the Continent—Francis may accompany him as an aide! Of course, at first, he would have to perform all sorts of menial duties, but it's a start. Francis left for London a week ago."

"How much did your father pay for his commission?"

"Oh...hundreds of pounds, I think. But Francis will be getting one hundred and fifty a year, which he's promised to pay Father, once he deducts for costs and mounts and such."

"I wasn't aware that your father had government connections."

"Didn't you know? He was himself a staff cornet with General Wills during the 'Fifteen, not much older than Francis. He was wounded at the siege of Preston, where the Scots surrendered. And he not only touched the hands of Marlborough when the Duke was alive, but was an escort at his funeral procession. He has all kinds of friends who have places in govern- ment, friends he made during the 'Fifteen campaign. And the stories he has to tell! Soldiering is a hard life, he warned Francis, even for the generals."

Hugh studied his friend for a moment. "You would like to follow your father and Francis to glory, wouldn't you?"

"Well, I don't know..." Roger stopped suddenly. "Wait!" He stooped to pick up a stone, and hurled it into a clump of brush ahead of them. A flock of partridges exploded from the brush, and Roger raised his piece and fired at the fleeing birds. None tumbled to the ground.

"You must do better than that," remarked Hugh, "if you want to don a gorget."

"Officers don't carry muskets."

"They may need to, in North America," said Hugh. "The French and the aborigines there don't exchange courtesies with us before instigating their butchery." He watched his friend casually reload his fowling piece with powder and a bag of shot. "And you'll need to improve your loading time. A good soldier can load and fire three times a minute. But I've heard that the Prussians can do five."

"Then it's a good thing they're on our side!"

Hugh laughed. "Oh? I thought that we were on theirs." The pair moved on through the field, paying less attention to the game around them than to their conversation. "What do you think of this war, Roger?"

The boy shrugged. "I hope it lasts long enough that I can get into it. I'd like to see some of life and the world before becoming a gentleman farmer."

"There is more to life than fighting," said Hugh. "There is the life of the mind, of sitting back and looking at the world and pondering what one wishes to do in it. I wish to go into commerce and trade, and grow richer for it." He paused to glance at Roger. "Glory is to be found in commerce, sired by honor and courage and riskier strategy than any employed by Saxe or Cumberland." He smiled. "Someday, after all the kings and princes and pretenders have exhausted their countries and their excuses for power, nations will boast instead of the size of their commerce and the comfort of their citizens. This is an age of reason, Roger, and it will advance, leaving the kings and princes far behind, ruling only over paper empires—in history books. England will be foremost among those nations, an England that will stretch from Margate and St. Peter Port to the Mississippi River. Mr. Pitt seems to be the only man in government who understands that, or who has a glimmer of it. He has a long view of things, and of what is at stake, and I admire him for it."

"Mr. Pitt is out of government now," remarked Roger.

"Not for long. He'll be back. Hold!" Hugh suddenly raised his piece, aimed, and fired at a rabbit that leaped from beneath a shrub. The rabbit dropped instantly. "Some stew for your table, Roger," he said. They walked over and inspected the rabbit.

"You got it in the head again," said Roger.

Hugh picked up the animal and put it into his bag. "There'll be less shot for your cook to pick out of the meat."

"Why do you think Mr. Pitt will come back?" asked Roger as they moved on.

"Because he is the only man, it seems, who has a policy. And, he is a friend to liberty. Liberty and empire are not incompatible. That is why France must lose, ultimately. It could not sustain an empire of peasants and serfs in North America or anywhere else. But an empire of liberty? That is a different matter! And that is where England has the advantage. God knows, England is not perfect, but it is closer to liberty than France or any other nation will ever be in a hundred years."

Roger glanced at his friend. "You seem to have profited much by your stay in London."

"Perhaps your father will allow you to stay with me there for a while. I could show you so much!"

"I would like that!"

Hugh saw too little of Reverdy during his idyll in Danvers. He called on her and the Brunes almost every day, and often supped and had tea at the Brune house, but she always seemed to be in the company of her family. Her mother, especially, made certain that she was present when Hugh was near her daughter.

Mrs. Brune's eagerness to have Hugh as a son-in-law had measurably abated since the Brunes' return from London. She was not so much concerned for Reverdy's virtue as for Hugh's influence on her daughter's comportment as a respectable, marriageable lady. She had broached the subject of Hugh's behavior with her husband, Robert Brune, and expressed subtle misgivings and doubts about Hugh's character. She reported to him Hugh's mockery of Alfred the Great's five axioms, and ended by comparing Hugh with a certain John Wilkes, the high sheriff of Buckingham and notorious libertine and rake, of whom she had heard in London gossip.

Robert Brune, confined to a wheelchair with the gout, had merely laughed in dismissal of his wife's worries. "If what you say is true, deary," he said, "our Reverdy can only become the wiser. Besides, James and the Baron and Hugh himself contradict you."

"He is not...normal," answered Mrs. Brune. "He is a troublemaker. There was that incident with the Duke, and now, I hear, he won't even speak to his uncle, the Earl. It's...scandalous."

Robert Brune refused to discuss the matter further. He did not like the Duke of Cumberland or the Earl of Danvers, while the Five Axioms of Alfred the Great had no special place in his ethics. Mrs. Brune, for her part, composed a letter to Duncan McDougal in Surrey that gushed with compliments for his son, Alex, and extended an open invitation to him and his family to stay at the Brunes's.

*   *   *

Hugh left the great house on a lone, two-day outing to inspect the rabbit warrens and hutches his father had had dug the past winter. He called first on Mr. Hanway, the warden, and received a report from that man that the cony population had increased dramatically, and that the only poachers were transient vagabonds. He gave Hugh a map of the hutches' locations, and advice on how to deal with poachers. Before Hugh rode from his lodge, the warden discreetly inquired if the Baron was satisfied with his management and policing of the estate. "My father is quite satisfied, Mr. Hanway, have no doubt about that. I wish merely to become more familiar with the grounds."

"Then, good day to you, milord, and may no harm come to you."

Hugh smiled, touched his hat, and rode off. He carried a fowling piece, two pistols, matches for a campfire, and, with other necessities in his saddlebags, some books and a notebook. He had volunteered to inspect the warrens, first, because he was curious about them, and then because he desired a quantum of solitude, a time away from everyone, including those he cared for.

At the end of the first day, he sat in a deserted tenant's cottage and wrote a proposal for his father to consider: Instead of maintaining warrens and hutches in the wild in which to breed rabbits, why not set aside an acre and build coops? This would save the grasslands and meadows for more important pasturing of sheep and cattle, and prevent poaching, and make more efficient use of the warden's and gamekeeper's time. It seemed to make no difference, he noted, where conies lived, so long as they were fed, and he did not think that artificial confinement would affect their multiplication. It was a modest suggestion, thought Hugh, but if implemented could save the estate the bother of letting land lie fallow until it recovered from the damage caused by the conies' appetites.

He sat at the door of the cottage until past midnight, staring at the moonlit landscape, glancing occasionally up at the stars, at peace with himself and with the world, not permitting memories of the past or thoughts of the future to disturb his inner tranquility.

It was late afternoon on the second day when he approached the end of his circuit around the estate and neared the property of the Brunes. He had passed through two villages and many leaseholds and farms, and forded two streams that wound their way from the Onyx River to irrigate the flat meadowland that was now giving way to heath. He had toyed with the idea of taking another day to ride south to the coast and skirt the cliffs as far as St. Aldhelm's Head, or even travel from Lulworth to Steeple.

The sun was warm and he decided to rest himself and his mount near the last stream. There was a cluster of young pines and shrubbery clinging to the banks of the stream, and beyond that he could see the dots of the Brune house and its outbuildings on the horizon.

As he neared the pines, he espied another horse, tethered to a shrub, and then a woman's garments and a straw hat atop one of the bushes.

When the stream came into sight, he reined his mount to a halt.

Reverdy Brune emerged from the water. Her black hair, longer than he had imagined, fell to her shoulders. Drops glistened on her face and bare arms. She was clad only in a cotton camisole that clung to a body whose planes and curves he had only guessed at—and had, he knew, guessed correctly. She stepped onto the grass, closed her eyes, and raised her arms to let the warm breeze caress her. She stood that way for a long time, oblivious to Hugh's presence and everything else around her but her own being.

Hugh sat very still, enchanted by the sight, drawn to it, his desire to leap down and hold Reverdy fighting his desire to prolong this vision of her.

His mount shook its mane and caused the bridle to jingle.

Reverdy opened her eyes, but otherwise did not move. She recognized her observer instantly. Then, holding Hugh's glance, she lowered her arms to her sides. She made no attempt to flee, made no sign of false modesty. The breeze played with the camisole and sharply sculpted her legs and breasts.

Hugh dismounted, threw the reins of his mount over a bush, then removed his hat and coat and let them drop to the ground.

He walked up to Reverdy, then fell to his knees. He took her hands and kissed their palms, then allowed his own fingers to wander over her body to trace her legs, hips, waist, and breasts beneath the wet cotton. He looked up at her, and saw a faint hint of fear in her eyes, together with a hope that he would do with her what he would—and a courage to accept it. Instead, he encircled her with his arms and buried one side of his face between her breasts.

She heard him inhale deeply, as though to breathe her aroma and drink the water from her camisole. His arms tightened as he pressed her closer to him. She rested trembling hands on his head and greedily stroked his hair and the side of his face. They remained that way for a long while. Reverdy shut her eyes, thinking that this would dispel a new fear that was growing in her.

The next thing she knew, Hugh had risen and kissed her. He held her away. "We will be married next year," he said in a voice that rasped slightly, "and we will spend our wedding night here, on this grass. Can you wait?"

She nodded once.

He ran his hand once more from between her legs, up over her breasts, her neck, and finally her face and hair. She looked up into his intent eyes and face straining to control the violence of his ownership of her, and wished she could be smashed by them. Her own knees gave way, and she knelt before him to rest her head against the buckle of his sword belt. Then she sat back on her heels, undid the lace string that held the camisole to her shoulders, and let the garment fall. She pushed it away from her so that her hair dangled in the air beyond her shoulder blades. She held his glance, openly challenging him, testing his power over her and himself. She was unsure whether she admired or feared his control, for it was a servant of his own purposes, and she did not know if she approved of those purposes, or if she could ever influence them. She sat there, exposed to him, proud of what he was seeing, proud that it was hers and that she had it to submit to his sight and carnal enjoyment, wanting him to surrender to it and crush her here and now in the grass...because if he surrendered, she would know that a life with him was possible...and if he did not surrender, that she would be a helpless appendage to his life, a willing one but still helpless, and she was not certain that this would give her happiness. These thoughts came to her fast and unbidden, and were clouded by the throbbing in her temples and the blood racing through her veins, and were quickly dissolved by the ecstasy of expectation.

She was about to raise her arms in invitation, when he said, "You will look like this on our wedding night." He reached down to run gentle fingers over her forehead. Her hands came together to hold his hand and pressed the fingers closer. Then he withdrew his hand and stood to his full height. "Get dressed," he commanded in a hoarse near-whisper. "I'll escort you back as far as your west gate." He turned and walked back to his mount.

When she was finished dressing—and she resented the necessity of it, for she would rather have ridden back naked and flaunted her intimacy with Hugh to her parents—he tied the ribbon of her hat beneath her chin, then lifted her up onto her side-saddle. They rode in silence in the direction of her house, their hands clasped together. When they reached the west gate, he raised her gloved hand and brushed the palm over his cheek, then let it go. He said, "I'll come over for tea at noon tomorrow." Solemnly, he doffed his hat, then reined his mount around and rode off at a controlled trot.

Chapter 30: The Arrests

TWO MORNINGS AFTER HUGH KENRICK LEFT LONDON FOR DANVERS, POSTERS were found pasted to the great doors of Westminster Abbey and St. Paul's Cathedral, and were instantly and furiously ripped down by the deacons who found them. Knots of merchants, tradesmen, and other men able to read gathered to peruse similar posters that had appeared overnight on the pillars in the piazza of the Royal Exchange, on the doors of Westminster Hall, on some walls of the King's Bench Office, and on walls around the Inns of Court. The homes of some peers, and that of the Speaker of the Commons, boasted the posters. Soon watchmen and constables arrived and tore them down. Some spectators cheered, while others were silent. Bailiffs found bundles of the posters, wrapped in twine, deposited in front of Old Bailey and Newgate Prison. The watchguard on Westminster Bridge turned over to a justice of the peace bundles of the poster found in alcoves on both sides of the Thames.

The text of the poster read:

"Arise to establish a New Order! Liberty and Monarchy are eternal
enemies! Scripture is a Prescription for Tyranny, and Atheism is
England's only Salvation! Elevate and honor the Proud, and humble
God and his credulous sheep! Question the Legitimacy of His
Mongrel Majesty from Hanover! George's bloody reign rests on
a dung heap of sophist whirligigs! His heir the Prince of Wales
could not earn a farthing as a dustman or glover, yet will rule a
nation of his Betters! The Crown is a tiara of cobwebbed dogma,
but has the appetite of a pig, and consumes our sustenance! Join
The Society of the Pippin!

Londoners had heard of the Beefsteak Club, of the Robin Hood Society, of White's Club, of the Literary Club, and of Boodle's and Crockford's. Clubs and societies were as numerous as churches and chapels, and as diverse in their purposes and practices.

But no one had ever heard of the Society of the Pippin. There was some talk about the posters in the taverns and coffeehouses among that small portion of the public that had read the posters before they were removed, but the pressing matters of politics, war, and trade caused those men to forget the posters and what they had said. Some letters appeared in news-papers a few days later, complaining about the posters and calling for a gov-ernment investigation. The authorities, accustomed to mobs, riots and spontaneous demonstrations of public support or anger, fully expected to hear reports of a rabble marching through the streets to Parliament, and debated among themselves whether or not to recommend to His Majesty that he advise the army to be prepared to disperse it.

Nothing, however, happened, and for two reasons. No one knew any-thing about the Society of the Pippin, much less how to communicate with it or enlist in its ranks. And, while the statements on the posters were undoubtedly provocative, offensive, and even libelous, few who read them understood them. Except for the blasphemy against the Scriptures, and the aspersing of the royal family, the statements were too broad to be connected to any current or past subject of controversy or cause. The posters did not reappear, and the authorities concluded that they were the work of a tilted crackpot who had exhausted his funds in carrying out the mischief.

A poster had been put on the door of the residence of the Marquis of Bilbury. A servant took it down and brought it to Brice Blissom, who showed it to his father over breakfast. The elder Marquis was outraged, as was his son. The son assured his father that he would look into it and find out who was responsible so that legal action could be taken. The elder Mar-quis grunted in satisfaction, content that his son was maturing at last.

It was Brice Blissom who had put it on the door, after the family and household had retired. It was he also who, incognito, had paid a handful of men to put the posters up around the city; had paid to have them secretly printed; and had paid William Horlick to compose the call to revolution from the Society's ledger of minutes.

Two evenings after the posters appeared, he entertained, in a private supper box at Vauxhall Gardens, a junior attorney-general who was a dis-tant cousin and engaged to the religious daughter of an equally religious earl, and a junior solicitor-general, who was not related but who owed the young marquis a thousand pounds from a night-long game of faro. With the exquisite food and fine drink came two reputable and pretty courtesans, whose company the junior officials could not otherwise afford. A drunken orgy ensued, and the party made such a commotion that the manager requested that the Marquis and his party leave. As a favor, Brice Blissom paid the manager not to report the "delicate but damning doings" to anyone.

Early the next day, Brice Blissom called at the office of the junior attorney-general and presented to the hung-over man "some interesting documents." These were a copy of the poster and the minutes ledger of the Society of the Pippin. He stated that he wished to file informations of a conspiracy to disturb the tranquility of the government, and of published libels of the king, Crown, and Parliament. The posters, he explained, had been broadcast in many boroughs, as municipal authorities could confirm. He had knowledge of the date, time, and location of the next meeting of the Society of the Pippin, and, in conformance with his duty to His Majesty and the nation, wished to sue to bring the conspirators to justice with all possible dispatch.

The Society and its posters, he explained to the stunned junior attorney-general, could be a part of a larger, insidious French plot to incapacitate England with civil strife. The French, he said, had tried it before during the 'Forty-five with the Young Pretender. The Marquis pointed to the heads of the Scottish rebels—or what remained of them—visible through his distant cousin's window. They were impaled on poles over the Temple Bar Gate, and had looked down on passersby for ten years. He reminded his stunned cousin of his duty to the Crown and to the king, and also of the favor he had so recently done for him, and assured him that, even though it might seem a minor matter, the Crown and king would be grateful for any swift action taken.

The junior attorney-general sent for the junior solicitor-general, showed him the documents, and conferred with him on the urgency of the matter. He also mentioned the Marquis's late favor. The attorney-general and solicitor-general, who had delegated certain responsibilities to their subordinates, were away at their country homes for the summer, and would not, presumed the juniors, want to be consulted on so pedestrian a matter.

The junior solicitor-general, who represented any legal matters concerning the state, agreed that the documents were proof of a heinous attempt to disparage the king and the government; he also agreed that the authors of the documents were guilty of the chargeable crime of blasphemy. The juniors agreed that action was called for, action that would also be a credit to their careers. The young marquis promised the junior attorney-general his father's political support in the future, if it was needed, and proposed to write a note of waiver absolving the junior solicitor-general of his gambling debt—provided the culprits were in fetters the very night of their criminal meeting. Brice Blissom also offered to indemnify the solicitor-general, the attorney-general, and their subordinates from any suits resulting from a failure of the courts to find the parties guilty of any charge.

On that note, Brice Blissom took his leave. He had refrained from naming Hugh Kenrick, for he wished to surprise that party with an unexpected arrest; also, he was afraid that the Kenrick family might have connections in the government and be warned of the impending scandal. The junior attorney-general and his colleague wondered privately why their patron was so eager to see the Society broken and punished. But they had no need to wonder about the carrots he had dangled before them, or about the stick, which was their scandalous behavior at Vauxhall Gardens the night before. They concluded that they had been set up, that the young Marquis was a devil, and that they must pay him his due.

The junior attorney-general and his colleague made an urgent appointment with the secretary of state, northern department, to present the case and persuade him to sign a general warrant for the arrest of the members of the Society of the Pippin. This eminent person, however, was a member of the Board of Trade and Plantations, an overseer of the East India Company, and an advisor to the Duke of Cumberland, and at the moment was too embroiled in a multitude of other duties to chat with the subministers. After being advised that the matter did not personally involve the king or the present ministry, he delegated responsibility for its handling and resolution to Sir Miles Goostrey, an under-secretary of state.

The under-secretary of state listened to the arguments, read the poster, and became fixated on some of the leaves of the ledger. He was properly appalled by what he read, and ordered drawn up a general warrant for the arrest of the "authors, printers, and publishers" of the material.

That evening he included it in a pile of other documents requiring the secretary's signature, and it was signed by that eminence after only a cursory glance. "And what's this?" the secretary asked hurriedly. "More spouting club slander? By God! You teach some men to read and the next thing you know they're rewriting the Bible! Oh, yes, this was what you queried me about earlier, is it? I see, I see...Well, here, Goostrey, see this through, would you? And be sure these dolts are paid well for their crassitude! You know, pilloried, or hanged, or whatever the court sees fit as punishment. There's so much scribaceous cacodoxy about these days, you never know where it could all lead! We really oughtn't to encourage it...And this? Another arrest for rioting against the Militia Act? Let me see here…persons not yet conscripted? Damn it all! These ungrateful brutes ought to be tried under the Mutiny Act, ought to be whipped and strung up by their thumbs, like any deserter!… How much more have you? What time is it? Newcastle's expecting me for supper…"

The next morning the junior attorney-general filed the informations with the King's Bench, and deputized two king's messengers to carry out the warrant on the evening of August 3. These worthies in turn arranged to have several parish constables accompany them to the place of arrest— "the Fruit Wench public house on the Strand, at the junction of Villiers Street"—for the informations indicated eight conspirators. The messengers, the constables, and the under-sheriff who would lead them were all bewildered by the absence of names on the general warrants. Their instructions were to arrest anyone admitting to membership in the oddly named club, which would meet at eight o'clock the next evening. The messengers were told that the members went by secret names, and that one of the conspirators was a nephew of a peer.

"If that much is known about him, why does his name not appear on the warrant?" asked the under-sheriff.

"There must be a delicate political reason behind this action," replied one of the messengers, "and one of importance. It is not our privilege to pry."

"Begging your pardon, good sir," said the under-sheriff, "but it's a damned queer warrant you carry. Still, we'll do our duty." He turned to one of the constables. "We'll need a cart to carry them away. And cuffs. And a driver. Go and fix all that up, would you?"

On the evening of August 3, the Fruit Wench was as crowded and noisy as ever. The patrons' talk centered on the food riots in outlying counties, on the trouble brewing over the Militia Act, and on the Pitt-Newcastle-Grenville dispute over policy. There was even speculation on what steps England would take to aid Prussia, if Frederick struck against Austria and the Imperial Coalition. Mabel Petty welcomed Tobius and Claude, who arrived simultaneously, took their order for supper and port, and escorted them to the room in the rear. Elspeth, Steven, and Abraham arrived shortly afterward. They exchanged remarks about the food riots, the Militia Act riots, and the political turmoil. But they were oblivious to any news about the posters that bore their club's name.

The men awaited the arrival of Mathius, who would convene the meeting. Muir also was tardy. Steven brought a fresh new ledger in which to record the discussion, while Claude studied the notes for his address to the Society. Miltiades, they all knew, would be absent from this and the next meeting. Claude began to wonder out loud who he actually was, but Tobius reminded him of the rule never to speculate about the true identities of the members.

At eight o'clock they heard the clump of several pairs of boots approach the partitioned room. An under-sheriff, six constables, and two liveried men appeared and blocked the opening to the room. The noises of the tavern in front had diminished. The under-sheriff glanced at the men at the table. "Am I addressing members of an organization that styles itself the Society of the Pippin?"

The members looked at one another. Tobius rose and answered, "You are, sir. We are all members of that society. What is your business here?"

The under-sheriff nodded to one of the liveried men, who stepped forward, opened an envelope that bore the royal crest, and took out a large sheet of paper, from which he read:

"By order of the Secretary of State, Robert D'Arcy, Earl Holderness, and of the Attorney-General, Sir Charles Yorke, on the second day of August, 1756, in the twenty-ninth year of the glorious reign of His Most Gracious Majesty, George Rex the Second, you, gentlemen, confessed and acknowledged members of a private association styled the Society of the Pippin, are commanded to submit to arrest and detention without bail, for the purpose of answering questions put to you by the Secretary of State or his proxies, the Attorney-General or his proxies, and the Solicitor-General or his proxies, and to give truthful and verifiable answers to their queries under penalty of perjury."

The messenger paused. "What are your names, sirs?"

One by one, the members rose as the warrant was being read. The constables produced pistols and twisted their barrels to make them ready.

"On what charge, sir," demanded Tobius, "are we to be denied our liberty?"

"I cannot say, sir," replied the messenger, "for we do not know. It must be a serious charge to merit such an extraordinary warrant."

"I demand to know the charge!" said Claude.

The messenger shrugged. "The charge will be determined upon completion of your examination."

The under-sheriff held up his baton of office. "Will you gentlemen submit to cuffs, or must you be taken into custody by force and injury?"

The suddenness of the event paralyzed the members. Tobius noticed that Claude was fingering the pommel of his sword. He shook his head and said, "I recommend, gentlemen, that we go with these men, and resist this outrage through legal channels."

"That is a wise recommendation, sir," remarked the under-sheriff. "Unbuckle your swords, please, and present your wrists for cuffs."

As the members obeyed, Abraham asked, "Where are we to be taken?"

"To the Fleet Prison, and kept there until the Secretaries are ready to examine you."

As five sets of cuffs were snapped over five pairs of wrists, the messenger asked again, "What are your names, please?"

Tobius replied, "We will give our names to the Secretary, sir, when we are informed of the nature of our crime."

"As you wish, sir," replied the messenger. "I feel obliged to remind you, however, that this warrant does not represent a criminal charge. It is an attainder."

Claude laughed bitterly. "How could it represent a charge, sir, when it does not name a crime?"

The messenger looked offended. "I do not make the law, sir, but merely carry it out. You are suspected of complicity concerning whatever charges will be determined." He looked around. "Our information is that there are eight members of this society. Where are the remaining three?"

Steven glanced around at his friends. "We don't know," he said with emphatic finality.

The under-sheriff shrugged. "I should advise you gentlemen that if information is not volunteered to the Secretaries in civil conversation, it may be volunteered on the application of pressing stones, pelliwinks, or other machines of confession."

"We will volunteer our names when we learn the charges," said Elspeth.

The members were led out of the Fruit Wench, each constable grasping a prisoner by the shoulder. The under-sheriff led the way, carrying the new ledger, an armful of sheathed swords, and the walking stick. The tavern became as quiet as an empty church as its patrons paused to watch the somber procession pass outside to the waiting dray. Mabel Petty stood behind the bar, her eyes wide and her hands holding the sides of her face. Her daughter Agnes stood among the patrons with a hand over her mouth.

Chapter 31: The Criminal

ACROSS THE STRAND, IN AN ENCLOSED PHAETON ON THE OTHER SIDE OF A crowd of spectators, Brice Blissom watched with satisfaction as the members emerged from the Fruit Wench and were helped aboard the wagon by the constables. Dusk was sliding into darkness. The wagon was a heavy dray used to transport casks of ale and beer, hired by the under-sheriff. The young marquis frowned when only five cuffed men were taken out. The dray was turned around and escorted back down the Strand by the mounted under-sheriff, constables, and king's messengers.

Hugh Kenrick was not among the prisoners, and neither was the Negro man whose club name, Brice Blissom knew, was Muir. The Marquis wondered if they had already been apprehended. "What the deuce?" he asked himself. He leaned forward and shouted up to his coachman to drive to Windridge Court. This man did not hear him, for the crowd was noisy and he remained gawking at it and the retreating dray. Brice Blissom leaned out his window and yelled angrily up to the man. "To Windridge Court, damn you, and be quick about it!" The coachman heard him this time, and snapped his whip over the heads of the two horses. The carriage moved forward with a jerk and rolled over the cobblestones in the direction of Windridge Court.

Glorious Swain, standing in the crowd of onlookers, watched with trepidation as his friends were taken away, and with relief that he had been late arriving at the meeting. But he was close enough to the phaeton to hear its passenger repeat his order to the coachman. He seemed to recognize the haughty voice, and glanced in time to see the Marquis of Bilbury's face in the window of the carriage as it passed by. He watched the phaeton rumble away, and wondered what business that man could have at Windridge Court. With a last look at the dray and its escort, he turned and followed the phaeton as it rumbled slowly up the Strand to Charing Cross.

When it pulled up at the open gates of Windridge Court, Brice Blissom stepped down from the phaeton and ordered the coachman to wait. He patted one of his coat pockets for the pistol he had there, and strode purposefully over the flagstone court to the torches that lit the front of the house. He knew what he would do: Make a citizen's arrest! It was his right, and his duty! And if Hugh Kenrick resisted—if he answered with his biting words and withering contempt—he would shoot him, as would be his right!

When this thought came to the young marquis, he stopped and realized that he could have told the under-sheriff that one more conspirator could be had, here, in this house. This thought was followed by a doubt, for the house was the home of a peer, and no common bailiff or other officer could enter it on arrest business. "Damn!" he exclaimed. Still, he himself was the son of a peer, and there could be no legal objection to him detaining the nephew of one.

Brice Blissom's mind swelled with confusion and frustration. He so hated Hugh Kenrick, and was so furious that the young baron was not among those led out of the tavern, that he could not think clearly, he could no longer sustain the cool calculation with which he had plotted this entire affair. He wanted Hugh Kenrick on that dray, constrained by cuffs, immobilized, cowed, ordered about by commoners!

He ran up the front steps and banged the doorknocker insistently until a servant opened the carved oaken slab. The servant was in his nightgown, and looked perturbed in the light of the lantern he held. "Yes, sir?"

"I wish to speak with Baron Hugh Kenrick," commanded the Marquis.

"Who is calling?" asked the servant.

"A friend." Brice Blissom paused, then added, "The Marquis of Bilbury. He is expecting me. See to it."

"Oh." The servant looked apologetic, and bowed once. "Excuse me, milord, but I regret to inform you that milord Danvers is not at home."

"Where is he?" asked Brice Blissom, struggling to keep the anger and impatience out of his words.

"He has gone home, milord, to Danvers, of course. He left several days ago, and will not return until late next month."

"Damn you, you cretin! Why didn't you tell me that in the beginning!" The young marquis raised a gloved hand and slapped the servant hard across the face. "I ought to have you flogged for your impertinence!"

The servant's eyes narrowed. "My lord Kenrick is not at home, milord, and good night to you." He closed the door and turned the latch.

"You'll be taught manners by me, you ape!" Brice Blissom struck the door with a fist once, then kicked it once. With a last pounding on the door, he turned and went back down the steps, his mind a furiously boiling cauldron of malice for anything that stood in his way. It was intolerable! After all his planning, all the money spent! His thoughts flailed about for a solution. Would the prisoners give their names to the Secretary? Could they name Hugh Kenrick? No, they would not. Could not, if that foolish hack Horlick was right about the stupid rules of the club. He said that none of them knew the others' names.

Well, he could fix that! He would go to his cousin and name Hugh Kenrick! But would Kenrick deny membership in the Society? Yes, he could, thought Brice Blissom, but he could be identified by the prisoners, and so much for that lie! But—would he lie? No, thought the Marquis, he would not! His fool sense of honor would drive him to protect his friends! Yes! That was the solution! Name Hugh Kenrick to the Crown, and watch him squirm!

"You will bend, Hugh Kenrick!" shouted the Marquis to the empty sky and the walls of the courtyard. "Your own honor will break your neck, and I'll be there to watch you grovel and swing from a rope!"

Halfway across the courtyard, he stopped. A man stood in his path, his silhouette blocking out the lantern lights of the phaeton beyond the gates. Before he could say anything, the man struck a match and held it up. "Who are you?" asked the stranger. "Oh, it is you again!"

Brice Blissom squinted in the flaring matchlight. He recognized the Negro called Muir. "You!" he growled.

"What do you want with my friend, Hugh Kenrick?" asked Glorious Swain.

"I am the Marquis of Bilbury," spat Brice Blissom, "and your friend will hang with the rest of his friends for treason! As will you!"

"He will not hang, neither will the others, nor will I," said Swain calmly. "Are you responsible for their arrests?"

"I am," proclaimed the young marquis. He reached into his coat and drew out his pistol. He twisted the barrel and pointed it at Swain's chest. "I came here to make a citizen's arrest! You are arrested!"

Swain's match died and he dropped it. "Is this a new form of ambushing men in dark alleys, sir? The dark alleys of law? Of hanging them by their heels?"

"Yes!" laughed the Marquis, "and the law permits it! I will kill you now, and claim that you resisted! I will be exonerated!" Then he sniffed. "Unfortunately, it will be called manslaughter, for you are not a man, blackamoor!"

Glorious Swain did not reply. In an instant he knocked the pistol aside and punched the Marquis in the face. Brice Blissom fell backward, lost his balance, and crashed to the flagstones. The pistol flew from his hand as he tried to break his fall.

Swain jumped to pick up the pistol. He cocked it and waited for the Marquis to make the next move, holding the weapon level before him.

The Marquis thrust his hand out in the dark for the pistol, and not finding it, jumped to his feet and drew his sword. With an animal yell of rage, he raised the blade to strike.

Glorious Swain pressed the trigger. The pistol flashed, bucking in his hand, and the young marquis gasped, his other gloved hand jerking up to cover his heart. With another horrible gasp for air, followed by a guttural, unintelligible curse, Brice Blissom lunged at Swain, his sword arm sweeping down at Swain's head. Swain stepped aside, and the young marquis collapsed on the flagstones. The silver buckles on his shoes scraped the stone briefly in what Swain knew was his death throes.

A dog barked from somewhere. Swain saw the coachman alight from his perch and cautiously peer into the courtyard. Swain glanced at the dark, still figure at his feet, thinking fast. He dropped the pistol, stooped over the body, and turned it over on its back, then unbuckled the sword belt. The front door of the Earl's house opened, and a servant with a lantern appeared. "What's going on out there?" A lantern light flicked on in the adjacent stable and began to move in Swain's direction.

Swain jerked the sword from the Marquis' hand and sheathed it in its scabbard. It would look like a mere robbery. He quickly searched the dead man's body and found a purse. It was heavy with crowns and guineas. Swain allowed himself a smile; the money could be used to meet his friends' legal expenses. That would be justice! he thought. He rose and ran past the approaching coachman, out the gate, and around the corner in the direction of Charing Cross.

The London Evening Auditor, and other newspapers, the next day reported the murder of Brice Blissom, son of Guthlac Blissom, Marquis of Bilbury, in the courtyard of the residence of the Earl of Danvers. "A sword and possibly a purse of coin were taken in the robbery," said the *Auditor,* "and, as with so many other victims of crime in the metropolis, the young marquis erred by resisting his assailant. His presence at Windridge Court remains inexplicable, as he had never called there before, and was not known to be a companion of the young Baron of Danvers, after whom he had enquired. Mr. Horace Dolman, the Earl's steward, advanced the opinion that the young marquis was in an agitated state, and had been rude to him. Mr. John Tucker, the late marquis' coachman, was unable to offer an explanation for his employer's presence or behavior, except to say the Lord Blissom had wished to go for a drive in the evening for air. The assailant passed Mr. Tucker in the courtyard, but darkness prevented him from seeing much of the culprit."

The *Auditor* and other papers also reported the arrest of five men, on the same evening, "members of a club known as the Society of the Pippin, in connection with the recent appearance in public places of abusive and contumelious posters that proclaimed atheism and impugned the character of His Majesty and his grandson, the Prince of Wales. Their names were not given."

William Horlick, when he read in the papers of both his patron's murder and the arrest of his former colleagues, that very evening got roaring drunk, beat up his nagging wife, and went on a tour of taverns in his neighborhood. The next morning, when he was sober, he beat his wife again, and left his garret to call on the home of the Marquis of Bilbury. When he was admitted past the black crepe-bedecked door, he waited in an antechamber with other callers, in order to offer his condolences and suggest that he compose a eulogy for the Marquis' late son, to be published in some newspaper. The elder Marquis, touched by the offer, agreed to the idea, provided he could edit it. William Horlick smiled and conceded the privilege.

Glorious Swain made discreet enquiries about the fate of the Society of the Pippin. He learned only that Hugh Kenrick's name had not been mentioned in the general warrants, and that his friends had not been granted bail or the comfort of visitors. He remained ignorant of the posters—except for their mention in the newspapers—ignorant of the charges, ignorant of William Horlick's betrayal. In fact, he was ignorant of William Horlick. Mathius, he supposed, also just missed being arrested with the others, and had fled. He did not see him being led out of the Fruit Wench with the others.

Swain toyed with the idea of writing Hugh in Danvers and apprising him of the events, but stayed his hand. He suspected what Hugh's response would be, and he saw no reason why his friend should share the others' fate. He felt no more remorse over having killed Brice Blissom. That man had somehow learned of Hugh's connection with the Society, and that knowledge had died with the malefactor. He had watched Windridge Court for signs of official visits, but saw none. He picked up several pounds of contraband tea, and called on both Windridge Court and the Pumphrett residence next door on the pretext of selling some to the servants, but the staffs had nothing out of the ordinary to gossip about but the young marquis' murder.

Glorious Swain felt torn between wanting to help his friends, and hoping that whatever happened to them now, would happen before Hugh returned from Danvers. Trying to help his friends, he realized, would be suicide. And, he hoped that whatever happened to his Pippin friends would be beyond Hugh Kenrick's capacity to correct.

* * *

The Kenrick household received news of the young marquis' murder in their courtyard long before subscribed London newspapers reached Danvers. Friends, relatives, and even peers of the Earl's acquaintance all wrote the Kenricks about the incident. Benjamin Worley wrote the Baron about it, and sent with his letter several clippings from the *London Gazette* and the *Whitehall Evening Post* of items related to the murder, including one of an advertisement placed in many papers by the grieving Marquis of Bilbury offering a reward of five hundred marks for the person, public or private, who apprehended his son's murderer, or gave information that led to his apprehension. Horace Dolman, the steward, also wrote to the Kenricks, giving his first-hand account of the Marquis' visit, and crediting himself with having chased off the murderer before he could relieve his victim of his shoes, hat, and peruke.

The Kenrick family that month was too happy and busy to read newspapers, though Garnet Kenrick did show Hugh the clippings sent by Worley and others. Hugh had little to say on the matter, except to wonder why the late Mohock had been on the family grounds. His father said, "Your uncle is writing a letter of condolence to Bilbury, and would like us all to sign it, even Alice." He paused. "Will you oblige him?"

Hugh had shrugged. "Yes. It will cost me nothing."

Garnet Kenrick breathed a sigh of relief, and turned back to the matter of planning an excursion that Hugh wished to take with Roger Tallmadge along the Dorset coast the next week.

Basil Kenrick read the newspapers. Although he was faintly amused by the death of the young marquis, he had nothing to say on the subject.

Chapter 32: The Examination

THE MACHINERY OF JUSTICE, ONCE SET IN MOTION, MOVED WITHOUT THE man who had pushed it. It made no difference whether Brice Blissom was alive to see it function, or dead. Other than a tantalizing allusion to the complicity of the nephew of a peer, the late Marquis had not confided in his distant cousin and his colleague his true motive for bringing suit against the "Pippins," as officers, jurists, and legal functionaries began to refer to the imprisoned members. The informations had been filed, the suit begun, the warrant executed, and the suspects detained. The process advanced inexorably to a conclusion, just as the spark from the flint of Glorious Swain's pistol had ignited the powder in the pan to create an explosion that propelled a lead ball through the Marquis' heart.

Glorious Swain, a man of intellect moved by some Quaker principles of pacifism, did not have murder on his mind when he stepped into the Marquis' path in the dark courtyard. His purpose was to learn, and to stop a man from harming a valued friend, he knew not how. This man had tried to kill him, and he killed the man instead.

The laws of England of the period and the machinery for enforcing them were not so skewed that he, a commoner and a black man of dubious liberty, would have had no chance of acquittal on a finding of self-defence. What would have certainly condemned him was the reason he had had to defend himself; this was, in essence, his opposition to the prosecution of a law enforced by the same legal code and the same machinery, which punished those who voiced an idea that seemed to jeopardize a smugly corrupt political establishment. A distinction existed between English jurisprudence and English politics, and also a schism. English jurisprudence triumphed in the next century, reforming politics, endorsing free trade, and abolishing slavery. As for the latter evil, already many Englishmen had set their sights on its eradication. The schism and the victory would make England great, and virtually unrecognizable to even the most radical of the eighteenth century's freethinkers.

The Marquis of Bilbury did not think that his son's murder was in any way connected with the suit his son had only a few days before filed against some stray political club. The idea did not occur to him at all. Nor did the suspicion occur to either the junior attorney-general or the junior solicitor-general; nor to anyone else in the legal machinery. Political assassination was then an unimaginable phenomenon, even to an inmate of Bedlam Hospital and the most alienated manqué. It would not manifest itself until later in the century.

The junior attorney-general and the junior solicitor-general proceeded with the late Marquis' case on the assumption that the son had been acting on behalf of the father. They did not bother to query the grieving father on this point; that would have seemed churlish, or trite. Thus, action seemed imperative, and caused them to discover just how swiftly and efficiently the machinery could work. They had begun an action, and were legally bound to complete it, but that was another matter.

Near the King's Bench and Inns of Court, the Strand changed to Fleet Street. Elspeth ran his bookshop at this point, and lived with his wife and children in rooms above it. The under-sheriff was merciful, and, upon Elspeth's request, stopped the procession long enough to allow him to enter the shop with a constable and inform his speechless wife of his predicament.

The wife, the next day, called on a solicitor of her husband's acquaintance, a man for whom Elspeth had found some rare books on Salic law, and engaged his services in her husband's and his friends' names. The solicitor, however, could not act until he was permitted to see his clients, and this was not possible until they had been interviewed by the Secretary of State or his proxies; he could not act, in any event, until he learned the nature of the charges levied against his clients, and this was not yet determined.

The five men spent a miserable two nights and a day in the Fleet Prison, immersed in a world of murderers, extortionists, pickpockets, petty thieves, prostitutes, and other raw recidivists. They were kept in a cell apart from the other prisoners, many of whom had the freedom of the place. Tobius, once he had seen the inedible slop served to prisoners, pawned his gold watch to the jailer for food and ale for himself and his colleagues. They fell asleep on mats of straw in the dank, noisy, vermin-infested place, and awoke to find most of the money in their pockets gone, together with their pipe cases and tobacco pouches. They did not wonder how this could have happened to men segregated in a locked cell; the jailers and many of the criminals set the terms of incarceration and ran the place as a personal enterprise.

It was a filthy, sallow-faced group of men who were finally taken to the

King's Bench Office and led by a bailiff and his deputies into the junior attorney-general's sanctum. They stood before a desk in the cramped room, their handcuffs linked together by a chain, and were questioned by Sir Miles Goostrey, the under-secretary of state. The junior attorney-general and junior solicitor-general sat in chairs at the sides of the desk.

Goostrey asked, "What are your names, please?"

"With what are we being charged?" countered Tobius.

Goostrey glanced at his colleagues, then said, "Libel, blasphemy, and possibly…treason."

"On what evidence?"

Goostrey held up a poster for the prisoners to see. "Do you recognize this?"

The chained men shook their heads.

"Do you recognize the work of the printer?" asked the under-secretary.

Again the men shook their heads. Elspeth asked, "No, sir, we do not. And there is no printer's name at the bottom. That's a violation of regulation."

"Agreed," said Goostrey with a smile. "And, this?" He produced the ledger of meeting minutes and held it up.

The prisoners gasped as one. "Why, those are our minutes!" exclaimed Steven.

"How did you come by them?" demanded Claude.

"They must have been stolen from Mathius!" said Abraham.

And then it dawned on the five men the possibility that they had been betrayed.

"This constitutes an invasion of privacy and the liberty of association!" said Elspeth.

"Those points can be argued later," replied Goostrey with a sigh. "Will you now surrender your names, together with your club names?"

A single thought occurred to all five men: If they continued to refuse to give their names, their refusal would lend credence to the charges, especially to the one of conspiring to commit treason. They looked at one another and knew what the other was thinking. Tobius nodded. A clerk was called in to take down the information. Each man gave his name, club name, place of birth, parish of residence, profession, and address.

When they were finished, the officials witnessed a strange thing. The prisoners greeted each other and shook hands as if they were meeting each other for the first time.

"Well, sir! It's a pleasure to meet you at last!"

"You were born in St. Giles? What a coincidence! So was I!"

"You're a Jew?"

"Yes. What of it?"

"I merely wanted to say that you must have read the Talmud, it accounts for the rigorous precision of your mind."

"I hated reading Talmud, and have done my earnest best to forget it."

"I say, Brompton, my son would like to learn the violin. Could you give him lessons?"

"Of course. But, has he an ear?"

"How are things in the Old Sod, sir?"

"I wouldn't know, sir. Dull as deuces, as usual, I should say."

"Gentlemen!" barked Goostrey.

The prisoners broke off their greetings and turned with surprise to face the under-secretary of state. "Now, who are Mathius, Muir, and Miltiades, if you please?"

Sweeney shook his head. "You misconstrue our Society, sir." He chuckled. "Until now, we did not know each other."

"And so we do not know who owns those names," added Mendoza.

"Well, then...what are the descriptions of these persons?"

The prisoners consulted each other in silence. They were tempted to give a description of Mathius, but they had no proof that he had actually betrayed them. Meservy drew himself up and said, "We will not give those to you, sir."

The junior attorney-general, like his colleagues, was baffled by the rules of the Society. "Is this true?" he asked, "that, until now, you did not know each other's names, or anything else about each other?"

"That is true, sir," said Brompton.

"We must know who is attached to those other silly names," said the junior solicitor-general.

Sweeney snorted at the man's contempt. "We, too, are curious to know, sir, but will give you no information about their owners. Silly man!"

"We will not endanger their liberty," added Mendoza.

Goostrey grimaced. He studied the prisoners for a moment, then shook his head. "It is not one of you—that is obvious—but our information is that one of your absent colleagues, attached to one of these aliases, is a member of the nobility. Were you aware of that?"

Each of the prisoners knew who that must be. Each knew that the newest member of the Society was a scion of aristocracy. Who he was, they did not know. But it had always been quite obvious to them, too.

"We have never entertained his identity," said Brashears.

"It was the pedigree of his mind that dazzled us," said Meservy, "not his title or origins."

"He will be of more danger to you," warned Sweeney, "when he learns of our present circumstance, than you could ever imagine us to be."

"Hmmm…" Goostrey gestured once with his hands, and glanced at his colleagues. "Very well, sirs. Here it is, then. This"—he picked up the poster again—"was composed directly from this"—he slapped a hand on the cover of the ledger—"and a careful review of these documents has led us to conclude that the statements in them resemble nothing heretofore produced in all the licentious literature this country permits to be published. The statements in either document are unique and selcouth. You have admitted the collective authorship of the minutes. Therefore, you may be charged with libel and blasphemy, or some form or degree of those crimes, and possibly with conspiracy to commit treason. Seditious libel may also be construed by a court." The under-secretary paused. "A barrister must be selected for your defense. That is all. Bailiff, kindly remove the prisoners to King's Bench Prison to await arraignment."

"You cannot arraign a man without an indictment, sir," said Brashears.

"Do not tell me my business, sir," replied Goostrey.

"I will, sir, if you don't know it!"

"Your examination is completed," said the junior attorney-general abruptly. The prisoners were marched out of the office.

There was no peer, nor even the nephew of one, among the five prisoners, concluded the three officials. They reasoned that if there was one, he would have made himself heard by now; or perhaps he had decided to disassociate himself from the prisoners. Further, none of the prisoners was a member of Parliament, and so there would be no complications of privilege that could bog down the proceedings. They decided not to search too hard for the identities of the persons attached to the three remaining club names. The Crown side of the matter, it was seen, was shaping up very well. The junior solicitor-general scoffed, "How could that fellow doubt the likelihood of an arraignment? Why, a jury of weavers could not help but find for libel, unassisted by the prosecution."

Brashears' solicitor was waiting for the prisoners when they emerged from the King's Bench Office to board another dray. The bookseller had only enough time, before he was lifted bodily onto the wagon by two bailiffs, to tell the man what were the charges and the names of the lawyers to see. As the dray jerked forward, Brashears yelled back, "And be sure to learn the name of the party who gave the evidence!"

The solicitor stood for a moment, thinking. He strode inside the building, and, hours later, his purse lighter from fees and bribes, walked out with a copy of the general warrants, a copy of the order remanding the prisoners to the custody of the Secretary of State, a copy of the order sending the prisoners to the King's Bench Prison in Southwark—and with the knowledge of who had given the evidence to the Crown. He saw the sworn declaration, witnessed by the junior attorney-general. But he was not able to secure a copy of it.

It was late in the afternoon. He rushed to the nearby office of a barrister acquaintance who was a serjeant-at-law at the Court of Common Pleas. He explained the matter to him, and asked him to accompany him to that court to obtain a writ of habeas corpus, which would force the Crown to specify its charges and allow some bail to be set, and perhaps even to surrender the case to that court. This the barrister agreed to do, for costs and a gratuity. They rode a hackney together to Westminster Hall.

After making inquiries in the bustling hall, and paying the usher, the clerks, and the recorders, the serjeant-at-law was able to persuade a magistrate fresh from dinner at the Purgatory Inn nearby—both verbally and for the cost of his meal—to listen to his arguments and review the solicitor's documents.

The magistrate, Sir Oswald Huggens, listened keenly and read the documents carefully, alternating between using a fan to cool his face and flicking a horsetail swatter at a bothersome fly. He did not seem to hear the noises of the tradesmen's counters on either side of partitioned venue, nor the racket of workmen refurbishing the dilapidated accommodations of the Court of the King's Bench at the far end of the Hall.

At last, he looked dolefully down at the serjeant-at-law and his client. "This is an unfortunate turn of events for your client, my brother Simon. The evidence in possession of the Crown seems quite damning, though that needn't be so disheartening. However, the name you give of the party who filed the suit—taken on oath—together with his evidence, leads me to believe that the Crown is intent on proving a most evil deed or what it regards as such. The Crown seems to have attended to every detail." He paused to study the up-turned frowns below. "I am not saying I lack sympathy for your client's cause, brother Simon, but even were I willing to rule that a jury be called here to indict or no, the King's Bench, because of its apparent special interest in the matter, would likely invalidate my writ. Or, barring that, issue a writ of mandamus, directing this court to surrender your client to the King's Bench. Or, that venue might even issue a writ of certiorari, which, as you know, would allow the King's Bench, in this instance, to absorb this court. And I am reluctant to see my court so compromised and prostituted. I am very sorry, but I must deny your application for a writ of habeas corpus."

As the hackney drove them back to the Temple, the serjeant-at-law studied the worried, crestfallen face of the solicitor, who sat watching the Strand roll by. It had begun to rain, and they could hear the driver curse scurrying pedestrians who got in his way.

"I would plead your case," said the serjeant-at-law, "but, as you know, I practice in Common Pleas, and may not appear at King's Bench." He paused to take some snuff, and offered his box to the solicitor, who shook his head. "However, I know of a fellow at King's Bench who is a firebrand on these kinds of cases. He has had dismissed or reversed a number of private and Crown suits against printers and publishers. His name is Dogmael Jones. He's finally up for a knighthood, so I hear, though I don't believe he could be bought off with one. I'll gladly give you a letter of recommendation, if you wish, or even arrange a meeting between the two of you."

"What could he or anyone else possibly say in defense?" asked the solicitor. "The Crown's got my clients bound up tighter than a tea chest!"

The serjeant-at-law smiled, more to cheer up his companion than to be amusing. "Mr. Jones is Welsh, sir, and, as you know, Welshmen will not yield. He has made more than one King's Counsel rue his robes. I hear he is the son of a coal miner, and that he digs deep."

*   *   *

The solicitor was that evening permitted to see his clients in the King's Bench Prison; the visitation ban had been lifted. The prison was arguably a worse place than the Fleet. Here the unsalaried jailer operated his own tavern, while his colleagues ran such services as lotteries, card games, and prostitution rings. Henchmen of criminals awaiting trial came and went with the freedom of the jailers, as did families and relatives of the inmates. Children were everywhere and underfoot, the smoke from pipes and cooking stones created an acrid, unmoving haze in the place, and the air reeked of gin, cheap wine, and other, worse smells.

The solicitor reported his day's work to the men through the bars of their cell. He held his valise and cane close to his chest, and wished he had emptied his coat pockets before coming in. A ragged, feral pack of children watched him from a distance like hungry rats, while some men lounged too casually against the walls near him. He was obliged to pay not only the jailer and his clerk for visiting privileges, but a gruff lout who had marked out that portion of the prison as his own "borough" and charged a "toll."

He ended his report with the news that he had agreed to meet Dogmael Jones, a serjeant-at-law at the King's Bench, to discuss the case. Finally, he said, "I know who filed the informations against you, sirs. It was the Marquis of Bilbury. The son."

"Why?" asked Brashears. "And how did he obtain our minutes?"

"We'll never know," said the solicitor. He glanced nervously around, and lowered his voice to a whisper. "He was murdered by footpads the very night of your arrest!"

"Then, why prosecute us?" asked Sweeney angrily. "The interested party...is beyond interest, beyond care!"

The solicitor could only shrug his shoulders. "The Crown, like the king, sirs, can do no wrong. The action was begun on you, and must be completed."

"Mathius," said Mendoza. "It must have been Mathius."

"Yes," acknowledged Meservy. "He broke with us over Miltiades."

"He cannot have been such a shallow man!" countered Brompton.

"Well, perhaps he was."

"It must have been Mathius," said Sweeney.

"And very likely for thirty pieces of silver from the Marquis," mused Meservy.

*   *   *

Even as the nervous solicitor was making his way to the prison, Sir Miles Goostrey and several deputized clerks from his office were conducting warrantless searches of the homes and establishments of the prisoners. Two wives and one mistress demanded to know the whereabouts of their men, and were cordially informed by Goostrey himself. Two of the women also demanded to know by what right their homes could be entered and searched, and themselves rudely questioned. They were informed that it was the King's Right and a Crown matter.

Little incriminating evidence was found in four of the prisoners' places, except for some untaxed tea and spirits, and a few proscribed books, one of which was *Hyperborea*, copies found in three of the prisoners' homes. Notwithstanding the dearth of direct evidence, the clerks removed armfuls of books, ledgers, correspondence, and personal papers for examination by the junior attorney-general and junior solicitor-general. No copies of the poster were found in any of the homes or businesses. In Beverly Brashears' shop, which Goostrey himself had patronized many times, the secret shelf with the ten volumes of Society minutes was discovered, and the ledgers confiscated as evidence.

Chapter 33: The Crown Side

I T WAS A HUMID, LETHARGIC AUGUST. QUARTER SESSIONS HAD ENDED EARLY in July. The Chief Justice of the King's Bench was indisposed with a "distemper of the stomach." Most judges of the Bench were on holiday, or on the circuit of assizes in other towns. The Right Honorable Sir Bevill Grainger was accosted one morning at his home near the York Stairs and Water Tower, while he was puttering in his tiny garden, by two ardent and well-connected junior lawyers from the Attorney-General's and Solicitor-General's offices. In a most genteel but urgent manner, they requested that he sit at the arraignment and prosecution of some obscure freethinkers. Of the few justices remaining in London this month, they said, he was the Crown's first choice to oversee the matter.

Sir Bevill Grainger, aged sixty-six, and on the eve of his retirement, was Master of the Rolls for the King's Bench, M.P. for Craddock in Hampshire, a founding member of the Silks Club of jurists, and on the board of governors of the new British Museum. Also, he was a member of the Privy Council. He could sit in a judicial capacity, at his own discretion, when the Chief Justice and Lord Chancellor were absent or otherwise indisposed. He was at first put out by the visit and request, and said so, but he removed his gardening apron and cap and invited his callers inside for tea.

It was a highly irregular request, to convene a court out of sessions, but there were precedents for the action. And the circumstances were extraordinary. The offices of the Secretary of State, Northern Department, and of the Attorney-General, promised to underwrite all costs of the action, including Sir Bevill's compensation and that of the bailiffs, clerks, and other necessary functionaries. The murdered son of an influential and respected peer had filed the suit, so it would seem obtuse to put the matter in the regular queue with lesser cases. The king and the church had been libeled. The Secretary of State had signed an order for the Attorney-General to prosecute the case forthwith.

Sir Miles Goostrey, an under-secretary of state, addressed a very cogent letter, delivered by the junior attorney-general to Sir Bevill, that explained the many advantages of an out-of-sessions trial. Not the least of these was that a trial convened now could prevent the case from becoming a contentious subject on the floor of the Commons when that body reconvened in the fall during Michaelmas Term.

"This would likely happen if Mr. Pitt and his party re-enter the ministry," wrote Goostrey. "They are such tomtits on press liberty matters, and could make enough fuss that they might unduly alarm a populace already agitated."

There were other preponderant reasons for obliging the Crown.

It was the practice to confer upon a retiring Master of the Rolls a peerage, which the king selected. The rank chosen would depend heavily on the outcome of such a trial. Sir Bevill was to retire in three months, just as the new session of Parliament began; it would take him that long to prepare for his seat in Lords. Goostrey, in his letter, together with the junior lawyers, had assured him that the Crown's case was so secure that the session would last no more than three days. One of Sir Bevill's favorite barristers, Sir James Parrot, a King's Counsel, had accepted the brief for the Crown side, contingent on Sir Bevill's willingness to commission a trial, and would oversee the sitting of a petit grand jury. Alderman Richard Shrubb was free to form a quorum with Sir Bevill, before he left on business on the Continent, so that a trial could be properly commissioned, though he would take no active part in it. Magistrate Oswald Huggens of the Court of Common Pleas had rejected the accuseds' application for a writ of habeas corpus, thus eliminating both the chance of legal interference from that quarter and the necessity of invading that court's venue.

Sir Bevill had made up his mind to commission a trial, but he teased his visitors with the pious sham of not having done so. He raised with them two minor problems: where to hold the trial, and Dogmael Jones, a bothersome fellow who had accepted the brief for the defense. The grand facilities of the King's Bench at Westminster Hall were being repaired for the next term, while the trial stalls and rooms there were too busy with special Pleas business. Anyway, often he could not hear testimony or arguments being made by attorneys for all the noises and distractions emanating from the tradesmen's counters and adjacent hearings and trials. The schedules for Jail Delivery trials at the Sessions House of Old Bailey were crammed beyond endurance, and it would be difficult to rearrange them.

He hit upon the ingenious idea of holding the trial at the Middle Temple of the Inns of Court, in one of the reading rooms, where law students audited lectures and conducted moot trials. This was a feasible idea, he pointed out to his callers. The King's Bench, which once traveled with the king, could sit anywhere. Furthermore, most of the readers and students were away, between terms, and one hall he had in mind was commodious enough to accommodate not only all required personnel, but even some spectators. The more he thought about it, the more he savored the idea. It would be a salutary gesture, to have his last trial in that room, where ages ago he had been a student himself and participated in countless moot and word jousts. He knew he could persuade the Master of the Temple to let the room to the Bench for that purpose.

There was the matter of Serjeant-at-Law Dogmael Jones. Sir Bevill had never conducted a trial in which Jones was a plea counselor, but he knew the man's reputation for leading justices around by their noses in argumentation. The Crown felt its case secure, yet he wondered if Jones could find a vulnerable point in it. He decided that the threat was minimal; after all, if and when the jury—and it would be a jury friendly to the Crown, Counsel Parrot would see to that—indicted the prisoners, it would be left to him, Sir Bevill, to decide on the degree of the prisoners' guilt, and to prescribe the punishment. The trial would be over. The prisoners could appeal the decision, if they felt they could afford to, but their case would not be considered by a court of appeal for over a year. The junior attorney-general was adamant that no bail would ever be granted the prisoners; the junior solicitor-general confided that the prisoners were mere tradesmen, in no financial position to sustain a drawn-out legal battle with the Crown. In a year's time, he said, they would either succumb to the certain rigors of their confinement, or go bankrupt.

Sir Bevill thanked his visitors for their information, adding that it was time for his nap. He told them that he would send a messenger with his decision to the junior attorney-general's office later in the afternoon. He would make these impertinent puppies wait. He did actually take a nap, which was made all the more pleasant by reveries of retiring on wings of justice and glory.

*   *   *

Benjamin Worley was leaving his house on Mincing Lane for Lion Key two mornings later when a deputy under-sheriff rode up, asked to know his name and occupation, and handed him a summons to appear the next morning at the Middle Temple, to be examined and possibly chosen by lot to sit on a petit grand jury. Worley had served on juries in the past; he met the juryman's property qualification of £100 per annum. He also enjoyed the diversion. Like other merchants, he believed that merchants and tradesmen were the best protectors of property and commerce.

Worley dutifully appeared the next morning, along with a dozen other gentlemen of similar means, and was examined by Sir James Parrot for his views on libel and blasphemy. Two men were disqualified, and the remaining ten drew straws from the hand of Parrot's junior counsel. Worley and five others picked the shortest. They were told to report early next morning to be sworn in by the clerk of the court. "What is the charge we are to hear?" asked Worley of the junior counsel. "You will know that tomorrow, sir," answered the man. When Worley returned home, he instructed the kitchen to pack him a basket of cold meats and give it to him when he left for court the next morning.

*   *   *

That next morning, the Pippins were obliged to walk from the King's Bench Prison in Southwark, over London Bridge, to the Inns of Court, as no dray or lorry was available when they were summoned to answer the indictment. They walked this distance, under mounted escort, fetters on their legs, handcuffs on their wrists, and linked together by a chain. This wardrobe of iron ensured that no escape was possible.

All five men looked haggard from their incarceration, even though visitors had been allowed to bring them food and drink. Meservy, Brashears, and Brompton were married; Sweeney lived with a mistress, and these women appeared to give their men succor. Mendoza was a bachelor. The Fleet Prison had a provision for straw bedding for prisoners; the King's Bench did not, and so the men had slept on stone. The jailer told the men that morning that they must shave before appearing in court; as they were not allowed to shave themselves, a prison barber—a convicted grave robber serving a term—performed the task at a rate of six pence each. The wives and mistress had wanted to stay with their men until the day of their trial, but the men would not allow them to, for fear they would be assaulted by other prisoners. Mrs. Brashears, without the knowledge of her husband, was propositioned by the jailer himself, and allowed herself to be fondled by him in exchange for his promise to provide her husband with bedding and food. When she was gone, the jailer and his colleagues had a good laugh about it, and the promise was not kept.

The men who hobbled over London Bridge and through the streets to the Middle Temple did not have enough money left between them to buy a round of cheap port at the Fruit Wench.

They were visited two days earlier by Serjeant-at-Law Dogmael Jones, his clerk, and the solicitor in a dank private room in the prison to review the case against them. Jones asked them dozens of questions about the Society of the Pippin and its history, and so got a clearer idea of the matter. He expressed outrage at the Crown's actions. He had seen one of the posters and the ledger of minutes which the Crown was claiming was the source of the offending statements. He stressed that he disagreed with many of those statements—vehemently, he added—but he believed that the poster was not of the Society's making and propagation. The Society, he had become certain, was purely a private association dedicated to the exchange of ideas and beliefs and to the pursuit of knowledge, and not to the forcible abdication of the king or the dissolution of the present government.

He cautioned: "I cannot deny in court, sirs, that the statements on the poster are based on specific statements found in your minutes. Clearly, they are. The Solicitor-General has taken pains to match all of them, except for the gratuitous aspersions on the characters of His Majesty and the Prince of Wales, which apparently are significantly absent from the ledger." Jones paused to relight his pipe. "The point I shall argue before the jury is that it cannot be proven that your Society, or any member of it, had the poster printed, and that as the printer of it cannot be found who could confirm any communication between him and yourselves, the Crown cannot charge you with the printing and distribution of the poster."

Jones paused again, then added, "I shall argue, sirs, this: That while the Crown has ample evidence of libel and blasphemy between private parties, no effort was made by the Society or any member of it to propagate said libel and blasphemy or to perform any other kind of defamation in public." He smiled and remarked, "One may as well charge a knifegrinder or fishwife with swearing on the porch of St. Paul's."

The members nodded with satisfaction. "Thank you, sir," said Meservy.

Jones collected his papers and put them in his valise. He studied his clients for a moment. "In the last issue of the *Gazette,*" he said, "there appeared an item announcing your trial—one of many such items—and your names were given, as well as mine and the King's Counsel's. Last evening a Negro fellow came to my quarters and handed me a purse of coin. In it were nineteen guineas and several crowns. He insisted that the money be used for my fee and other expenses. I have used some of it to pay your solicitor here, Mr. Bucks, and some for your prison charges. The amount remaining more than meets my own fees. This fellow was tall, with an extremely ebon complexion, very well dressed, and courtwise articulate. An admirably splendid fellow, all in all. He would not give his name, though he claimed to know mine through reputation. Are any of you acquainted with him?"

The Pippins shook their heads. Sweeney remarked, "He must be a friend whom we have never met."

Counselor Jones hummed in doubt, but did not pursue the matter. "I mention the incident only to assure you that your debts have been paid, and can be paid once this nasty affair is concluded."

Brompton asked, "What kind of case are they constructing, Counselor? Have they witnesses against us? Have they bought anyone to say he saw one or all of us put up these posters? And, have you any witnesses of your own?"

Jones shook his head. "I do not know what other stratagem Mr. Parrot has fabricated, other than the connection between the poster and your minutes. Of course, perjurers can be bought; I can do nothing about that. I have had my junior counsel here take depositions from your families, associates, and customers. Many of them have volunteered to testify in court on your behalf. I shall call them, if needed, and if permitted by the bench. But their word may not count for much. You are in the custody of the Secretary of State, and that office is establishing the rules. Witnesses for either side may not even be considered or allowed." The serjeant-at-law smiled again, but it was not a happy smile. "The Crown wishes to dispose of this matter quickly, sirs. If the jury acquits you, then it is over, and you may commence a suit for damages, and I would happily represent you. But the jury impaneled by King's Counsel is likely to be a stalwart one, composed of your peers, but not so, well, freethinking. Honest and upright, according to their lights. They will be swayed by arguments I engage with the bench, but not much by any arguments I put to them."

*   *   *

Two of the men, Brashears and Brompton, looked more haggard today than the others on their march to the Middle Temple. The junior attorney-general was tempted to force a plea from one or all of the Pippins, and perhaps get descriptions of the three missing members. A day after Serjeant-at-Law Jones' visit to his clients was reported to him, his deputies arrived at the prison with orders to interrogate Brashears and Brompton in the press yard. Brashears was stripped and staked to the floor of the yard and measured stone weights were put on his chest. He was informed that five pounds would be added to the weights, every hour, if he remained silent when questioned about a plea or the descriptions. In the throws of agony, he maintained enough of a presence of mind to break silence and assault the deputies and prison hangman break with choice Shakespearian epithets, such as "Weigh on, you milk-livered ratsbane!"

Brompton, meanwhile, was strapped into an iron chair, and pelliwinks—iron clamps that could be tightened with screws—were applied to all his fingers and some of his toes. The pelliwinks crushed first his nails, then the bone, as the pressure was increased each time he refused to answer a question about a plea or the descriptions. He, too, assailed his torturers, with more contemporary epithets, such as, "No betrayal from me, you lumpish, dog-hearted dewberries!" He fainted after half an hour of questioning, and was carried back to his cell.

After ten hours of pressing, Brashears nearly died from asphyxiation, and he, too, was returned. Brompton, when he recovered, looked at the throbbing pulps of his mashed fingers, and knew he would never again play an instrument. Brashears coughed violently for a while, spitting up blood, and later complained of a sharp pain in his chest. He did not know that he had a broken rib, and that it was lacerating one of his lungs, until Meservy probed his torso.

The deputies did not molest the other Pippins; they felt abused by the prisoners.

When the Pippins arrived at the Middle Temple, they were taken to a small room adjacent to the courtroom, and allowed to sit on a bench as best their fetters would permit. They heard voices in the courtroom, but could not distinguish the words being spoken. Mr. Bucks, the solicitor, came in, and got permission from the sheriff's men who were guarding them, to give the prisoners draughts of brandy and a pipe of tobacco to share. He gave his clients a look of reassurance, then returned to the courtroom through the connecting door.

*   *   *

Sir James Parrot, King's Counsel, had nearly completed his arguments for the Crown side when the Pippins arrived. Serjeant-at-Law Dogmael Jones, advised by Mr. Bucks of the arrival of the prisoners, interrupted Parrot long enough to ask the bench if they could be brought into the dock. Judge Grainger replied that this could be done when King's Counsel had finished his arguments.

Parrot had produced a copy of the poster, and, statement by statement, was tracing their origins back to the ledger of minutes. The poster statements, together with their sources, were unique and dissimilar, their likes not to be found anywhere else in the corpus of English political and religious writing, and could have no other origin but the Society's minutes. Therefore, he argued, no one else but a Pippin could have composed the poster statements. No one but a Pippin would even possess the "peculiarly addled mental talent for adapting the ledger statements for propagation to a literate but an unfamiliar and impressionable audience." Parrot digressed for a while, to read off, in terms of offended righteousness, the locations where the posters had been found and where bundles of them were discovered by the authorities.

Judge Grainger, at this point, glanced at Serjeant Jones, expecting him to note a discrepancy. Jones, however, gave no sign that he attached any special importance to the oversight.

Parrot continued. "The fact that the Crown has been unable to locate the printer party of the felony in no way dilutes the culpability of the Society or its members. It is the only aspect of this matter that has foiled the best efforts of the Crown's investigation. It may be taken as a mere measure of the stealth with which the accused have acted, and I commend them for it."

All in the courtroom chuckled at this remark but Jones, his junior counsel, Mr. Bucks, and an elegant black man, who sat far in the rear of the room. Jones had noticed the black man earlier in the proceedings, but, not wishing to call attention to him by acknowledging his presence, studiously ignored him. He suspected that he was one of the missing Pippins, or at least was a servant of that person.

The moot room of the Middle Temple had been designed to resemble an actual courtroom. The jury sat on a bench on one side of the modest room, the counselors and their juniors at tables facing the dais and

Grainger's bench. Recording clerks and officers sat below the judge's bench. Opposite the jury were two raised docks, one for prisoners and one for witnesses. On the walls were emblazoned the coat of arms of distinguished members of the Middle Temple, alternating with portraits of some of England's most famous jurists. About thirty spectators, including friends and family of the prisoners, sat listening in benches and pews allotted for the public. Grainger so liked the venue that he entertained the idea of campaigning to have the King's Bench moved here permanently.

Parrot began his summary. "In conclusion, the Crown begs the court to indict the members of the Society of the Pippin"—here he paused to read off the names and club names of the prisoners—"for having falsely, seditiously, maliciously, and factiously printed and distributed in public, or for having caused to be printed and distributed in public, on the night of August the first of this year, a poster inviting a general uprising and the forcible and violent dissolution of the monarchy and of the church, mocking the sacred moral foundations of our tranquil polity, and libeling the character of His Most Gracious Majesty, George Rex the Second our Sovereign, and of his grandson, George William, the Prince of Wales. The Crown begs to ask for the most severe penalty that may be lawfully imposed upon the accused."

Sir James paused, glanced slyly at Jones, then gestured to his junior counsel, who took a mass of papers secured with red velvet cord from a red bag, and handed it to him. "The Crown has elected not to call witnesses, milord, as it would consume time and contribute little to the Crown's case, although it reserves the right to call witnesses later in these proceedings." He hefted the papers in his hands. "I present to the court a dozen affidavits, taken and sworn before officers of the Secretary of State, attesting that their signatories heard the statements on the poster, together with other, similarly scurrilous statements, uttered by the accused in the public house known as the Fruit Wench, on various dates preceding the appearance of the poster itself." He approached the bench and handed the papers to a clerk, who in turn handed them up to Grainger. Parrot smiled and bowed to Jones. "My worthy opponent may choose to have these affidavits read in court at any time, at his own risk." He stepped away from the bench and bowed to Grainger. "Milord, the Crown rests." With another bow to the jury, he went to his table and sat down next to his junior counsel.

Justice Grainger untied the papers and glanced through a few of them. He then said that the defense would be heard after an hour recess, and rose to retire. Jones sat for a moment, and smiled. The stranger in the rear of the room had given him an idea for a better opening statement. He stood up and left the courtroom to see his clients.

His eyes narrowed when he saw them. Brompton's hands were an obscene sight, wrapped in bloody bandages, while Brashears looked like he was at death's door. "Were you interrogated?" he asked the men.

"Only Peter and Beverly," answered Meservy.

"I see." Jones knew that it would be useless to protest the torture, even though the men responsible for it, the junior attorney-general and the junior solicitor-general, were present in the courtroom, seated at their own special tables. His protest would not even be recorded by the clerk. He turned to the solicitor, who had accompanied him, and reached beneath his gown into his coat for some coins. "Find a market, please, and get these men something to eat and drink." Mr. Bucks nodded and left. Jones glanced at the sheriff's men, then said to his clients, "The generous friend whom you have never met is auditing the trial, sirs." It was a warning to the men, when they were taken into the courtroom, not to give any sign of recognition.

"And no one else?" asked Sweeney cryptically.

"No one but your wives and mistress are among the spectators, and some of your tradesmen colleagues. And some students. No one else," he added just as cryptically. Jones noticed that Sweeney's shirt was in tatters. "Mr. Sweeney, did you bandage Mr. Brompton's hands?"

"No, sir. Dr. Meservy here did the honor. The prison surgeon wanted half a pound for the service. I merely provided the cloth."

Jones grimaced in disgust. "I'll see if I can get a surgeon to properly attend to you, Mr. Brompton, after the trial."

When Mr. Bucks returned with some fruit and bottles of port for the prisoners, Serjeant-at-Law Jones briefly reviewed his arguments with his junior counsel, then stepped outside for a pipe and fresh air.

Mr. Bucks joined him a few minutes later. "What do you think, sir?" he asked.

"Sir James is in his best form today," answered Jones.

"Those affidavits—do you think they are genuine?"

"Some may be," answered the serjeant-at-law with a shrug of his shoulders. "He would need only one to prove intent to breach the peace, but apparently he has decided that, for flavor, a thick sauce is preferable to a humble herb."

After a moment of silence, the solicitor remarked, "He's eligible for an elevation now, you know—Milord Grainger, that is. Word is it might be the Viscountcy of Wooten."

"That fact sits dully in my mind every minute, sir."

A clerk came out and informed them the prisoners had been taken to the dock, and that the trial was about to resume. Mr. Bucks followed the clerk back in. Jones tapped out the contents of his pipe, tucked it away, patted his wig, and smoothed the folds of his gown, then turned and marched through the doors after them.

Chapter 34: The Defense Side

"**T**HE DEFENSE SIDE CASE MAY NOW PRESENT ITS ARGUMENTS FOR WHY the accused should not be indicted for and charged with the crimes cited by King's Counsel, which are," said Justice Grainger, turning to the jury, "libel, blasphemy, and conspiracy to breach the public peace. Other offences may come to light in the course of these proceedings." He turned to face Jones. "Counselor, you may proceed."

Serjeant-at-Law Dogmael Jones rose and bowed to Grainger, Parrot, and the jury. As he bowed, he felt a twinge of apprehension. He was thirty-six years old, Parrot was fifty-one, and Grainger, sixty-six, but he did not think his relative youth was a disadvantage here. He did not think that his experience, stock of legal knowledge, and powers of argumentation were at a disadvantage; he had, in the past, won victories over jurists and counselors with twice his tenure at the bar. He did not believe that the jury was prejudiced against him or his clients, or at all predisposed; his junior counsel had ferreted out information about the jurymen, and identified all as upstanding, honest, reputable merchants, above bribery and subornation.

He was Welsh, and even though he had spent much of his youth and all of his adult life in London studying and practicing law, he still retained a faint lilt in his speech. But he did not place much importance on it, and did not think his colleagues at the bar did, either. Scottish and Irish barristers and attorneys practiced in London, and won and lost suits and cases with the same frequency as did English lawyers. That was one reason why he loved his profession: It was a sieve of absolutes that could block all irrelevancies, and through which only justice was allowed to flow.

Could, he reminded himself. Now he was caught between the pelliwinks of an expected peerage, on the one hand, and the Crown's resolve to smother and discourage any affronts to it, on the other, without seeming to be an enemy of the liberty of speech. He had fought the latter phenomenon before, sometimes winning, sometimes losing. Yet, today, he felt at a disadvantage, for while everything looked proper and in its rightful place, he felt somehow, for the first time in his career, that he was a party to something counterfeit, and, because of that, he must lose.

With a nod to his clients in the dock, he turned to Grainger. "Milord, before I begin, may it please the court if I pose a personal but relevant question to my knowledgeable colleague, the King's Counsel?"

Judge Grainger merely gestured with a hand in the affirmative.

Jones smiled at Sir James Parrot. "Counselor, would you agree that the alleged actions of the accused were worthy of Iago?"

Parrot frowned. "Excuse me, sir?"

"Iago," prompted Jones, "the villain in *The Tragedy of Othello*?"

"Oh," replied Parrot. He frowned again, wondering what trick Jones was playing on him, then managed an amused smile. "Why, yes, sir, I must say that their actions were worthy of that wretched, unworthy creature."

Jones smiled at the expectant face of the barrister. "Thank you, learned Counselor."

Neither Parrot, nor Grainger, nor anyone else in the courtroom could see the purpose of the question. Many thought that it could only damage his case.

Jones then launched his arguments, subjecting the Crown's case to a barrage of consecutive challenges. He first expressed serious doubts about the legality and even moral appropriateness of general warrants, a subject on which the Crown had always been sensitive.

Judge Grainger ruled that while the legality of general warrants had been a longstanding and difficult question, this was not the time or place to ponder their legality or their moral provenance. "That issue, Counselor," he explained with some condescension, "is a proper subject of discussion for legal philosophers."

"And where, milord," replied Jones, "are these sages? If they have been remiss in addressing this subject, or have swept it under the scholar's rug for their heirs to find, it seems to me that a court of law comprises the only time and place to address it. If we have been abandoned by philosophers, ought not common men, such as ourselves, to become their own philosophers, readers, and guides?"

Judge Grainger grunted once in dismissal of the idea. "Perhaps, Counselor," he said gruffly, "but not today, nor on this matter. The point is nullified."

Jones renewed his attack on general warrants, questioning the power they gave a government to punish all manner of expression, and concluded by positing that the sustained legality of the warrants could, hypothetically, enable an offended subject to sue "printers, publishers, and authors, who would never otherwise presume to offend the Crown, for but wearing clocks on their hose or rings on their ears."

King's Counsel rose to object to this line of argument, claiming that it introduced an element of levity into a very serious matter, and also subjected the power of authorities to mockery. Judge Grainger sustained the objection.

Jones smiled wickedly. "*Levity*, milord? Then I must apologize to the court for its introduction, and conform to the *gravity* of the moment." He took from beneath his gown a folded sheet of paper, opened it, and said, "I now read to the court an excerpt from a most calumniatory libel, only one of innumerable inventions by a notorious scrivener." He began reading from the paper in his hand, but soon was gesturing to dramatize the lines. He became an actor, and the whole court sat stunned and mesmerized by his performance. Occasionally he would glance pointedly at Judge Grainger, as though communicating some parallel between the magistrate's situation and the lines.

> I'll make my heaven to dream upon the crown.
> And whilst I live, account this world a hell,
> Until my misshaped trunk that bears this head
> Be round impaled with a glorious crown!
> And yet I know not how to get the crown,
> For many lives stand between me and home.
> And I—like one lost in a thorny wood,
> That rends the thorns and is rent with the thorns,
> Seeking a way and straying from the way,
> Not knowing how to find the open air,
> But toiling desperately to find it out—
> Torment myself to catch the English crown.
> And from that torment I will free myself,
> Or hew my way out with a bloody axe!

Jones omitted the rest of the soliloquy, and ended with, "Can I do this, and not get a crown?" He looked around, and saw that the courtroom was waiting for him to continue. He calmly refolded the paper, and put it in his gown pocket. "Am I not right, sirs!" he exclaimed, turning suddenly to the jury with a pointed finger, causing its members to shrink back. "The man who put those murderous words into the mouth of a king, ought to be brought in on a general warrant, and made to eat every page of his poisonous pen, for he had a habit of libeling, in that manner, more kings and princes than any of us will ever see in our lifetimes!"

"What king?" demanded Grainger impatiently. "What is the point of all this?" He had never before in all his career witnessed such a display in court.

"Why, Richard of Gloucester, milord," answered Jones amiably. "In *Richard Duke of York*, act three, scene two. Surely you knew that. Forgive me the compressed fragments of his address." He paused, then addressed the jury again. "And my point is this: It is calumny!" he roared with a passion which no one could be sure, least of all Judge Grainger, was genuine or feigned. "It is a libel on the dead, who cannot bring action against the living! There is Richard the Third, a perfectly good king for the time, no better and no worse than any who preceded or followed him, painted in the blackest of tones as a grasping schemer and cut-throat! It is mere lore that he possessed a 'misshaped trunk' and a withered arm, and mere conjecture that he ordered his nephews murdered in the Tower! As for his other infamies, well, these were the common practices of his day. And how many worthy men today become intimate with their nieces, and consume them on dubious bridal beds, and risk no public censure? That prince, I say, was blameless, and his good name and reputation ought to be restored! However, Mr. Shakespeare is beyond the reach of general warrants—but not all the actors, theater managers, and publishers who even today perpetuate the lies! If the Crown wishes to be consistent in the prosecution of liars and libelers and besmirchers of good names—"

Grainger picked up his gavel and angrily struck it once. "Counselor, you are again mocking these proceedings, and I insist—"

"—If the Crown be consistent," Jones bellowed over the judge, "it would punish all men party to those lies and libels, and banish the Bard from our lives! Was not Richard a king of *this* nation, but is not the universal portrait of him a libel and a blasphemy? Is he not deserving of the respect paid our present sovereign, and of the protection afforded by our laws and courts? Yet, he has been put on an eternal pillory—with Iago!"

Parrot, his mouth pursed in fury, jumped up and strode to the bench. "Objection, milord!" He turned and wagged a shaking finger at Jones. "Everyone knows, sir, that Mr. Shakespeare's tragedies and histories are mere drama, and do not advocate any particular religion or mode of politics or ethic!"

"Perhaps, esteemed Counselor!" replied Jones. "But you yourself conceded a damning judgment on Iago, who is no less a fictive portrait than that of Richard! No less than the one the Crown has created of the accused!"

Parrot's face grew red, and his eyes became orbs of hate.

Jones continued. "You cannot deny that a damning judgment was passed on Richard! Why, more citizens have cringed at his cadent, blazoned evil than have been lured and duped by the statements on the poster wrongly attributed to the accused! And those statements, by the bye, are far more peccant and confusing than the worst speech by the Bard's maddest creation!" Jones flapped his arms once in seeming outrage. "Shakespeare has committed a grosser libel than have the accused, yet while his libel is repeated to paying audiences, and called nonpareil prose, the accuseds' alleged libel is called hurtful and perilous to the Crown, and subject to punishment!" He turned from Parrot and addressed Grainger. "Where is the equity in that, milord? I say, impound and impeach the Bard, just as the Crown has the accused—or pass not judgment at all, and stay the busy pens of men who sign general warrants!"

Grainger banged his gavel three times in anger. "Cease, Counselor! The objection is sustained!" With a glance at Parrot, who smiled in triumph despite the quivering redness of his face, he sent that man back to his table, then turned to glower down at Jones. "You, Counselor," he said, pointing a finger at the barrister, "will cease these theatrical displays! If you engage in another instance of histrionics, I shall forbid you to speak further, and instruct the jury in its duty! You will observe the comportment required in this court! Is this clear?"

Jones nodded and bowed modestly. "Forgive my theatrics, milord." He turned to address the whole court. "But before I took up the heavy tomes of the *Areopagus* to puzzle out justice, I contemplated taking up the prompt-book to seduce the gallery. On occasion, I succumb to the sweet memories of that juvenile affection."

A man in the jury clapped once, then remembered where he was and quickly folded his arms. Grainger threw the juror a contemptuous look, but Jones faced the man with a smile and performed a stage bow. Parrot muttered to his junior counsel, "He ought to have followed that ambition!"

Grainger let out a sigh of relief, and sat back in his chair as though tired from some physical exertion. "Continue with your arguments, Counselor," he ordered, "and mind what you say."

Jones bowed again, then turned to address Parrot. "A question for the King's Counsel," he said, assuming a more restrained, business-like demeanor, though with the faint suggestion of a friendly challenge on his face. "When copies and bundles of the poster under consideration were found in all the places claimed by the Crown, did the Crown find any on the persons of the accused, or in their homes or places of custom?"

A collective gasp rose in the courtroom. Parrot glanced quickly up at Grainger. The judge briefly shut his eyes, regretting the self-deceit that had allowed him to believe that Jones overlooked this point. Parrot rose and said, "Objection, milord! The question is…irrelevant."

Jones chuckled. "Irrelevant, Counselor—or late in the asking?"

Grainger's eyes slid darkly to silently reprove Jones, then he grimaced and shook his head. "Objection overruled, Counselor," he sighed. "King's Counsel must answer the question."

Parrot bit his lips and faced Jones. "No, sir, not on their persons, nor in their homes or places of custom."

"Nor anywhere in the vicinity of places frequented by any of the accused, such as the Fruit Wench, or the Royal College of Surgeons, or Mr. Brashears' club of booksellers on Chandos Street?"

"No, sir."

"Were any of the accused observed placing the poster in the places cited by King's Counsel?"

"No, sir."

"Has the Crown any witnesses it might have called who would swear to having seen any of the accused place the posters in these or other public places?"

"No, sir, it does not." Parrot looked up at Grainger, hoping to be rescued from the line of questioning.

"Who filed the suit against the accused, sir?"

Grainger leaned forward and said, "King's Counsel need not answer that question, as the answer may subject that person to recriminations or vendetta suits."

"Brice Blissom, the Marquis of Bilbury, is deceased, milord," advised Jones, "and beyond recrimination or redress of the injuries and costs borne by the accused."

Grainger snorted. "You have violated a Crown confidence, Counselor, and the court will take that violation into consideration when it weighs the jury's return."

Jones shrugged, and faced Parrot again. "Other than signing documents necessary to the filing of a suit, Counselor, did the late Marquis sign a deposition or affidavit swearing that he observed one or any of the accused placing a poster in a public place?"

"No, sir. That worthy lord was brutally murdered by persons unknown, before he could sign anything other than the sworn and witnessed documents necessary to begin this suit."

"And am I not correct in assuming that among the affidavits now in Milord Justice's possession, none is signed by the late Marquis?"

"You are correct in assuming that, sir," answered Parrot.

Jones nodded. "Thank you, Counselor," he said with a broad smile. "You have been most cooperative."

Jones turned to address Grainger. He wondered why he had not intervened to block the questioning, as he knew Parrot was praying for Grainger to do. "The Crown has already examined the accused, milord, and read to the court each of their admissions to the authorship of many of the statements to be found in the Society's minutes and which subsequently found their way in twisted forms to the poster. However, this was done while the accused were being brought here. I therefore beg permission to introduce these gentlemen to the court and jury."

Grainger shrugged his shoulders. "Certainly, Counselor. The court would not ask the jury to indict mere names, without offering those gentlemen a chance to associate those names with the actual persons."

As he turned away from the bench, Jones muttered beneath his breath, "Milord is too kind."

The prisoners remained standing in the dock. Jones asked each one for his name, club name, and profession. When this was done, Jones invited King's Counsel to question the prisoners. Parrot declined. "The Crown has asked the accused all the questions it need ask, Counselor. Thank you, though, for the opportunity."

Jones turned to the jury and repeated Parrot's earlier description of the Society of the Pippin, but without insinuating that the club was a sinister band of conspirators. "It was no more than an association of private persons who enjoyed exercising their minds on a wide field of mental play and inquiry," he explained. He went on to state that three of the members had not been identified and found, and so could not be questioned. "The venue of the Society's meetings is immaterial," he continued. "If the Society had conducted its meetings in a private home, there is no guarantee that this trial or hearing would not have taken place, given the intrusive scope of Crown authority over our lives. But it is my firm conviction that the accused were betrayed by one of the three missing members. The late Marquis, who brought this suit, would certainly have not been invited into this Society. Metaphysical speculation could be said to be his foible, rather than his forte. It is on record with a number of justices of the peace that he was arrested and charged on three separate occasions for molesting citizens and disturbing the peace, but went free upon payment of the fines."

Parrot rose to lodge an objection. "The late Marquis' character is not in question here, milord, and the Crown asks the bench to instruct the jury to disregard the Counselor's remarks on that matter."

Grainger sustained the objection, and so instructed the jury.

"Be that as it may," continued Jones, "the late Marquis could not have possibly come into possession of the Society's minutes, not unless they were either stolen, or given to him by a member of the Society—that is, by a false friend of the accused."

Jones turned to Parrot and said, "Therefore, I concur with King's Counsel that only a 'Pippin' could have authored the statements on the poster. However, that 'Pippin' could not have been one of the accused. Of the three members known only as Muir, Miltiades, and Mathius, the accused agree that only Mathius had reason and opportunity to betray them to the late Marquis. He was the last 'Pippin' to have had the ledger of minutes in his possession."

Grainger interrupted Jones. "The court objects to the Counselor's characterization of this missing member as a traitor, for it casts further doubt on the character and motive of the late Marquis. The late Marquis exercised his right and duty, as did, apparently, the missing member."

Jones said, "I beg permission to call character witnesses for the accused, milord. They are here and eager to testify."

Grainger granted permission. For the next hour and a half, the prisoners' wives, friends, and business associates were examined by Jones. They all gave glowing appraisals of the accuseds' characters and lives, though all confessed ignorance of the Society of the Pippin and the accuseds' memberships in it. When the last witness returned to the spectators' section, Jones paced thoughtfully before the bench. "The one witness, other than the missing members, who could have told the court something about the benign character of the Society, is Mabel Petty, proprietress of the Fruit Wench tavern, where the Society held its meetings. Unfortunately, she is not free to testify in this matter, as she has been promised prosecution by the Crown for harboring and abetting, should she appear as a witness for the defense, or even sign a deposition for it."

Grainger glanced at Parrot, who rose and objected to the suggestion that the Crown had pressured or threatened Mrs. Petty. "That is not true, milord. Mrs. Petty's establishment is under investigation for encouraging lewd and bawdy behavior and so for disturbing the peace. She is not eligible to testify."

Grainger sustained the objection.

Jones persisted as though the objection had not been raised. "I have it from Mrs. Petty, from her daughter Agnes, and from their serving boy, Tim Doody, that they were obliged to give descriptions of both the accused and the missing members. Under duress, I should note. Yet King's Counsel has not seen fit to read these descriptions in court, nor to my knowledge cause them to be a matter of record. I would like to see them myself. I ask King's Counsel to explain to the court the reason for this unusual oversight."

Parrot rose once again to object. Grainger overruled him, for he, too, was curious about the omission. Parrot said, "The descriptions obtained from those persons are not relevant to the Crown's case, milord. The Society has been exposed, and its key members named and arrested. The Crown is satisfied with what persons it was able to lay hands on. That is all the Crown is obliged to say on that matter."

Jones wondered if the black man in the rear of the courtroom matched one of the descriptions. Parrot and his junior counsel had not looked much at the spectators, and probably had not yet noticed him.

Jones turned to Grainger. "Milord, before I conclude my arguments, I beg the court's permission to review the affidavits presented by King's Counsel."

"Certainly," answered Grainger. "But all you will read are the sworn statements of the witnesses, who overheard the most imbenign remarks made by the accused about His Majesty, our Church, and even common Christian decency."

"Still, milord, I wish to review them, if only to know who accuses my clients."

Grainger sniffed in superiority. "The affidavits do not accuse, Counselor. They merely attest. The prisoners know who accuses them. It is the Crown." He paused. "I have read the affidavits, and must assure you that if you are searching for something amiss, you will not find it. Those statements heard by the signatories in the Fruit Wench are linked to statements in the Society's minutes and those which appeared on the poster, and have been clearly marked by King's Counsel."

"I am certain they have been, milord," replied Jones with irony.

Grainger recessed the court for two hours. Jones signed a receipt for the affidavits and for the ledger of minutes, and promised not to remove them from the courtroom. The chamber was emptied, and the prisoners taken back to the anteroom for the duration of the recess. The only persons left in it were Jones, his junior counsel, Mr. Bucks, and a bailiff who remained to ensure that no one absconded with the documents.

*   *   *

When the court reconvened, Jones noticed that the black man was absent. He had heeded the warning. Jones was certain now that the mysterious stranger was one of the missing Pippins.

He, his junior counsel, and the solicitor, Mr. Bucks, had waded into the affidavits, and indeed confirmed that nothing was amiss in them. Everything was in order—in too perfect order. Many of the statements were apparently taken down by a clerk verbatim; these he did not doubt the authenticity of. Five of the affidavits, however, were written in too perfect language, and signed by men and women whose professions were "chandler," "publican," or "seamstress." And he recognized the names of three of the signatories.

He approached the bench with a grim set to his face. "Milord, the defense thanks the court for allowing me to peruse the affidavits and the Society's minutes. I must commend King's Counsel for the care with which he has prepared his case." He laid special stress on the word "prepared," as though he wished to say "fixed." Grainger narrowed his eyes at this, and looked innocently away. "However, three of the signatories are the names of persons I have encountered in past cases, and I know them to be men of ticklish, if not doubtful, veracity." He glanced at Parrot. "I mention this only to advise King's Counsel that, in this respect, he has not been careful enough." He turned back to address Grainger. "I wish, therefore, to call these persons so that they may repeat their statements for the benefit of the court."

Grainger threw another disgusted look at Parrot, and then addressed Jones. "Fortunately, Counselor, you were wise enough not to utter the names of these persons here. But you are again imputing that the Crown and King's Counsel have stooped to bribery or other illegal practices, and thus you yourself are verging on slandering the Crown. On that account, permission is denied."

"Then, milord, I beg permission to examine those persons whom I do not suspect of perjury."

Grainger shook his head. "King's Counsel has waived the privilege of calling witnesses, Counselor. In all fairness, I must deny the defense side the same privilege. Defense was permitted to call witnesses to the character of the accused, and that was done from a sense of mercy."

Jones had expected it. This, then, was the beginning of the end. He could only hope now that he had damaged the Crown's case enough in the minds of the jury, and given the six men great pause for thought and doubt. Grainger sat waiting for him to speak. "I shall now present my closing arguments, milord."

Grainger sat back to listen. "No more histrionics, please, Counselor, or I shall rule you out of order."

Jones faced the jury, and deliberately held for a moment the glance of each man in it. Then he smiled. "There you have it, gentlemen. The Crown, represented by the able King's Counsel, has presented you with a fine conundrum with which to wrestle! It has proven beyond doubt that the statements on the infamous poster are but crude versions of statements recorded in the Society's minutes. Their relationship is undeniable. Bear in mind, however, that this is all King's Counsel has proven."

Jones pointed to the five men standing in the dock. "There stand the accused, who admit—not confess, mind you—admit to being authors of many of the statements found in the minutes. Yet, it is not proven by the Crown that these men authored the statements on the poster. The accused deny authorship of those same said statements. They do not know who wrote them. King's Counsel does not know who wrote them. I do not know who wrote them. I have argued from the likelihood that one of the missing members of the Society authored them, for reasons and motives unknown to anyone here today. The accused, most of all, remain ignorant of the reasons and motives, for they inform me that, to their knowledge, no man in that Society bore his brothers ill will.

"However, rude inference rules that one of their number turned Judas, and resorted to the power of the Crown as a means of venting his reprobation. Thus the late Marquis of Bilbury came into possession of a private document, the meeting minutes, and for his own questionable reasons filed a suit against the Society. One or another of these parties informed the authorities where and when the Society could be arrested. Without those meeting minutes, may I point out, the Crown would have no arguments. That underhanded commerce was the only way the Crown could have even gained knowledge of the Society."

Jones paused. "I argue that the Society not once, in its forty-year life, ever contemplated active disloyalty or revolt against His Majesty, the Church, or Parliament; not once engaged in organizing protests against the Crown, its policies, or institutions. The Society's members have themselves, in fact, been victims of organized protests as a result of Crown policies. Mr. Brashears' wife was last year stripped nearly naked by a mob of silkweavers protesting the importation of French silk, on the street outside her home. Mr. Mendoza, a lapsed Jew, two years ago nearly had his shop burned to the ground by intolerant Christians celebrating the repeal of the Jewish Naturalization Act."

Jones pointed to the prisoners again. "There are men who were in regular correspondence, not with this nation's enemies, but with the brightest lights in Europe, with philosophers and scientists and men of letters—men who are persecuted by their own governments, and who envy an Englishman his liberty! Are we to emulate the French now, and punish Englishmen for their private perorations? If we do, gentlemen, then we cannot but turn this nation, in time, into an island prison!"

Jones paused to study the jurymen's faces again. "The Crown rightly claims that the statements on the poster are offensive and tend to incite revolt. I concur wholeheartedly with that claim. The statements are vile and odious, and test my own endurance and practiced toleration. Yet"— Jones raised a finger high in the air—"the Crown is wrong, for it has not proved that the accused authored them! The Crown has produced no witnesses who saw any of the accused put up the poster. No copies of the poster were found on their persons, or in their homes or shops. The Crown cannot even identify the printer of the poster. In sum, the Crown has established no irrefutable link between the accused and that cursed poster. All the Crown has proven is that the accused unwittingly provided some knavish coward the material and opportunity with which to concoct a premeditated, fearful, and malign plagiarism!"

Jones waved a hand and gestured to himself. "My purpose here, gentlemen, was to point out the lapses and inconsistencies in the Crown's evi-

dence and arguments. As I am not persuaded by the Crown of the culpability of the accused, I pray most fervently that you are not persuaded.
Thank you, sirs. That is all I have to say." He bowed once to the jury, then
turned and bowed to the bench. "Milord, the defense rests." Jones returned
to his table, sat down, and shut his eyes for a moment.

Grainger consulted his pocket watch, and pursed his lips. It was seven-
thirty. He ordered a ten-minute recess.

Jones suddenly felt the weight of exhaustion, coupled with a pang of
hopelessness. He had expected Grainger, because of the growing darkness,
to recess until tomorrow. The short recess was an omen of his worst fears.
He glanced over at the prisoners and tried to give them a look of reassurance. When he looked at his junior counsel, that man slowly shook his
head.

Chapter 35: The King's Bench

SIR BEVILL GRAINGER ADDRESSED THE COURT, HIS SIGHT ALTERNATING from Sir James Parrot, Serjeant-at-Law Dogmael Jones, and the jury. His manner of address was officious, but benevolent. "The bench of this court is satisfied with the evidence and arguments offered by the Crown side. I wish to commend King's Counsel for his succinct and masterly presentation." He paused to clear his throat and adjust the spectacles he had put on; the diminished light was beginning to hurt his eyes. "However, the bench is not happy with the conduct of the defense side, and so it will exercise its privilege of examining defense counsel and reviewing certain gaps in his arguments." He looked down at Jones. "I do this so that the jury may consider all relevant aspects of the matter in the course of their deliberations, and for no other reason than to attain justice."

More sconces had been lit by the Temple caretaker, and lanterns brought in to counter the fading daylight. Three of these were French pump lamps, which produced a steadier, non-flickering light, and had been donated to the Temple by successful barristers and alumni; one sat on either side of Justice Grainger. Many spectators had gone, having left during the recess to reach home before dusk and darkness increased their chances of being robbed or waylaid.

Jones, seated at his table, envied them. He thought: They had left this place, and what could possibly be taken from them would never equal what was about to be taken from me. He had requested that the prisoners be allowed to wait in the antechamber during this part of the proceedings. Beverly Brashears had collapsed during the recess, and the force of his fall broke the flimsy bar the tired men were leaning on. Grainger agreed to the request, and Jones had promised to pay for repairs. The serjeant-at-law looked around at his surroundings. In the quickening darkness, furniture and men's bodies were vanishing, leaving behind only yellow attentive faces and yellow rectangles of the papers before them.

"Counselor, you may remain seated during questioning. I know you are tired. We are all tired. But it is nearly over." Grainger cleared his throat again. "As the affidavits will be made available to the jury, so that those gentlemen may see for themselves, I have some questions to put to you about their importance." He paused. "You have read the statements of the signatories. Were the sentiments reported by them voiced, or uttered, in a private home, or in a public place?"

"In a public place, milord," answered Jones, "but in private intercourse."

"Then, you concede that they were uttered in a public place?"

"Yes, milord. But not for all in that place to hear."

"They were expressed in a public place, Counselor, where all or any who wished to hear, could." Grainger tapped the pile of affidavits that lay before him. "And did."

"No one but members of the Society heard them, milord. For otherwise, the Society should have been brought to brook long ago—without the excuse of a poster."

"You cannot prove that, Counselor, whereas the Crown has proved the contrary—with these affidavits."

"I was merely pointing out a flaw in the bench's logic, milord."

"Do not instruct me in the art of reasoning, Counselor," growled Grainger. He snorted once, then reached over to drag the heavy ledger of minutes before him. He opened it and turned to a page at random. "I read now from the minutes of May twenty-second last: 'Discussed this evening conscience. Muir'—whomever that is or was—'gave the address on this subject and averred that a conscience, especially one of a Christian nature, is a fabric woven of inane tenets that cripple a man's potential for true character..." Grainger turned to another page. "From the minutes of July first last: 'Miltiades claimed that a better foundation for liberty should be found, other than on Scripture...He inveighed not against Milton, but against his method of defending Liberty by almost exclusive reference to Scripture...' And here," said the judge, turning to another page, "from June ninth last: 'Elspeth averred that no sovereign could claim kingship, neither on Scripture, nor on the most liberal interpretation of Genesis, nor on the modern arguments of conquest and interlocking royal marriages...If a sovereign cannot logically claim divine right on the basis of personal selection by God, then by what right does he rule?...'"

Grainger made a face, then slapped the ledger shut. "I could go on, Counselor, but at the risk of offending the ears of the clerks, the jury, and our public auditors. The jury will see it all soon enough. In all instances, the accused agreed to a man with the sentiments expressed in these minutes. I did not note a single instance of disagreement or dissension. What I have just read is reported in some of these affidavits. I am sure that if the Crown began a search, it could in time produce perhaps ten score more of affidavits from persons and thereby match every one of the heresies and libels recorded in this document. Fortunately, for the Crown's purposes, only a handful are needed. In fact, only one."

Jones had nothing to say. There was nothing he could say.

"Now, on to the device of the Society's club names. This device, Counselor, by itself, suggests conspiracy and other dark purposes."

"The device was adopted to protect members from harm or betrayal," answered Jones.

"Not successfully, it would appear," replied Grainger.

"It was successful for forty years, milord. It is a private association, with its own private rules. I must object to your suggestion that employment of that device imputes dark purposes."

"What is the substance of your objection, Counselor?"

Jones rose to speak. "How can the court charge the accused with any species of libel, milord, when, before their arrest, their club's minutes were never printed, never made public, when these records now in your possession were for the exclusive, private perusal of the Society's members? No attempt was made by them individually or corporately to publish those minutes, nor to propagate the sentiments recorded therein."

"But the minutes did come into the hands of a member of the public, Counselor, and so greatly distressed him that he felt it his duty to bring them to the attention of the Crown."

"But had the minutes not come into that person's hands, milord, no one would have learned what was said or recorded at the Society's meetings. Indeed, we would not know of the Society. We would all be in ignorance of what was said, heard, and recorded, and none the worse for it."

Grainger shrugged. "The fact remains that the minutes did come into that person's hands, and were made public in part on the poster, and we are all the worse for it."

Jones shook his head once to rid his eyes and mind of the cobwebs of exhaustion. "I insist now, as I have insisted in my arguments today, that the poster was printed and put up by someone hostile to the Society, milord. It was done without the leave, knowledge, or sanction of its members. I must labor this point. You have seen these men, and sampled their prose in the minutes, and must know that they are cautious men, sensitive to the legal consequences of their statements. Why would they invite certain arrest, incarceration, and trial by advertising themselves so immodestly, so wit-lessly, so injudiciously? They had gone to great lengths to ensure and pro-tect the privacy of their thoughts and company."

Grainger scoffed. *"In a public place?"* He shook his head. "Besides, Counselor, that is begging the question. However, even if I conceded your points, may I stress the matter of this public place?"

"Their privacy there was violated."

"Violated, if I correctly recall your closing argument, from a motive of malice and discontent by a member of this Society?"

"Yes, milord. It was as malicious an act as is gossip or slander, though with graver consequences for its victims. And now the court is acting as a cat's paw in a scheme by some craven person to exact a personal vengeance."

Grainger looked thoughtful for a while. "As with many instances of gossip and slander, Counselor, so it is with libel. Much gossip, to be sure, speaks the truth, regardless of the moral standing of the gossiper. That is why I place no importance on the motives of the discontented member of the Society or the late Marquis. In this instance, the court cannot find fault in the person who felt malice for the sentiments he discovered in these minutes. Malice is not altogether an evil thing for a man to harbor, if it impels him to perform a public duty. The court may even extend this understanding to the colleague of the accused who made these minutes available to the late Mar-quis. For all we know, he may have been smitten by a revived conscience, and seen the error of his ways. However, this is all irrelevant. The intentions of those parties are moot, the evidence is quite real, and the law is quite specific and plain. Very little justice would be achieved if the courts relied exclusively on the unimpeachable character of the provenders of facts and evidence. The accused unlawfully availed themselves of a public place."

Jones said, "I protest the court's conjectures on the benign motives of the parties responsible for the accuseds' present predicament," he said, the contempt evident in his words. "And I maintain that the Crown has not proved its case against them."

"In the opinion of the bench, Counselor, it has. And conjecture is the privilege of the presiding judge," replied Grainger. "Should you someday find yourself in such a role, I am sure you will exploit that privilege yourself."

Jones' eyes narrowed. "That was a gratuitous slander of my character, milord, and I protest it, as well."

Grainger's only response was a smug smile. He said with finality, "You may be seated. This examination is concluded. I shall now instruct the jury."

Jones took his seat, knowing too well what damage had been done to him. Parrot, the junior attorney-general, and the junior solicitor-general sat up in their chairs. The jury braced itself. One of the jurymen nudged awake a neighbor who had begun to doze off.

Grainger turned slightly in his chair to face the jury, and read from his notes. "Gentlemen of the jury: I recommend that the accused, named Robert Meservey, Beverly Brashears, Peter Brompton, Daniel Sweeney, and Jacob Mendoza, members of a private club styled the Society of the Pippin, be on this day indicted for fracteous and odious calumnies against His Majesty, George Rex the Second, our king and sovereign of his dominions, against our most perfect Church, and against the general and tranquil civil order of His Majesty's dominions, calumnies uttered in a public place known as the Fruit Wench in this city of London, or the county of Middlesex, on any and all dates noted in their own recorded proceedings together with those noted in affidavits assembled by agents of the Crown."

Jones sat aghast, as did his junior counsel and the solicitor, Mr. Bucks. King's Counsel cocked his head in triumph, while the junior attorney-general and junior solicitor-general exchanged looks of relief.

One of the jurymen leaned forward and opened his mouth to speak, but Grainger raised a finger to silence him. "I have not yet finished my recommendations, sir. Patience. I continue: The accused should be charged under the Act of 1661, the Act of Settlement of 1701, the Act of 1707, and under various other Acts of Parliament and on precedents established in this and other courts in His Majesty's realm, with these specific offenses: Questioning the right of His Majesty to his station and office as sovereign of his dominions; questioning the competence of His Majesty and probable heirs to govern said dominions; casting aspersions upon His Majesty and certain of his immediate family; libelous statements intended to elicit contempt for the person of His Majesty among the public; expressing like contempt for both Houses of Parliament, and voicing doubts concerning their right and competence to govern the nation; claiming that Parliament may sit without a sovereign, and that a sovereign is a redundant but dangerous ornament as a supreme executive of legislation and law; assailing and aspersing the veracity of Christianity and the Scriptures, the moral foundation of the nation, in such a quantity of statements, and in such evil terms, that to read them in this court would simply be to repeat the offense; and inadvertently, by the accuseds' hands, or by the hand of an unknown party—it matters not which—making known these libels and blasphemies to the public by their utterance in a public place and by dissemination of them on posters put up in public places, consequently tending and intending to incite public dissatisfaction and a breach of the public peace."

Jones shot up out of his chair and exclaimed, with a raised fist that shook as violently as his voice, "Milord! Half of your recommended offenses were not—I repeat, were not—the subject of these proceedings! The subject was the poster, not the affidavits. I rebutted the Crown's arguments! Your recommendations are as calumnious as that poster, and I am not—"

The recording clerks, after a short pause, rushed ahead with their tasks. Parrot, the junior attorney-general, and the junior solicitor-general all leaned back in their chairs, as though to duck an explosion. Grainger banged his gavel so violently that its head cracked. "You will be seated, Counselor, and you will maintain silence until I am finished, or I will order you ejected from this court until I am finished and the jury has retired!"

Jones, smoldering from self-control, felt a tug on his gown sleeve from his anxious junior counsel, and allowed himself to be pulled down.

Grainger waited a moment, then said, "Clerks will strike Counselor's outburst. It is not worthy of record." He adjusted his robes, picked up his notes, and turned to the jury. "To continue, gentlemen: Altogether, while your findings may comprise blasphemous libels against the Crown and the Church, which could even be said to be seditious libel, I recommend leniency by not calling it treason." He glanced once at Jones, almost as though he were inviting him to protest. Jones glared back up at him. Grainger smiled. "As the accused took no direct or observable action on their oppugnant words, and seem to be inclined more to speculative inquiry than to active rebellion and public mischief, I instruct the jury to limit their findings to blasphemous libel. I advise you gentlemen to keep in mind this dictum: 'When a man doth compass or imagine the death or demise of our sovereign…' Well," said Grainger, waving a hand, "you see how merciful the court wishes to be in this unfortunate affair." He put down his notes and folded his hands. "That is all, gentlemen. You may now retire and decide the matter. The clerk will hand you the pertinent evidence and documents with which to aid you in your deliberations."

The six men rose and were led out of the chamber to another room. Grainger busied himself with reading documents. Jones sat with his head in his hands.

Chapter 36: The Jury

THE JURY SAT IN A SMALL ROOM AROUND A TABLE LIT BY A SINGLE LAMP. The room was hot and airless, made more so by the restlessness of the jurymen. Benjamin Worley said, "I do not like the way this thing is being handled."

"Nor do I," said another juryman, yawning. "But, there you are."

The foreman picked up the poster and held it up before Worley. "Do you agree with this tripe, sir?"

"No," said Worley. "It is vicious pap. But the Crown did not prove that these men made that poster, not to my mind."

"Oh, but the Crown did prove it," said another man. "They thought the thoughts, and made the poster possible."

"They spoke the thoughts, as these affidavits prove," said another, glancing at the daunting pile of documents that sat in the center of the table.

"And their thoughts were made public."

Worley glanced around at his fellow jurymen. "The one thing has nothing to do with the other. Justice Grainger mixed them all up. I've never heard anything like it before. It's as wrong as old fish."

"I see," said the foreman. He had been specially selected by King's Counsel for his known powers of persuasion. Parrot had used him before on similar but more minor cases. The foreman had had some property judgments ruled in his favor as a result. This time, though, in a note slipped to him by the bailiff—who had accepted a crown for the favor—Sir James had promised to endorse his candidacy for alderman of his parish on the next election, and to contribute to it, if he could deliver this jury. The note was safely tucked away inside his frock coat, to be used to remind Sir James of his promise.

The other jurymen, like him, were tired, though their minds seemed to be numbed, too, by the amount of argumentation thrown at them today and the prospect of having to wade through it here. Only Worley seemed to be pulled by the strings of propriety and fairness. The foreman was certain he could wear him down, so that they could return a unanimous decision. He opened the Society's ledger of minutes and smiled at Worley. "You say it's as wrong as old fish, sir. We say it's as right as rain. Let us see if we can reason this out."

*   *   *

After a while, Justice Grainger looked down on Jones with an expression of sympathy. "Forgive me for not first explaining my method to you, Counselor," he said with conversational kindness, "but I have decided here to test the waters of collateral justice." Parrot and the lawyers looked up with interest.

Jones raised his head. "Collateral justice, milord?"

"Yes. It is a novel notion. I first heard it voiced by a member of the Commons at a concert some time ago. I believe it was at his own house, but cannot remember the fellow's name. Sir Henry Parnell, or Panelli, or some such." He paused in an effort to remember the name, the place, or the occasion, but could not. "By it," he continued, "provable crimes may be collected and punished together with proven felonies, in a form of gross attainder, so to speak. Its purpose is economy and the swift administration of justice. So many men commit multiple crimes, that we are forever prosecuting them, and see them too often in the dock. You objected to the wording of my instructions to the jury, no doubt from surprise." He shook his head. "Of course, the notion cannot be applied to all cases, only to special ones, such as this one, at the discretion of the presiding magistrate."

Jones said, "I demolished the Crown's case, milord." His eyes narrowed in thought, and he added, "The notion you have explained and introduced is insidious. It would eat its way down to common law and destroy all justice."

Grainger sighed. "You find the notion of collateral justice noxious to you now, Counselor, but later in your career you may find it a useful device. Do not reject it with such passionate foolhardiness."

"I would sooner give up the law than indulge it, milord," replied Jones.

Grainger clucked his tongue. "I, for one, would be sorry to see you go."

Sir James Parrot chuckled and leaned forward to half-whisper in mock confidence to Jones over the space that divided their tables, "If you go, sir, I suggest haste. I understand by the advertisements that Mr. Garrick is seeking players to stage *Much Ado About Nothing*, at Drury Lane, and that the clownish role of Constable Dogberry has yet to be assigned."

Jones smiled, and replied so that the whole court could hear, "Like Richard of Gloucester, learned colleague, you mistake base gloating for wit and honor. It does not become you." The serjeant-at-law rose and left the room to have a pipe outside.

*   *   *

An hour and a half later, the foreman handed a folded paper to the bailiff, who handed it to a clerk, who handed it up to Grainger. The judge said, "The accused are summoned to the bar."

When the prisoners were returned to the dock, Grainger looked at them and said, "The jury has found for an indictment of you men for blasphemous libel, and I so charge you with the felony. How do you plead? One at a time, please. The clerk will read out your names."

And, one by one, the prisoners answered, "Not guilty, milord."

"You men are summarily arraigned. The marshall of the court may dismiss the jury." Grainger turned to the jurymen. "Thank you, gentlemen. You are discharged from your duties, which you performed admirably."

All but one of the jurymen rose and bowed in acknowledgment. Benjamin Worley simply blinked at Grainger with incomprehension, then glanced up at the prisoners, and finally at Counselor Jones. He dropped his head in shame. The foreman and the others had browbeaten him and worn him down so that he could no longer think clearly, and he had agreed from exasperation to the indictment. The words on the poster, in the minutes, and in the affidavits were still swirling in his mind. The marshall of the court bent to take him by the arm and led him out after the others.

There was a general rustling of paper and garments as the court settled back to listen to Grainger. The magistrate toyed with his spectacles, then said, "As you know, this court, in this particular case, which dealt with matters crowding the subjects of libel and treason, is vested with the power of reaching a verdict of innocent or guilty if the grounds of the indictment warranted it, and of proclaiming that innocence or guilt on the court's own recognizance, in lieu of a trial by full jury, and contingent upon the evidence presented by the Crown. It is my judgment that said evidence, in a full jury trial, would only be reintroduced with the same likely finding. I therefore arraign and charge the prisoners with blasphemous libel, and in so doing find them guilty of that felony—"

Jones rose so quickly that he nearly toppled his table.

Grainger frowned. "What now, Counselor?"

Jones could barely control his stammering outrage. "On what grounds do you...does the court assume this...power?"

Grainger leaned forward as though he wanted to spit the words into the barrister's face. "On the grounds of the prisoners' obstinate refusal to surrender the names of their three accomplices, and that refusal comprises willful contempt of this court, and that empowers me, sir! Read your statutes!" He swept up his gavel and struck it once. "I fine you five pounds for interrupting the reading of a sentence!"

"But the prisoners do not know those names—"

"Ten pounds!"

"Milord, the prisoners are not—"

"Twenty pounds!" shouted Grainger. "How much are you worth, Counselor? We can go on all night, if you wish!"

Jones looked at the prisoners. Robert Meservey smiled sadly and shook his head. The barrister sank to his chair. His junior counsel fidgeted with the paperwork before him. For a while, no one in the courtroom looked at anyone else.

Grainger put down his gavel, cleared his throat again, and continued. "—With blasphemous libel, and in so doing find them guilty of that felony. This conviction entails a fine of one hundred pounds, in currency or in kind, for each prisoner, in addition to seven consecutive days on the pillory at Charing Cross, at the convenience of the sheriff, from sunrise to sunset, that place being nearest to the scene of the prisoners' perfidy, and to three years each of labor in one of His Majesty's prisons, employed in a manner deemed by the executive of that place most beneficial to the nation and conducive to penance and redemption. The prison terms are commutable to transportation to one of His Majesty's possessions in North America, contingent upon opportunity and the discretion and convenience of the authorities."

Grainger set aside his notes. "Have the prisoners anything to say for themselves?" It was the first time he had addressed the men in the dock. He could see only five pale faces and the bare suggestion of their bodies in the gloom. From outside, through the high window of the hall, came the sound of the bells of St. Mary le Strand, marking the hour. It was nine o'clock.

The prisoners were silent. Grainger could see that their faces were drained of care and hope. His mouth twitched into a smile of approval. This was right and proper, he thought: The men who had so much to say in the ledger of minutes were rendered speechless. He waited another moment, then reached for his gavel to adjourn the court and to order the marshall to arrange the prisoners' transfer of custody. He noted the crack in the head of the gavel, and smiled wryly. It was Temple property, and he must remember to reimburse the Master of the Temple for a new one.

A voice boomed from the darkness far in the rear of the hall: "Long live Lady Liberty!"

The prisoners' heads jerked up at the words, and their faces became alive with recognition. Serjeant-at-Law Jones was also roused from his own morose thoughts: He, too, recognized the voice.

The prisoners stood straight, and raised their cuffed hands together, as if they were holding tavern glasses. As one, they answered, "Long live Lady Liberty!" Then they laughed, and tossed the imaginary glasses over their shoulders.

Grainger was stupefied by the incident, and too late ordered the bailiff to investigate the disturbance. By the time that man rushed with a lantern to the rear of the hall, everyone heard footsteps and a door slamming shut.

*   *   *

The incident enabled Dogmael Jones to console the sobbing wives and relatives of the prisoners, and to caution the solicitor, Mr. Bucks, and the spectators about their muttered curses and epithets. It gave him the strength to speak with the prisoners in the antechamber, where they were to wait until taken to a new prison. Robert Meservey said, "You defended us at some cost to yourself, sir. We had not expected that."

"Do you wish me to file an appeal? It would be heard in King's Bench again, but not for some time. I'll speak to your families."

The men shook their heads. "Even had we the means, sir," said Brompton, "it would do us no good."

"Justice was not their object," said Sweeney.

"It was silence," said Brashears in a labored voice. He managed a smile. "But we had the last word! Thanks to Muir!"

Jones smiled tentatively, sharing the secret knowledge with the men. Then he frowned, and said, "I have failed you, as he did not."

"No," said Mendoza, reaching out to pat Jones' arm. "No, sir. Don't think a bit of that. My excellent man, you were royally sponged!"

When Jones returned to the courtroom to gather his things, Grainger paused in the midst of signing papers and documents. He said, "A word with you, Counselor." He shooed away the clerk who was assisting him.

Jones approached the bench, and waited.

"While you conducted a very thorough defense of these villains," said the magistrate, "you seem to have forgotten an important aspect of law. I know your record, and have heard of your style. The line of questioning you employed may have served ordinary matters very well. This, however, was an important Crown matter, and Crown matters of this type demand arguments and conduct of the prosecution, defense, and bench that are above ordinary reasoning."

Jones' brow furled in thought. After a moment, he asked, "Above it, milord, or apart from it?"

Grainger sniffed once, then said, "You forget yourself, sir." He waved the clerk back, and bent to read a document, absently reaching for a quill. "Goodnight to you."

Chapter 37: The Oath

WHEN THE SARACEN GENERAL AMROU CAPTURED ALEXANDRIA IN 638 A.D., he ordered the surviving books in its great library to serve as fuel for the conquerors' heated baths. Neither he nor his lieutenants, nor any member of the numerous rival Christian sects now subject to Mohammedan law, bothered to ponder the fate of the knowledge recorded on those rolls. Amrou regarded himself as a practical man, and was not content to merely burn the ancient repository. Fire was a useful thing: Why waste it on showy destruction? The books kept the baths warm for many months, until the last word was consumed, never to be recovered. It was a signature event of the Dark Ages.

Once the Pippins had been disposed of by the Crown, they were remanded to the custodial quicksands of criminal administration, and forgotten. The proscribed books and the eleven volumes of the minutes of the Society of the Pippin, seized by the Crown, were sold to a ragman's concern to be repulped into paper and reconstituted for official forms and documents. Words of wisdom and tantalizing insights dissolved in the ragman's boiling vats, to be replaced by words of permission and command. In the Age of Enlightenment, it was an instance of the doomed bicameral alliance of church and state.

The London Gazette, and a handful of other newspapers that regularly reported official news, briefly mentioned the special session of the King's Bench and the conviction of the five men for blasphemous libel. The item was inserted in columns devoted to Commissions of Bankrupt notices, property disposals ordered by the Courts of Chancery and Exchequer, and advertisements for the public auctioning of property.

Among these mundane items was the announcement of the revocation of the license of "a public house, formerly known as the Fruit Wench, at the head of Villiers Street. Prospective bidders may inspect the property and its contents and register for the sale upon payment of a fee of five shillings." Mabel Petty had been found guilty by a justice of the peace of having encouraged lewd and bawdy behavior, and fined eight pounds. She and her daughter sold the property to a speculator and eventually moved to Bristol to begin anew.

Sir Bevill Grainger retired to await his expected peerage, and divided his time between his garden and developing the idea of "collateral justice." The junior attorney-general and junior solicitor-general returned to the humdrum business of conventional legal matters, and occupied themselves with preparing less spectacular Crown cases for the opening of the Michaelmas Term in the fall.

Serjeant-at-Law Dogmael Jones, haunted by the trial, lost much sleep. He tortured his mind in an effort to understand the disadvantage under which he had conducted his defense of the Pippins. He managed to narrow it down to a conflict between the notions of liberty of speech and public places, but the legal resolution maddeningly eluded him. He became a close friend and advisor of the families of his former clients, and even helped Beverly Brashears' wife manage her husband's bookshop. His reward for losing the case was a summons from the Court of St. James' to receive a knighthood. He was tempted to spurn the honor, but knew that to do so would imperil his career. He became Sir Dogmael Jones.

There appeared in the *London Evening Auditor*, shortly after announcement of the convictions, a verbose tribute to Brice Blissom, late son of the Marquis of Bilbury, by William Horlick, for which he was paid £50 and a promise by the father to subsidize the writing of a new parable, in poetic essay form, about a prodigal son turned repentant.

There also came by post to the office of Sir Miles Goostrey an anonymous letter describing two of the missing Pippins. "Pshaw!" scoffed the under-secretary of state to the junior attorney-general. "Here's another crank missive from someone who claims that Miltiades and Muir are a young man of fair appearance and plumb means, and a tall Negro man with the airs of an Ethiopian prince! Yesterday one came in swearing that they were the Young Pretender and the grandson of Algernon Sidney! Gadso, what some people won't do to puff themselves up!" The letter had been sent by William Horlick, who was both disappointed that the Crown did not press its search for the missing Pippins, and fretful about a chance encounter with one or both of his former colleagues in public.

The Pippins were condemned to wait their turn at the pillory in the sweltering, fetid confines of Newgate Prison, as other felons had been scheduled for the punishment long before their own arrests. Newgate differed not a whit from the Fleet and King's Bench Prisons. It was governed by the warden and his staff of turnkeys, but ruled by the underworld.

The Pippins, accustomed to freedom, did not easily adjust to the arrangement established by the more brutal elements of the place, and were marked as fair game by both the governors and the rulers. Two weeks after their arrival, Beverly Brashears verbally objected to the larcenous ethics of a turnkey, and was put into the prison's own stocks in retaliation. When guards came back to release him, he was dead. The broken rib had punctured a lung, and he drowned in his own hemorrhaging. Jacob Mendoza, already weakened by enteric fever, was beaten up by two inmates arrested years before during the anti-Jewish riots, when they discovered his "origins." When he protested that he was an atheist, they nearly killed him. He did not awaken the morning after the assault. Robert Meservey was unable to determine whether his friend had succumbed to his injuries, or to the fever.

Sir Dogmael Jones, when he heard of the deaths, tried to use his new influence to have the three surviving Pippins transferred to Ludgate Prison, which he knew was a far more humane and civilized place. His requests were rebuffed in a manner he could not decide was indifference or spite.

Glorious Swain waited. His world had been shattered, leaving him lonely, isolated, and voiceless. He had written a letter of thanks to Dogmael Jones, expressing his appreciation for the barrister's courage and care, and confessing that he had been the one who led the Pippins in their final toast, "having taken advantage of my complexion and some darkish attire to retire to the darkest recesses of that now ignoble hall, to hear the progress of the trial. I know that our *faux bonhomme*, Mathius, is at liberty, and can identify me. I shall keep my public business to a minimum. I enjoyed your rendition of Richard of Gloucester; it was almost as worthy as Mr. Garrick's, though I believe you made no friend of Justice Grainger, whom I am certain did not miss the parallels you were imputing. Your most gracious admirer, 'Muir.'"

Swain knew that he could roam the streets of London at will, without risk; and also that if he made a single move to help his friends, he would be crushed by the same machinery that had crushed them.

"What ails thee, friend Swain?" asked a Quaker acquaintance one day when he had finished teaching a class of children at a nearby chapel. "Thou was once a sun of smiles and good cheer. Lately, thy visage is as warming as a gibbous moon."

"Some Titans have fallen in mortal combat with the gods," Swain answered plaintively, "and I am unable to offer them rescue or succor."

He kept as close a watch on Windridge Court as his unpredictable employment allowed. He was determined that the gods would not claim the Titan most precious of all to him.

*   *   *

Hugh Kenrick returned to London on the sixth of September, in the early evening, a week earlier than he had planned. He was happily occupied for a number of days with school, business, and family matters. His family, including his uncle, would follow soon, and he had been charged with readying Windridge Court for their arrival. The house needed to be cleaned, victuals restocked, Horace Dolman promoted to major domo, and a new man hired to replace him. His parents were planning to have concerts this season, and he interviewed several troupes of musicians. His uncle would be sitting at Lords again, until Parliament recessed the next year, and so he visited Mr. Rickerby on Cutter Lane to renew the arrangements for his room there. His father wanted him to divide his time among school, Lion Key, and Formby, Pursehouse & Swire's Bank; Hugh called on Mr. Pursehouse and began his introduction to the business of loans, interest rates, and capital investments. It had been decided that he would attend Leyden University in another year; he visited Dr. Comyn to inform him of this decision, and to learn from the instructors the new term's schedule of instruction.

It was only when he noticed, from the window of a hackney taking him to Lion Key, a painter atop a ladder blotting out the signboard of the Fruit Wench that he sensed something was amiss.

At Lion Key, Benjamin Worley greeted him effusively, and during a walk along the Keys brought him up to date on the business. "Oh, everyone's in a mad rush to fill orders for the colonies and Europe and load up the merchantmen before things get testy at sea between our navy and the French! Insurance rates have gone up, as you can imagine. Why, even the French are insuring their merchantmen against damage and capture by our own navy, right there in the Royal Exchange! The bloody cheek of it! I've had news that Frederick's occupied Dresden and beaten the Saxons and Austrians in a terrific battle near Lobositz, and that Russia might side with the French just to spite us."

Hugh and Worley stepped out of the way of a dray carrying bales of cotton. "But," continued Worley, "as if that weren't enough, fate picked me to sit on a grand jury to indict some freethinkers, and that ruined me for two days, and let my sons make some blunders in the office. Couldn't sleep much after the trial, milord! Even lost my appetite, big as it is!"

"A trial of freethinkers?" queried Hugh.

"Yes. Some club of them known as the Society of the Pippin, or Pippins. Charged with putting up a most scandalous poster in parts of the city that libeled His Majesty and his ninny of a grandson, and practically called the Bible the devil's work. No small beer, wouldn't you agree, milord? Well, I only saw the thing during the trial, not where it was said to be posted. King's Counsel and the defense had a right good dust-up over it, one claiming that the men put the poster up, or at least were responsible for the words on it, the other, a lively fellow called Jones, claiming that the Crown hadn't proved its charges. I would have laid a pound in Jones, and I was ready to acquit, and thought the others would, too. But in the end, it became so confusing, and I was tired, and the foreman argued that, all things considered, their mere denial of action wasn't proof that the Pippins didn't put it up... So, we found for blasphemous libel." Worley sighed. "Somehow, we were flammed, and so was that advocate, Jones, but I don't know how. The judge had the rum lay on the matter, I can tell you! Put a hex on the advocate's case. I could tell that right from the beginning..."

Hugh asked, "Where are they now?"

"The Pippins?" replied Worley. "At Newgate, I hear. But they won't be there for long. They were ruinously fined—a hundred pounds each!—and will probably end their days trimming timber at the Deptford docks, or beating hemp at Bridewell. Were given three years apiece. It's not a hanging offense, but once the Crown's finished with them, I'll wager they'll wish it was one!"

"How many men were charged?"

"Five, milord."

"At which court?"

"King's Bench, in a special session at Middle Temple, which was convenient for me. Didn't need to traipse all the way up to Westminster Hall." Worley hailed a passing fruitseller and bought an apple from the woman. "The whole matter put a sour taste in my mouth, milord, I don't mind saying," he said, examining the reddish orb in his hand, "unlike these beauties. Extraordinary experience!" he remarked with a shake of his head. "Wish I hadn't been summoned that time!" He took a bite from the apple.

"What was the barrister's name again, Mr. Worley?"

"Jones, milord. Odd first name. 'Dog meet,' or was it 'Dogs ale'? Or some such," said Worley. "Oh, yes! I remember! Dogmael! Dogmael Jones!"

Hugh turned to the merchant and said, "Forgive me, Mr. Worley, but I must look after something. I shan't be back today." Without waiting for a reply, he turned again and strode quickly back up Thames Street.

On the Strand, he stopped the hackney and ordered the driver to wait. The painter had by now finished drawing the outline of a ram's head on the signboard. Hugh went inside the tavern and asked for the proprietor, who told him that Mabel Petty's license had been revoked, that she had sold the place to him, and moved from the quarters above. "To Bristol, sir, if I recollect. She has relatives there, I think she said." Hugh nodded thanks to the man, and walked out. "Hope to get your custom, sir!" the proprietor called after him.

Hugh stood, immobile, outside the tavern. His world was vanishing. Two porters carrying a sedan chair brushed by him, almost knocking him down. He barely noticed the jostling.

His mind was bursting with questions, throbbing with building anger, more anger than he had thought himself capable of feeling, an outrage more intense than that which he felt toward his uncle. He could not decide which answer to his questions was more important: Why had he not been arrested? But Worley had given him no sign that he even suspected he was connected with the Society. Why were his friends arrested? For a poster? What poster? Only five men had been arrested, tried and convicted. Which ones, and where were the other two? Had they fled? Were they to be tried separately?

He looked up at the waiting hackney driver. Hugh told him to take him to Windridge Court. He would recover from the shock there, collect his thoughts, and decide on a course of action.

But Dolman met him as he came into the house, and handed him a sealed note on a salver. "A dusky gentleman called about an hour ago, milord," he said, "and asked me to give this to you the instant you returned."

Swain! Hugh recognized the handwriting in the address. He snatched the note up and opened it. "See me at home," it read. "Most urgent. G. Swain." Hugh turned and raced back out the door and across the courtyard to hail another hackney.

*　　*　　*

He found Swain in his garret, sewing silk parcels of tea to a false lining inside his frock coat. The man expressed surprise and relief at seeing him. "You are safe!" they exclaimed together to each other.

After they had exchanged greetings, Hugh asked, "What has happened?"

Swain told him the whole story, and showed him the newspaper accounts he had saved.

Hugh read them, and set them aside. "Who filed the suit? That is not mentioned anywhere."

"Our mutual friend, the Marquis of Bilbury," answered Swain. "The son."

Hugh paced back and forth for a moment, thinking. "Somehow, he learned of my association with the Society." He shook his head. "It was me he was after, not any of you."

"Yes," agreed Swain, who sat on his bed. "I know."

Hugh stopped pacing and faced his friend, his expression inviting an explanation.

In the manner of a man confessing his sins, Swain told Hugh about his encounter with Brice Blissom at Windridge Court. "I killed him, my friend, I—a man who has never so much as spanked a beast of a child or cursed a man who cheated me!"

After a long moment, Hugh said, "That was justice, sir. He was going to kill you. I do believe he would have contrived to kill me. However, I do not think you would get justice in the law courts."

"No," answered Swain. "I was a Pippin. I resisted arrest and killed the man who wanted to arrest me. I would be hanged, as surely as the Thames tide goes out."

"And he was a marquis," added Hugh. "A thousand marks are on your head. I read about that in Danvers. The man who could offer that reward could also afford to have you killed before you came to trial." He stepped forward and gripped Swain's shoulder. "I do not know how to thank you, Mr. Swain. You have my gratitude. You rid me of a nuisance. But you did it to save yourself. Feel no guilt about that, or I shall be angry with you."

Swain managed a weak smile, and nodded.

"So," said Hugh, pacing again, "the Society was betrayed. One of us gave him the minutes."

"It must have been Mathius," sighed Swain. "As I recall, it was he who had them last, for that meeting. And he is now notably absent."

"He, too, bore me ill will," remarked Hugh.

"If, like me, he is hiding, or not going about publicly, because he fears me... Well, if I saw him, he need fear nothing from me but my pity."

"A dire retribution, to be sure," said Hugh, studying his friend. "A better one would be contempt." He smiled a smile as cold as marble in winter, and Swain knew that he had not been paid an empty, patronizing compliment.

Swain said, "I have been communicating with the advocate, and so I know this: Elspeth and Abraham have perished. They are gone. In two weeks, Claude, Tobius, and Steven are to take their turns on the pillory, for seven days. They could not be scheduled sooner. They have been sentenced to three years of labor for the Crown, or transportation if it suits their wardens. Abraham's watch shop was seized in lieu of his fine. Elspeth's bookshop—he dealt mostly in law books, I learned—has been shunned by lawyers and barristers and students, and is near bankruptcy. Tobius has been banished by the College of Surgeons, and his wife impoverished. Claude's mistress made off with all his possessions, or what was left after the Crown took its due. And poor Steven will never again play music, for his fingers were smashed almost beyond use."

Hugh was silent for a while. "Where are they to be pilloried?"

"At Charing Cross," answered Swain, "'that place being nearest to the scene of their perfidy,'" he added, quoting Judge Grainger in a mocking impersonation of the judge's voice. "I would not tell you that, except that you would learn of it in any case."

Hugh stared out the tiny rectangle of waxed paper that was Swain's sole window. "I shall visit them in prison," he said ominously. "I shall see them on the pillory, and ground any man who taunts them or throws a single stone. I will call on this advocate and demand to know why he lost."

Swain looked up at Hugh, his eyes now alert. "He would not be able to tell you why he lost. He tried to win, but the trial was foreordained to conclude as it did." He paused. "You pass the pillory every day, sir. There are wretches there now, enduring public censure. 'Tis the season to exhibit them. Why do you not feel that same anger for them?"

Hugh shrugged, and did not turn around. "Because they are thieves, and reprobates, and larcenous scum. Why should I feel anything for them?" His hands balled into fists, and he leaned against the edges of the windowsill. "Our friends, however, are the benefactors of the men and women who censure them, and they do not deserve to suffer for their generosity!"

He whipped around and shouted, brandishing a fist that punched the air with every word he spoke, "I will accost King's Counsel and tell him who I am! I will dare—no, challenge—him to file charges against me! I will secure the release of our friends, before they perish in captivity!"

Swain calmly studied a face animated by murderous fury, a face that would perish in the very hell its owner presumed he could destroy. He had been afraid that this would be his friend's reaction. Now he knew it. He was determined to abort that certain tragedy. "And who are you?" he asked in a mocking tone.

"I am Miltiades, who triumphed over the Persians!" shouted Hugh with a grim, dreadful recklessness. "I vanquished them, and I'll vanquish the Crown!"

"No, you will not." Swain rose and approached Hugh. He towered menacingly over his friend. "You may thank me by not doing anything foolish!" he commanded. "You will not attempt to see our friends, or even rescue them. You will not try to help them. The Crown does not wish them to be helped. You will make no move that would identify you as one of them, young sir!"

Hugh's brow furled in surprise at these words and their manner of utterance. He began to reply, but Swain wagged a finger in his face.

"You will do nothing," said Swain. "For if the Crown learns your name, and the name you were known to us by, it will know who made the statements on the poster it most objected to—and then a greater conspiracy would be imagined by it than the mere gluing of inane posters to columns and doors! I observed the entire trial, sir, and saw how men wedded to the Crown would flout reason and mislead honest men! The Crown would go mad, and unleash the dogs of war on everyone, and begin arresting men without cause, reason, or protest! Your family would not escape examination, and your teachers, because they are mere commoners, would be interrogated with the same kindness and respect as were Elspeth and Steven! Men of your own rank would be suspected, and friends to our cause in all the strata of our strange society abused with general warrants, only to disappear after hurried trials and be consumed as our friends are fated to be!" Swain paused. "You credit me with having a fresh mind, sir. Then honor me by owning to that harrowing scenario!"

"So be it!!" shouted Hugh up at Swain's face. "But I will not stand idle and watch them be degraded and lawfully murdered! I could not live, knowing that they—"

Swain raised an arm and shoved Hugh roughly against the wall. "But you will stand idle, sir! That will be your pillory! And mine! See this: Your sword cannot help them, and neither can your rank! You would not have enough money to purchase all the places owned by the Attorney-General and the Secretary of State, and even if you had, would it guarantee you justice? Do you believe that the men who wield that kind of power would relinquish it by admitting their error, and defer to your reason? No? Then you will be silent, and settle for saluting our friends at the pillory, to let them know that you are free, and will someday avenge them! You will live, my young Baron of Danvers, and enjoy living, and know when it is the right time to vanquish the supreme Mohocks who ambushed them!"

Hugh's eyes narrowed and he steeled himself. "I'll avenge them now!!" he growled. "And you are in my way!" He raised an arm and made to push Swain aside.

Swain's hand rose and his palm slapped Hugh roundly across the face. "Be silent, younker!" he commanded. "Be still, and obey me!"

Hugh fell back against the wall, shocked by the act and by the violence of Swain's words.

Swain moved his face closer to Hugh's. "You wonder why I oppose you? This is why, sir: You are something I struggle to be. All of us in the Society have had a glimpse of it. Before you joined us, we merely tinkered with the trappings of what you are, groped futilely in its shadow with the weak candles of our minds, danced to music we could hear only faintly beneath the commotion of our own confusion! We are all drawn to it, except Mathius, whose fear of it caused him to turn Macbeth on us! You could not have had that effect on us, were you not what you are. Yet you do not know what you are. You have had no reason to think on it. The name for you has not yet been devised. The answer lies in you, and only you can put it into the right words. Someday, you will. I may not witness the moment, nor ever hear the words, but I will live happily knowing that they will be discovered and spoken! Somehow, they will justify our own cruel pillory and demolish it at the same time! And I will not allow you to jeopardize that moment!" Swain now saw in Hugh's eyes the thing he could not identify, together with a knowledge of itself, and rebellion against his words.

Swain bit his lip, then clasped Hugh to him and held him tightly. "You are the future, my friend! And I forbid you to die until you have lived it!" He held Hugh away from him, gripping his shoulders with a strength he had never tested before. "Promise me, as a Pippin, and as my dearest friend, that you will heed my wisdom! Swear to me!"

Hugh did not understand the conviction that took hold of him. It compelled him, after a long moment, to whisper with solemn honesty, "I swear it." He did not think his words had anything to do with the intensity of Swain's eyes, nor with the tears that glistened in them. All he could understand, at that moment, was that Swain had touched some part of his soul, and that he felt an unquestioned duty to acknowledge the act with a commensurate promise.

Chapter 38: The Pillory

HUGH KENRICK KNEW THAT GLORIOUS SWAIN WAS RIGHT—RIGHT, AT least, about the consequences of rashly identifying himself to anyone as one of the missing Pippins. Upon cooler reflection, he privately conceded Swain's points, but their rightness only magnified his sense of helplessness, which in turn fed his anger. He had taken an oath, but now wondered if, in the act of not breaking it, the oath would instead break him.

It was dusk when he paid the driver and stood to watch the hackney leave the courtyard. He walked over to the spot where Dolman and the stablemaster said they found Brice Blissom. Rain had washed the blood away. What happened here many nights ago did not seem real to him, either. Nor did the idea of Glorious Swain committing the act. Then he remembered his friend's warnings in the garret, and the slap on his face. The reality of Brice Blissom's death returned.

That evening, Hugh sat at an open window in his darkened room and watched the lights of vessels move up and down and across the Thames below, and let the distant rumble and rattle of wheels over Westminster Bridge soothe his mind. He had accepted all of Swain's arguments, but one: that he was the future. That is, he did not reject it. His life and future were his, as much as were his hands and feet. It was not an issue of accepting or rejecting such things; they were simply there. He did not know that there was something to be glimpsed, or something others struggled to be. The notion was so alien to him that he could not grasp it; it was as foreign to him as was the *Corpus Mysticum*. That, at least, he could grasp, for it was something he could observe, analyze, and abstract. He did not know how to observe and abstract himself. The idea smacked of vanity. He could not decide whether it was ludicrous or sublime.

It must be sublime, he concluded; Swain was not a man who wasted time on absurdities. And it must be wisdom, an elusive fragment of it he would perhaps acquire in the future that Swain had forbidden him to forsake.

* * *

Hugh had promised Swain not to reveal his association with the convicted Pippins. Such a promise, under such circumstances, is merely a lid fixed atop a boiling caldron of anger. Either the lid will be shot away by the mounting pressure, or the caldron will explode, leaving the lid intact. The first sign of the oath's inadequacy occurred two days later, when Hugh allowed himself an innocent exception to the oath, took time away from his duties at Swire's Bank, and went to Serjeant-at-Laws Inn to enquire after Dogmael Jones. He found the man in the near-empty library of the Inn, sitting at a table laden with law books and documents. He introduced himself, saying that he had been one of the spectators in the courtroom.

Jones was not wearing his wig and gown. He was a tall, lean, pock-mark-scarred man with silver-streaked black hair tied in back with a plain ribbon. He bowed cordially to Hugh, and gestured for him to sit across the table from him. A bottle of wine and a half-filled glass stood on top of an ancient, worn tome. "What is your interest in the matter, milord?" asked the barrister.

"I thought you should have won," answered Hugh.

"As did I," replied Jones. "Do you know the men?"

After a pause, Hugh answered, "I was acquainted with them, through their trades."

"I see." Jones scrutinized Hugh for a moment. "Did you see the poster?"

"Only in the courtroom, sir."

"Of course."

Swain and Benjamin Worley had told Hugh enough about the trial that he could ask informed questions. These he put to Jones, together with some on points of law. Jones smiled in appreciation of the questions. He gestured to the books and papers. "You catch me here in the midst of preparing a reading for students, come the next term. Statutes and precedents and rules of law." He paused to pour more wine into his glass. "Here's to public places." He tilted the glass back and swallowed the red liquid.

Hugh knew then that the man was half-drunk.

Jones noted the observation on his visitor's face. "Physicians bleed their patients to purge them of infirming humors. Why can't a man bleed a bottle to purge himself of pain?" He grinned. "Well, do you want to know how injustice was done? All right. On paper, I won the case. There was no doubt in anyone's mind about that. King's Counsel would even concede that. But when Milord Grainger examined my own arguments with malice aforethought, he lost it for me. I had not expected that tactic. I had heard he was a fair man."

"But, how?"

Jones shrugged. "He made an issue of public places, and those secret names. You were there. You heard him. I neglected both matters in my presentation, as they were not germane. But he flung them into the air for the jury to see, like a juggler at St. Bartholomew's Fair, for the mob to coo and crow over—while the twin thieves of protocol and privilege picked our pockets! Of course, he did not instruct the jury to disregard his own digression, and I could not instruct him to…instruct." Jones picked up the bottle again and poured another glass.

"Why would he want to sabotage your case?"

"Why?" chuckled Jones. "Why, indeed? To get himself a crown," said the barrister in the manner of a quotation, "or, at least, a coronet. Milord Master of the Rolls, I have it on good authority, is to be bestowed the Viscountcy of Wootton and Clarence, in Staffordshire, by a grateful king acting on the advice of those who have heard something of his prudence. Well, sixteen silver balls on a hat, versus the lives of five men—who could quarrel with such a trade?" Jones leaned back in his chair and passed a hand over his eyes, then studied the glass of wine in his hand. "Well, there's some justice in that reward. 'The last was I that felt thy tyranny,' said the ghost of Clarence to King Richard on the eve of battle. 'Despair and die!'" Jones emptied his glass again, and set it down with a thump on the tome. "I'll bet he never reads that tragedy again, the right honorable bastard!"

"That was the ghost of Buckingham," corrected Hugh.

Jones shut his eyes for a moment, then smiled. "Milord, you are right. Wrong ghost, wrong crime! I've misplaced my lines. Here, then, is Clarence: 'I wash myself to death with fulsome wine.' Slightly paraphrased, as Mr. Cibber and Mr. Garrick are wont to do on the stage." He picked up the bottle again and drained the last of its contents into his glass. "Is that all you wish to know, milord?"

"Yes," answered Hugh. "Thank you."

Jones rose, holding his glass. "Then you will please excuse me, while I imbibe my certain quietus, prepare to stump my students, and ponder the prerogatives of public places."

Hugh rose also. "Public places? That is the third time you have mentioned that, as though it were a lesion that inflamed your mind."

"I confess the notion confounds me, milord."

Hugh looked thoughtful. "Perhaps the confusion lies in its definition, sir," he suggested.

Jones was about to taste the wine again, but he paused to study his visitor. After a moment, he grinned and winked. "Spoken, milord, like a true Pippin. Thank you. I shall harry that definition." He bowed in deference.

"Good day to you, sir," said Hugh. He turned and walked away, but glanced back at the barrister. The glass, still full, now sat on top of the ancient tome. And Sir Dogmael Jones still stood, his back to him, fingers drumming a tattoo on the table, apparently deep in thought.

*　*　*

Between the soaring twin turrets and weathercocks of Northumberland House at Charing Cross strode a gold-plated bronze lion atop a rococo pediment, looking as though he were stalking prey below. Just south of the long facade of this building, the statue of swordless Charles I commanded the juncture of Whitehall with Cockspur Street and the Strand. The space there was wide enough to accommodate the pillory and the crowds it attracted. The pillory itself was not a permanent structure; it was dismantled and stored near a bailiff's house until the courts produced a fresh batch of felons. When it was up, merchants and tradesmen who leased shops at the crossroads rarely complained of the ruckus and inconvenience of the crowds; an excursion to the pillory was regularly fitted into many a lady's and gentleman's daily itinerary of shopping, social calls, and idleness.

Every six weeks, the hangings at Tyburn Tree near Hyde Park on the western outskirts of London drew thousands of spectators. The punishments at Charing Cross drew mere hundreds. Always there were men and women on the pillory, at times only two, often as many as six. Their sentences ranged from two hours to a whole day. The size and character of a crowd depended on the notoriety of the crimes or the felons. Whatever was not a hanging offense was a punishable offense. Adulterers and adulteresses were exhibited here to endure the ribald and coarse catcalls of the crowd. So were buggers and mollies—sodomites—who provoked so furious a wrath that often they were fortunate to be released from the pillory alive, barely able to see through their own blood. So were prostitutes and wagtails, or any women found guilty of lewd behavior. False cambists, or forgers of bills of exchange or other money instruments, took their turns at the pillory, as did receivers of stolen goods and defrauders of tradesmen.

Apprentices who beat their masters, and artisans who beat their apprentices, were exposed to public judgment. Servants lucky enough to win a jury's sympathy, when the appraised value of the property they stole was less than forty shillings, were sentenced to stand here instead of on the hangman's cart beneath Tyburn Tree.

And like Tyburn Tree, pillory days took on the character of a street fair. Enterprising vendors put up food and drink stalls nearby, or circled the crowds noisily hawking fruits, refreshments, potions, and snuff from wheelbarrows. Touts roamed the crowds selling places closer to the pillory, or illegal lottery tickets, or programs listing the schedule of felons and their crimes. Others, working on commission for the felons themselves, or for a prison chaplain, hustled to sell the prisoners' personal confessions, histories, or protestations of innocence in penny pamphlets, for there was a great market for the printed lives of criminals. Pickpockets and cut-purses, drawn naturally to great numbers of distracted people, worked stealthily and discreetly in the crowd, and joined in with their own curses and epithets. A handful of constables, watchmen, beadles, and mounted javelinmen with their red-tasseled spears were posted around the pillory by the presiding sheriff or bailiff to prevent rescue attempts and to control the crowds. If a felon or his family was rich enough, private guards could be hired to keep the crowd far enough away from the prisoner to reduce the risk of harm to him.

For many felons, time on the pillory was tantamount to the death sentence, for there were those among the spectators who, for lack of any other amusement or diversion, were professional tormenters. These were usually street urchins and idle men. They would come ready with bags slung over their shoulders crammed with the dross and scourings of the city: stones, dead cats and rats, blocks of wood, horses' hooves, rotten eggs, dung, and slaughterhouse offal. Their aim was practiced, accurate, and often deadly. What they did not themselves hurl at the prisoners, they sold to game or roused spectators. For some of these rogues, pelting the pillory was the only cathartic of their aimless, abridged lives; for others, the gross sales of missiles for the use of lawful mobs enabled them to sustain themselves for another day or week.

If a prisoner was maimed, or died from his injuries at the pillory, the law, age-old custom, and public approbation allowed it. The possibility was integral to the punishment. When a prisoner expired on the pillory, a coroner's jury would simply return a finding of "willful murder by persons unknown," and no investigation would be made. *The London Evening Auditor* was not the only newspaper to note that, on pillory days, "there are usually more criminals and miscreants in the crowds, than there are on view."

The pillory itself was a marvel of simplicity. It consisted of as many upright posts as a platform would accommodate. Attached to each post were two transverse boards, an upper one, hinged, and a stationary lower one. The upper board could swing up to allow a prisoner to place his neck and wrists in the sockets of the stationary, then swing down to complete the holes and be locked to the lower. The average height of the boards forced most men and women to stand in a bending position. The posts were often connected at the base to an iron bar that would permit a hangman, safely out of the way of missiles, to turn the posts, and thus the prisoners, for the crowds on all sides to see.

Swordless Charles, sitting high above the pillory, did not witness what transpired beneath the nostrils of his steed. The golden lion of Northumberland House, gazing down on it all, seemed to give it his kingly consent.

From Windridge Court, Charing Cross was Hugh's only egress to Worley's offices on the Lawful Keys and Swire's Bank on Lombard Street. He could have paid a waterman to row him from the Whitehall Stairs to Lion Key downriver, but he chose to pass through the juncture every morning. He thought he could accustom himself to the spectacle, so that, when their time came, the sight of the Pippins, standing with their heads and wrists locked between the boards, and exposed to the taunts and abuse, would be bearable. He had never ventured to Tyburn Tree, for he thought that a fascination with the executions there was morbid, strange and unhealthy. He had seen pillories before—in London, in Danvers, in Canterbury—and, without pausing in his business to gape, assumed that justice was being done. Nor was he a stranger to the gibbets that travelers encountered on the roads and turnpikes, those iron cocoons of the decaying remains of brutal highwaymen, planted aloft at the scenes of their crimes.

Soon enough, though, he realized that he was deceiving himself. He could endure the sight of a pillory and the raucous crowds that surrounded it. He knew that what he could not endure was the sight of the Pippins on one. They had been found guilty of blasphemous libel, of putting up seditious posters, yet they were not criminals. The Crown said they were. He knew they were not.

They would be pilloried—because of him. Elspeth and Abraham were dead—because of him. The Society had been the excuse for striking back—at him. It was he who had been the object of malice, that of Mathius and of Brice Blissom. How could he abandon the three surviving Pippins? How could he not share their punishment? He began to feel absurdly guilty for not having been arrested, tried, and sentenced to the same punishment. Then he thought of Glorious Swain, who felt guilt neither for his freedom, nor for having killed the Marquis.

His guilt fought quietly with his sense of injustice. Laws existed that could punish men for thinking. Men could use those laws to punish others. Men could corrupt a court to seek an end that would get them some lucrative preferment—such as the Viscountcy of Wootton and Clarence. The guilt clashed also with his shattering disappointment that such a thing could happen in England. But, he asked himself: Why should he be so surprised? There was his uncle, who could sit in Lords and wield power. There was Henoch Pannell, who could sit in the Commons and wield power.

I do not wield power, he thought, and yet I am feared. Is that such a vain observation? John Hamlyn had tried to crush him. His uncle had tried to crush him. As had Brice Blissom. Yet Glorious Swain said that he was the future. Did his uncle and Pannell see that, too?

Hugh spent many evenings at home, sitting at his desk, spinning his brass top on its cleared surface, thinking, pondering, attempting to reconcile a host of opposites. He could not. The top would spin until it began to wobble, and he would put a finger on it so that it would not fall.

Chapter 39: The Lawless

"**O**NE MAY CURSE IN FRENCH, AND STILL SOUND BEAUTIFUL AND profound."

"Oh, no! One may not curse properly in French at all!"

"Depend on it, gentlemen: If you are cursed by a Frenchman, you would not need to understand a word he says, to know that you are not being called beautiful or profound!"

The guests and hosts at the table of the supper room at Windridge Court laughed at this exchange between Garnet Kenrick, John Swire, and George Formby. James Pursehouse, the fourth partner of the bank, had bitten into his mince pie and found a stone. His muttered curse in French had provoked the exchange. Hugh was present, sitting next to his sister, Alice, now ten years old. Garnet Kenrick sat at the head of the table, next to his wife. Swire's and Formby's wives were also at the table.

Hugh merely smiled. His uncle arrived first at the London home, followed by his parents and sister two days later. He had already moved most of his things to Cutter Lane, and had seen the Earl only briefly in one of the hallways. In a week, he was to begin a new term at Dr. Comyn's school. Hugh would not speak to his uncle under any circumstances, except in reply. His uncle would not tolerate being snubbed by his nephew, at least not in company or in public. Effney Kenrick worked hard to keep them apart. Hugh was here tonight because the Earl was not.

Neither Garnet Kenrick nor his wife could penetrate the grim reticence of their son. They had never seen him so preoccupied before, and they knew not with what. They were certain it had nothing to do with the estrangement between their son and the Earl.

"Has Reverdy slighted you in a letter?" asked the Baroness gently one day.

"No," Hugh had said with a warm, incredulous smile.

"Has Mr. Worley done something I should know about?" asked the Baron. "In the business, that is."

"No," said Hugh. "His sons lost some wares that were to go to Spain while Mr. Worley was serving on a grand jury, that is all."

"Are you in any trouble...or difficulty?"

"No," replied Hugh. "Aye, there's the rub," he added, more to himself than for his parents' benefit.

"What do you mean, Hugh?" asked his mother.

"Yes, what do you mean?" echoed his father. Mistaking Hugh's quotation from Hamlet for some attempt at wit, he tried to use wit to coax an explanation from his son. "Leave moping about to the likes of that morose Dane, and drop that Melpomenic mask!" He followed this with a laugh and an inviting smile.

Hugh had merely grinned weakly, shaken his head, and would not explain what he meant.

The Baron remembered that his son had boasted of having friends in London. Some suspicion he could not explain to himself caused him to ask, "Well, what about these mysterious friends of yours, Hugh? I'd like to meet them, if I may. And your mother, too."

Hugh shook his head again. "Not now, Father. The time is not right."

It was not as though his reticence was deliberate. He seemed to be his usual, exuberant self—except that they detected a lag between his words and actions, as though he were struggling against some torpid melancholy that warped his normal behavior. This, in their son, meant that something was bothering him. He played chess with his sister, taught her some mathematics, and read stories to her. He seemed to take delight in being called "brother" by her. He spoke with some animation about his work with Mr. Worley, and the new things he was learning at Swire's Bank.

Still, Hugh's parents were certain that something awful, perhaps even tragic, lay beneath the confident exterior of their son.

Tonight, after all the guests had gone, and as Hugh was preparing to leave, his mother said, "We are planning to row up to Hampton Court early Tuesday morning to see the Palace and the Chinese Bridge, and then perhaps stop at Richmond and Chelsea on our return, and stay the night. Please, Hugh, come with us!"

"Your uncle will be at Bedford's all day," said his father. "You could meet us at the Manchester Stairs. I'm sure the fresh air will perk you up."

Hugh smiled. "Perhaps it may." He paused. "I must think about it. Perhaps you are right." He bussed his mother on the cheek, and shook hands with his father. "Good night."

When he returned to Cutter Lane, Mrs. Rickerby handed him a sealed note. It was from Glorious Swain.

"I have it from a bailiff's groom of my acquaintance that our friends' pillory sentence has been abridged to mornings until noontime, and reduced to five days only. There appear to be too many felons, assigned the same punishment, to oblige the court's original sentence. Their first morning will be this next Tuesday. Let us go together. G. Swain."

Hugh knew that he could not trust himself to go alone to the pillory. He would need Swain's cooler head and steadying hand. On his way to Lion Key the next morning, he stopped by Swain's garret to fix a time and place for their rendezvous. Their meeting was brief and hurried. Swain was going to Stepney to work with other hired men to assemble bags of smuggled tea, sugar and salt for sale on the streets; Hugh was to meet his father at Lion Key, where the Baron planned to review family accounts with Mr. Worley. When he left Swain's place, he had to smile. As he was a brother to his adoring sister, and even, if only in name, to Roger Tallmadge, Swain seemed to be one to him.

When he met his father in Mr. Worley's office, he told him that he had pressing personal business the next morning, but that he would either take a coach from the Bear Inn, or ride one of the mounts from the family stable, and join the family at Hampton Court later in the day. He would want to leave the city for a while, he thought, after seeing the Pippins on the pillory.

Then he lost himself in the task of preparing a customs cocket for one of the loaded merchantmen, the *Antares*, which was ready to weigh anchor and be piloted back down the Thames. At the end of the day, before he left with his father for supper at the Angry Angel, he reviewed a list of merchantmen, compiled by one of Worley's sons, waiting to be unshipped at Lion Key. Among the names was the *Sparrowhawk*, returned from her latest voyage. He thought that it would be pleasant to see Captain Ramshaw again.

He slept fitfully that night. He tossed and turned in that purgatory of rest that lay between nervous exhaustion and dreadful expectation. His body wanted to sleep, his mind would not. And when he managed to sleep, vivid nightmares raided his head, and hurled him toward calamitous near-death, only to vanish, without memory, when he woke up in panicked surprise.

*   *   *

On Tuesday morning, Hugh left his room on Cutter Lane, bid the Rickerbys good day, and strode over to St. Martin's Lane, which let out on the Strand opposite Northumberland House. He was to meet Glorious

Swain in front of Corsan's Book and Print Shop at nine; the Pippins—
Claude, Tobius, and Steven—would have been on the pillory for an hour.
Ahead, through the rumbling traffic of coaches, drays, and wagons passing
through Charing Cross, he could see a throng gathered around the place.
The city marshall, an under-sheriff, and some constables on foot and a few
javelin-men had stationed themselves loosely around the pillory. Some boys
sat on the pedestal beneath the hooves and belly of Charles I's prancing
steed for a better view. Hugh turned his back on the sight. He would wait
for Swain. He tried to study the etchings and prints displayed in the shop's
bow window, then stepped near the shop door to get out of the way of the
stream of people heading for the pillory.

Two men walked briskly by. "Well, sir," said one of them, "what miscreants do you think we'll see today? They must be special, to bring you so
far out of doors. And, look at this mob!"

"Three capons turning on the hangman's spit, Mr. Gould!" exclaimed
the other. "They crowed and strutted themselves right into the king's vise!"

Hugh turned sharply at the sound of the second voice, and stared at the
backs of the pair. He recognized the voice. He recognized its owner.

"Who are these capons, sir?"

"Caitiffs who took God's and His Majesty's names in vain! Two others,
I have heard, have perished already and gone to hell! And two more of their
fellows are at large. One of them, I am certain, murdered my patron for
having informed His Majesty's servants of their depredations!"

"And that is a sad thing, sir, to lose one's patron—and to such a terrible
crime! I don't wonder at your eagerness!"

"Much of a muchness, sir," commented the man. "The father is as good
as the son, and more generous."

"Perhaps their cronies will be here this morning."

"Not them, Mr. Gould!" scoffed the man. "No! They would not dare
show their faces! They are cowards!" The men threaded their way through
the coach traffic. The man spotted a boy in rags who was hawking missiles.
"Here, you! What are you asking?"

"Stones!" answered the urchin. "Broken bricks! Addled eggs! Cow and
horse hooves! Penny a toss, sir!"

William Horlick chuckled and reached into his coat. "Seven stones,
boy, with sharp edges, now!" He held out a handful of pennies.

The boy hunted through his bag and produced seven stones, handed
them to Horlick, and snatched up the proffered coins. Horlick dropped the

stones into one of his frock coat pockets.

"Only seven, Mr. Horlick?" asked Mr. Gould. "Why only seven?"

Horlick looked thoughtful. "Oh...I would say in honor of the seven hills of Rome, which did Rome no good, by the bye! Or, in honor of the Seven against Thebes, who all perished! Or, in honor of the seven Pippins who provoked the Crown—who will be slain by Orion, or swallowed up by the earth!"

The pair moved around the outskirts of the crowd, which was between one and two hundred people. Objects flew through the air now and then, mostly rotted vegetables and fruits, and missed their mark. A number of men in clerical garb were present. Mr. Gould addressed one of them. "Reverend sir, what are their crimes?"

"Only one, sir," replied the cleric. "Blasphemous libels uttered and published in public places. That was the charge the good sheriff read out to us."

"Thank you, reverend sir." Gould smiled at his companion as they moved on. "You seem to be especially in earnest about these fellows," he said. He gestured to the crowd. "But the mob here does not seem to know what to make of them, or how to hate them. Not even the regulars."

Horlick made a face. "Well, look at them, Mr. Gould! Mere artisans, and barrow-pushers, and common women in trade, and servants, and untutored boys! How often do you think they encounter atheists, doubters, or pagans? Cheats, and extortionate letter-writers, and cuckolding wives, and false witnesses—these they know! But half these people haven't the noodle to distinguish between the plainest verity of John Locke and the obscurest anagogy of the Rosicrucians! They will, however, punish whoever is put on the pillory, for they believe that if a man did not commit a wrong, he would not be there! They need but one example!" He put on a sly smile, and reached into his pocket for a stone. He glanced at it once, then hefted it. "Watch, sir, as I ignite a fusillade!" He drew his arm back and hurled the stone. It arced over the heads of the throng and struck a board near Robert Meservy's head with a loud smack that could be heard in the rear of the crowd.

"Bravo, sir!" exclaimed Mr. Gould. "You are in earnest!"

As they watched, more stones shot from the crowd, some hitting the Pippins, others falling into the crowd on the other side of the pillory. The marshall, under-sheriff, and guards moved discreetly away from the platform.

Horlick laughed in triumph at the sight, and reached into his pocket for another stone. But when he brought it out, something sharp pricked his wrist and caused him to drop it to the ground. He glanced at his wrist; it was bleeding. Then he turned and saw Miltiades looking at him, sword in hand. "You...!" He raised his hands in the air, as though he was being robbed.

"Good morning, Mathius," said Hugh. His face was a pale, rigid visage of contempt and unholy purpose that did not invite a reply from the object of its study. "You are wrong about the Seven of Thebes. They did not all perish. Adrastus, king of Argos, survived."

Mr. Gould also turned, and was about to protest, but Hugh said, "You, sir, will say nothing. This man knows me. I know him as Mathius. He belongs up there, on the pillory, with his friends. This is a personal matter, between him and me. Begone, or stay as a witness."

Mr. Gould glanced at the dumbstruck face of his companion, and knew that this was no affair of his. He muttered some apology, and slipped away into the crowd.

"Miltiades, I—" began Horlick.

"Who was he?" asked Hugh.

"Him? That was Mr. Gould!" stammered Horlick. "He composes tradesmen's cards, and advertisements."

"A more honest dealer in words than you, you must own," said Hugh. "He conveys plain information. You compose bilious verse, froggish fables, and libelous forgeries—William Horlick."

"You misjudge me, Miltiades!"

"Do I? I know what you did with the minutes, Mr. Horlick. I know your authorship of the poster, and of your connection with the Marquis of Bilbury. I waited until you tossed the first stone. That action marked the conclusion of your treachery, that you have turned against all that you believed in, that you have traded Olympus for a sack of guineas."

"But, I—"

"I am not finished, sir." Hugh had not moved a step. He stood with his sword grasped at both ends, by pommel and tip. "Do you know who I am?"

Horlick shook his head. "No."

"The Marquis did not tell you?"

"No, dear, merciful sir, he did not! He was very secretive..."

Hugh scoffed. "Perhaps he did not trust you enough with my name. Perhaps he suspected you would betray him just as you betrayed your friends. Still, I cannot blame you for his part of the crime—unless you knew what he planned to do."

"I didn't know what he planned, gracious sir!" said Horlick. But then his face wrinkled in confusion. "What crime?" he asked, partly in fear, partly in disdain.

"The crime of not being man enough to be a man."

"I—"

"How much were you paid to invent the poster?"

Horlick glanced around. People had gathered to watch and listen. He saw curiosity and fascination with his predicament in their faces, but no sympathy. He did not wish to give forthright answers to the questions, but the threat in Miltiades' carriage and in his voice compelled him to be truthful.

"How much?" repeated Hugh, tapping the blade end of his sword in the palm of his other hand.

"Twenty guineas," whispered Horlick.

"Well, at least that is more than thirty pieces of silver," remarked Hugh. He sighed. "I had a score of other questions for you, Mr. Horlick, but your admissions have answered most of them. I have not seen the poster for which your friends are being punished. Few people have. Perhaps you have copies in your own home, whereas your friends did not, and they are up there." He indicated the pillory. "But—" Hugh interrupted himself to ask in a mocking voice, "Why do you stand with your hands up, Mr. Horlick? I am not the royal scamp here."

The spectators around them laughed. Horlick, surprised, glanced at his hands, which were shaking, and quickly lowered them.

"But," continued Hugh, "the poster was merely a device to strike back at me, and at our friends for accepting me. Is this not true?"

Horlick blinked in answer.

"You did not mind the company of freethinkers, so long as their free thought did not put you in jeopardy. Is this not true?"

Again, Horlick did not answer.

"Your silence speaks volumes, which you lack both the talent and courage to write." Hugh paused. "Confess it, Mathius: You hated me, and feared me, from the beginning, because I am what you are not, but knew you ought to be."

This time it was Horlick's turn to express contempt. "You are vain," he spat.

"Vain? No. Observant, perhaps. But I know my own worth, sir. It would appear, however, that you have no worth to know. Not to yourself, at least. Others know that your pen may be prostituted, and that is your worth to them." Hugh sighed. "You have only five stones left in your pocket, Mr. Horlick. Surely you would want to move closer to your friends, so as not to miss them."

Horlick gulped.

"Do you stand so far away because they might identify you—or is it because you cannot face them?"

Horlick looked at his shoes.

Hugh used the tip of his sword to tap the cleft of Horlick's chin. "If you cannot face them, sir, at least have the bottom to face me. I am only one."

Horlick's face grew livid. He instinctively reached for the pommel of his sword, then changed his mind. He remembered how he came to know this young man. He remembered whose life this man had saved from three brutal Mohocks.

"Why do you not draw it, sir?" asked Hugh. There was no answer. "I understand. You remember the circumstances under which I made your acquaintance." He raised his sword again and pressed it against a button of the man's waistcoat. "Enough talk, sir. Let us move closer to the pillory. There I will identify you to the king's men there, and to the crowd. And you will identify me."

Horlick's body stiffened. "No," he said.

"No?"

"You must cut me to pieces here, for I will not do it!"

"Very well," said Hugh. "You are of the public, but afraid of it. So I shall mark you for the traitor you are—a traitor to freethinkers, a traitor to Lady Liberty." Before Horlick could comprehend the words, Hugh's blade flicked up, and in two deft strokes, cut a capital T on the man's left cheek.

The spectators gasped, and Horlick cried out in pain. His hands flew up to cover the bloody wound. Horlick could not see the wound, but knew by touch what letter had been carved into his face and would disfigure him for life. He looked at Hugh with eyes round with a new terror. Still holding his face, he took two steps back, then turned and bolted through the crowd.

"Run to your patron, Mathius," shouted Hugh. "Perhaps he will reward you with a coward's purse."

Horlick's abrupt departure left Hugh with an unobstructed view, over the heads of the throng, of the pillory. He could not distinguish the faces of the three men whose heads protruded through the holes. He sheathed his sword and moved forward, not knowing whether he was drawn to the sight or drawn to it by some irresistible force. There were people in his way; his hands grasped their shoulders and firmly pushed them aside. All anyone could see was a young man in an immaculate pearl gray coat and black tricorn who did not need to excuse himself or acknowledge their presence or existence, for they knew that he was an aristocrat and that he had better reason to be here than anyone else.

He stood in front of the crowd now, and could see the faces of his friends: Tobius, Claude, and Steven. They were sallow, unshaven, and filthy. Their faces were marred with bruises and smeared with blood and dung. Steven's hands were wrapped in dirty bandages. Tobius's hose was in shreds. Claude was barefoot. And the eyes of the men were lifeless; from shame or from resignation, Hugh could not tell.

There were some men and women near him who did not jeer at or taunt the prisoners, nor toss missiles at them. They stood looking up at the men with dull, helpless expressions, or with incredulous wonder, or with tears. These, Hugh presumed, were friends or relatives of the men who had not abandoned them.

When he looked at the men again, he saw that they were looking at him. He did not smile, but they seemed to smile in answer to him. He nodded once in acknowledgment, then made up his mind.

There was only one constable at the foot of the steps leading up to the pillory. Hugh crossed in front of the crowd and approached him. The constable was an old man, armed with only a stave. Hugh made as though to pass him, but turned and dashed up the steps. The constable began to follow him, but changed his mind when he saw the gleaming sword in Hugh's hand. He raised his stave in the air to signal the under-sheriff and city marshall, who sat together on their mounts beyond the crowd.

The crowd stirred when it saw a young man sheath his sword and walk with authority across the platform to the prisoners. And, until now, it had been a relatively tame mob that could not decide what to do about the prisoners. Horlick was right, thought Hugh: What was blasphemous libel to this mob? It was not lurid, gross, or contemptible. There was not a man in the crowd who had not blasphemed, or cursed the king, or questioned the competence of God, George, or Parliament. The men on the pillory could just as easily have been punished for disputing a mathematical theory, questioning the existence of ether, or refuting Ockham's razor. The proclaimed offense was too intellectual. Where was the cuckolded husband?

Where was the receiver of threatening letters? Where was the buyer of diluted cream?

Where was the victim of this crime? And what was the crime? Where was the outraged, offended victim who could lead the mob in the physical and verbal abuse of these pilloried felons? There were clerics in the crowd, more than the usual number present on such occasions. Some of them explained to fellow spectators what was meant by blasphemous libel, and why the men on the pillory this morning deserved to receive the full wrath of public outrage. As shepherds, they themselves were barred from tossing a single stone; it was their frank hope that their sheep would do it for them. But, because God was invisible, the king was at the royal palace in Kew, and Parliament had not yet reconvened, they could not point to a victim, and their humble diatribes came to naught. The crowd wanted a flesh-and-blood victim with whom to share vengeance, not some collection of sermonized abstractions. Some stones had been thrown, but only, as everyone knew, from the sport of the thing; bets had been made, that was all.

The young man who stood on the pillory now had an electric effect on the crowd. Everyone assumed that he would enlighten them about the depth of the prisoners' crimes, and name the victims of their felonious actions. The crowd's murmured speculations ceased as it noticed the city marshall and the under-sheriff edge toward the pillory, while several javelin-men coaxed their mounts back through the throng.

"My friends," said Hugh to the Pippins, who seemed both glad to see him, and afraid for him, "I apologize for not having joined you here sooner. I did not know this evil thing had happened. But I am here now, and will not leave until you do."

Meservy shook his head. "It is not necessary, Miltiades," he said with urgent gratitude. "Please, leave us! Go now, before they can reduce you to…this!"

"Live as we would live," said Sweeney. "As you have."

"But do not die as we are sure to die," said Brompton, "with more iron to keep us warm, than cloth. Die in glory. But live first, as we have lived!"

Hugh went to each man. "Long live Lady Liberty!" he said as he grasped the hand of each man and shook it.

"You, sir!"

Hugh turned to face the now strangely quiet crowd, only to meet the stern, priest-like scowl of the city marshall. "Sir," said this man, "you may not stay here!"

"I belong here, sir," replied Hugh. "I should have been arrested with these men, and similarly punished. They are my friends. So I have come to take my place with them."

"What do you mean?" asked the under-sheriff.

"I am Hugh Kenrick, a member of the Society lately dissolved by the Crown."

"I know nothing of that, sir," said the city marshall. "These men are guilty of blasphemous libel, of besmirching God, the king, and the constitution."

"Then I was tried *in absentia*, and am likewise guilty."

The under-sheriff pointed a finger at Hugh. "If you stay, sir, you will be arrested for trespassing, disturbing the peace, and interfering with the lawful punishment of felons!"

"I will leave when my friends' time is up. I will resist any attempt to remove me."

"Let 'im be, your honor!" shouted a man in the crowd. "We'll take 'im down!"

The under-sheriff turned in his saddle to glower at the crowd. The city marshall studied Hugh for a moment, and fidgeted with the reins of his mount. "Your loyalty and bravery are laudable, sir, but you are violating law. You will please step down, or I will order the sheriff here to remove you by any means he sees fit to employ."

"If these men are to be punished, then I will stand with them. However," cautioned Hugh, "I can and will brain any man who abuses them."

"You are inviting riot, sir!" shouted the under-sheriff, "and I am thereby empowered—"

A stone flew over the heads of the officers and struck the board below Sweeney's chin. Hugh picked up the stone and threw it back at the crowd. It sailed cleanly between the heads of the officers' mounts to hit a man on the forehead.

This man yelped in pain. The crowd responded with a roar of anger. Instantly a barrage of missiles rained on the pillory, striking the prisoners, the officers, their mounts, and Hugh. Hugh ran back and forth between the pilloried prisoners, trying to protect them and hurl back as many stones as he could. His madness rose with that of the mob, yet he felt a sense of power over the mob and hopelessness at the same time. All he knew was that this was something he must do, without thought of consequence, future, or harm to himself.

At some point in the noise and confusion he saw that his friends' faces were bloodied. Their mouths, heads, and ears were bleeding. A great sob of futility welled up inside Hugh. A stone struck his forehead. It was not the first missile to hit him, but he felt its thick sting more than he had any of the others. In murderous rage, he bent and found the stone. It was red with blood. It could have been the one that struck him, or one of the prisoners. It did not matter. He rose and shot it back with all his strength, not caring whom it hit.

It struck the nose of a fat, sweating cleric, who howled in pain.

The under-sheriff had signaled the constables and javelin-men to form a cordon around the pillory. He and the city marshall had also taken pistols from their saddle cases.

Then Hugh noticed a familiar face at the front of the crowd. Glorious Swain! Swain was shouting something up to him, and gesturing for him to leap down from the platform. Hugh could only stare dumbly at him. Then he saw the man bolt from the crowd, knock aside the old constable, and dart up the pillory steps. Swain rushed up to him, glanced once at the pilloried men, then grabbed Hugh by his shoulders. "You must go, my friend! Go now! You are hurt! Go, you damned fool, before they can—"

A javelin-man reached out with his spear and prodded Hugh with it. Swain whirled around, yanked the weapon from the man's hands, then raised the butt end of it and jabbed the man on his chest, tumbling the officer from his horse.

There was a pistol shot. Swain gasped, the javelin dropped from his hands, and his legs crumbled from beneath him. Hugh saw the under-sheriff sitting with his pistol still raised, a cloud of smoke drifting away, and at the same time became aware of a new silence.

He rushed to Swain. There was a look of surprise on the man's face, rather than one of pain. Hugh knelt, removed Swain's hat, and rested his head on his lap. He saw the spreading blob of blood on his friend's waistcoat, close to the heart.

"Go...Hugh Kenrick," said Swain. "Go...I am going, too..."

"No!"

"It is necessary," said Swain. "And...proper. Haven't you noticed the sky? It is blue. It is a 'glorious' day, today, this day...I come and go...on glorious days...Look," said the man, nodding to the sky. Hugh glanced up, and back down at Swain.

"Glorious," repeated Hugh, "and so you will not go! I command it! I command you to stay! To live!"

With difficulty, Swain chuckled. "I give such commands, young Baron of Danvers! I give commands to a baron!"

"As...an older brother," whispered Hugh.

Swain looked up and smiled into Hugh's eyes, and took one of his hands. "Thank you, my friend...my younger, most impetuous brother," he said softly.

The under-sheriff and city marshall had dismounted. Their boots thumped on the boards of the pillory and came to a stop. The officers stood over the young man and his dying friend.

"Listen, now," said Swain. "I know I have not long...before I go to our Olympus. My room...all that is there...is yours... The book, and my own scrivenings... They are of some value. Promise me they will live on...at least...I can no longer protect them..."

"I am responsible for this," said Hugh.

"No... It must have happened, sooner or later, my friend...one day or another... Our minds cannot be contained, our minds, our spirits—" Swain coughed violently. Blood spurted out of his mouth and wound with each spasm. "Be sure to construct our golden orrery, younger brother..." Swain's sight moved to look up past Hugh. "The sky is growing more blue...a royal cobalt...the canopy of Olympus..." Swain's eyes moved sluggishly to hold Hugh's. The grip on Hugh's hand became desperate. "Do not...regret what has happened here, Hugh. I thank you...for in thanking you...I thank myself... We were worthy of each other..." He gripped Hugh's hand more tightly. "Long...live..."

"...Lady Liberty," whispered Hugh.

Swain's grip loosened and his head rolled to one side, and it seemed that he was staring at the under-sheriff. But Hugh knew that his friend had died. The dead hand fell to a plank of the platform, and Hugh raised his head to look at the sky. Then he moved his own hand to close Glorious Swain's eyes.

Chapter 40: The Prisoner

THE CITY MARSHALL ORDERED THE CROWD TO DISPERSE. THE MOB, SILENCED by the pistol shot, obeyed; it broke up and drifted away. Some left in shame, some in spent righteousness, some with slaked curiosity. A man had been shot on the pillory, another was arrested. It was not yet noon, but the keeper from Newgate Prison had pulled his cart up to the pillory and the prisoners were being taken off the platform. One had to be carried to the cart by two constables. Another cart appeared with its own escort of constables, carrying three new occupants for the pillory. And behind that cart, another one, from the College of Surgeons. This one was empty; the surgeon and his assistant on it hoped to return to the College with at least one corpse. A tout scurried among the departing spectators, hoping to sell a list of the names, ages, trades, and offenses of the new felons. The boys had climbed down from under the belly of Charles I's steed.

Three men had observed the event from a distance: Sir Dogmael Jones, Sir Henoch Pannell, and Alden Curle. Jones had come out of a sense of penance for having lost a case, and also because he suspected that the mysterious black man, who called himself Muir, would be here today, and perhaps even his intriguing visitor in the library at Serjeant-at-Laws Inn. Sir Henoch was returning from a meeting with some allies in the Commons, during which they had agreed on the wording of some new bills to be introduced at the next session. He did not attend pillory days, but had stopped on his way back to Bucklad House when, to his astonishment, he saw his neighbor on the pillory, tossing stones at the crowd. Alden Curle, taking advantage of the absence of the Earl, who had gone on another visit to the Duke of Bedford, and of the Baron's family, who had gone to Hampton Court, was about to stroll down the Strand to visit his favorite tavern, when he, too, noticed his master's nephew on the pillory.

Jones walked away from the pillory in a thoughtful daze. Pannell could hardly contain his glee. Curle rushed back in alarm to Windridge Court.

*   *   *

A peer could expect no actual punishment for any crime but murder and treason. All else was, for him, vaporous misdemeanor. Hugh Kenrick was denied the honor of sharing the Pippins' punishment. He was escorted to a local magistrate's home by the city marshall and two constables to be charged with whatever the magistrate decided was the offense, once that worthy heard the marshall's account.

From a distance, they were followed by an elegant stranger.

Before entering the magistrate's house, the city marshall asked Hugh to remove his sword. Hugh obliged him. The officer eyed with some suspicion the coat-of-arms engraved below the pommel of the weapon. The lad was a gentleman, to be sure. But of what degree? He approached this subject cautiously. "What was your dead friend's name...sir?" he asked.

"Muir...Glorious Swain," answered Hugh.

"Had he family?"

"I am his brother."

The city marshall looked startled by this reply, then doubtful. "Hmmm..." He cleared his throat. "There will be no inquest or coroner's jury concerning his death. He was shot lawfully by the under-sheriff in the course of his duty."

"I wish to have him buried," said Hugh. "I will purchase a plot and a gravestone."

The city marshall shook his head. "I am sorry, sir, but the College of Surgeons has already claimed him...for study, you know. Two of their number arrived at the punishment, and took your friend away immediately in their cart."

Hugh sighed in resignation. "I see... Well, Muir was a great lover of knowledge. He would be glad to know that he will help advance the science of anatomy."

The city marshall blinked in surprise. He had expected any response but this. "Now...as to your name, sir," he broached.

"I am Miltiades, of the Society of the Pippin," stated Hugh.

The city marshall examined the sword. "How did you come by this fine steel, sir?"

"I purchased it in the thieves' market," answered Hugh.

"It is the property," said a third voice, "of Hugh Kenrick, Baron of Danvers, whom you address, sir."

Everyone turned to face this person.

This person wore an oddly apologetic, but satisfied smile. "Sir Dogmael

Jones, serjeant-at-law, King's Bench, and a recent acquaintance of the gentleman now in your custody, sir," he said.

"What is your interest in this matter, sir?" inquired the officer.

Jones shrugged. "My interest? To ensure that his galliard lordship here
sees better days, so that he might hurl bigger stones at greater Goliaths.
That is my interest."

Hugh frowned. "Why are you doing this? This is not your affair."

Jones raised his eyebrows. "Not my affair? It was my affair when I
accepted the brief for the defense, milord. Forgive me the contradiction, and
for the intrusion. I merely wish to see at least one Pippin escape the
Crown's attainder. And my compliments to you, milord. I have witnessed
what is likely to be the one and only time the pillory has struck back." He
bowed slightly, and tipped his hat. Then he addressed the city marshall.
"Do you wish me to vouch for his lordship's identity and character for the
magistrate, sir?"

"No, thank you," answered the officer after a moment. "That will not
be necessary. Thank you for the information."

Jones tapped the brim of his hat with the shoe of the cane he carried.
"Then, good day to you, gentlemen." He turned without further word and
strode away, knowing full well the consequences of his action. He had
acted, partly from a sense of justice, partly from a sense of vengeance, partly
from a sense of admiration. The moment gave him a bracing quantum of
contentment. The young baron would be protected by the same phenomenon that had cost him the case.

The city marshall regarded Hugh for a moment, then stepped back
from his captive, and held out his sword in its scabbard. "Milord, a thousand apologies, but I must still have you charged and held in custody."

Hugh was arraigned by the magistrate for disturbing the peace and
obstructing officers of the law in the performance of their duties. The first
offense could be discharged with the payment of a half-crown fine. The
second was more serious and neither fine nor bail could be set.

*   *   *

The Tower of London, east of London Bridge, served many purposes
then. It housed a menagerie, the Royal Mint, an arsenal, and important
prisoners. Among its more famous detainees were the two nephews of
Richard the Third, who were murdered, and Sir Walter Raleigh, who was

executed. Hugh had the dubious honor of being briefly confined there. The city marshall and the authorities above him were taking no chances. If the prisoner must be incarcerated, it would need to be in comfortable circumstances. Hugh was escorted to a cube on its fourth floor that was more a drawing room than a cell. It contained a bed, chairs, a desk, an empty bookshelf, and a washstand. Only the padlocked door and a barred window that overlooked the Thames defined its true purpose. For a gratuity, the jailer, turnkey, and their subordinates were at a prisoner's beck and call.

Hugh lay down on the bed and stared at the stone ceiling. He was immobilized by a kind of trauma, a mental and emotional daze the result of experiencing a great, soul-shattering event. His mind could dwell only on what had happened, not on what was happening or what was to happen. It was not fixed on the future. The future was on others' minds.

*　　*　　*

Basil Kenrick returned early from the Duke of Bedford's informal meeting with other peers on what agenda the Lord Chancellor ought to establish for the upper House to address in the coming session, especially on how to settle some bothersome divorce bills left over from the last session. The Earl was sitting on the terrace of Windridge Court, sunning himself, wearing only a gown and a daycap, reading William Horlick's *Twenty Moral Fables*, when Alden Curle appeared and begged his forgiveness for interrupting his leisure.

Curle was unsure about which would incense his master more: his own absence, or his news. He had invented a story to tell, if he was asked—about going to the market to procure some fresh fruit for the supper table this evening, when the Baron and his family were expected to return from their outing. He stood some distance from the Earl, and when asked, conveyed the facts of what he had witnessed at Charing Cross.

Basil Kenrick did not immediately respond. After a moment, he asked, "Where was he taken?"

"I do not know, your lordship."

The Earl merely looked at his servant.

"Yes, your lordship." Curle bowed, and hastened away on his new task.

Twenty Moral Fables dropped from the Earl's hands to his lap, and from his lap slid to the flagstone. He had been reading it because the book was written by a favorite of the Marquis of Bilbury, and he wished to prove some knowledge of it when next he spoke with the man. He was entertaining the idea of patronizing literature himself. It would be a suitable pastime.

He rose from his chair, and in the act knocked over the little stand that held a tea service. Annoyed by the clatter the crashing silver and porcelain made, he kicked the overturned stand with a slippered foot, breaking the teakwood beyond repair. He paced back and forth and in circles, stepping on the broken porcelain and spilled sugar and splashing the spreading tea. He was wrath out of control, unaware of anything else around him, even of his own body. The sun glinted on the teapot, blinding him for a moment. He glared at it but was unable to perform the simple task of picking it up. He kicked it, then tried to crush it with his feet. He began to curse, and his curses gave way to babble.

Some servants watched this raving from a window above. Curle told them the news, too, instructing them to decide who would inform the Earl that he had an important visitor in the waiting room, Sir Henoch Pannell, who had arrived just minutes before. Then he gladly slinked out on his chore to locate the young Baron.

The servants withdrew to the kitchen, and drew straws.

*   *   *

Hugh became fully conscious of his surroundings later in the afternoon. His mind, having tortured itself to exhaustion reliving the events at Charing Cross, came to rest, and allowed him to become aware of the bed, desk, and other furnishings. The cell was not unlike his room on Cutter Lane, though it was smaller by half. He rose and went to the window. Across the tops of the masts of the merchantmen at anchor in the Pool of London, he could see the smokestacks of the tanneries, candle factories, and soapmakers across the Thames in Southwark. And there was London Bridge, where Glorious Swain had been born. The house that was once his was gone, too. An idle thought came to him then, on how the city could consume so many men and things.

His body began to register his injuries. A throbbing pain on his forehead was particularly acute. There was a small mirror fixed over the washstand. He went to it and saw that his face was blotched with dried blood and dirt. He took the pitcher of water and filled the basin with it, then dipped a cloth into it to dab his wounds and scrub his face.

At seven o'clock, as he was listening to the city's church bells mark the hour, he heard voices and steps outside the door, and a key play with the lock. Two guards came in with an assistant jailer, who informed him that he was free to go.

"Why?" asked Hugh.

The jailer and guards looked at him as though he should know why he was being freed. The jailer said, "The charges against you have been settled, milord."

"How?"

"We do not know, milord."

The guards escorted Hugh without further comment from the cell and out of the Tower.

At the gate waited the Kenrick family coach. A footman rushed to open the door. Inside was Hugh's uncle, who looked at him once, then away. "Get in," he said.

Hugh obeyed.

The Earl wasted little time and few words. As the coach moved away from the Tower, he said, "I have bailed you out, bought off the law, and purchased silence, sir. Not for any love of you, but for our family name. You will now pay me the courtesy of explaining to me why such expense was necessary." He did not look at Hugh as he spoke.

Hugh told him about the Society of the Pippin, the young Marquis of Bilbury, the arrests, the trial, and the pillory.

When he had finished, his uncle said nothing for a long moment. "You will repair to your own place for the time being. I will speak to your father when he returns. We will decide then what is to be done with you."

The coach rolled on. Hugh asked, with incredulous contempt in his words, "How could one buy off the law?"

"Any magistrate may decide he is mistaken, for a handful of silver."

"That is corrupt."

"No, sir. It is power. Accustom yourself to it." The Earl paused. He braved a look at his nephew. "I am waiting for a word of thanks, sir."

"You will not hear one," said Hugh. "I wish to leave the coach—now, please."

The cane in the Earl's hand shot up and struck the roof twice. The coach stopped. Hugh opened the door on his side and jumped to the ground.

"You will not enter Windridge Court ever again, sir!" shouted the Earl after his nephew.

Hugh shrugged. "Father will know where to find me." He shut the coach door and walked away. In the distance and growing dusk, he could see lamps being lit between the columns under the dome of St. Paul's Cathedral ahead. He walked rapidly in the direction of Quiller Alley.

*   *   *

"You cannot assign any blame to me for this scandal!" said the Earl to his brother that evening in his study. "This incident is entirely of his own manufacture!"

"I have not assigned blame to you, dear brother," replied Garnet Kenrick.

"It is disgraceful! First, his association with this freethinking, libertine rabble, and then, his disruption of their deserved punishment! I told you, more than once, Garnet, that you were too coddling with him and his ways! Did you know about these Pippins?"

"No."

"God, I wish that puppy had thrashed him at Eton! You would have had a better son today!"

Garnet Kenrick narrowed his eyes menacingly. "I would have a simpering wastrel, and he and the late Marquis would have been fast friends."

The Earl sat at his desk, and felt thoroughly in command. His brother paced back and forth before him, hands behind his back, hearing only half of what his brother was saying. The news the Earl had given him left him numb.

"Perhaps," said Basil Kenrick. "But he would be obedient! Have you any notion of the damage that news of this could cause us in Lords?"

"It had not occurred to me."

"No, it wouldn't! We would be ostracized there, and in society! There go the Kenricks, breeders of fugitive rabble! Friends of plotting regicides! Why, we would be so despised that we would not be invited to attend a whore's ruelle! Why? Because your precious son must be allowed his precious books and his brain-steamed friends!" The Earl snorted once. "Well, you can count the Brunes out, dear brother, once they hear of this! They would no more want him in their family than they would a…fishmonger's son!"

"No doubt," remarked the Baron absently.

"That rotund fool Pannell is the only other person who saw it! He called on me to tell me so. I nearly thrashed him for the impertinence!" The Earl paused. He wished his brother would stop pacing. "It was necessary to purchase his silence, too."

"And how did you manage that?"

"I promised him discounted shares in your blasted bank."

Garnet Kenrick stopped pacing and faced his brother. "You had no right to promise him such a thing."

"Don't speak to me of rights, dear brother!" Suddenly the Earl's eyes grew brilliant, and the madness that had seized him in the afternoon welled up in him again. He rose and leaned forward over his desk, his hands balled into fists that rested on the baize blotter propping up arms stiff with self-control. "I do not ever wish to see your son again, Garnet, nor ever hear his name mentioned in my presence again! He has disgraced this family for the last time! Disown him, or send him to the Continent, to Italy, or the West Indies! I don't care where! Just remove him, get him out of my sight!"

"Remove him?"

"Before I harm him with my own hands!"

"Why should I banish my son from my own and Effney's lives?"

"You will do it, or I will tell him about the Lobster Pots, and how much he owes to the corruption he deplores, the dear boy!" The Earl stood to his full height. "Perhaps I should tell him! The pure saint would likely drop dead from sorrow and dismay! Then I would be rid of him!"

Garnet Kenrick raised his hand to slap his brother in the face. Basil Kenrick saw the desire, and smiled, pleased that he had driven his brother to this. He moved his face closer, daring his brother to do it.

The Baron narrowed his eyes and lowered his hand. "You overstep your privilege, dear brother." He turned and left the room, knowing that his brother was right.

*   *   *

It was late when the Baron called on his son in his room on Cutter Lane. The father was resolute but resigned; the son, guarded, distant, and tired. The Baron asked him for the whole story. Hugh told him everything, beginning with the night he rescued Glorious Swain from Brice Blissom and the Mohocks, and ending with his own unsolicited rescue by Dogmael Jones.

"I see," said the Baron. He was quietly astounded by the quantity and variety of his son's adventures.

"What is to be done?" asked Hugh.

Garnet Kenrick shook his head. "I have not yet decided." He glanced around the room. "But—you will go home, to Danvers, and await me." He spoke now with disorganized thought. "I will interrupt my stay here, and also return." He paused. "Your uncle is near to throttling you, Hugh, with his bare hands. There is no placating him. And, well, in a sense, he has a right to be...outraged. This is a serious matter. Your mother was in tears, not because of what you had done, but because she is afraid for you. As am I. Even if you stayed here," he said, gesturing to the room, "you would be in, well, danger."

After a moment, Hugh nodded. "I know it."

They were silent for a while. The Baron, seated across from Hugh at the window, espied a pair of books on Hugh's desk, sitting atop some notebooks. It was a copy of *Hyperborea*. "Where did you find that?" he asked, nodding to the volumes.

"It was Mr. Swain's," said Hugh. "He left it to me...before he died."

"I see. What kind of fellow was he, this Mr. Swain?"

"Like an elder brother." Hugh looked at his father. "They were all good men, Father. The best men I have ever known. They were alive. And now they are dead, or condemned to work as slaves with brutes, for brutes, for men who wield whips, not wisdom." He glanced out the window. "I shall hate England for what it has done to them."

"Do not hate England," said the Baron. "We are England."

"I shall hate the corruption that permeates it, the corruption of men who fear what my friends were...men who could never be what they were..."

Garnet Kenrick glanced away, as though wounded. He leaned over and touched his son's face. "You have been hurt. Have you seen a physician?"

"No," said Hugh, passing a finger over the cuts and bruises. "These will heal."

The Baron sat back. "As will, I hope, your soul, Hugh."

"It is very strange, Father," said Hugh. "Mr. Worley was on the jury that indicted my friends, yet he is somehow blameless, and I cannot hate him. And Jones, the barrister, lost the case, and I hold him faultless. They were dupes of something I cannot yet name, something that is more insidious than corruption."

His father winced again at the word. He sighed. "I am certain that you will someday find a word for it." He shook his head. "Hugh, I can't say whether I am ashamed of you, or proud of you. I know only that this entire matter has your...stamp on it." He rose and stood over his son, and caressed his face. "You are an exasperating burden to your mother and me, but we would not wish you to be other than what you are, and have been always, it seems... We knew from the first that if we attempted to force you in a conventional direction...as your uncle wished, and still wishes...we should kill you, or maim you somehow... We could never bring ourselves to do that... You are something more than what we ever expected or could explain, though we do not know what it is... We have not known how else to assist you, or guide you, other than what little we have done... My son, we are sorry for you, and concerned for you, and glad, and content...all at the same time... Please, do not regard that as cruelty, or indifference, or neglect..."

Hugh stood up, and, for the first time ever, embraced his father. "I never thought that, Father, and I am grateful to you both..."

Garnet Kenrick experienced a violent tangle of emotions—among them, gratitude. He patted his son's back, then held him away, not because he objected to or was uncomfortable with the display of affection, but because, secretly, he did not feel worthy of it. For a moment, his brother's threat flashed through his mind.

With a reminder to Hugh that he would settle his rent with Mr. Rickerby, have his things in the room packed, and a caution not to speak of the pillory incident to Mr. Worley in the morning, Garnet Kenrick took his leave. It was only when he was in the hackney on the way back to Windridge Court that he remembered his chief purpose for visiting his son, which was to rebuke him for not thanking his uncle for purchasing his release. But when he had entered Hugh's room, he saw a man, and not just a son, and that purpose suddenly seemed churlish and irrelevant, and he forgot it. He talked with his wife late into the night about Hugh, about his brother, and about what must be done.

Chapter 41: The Departure

TWO DAYS LATER, HUGH KENRICK ARRIVED IN DANVERS BY COASTAL PACKET. His last view of London was from an inn coach bound for Canterbury and Folkestone. He looked back at the city with a pained wistfulness, which combined a regret for having to leave it, and relief that he was escaping a nightmare. He did not know if he would ever see it again, or want to see it again. He was once its master; he had done great things there, splendid things. Now it was spurning him for those very reasons. He did not feel disgraced. He felt wronged.

Yet nothing had happened to him. He knew that his exclusion from sharing the Pippins' punishment was to become his own pillory, just as Swain had predicted. He felt like a doomed man, a banished renegade, as unwelcome as a band of cutthroat highwaymen.

Owen Runcorn and the staff of servants were surprised to see Hugh arrive in the merchant's sulky he had hired to bring him from Poole. As Runcorn unpacked his three valises, Hugh briefly explained his presence to the major domo, then promptly retired. He slept for three hours, and awoke late in the afternoon. Runcorn brought him tea and biscuits, and some of the London newspapers that had come by the post. Hugh read through these, and in one saw a cartoon picturing William Pitt and the Duke of Newcastle as a man and woman quarreling over their marriage contract, the both of them being offered inducements and strenuous and contradictory advice by other political caricatures.

The cartoon gave Hugh an idea. He found a pencil and a sheet of drawing paper, and began to sketch the members of the Society of the Pippin. It consoled him that he could at least preserve their likenesses. It was the only memorial he could think of giving them. He smiled for the first time in days.

By early evening, he had drafted the figures, assembling them all on one sheet of paper. There was Tobius, dapper-looking with the Society's silver apple-ornamented cane. There was Steven, with a violin. There was Claude, with his ever-present clay pipe. There was Elspeth, looking over his bifocals. There was Abraham, looking pensive. There was Muir, smiling back at him.

And there was Mathius, whom he set apart from the others, his back turned, walking away, his head turned to glance furtively over his shoulder, a petulant scowl on his face, and a copy of *Twenty Moral Fables* in his hand, the title visible.

Beneath each figure he wrote the name, club name, and profession of the members, and over them he inscribed, "The Society of the Pippin. Convened at the Fruit Wench Tavern, the Strand, London. 1756. Betrayed to the Crown by Mathius, for a fizzle of fame and security. Long Live Lady Liberty!"

He looked at his handiwork for a long time. He paid one of his father's workmen to frame it.

* * *

The next morning he called on Reverdy Brune. She gasped when a servant admitted him into the family's drawing room. "Hugh! What are you doing here?" She put a hand to her mouth when she came closer to him and saw his face. "Hugh! What happened to you?"

"Stones hit it," he said simply.

"Why...?"

"Because I threw them back."

"When...where?"

"A few days ago, at the Charing Cross pillory."

"I don't understand."

They sat down together on a couch. Hugh said, "Some friends of mine were convicted of an offense against the Crown. I tried to defend them from a mob."

"Were you arrested?"

"Briefly." Hugh paused. "I will not be returning to London, Reverdy, not for a long time. My father is sending me away. Perhaps to Leyden, or Edinburgh." He grimaced. "Away from my uncle."

"Hugh...!"

"We may not see each other for a year or so." Hugh took one of her hands. "I must tell you this before your parents hear it first, and before you hear it from them. It may affect things between us."

"How could it?"

"That will be for you to decide." Hugh smiled. "What I feel for you, Reverdy, will never change. What you feel for me, I do not think could change either. I wanted you to know, to hear it from me, so that you may judge for yourself."

Reverdy leaned over and kissed him lightly. "Let us walk in the garden."

As they walked arm-in-arm among the flowers and hedges, Reverdy asked, "Who were these friends, Hugh?"

He told her about the Society of the Pippin, how he had met its members, what had happened to them, and why. He finished by saying, "I will be leaving on the command of my uncle, with whom, I believe, Brice Blissom had much in common. He has threatened my life. My parents have resolved to move out of our house here. There is a vacant one in the town that is owned by the family, and they will stay there until a new place is built for them, on the other side of our grounds. They are more intimately tied to my uncle than I could ever permit myself to be." He sighed. "Your parents? Well, I don't know how they will now view a marriage between us."

"I don't think it would make a difference to them what you did, or what your uncle does."

Hugh looked at her. "You mean, it should not make a difference. But it may."

After a moment, Reverdy nodded in concession. "Yes, that is what I meant." She stopped to face him. "Hugh, why can you not reconcile with your uncle?"

Hugh shook his head. "It is not possible, ever. If it were possible, it would be only at grave risk to myself. And then you may not want to know me, or marry me. I would not want to know myself. In the end, I would grow to be like him. But—I would not do it. I could not do it."

Reverdy frowned. "Then I think he should make his peace with you! Pardon me for saying this about his lordship, your uncle, but I don't believe it would cost him anything! He is a vain, empty, pompous...fool! There! I said it! Everyone says so! He would add something to himself, if he apologized to you...and let you be. I would think better of him. Everyone would."

Hugh smiled. "He would needs be a man of substance to apologize to me, Reverdy, and my uncle is a man in name only." He took her into his arms and held her closely.

"Were you put into one of those awful prisons, the Clink, or the King's Bench?" she asked. "I've heard the most dreadful things about them."

"No. The Tower."

"Oh! You were treated like a prince!"

"But my friends were not," said Hugh darkly, "and they will not survive."

Reverdy changed the subject. "Have you seen Roger?"

"Not yet."

"His brother is home on leave, and parades around in his uniform. He is only a cornet, but behaves like a colonel. Mr. Tallmadge is quite proud of him, and Roger is dazzled."

* * *

Hugh waited for Roger Tallmadge outside until the tutors dismissed their students for the day, and met him in the yard in back of his friend's house. After they had finished their greetings, Hugh told Roger why he was home.

Roger was dumbstruck. "I had heard you were home, but could not understand why."

"Now you know."

"Were you actually friends with these men, and you stood on the pillory, and defied the crowd?"

"Yes."

Roger did not know whether to be envious or disapproving. "Hugh," he said, "you do the most fantastic things!" His face lit up. "Defying the Crown, and all those people! I wish I could have been there to see it!"

They sat down on a bench. Hugh asked, "Would you have joined me?"

"Yes," replied Roger. "I suppose I would have. But...I didn't know your friends. I don't know..." He paused. "At least, I would have tried to defend you. You do things that I suppose are right, but no one else understands them."

Hugh squeezed his friend's shoulder once. "I'll show you the pictures I drew of my friends. You won't meet their like in Danvers, or Poole."

"And you were locked in the Tower! Who else was there?"

Hugh shook his head. "I did not notice."

Roger studied his friend's face. "Battle scars!" he laughed. "Francis hopes to get one, to impress the ladies." Then he sighed. "He is home on leave. We had better not tell him about this. The Duke spoke three words to him, and now he is all full of fire."

"He will learn of it sooner or later," said Hugh. "But—you would like to be in his place, would you not?"

"Well…no. He is treated like a valet by most of the senior officers of the regiment. He must even run errands for the Duke's new mistress, and some of the lieutenants keep playing pranks on him and try to get him into trouble." Roger paused. "Did your uncle actually threaten you?"

"So my father said. Do you know the old Milgram house in town?"

"Yes."

"My parents and sister will move into it, when they return. They have decided not to live with my uncle. Father plans to erect a new house some-where in the western part of the estate."

"And where are you going?'

"To Leyden, or Edinburgh. I will know when my father returns. He is coming back only to see me off, and then he will return to London on busi-ness matters."

"How long will you be away?'

"Perhaps a year." Hugh rose. "I'm certain that your parents will be invited over for supper when mine return, Roger. I'll show you the render-ings I did of my friends in London."

"I'd like that." Roger stood up. He looked apologetic, then blurted, "Your uncle is a flagitious hick, for all his manners and airs! Strike me down, if you must, but that's my opinion!"

Hugh smiled. "Say anything you wish about him, Roger."

*   *   *

It was Hugh's turn to be surprised when, on returning two days later from a ride through the hills above Danvers with Roger and Reverdy, he found both of his parents and his sister at home.

"We decided to forgo a season in London, rather than stay," said his father. "We cancelled the dinners and concerts. Under the circumstances, we could not have much enjoyed ourselves."

"By the time your uncle returns, after Parliament has recessed, we will have settled into the Milgram place," said his mother. "It is less com-modious than our home here, but we will be spared the distraction and the awkwardness."

"And the annoyance," added the Baron.

Hugh was sitting with his parents in the orangery. "I'm sorry you chose to leave," he said. "I know how much you look forward to the season."

"Don't be," said Effney Kenrick. "It was our decision. It will cause talk here and in London, but that is as it may be." She reached over the table and took Hugh's hand. "Besides, I couldn't bear the idea of not seeing you again, before you go."

"Have you told Reverdy?" asked the Baron.

"Yes."

"What did she say?"

"That it does not matter."

"And...her parents?" asked the Baroness.

"I don't know that she has told them yet," said Hugh. "I'm still welcome at her house."

"I see," said his father.

"Hugh," said his mother, "please don't be...disappointed if they do not understand, or if she is reluctant to tell them about Charing Cross...and everything else. Her parents may press her to change her mind about you. It is not entirely a matter of her choice."

Hugh looked away, then faced his parents again. "I knew from the beginning that ours was a marriage of property, and not simply...a marriage. But Reverdy has expressed her love for me, and I don't believe she would be able to, well, smother it to suit her parents."

"I hope that is true," said the Baron. "But your mother tells me that she knows that Mrs. Brune has other...prospects in mind for Reverdy, should the two families find serious grounds for disagreement." He shook his head. "For my part, the Brunes' property, attractive as it is, weighs nothing in a scale between it and your happiness. Your mother and I wish you to understand that."

"All we are doing is warning you, Hugh," said the Baroness. "And it may be that our concern is baseless. You and Reverdy were not to be married until you reached your majority. Even though she may seem hesitant or confused now, it may mean nothing. She and her parents will have some time to, well, accept this new situation. No time will have been lost."

Hugh shook his head. "She has been neither hesitant nor confused."

His mother managed a smile. "Then perhaps she is stronger than we had imagined."

The Baron sighed and poured himself another cup of tea. "Here is what I have arranged, Hugh. In two weeks' time, the *Sparrowhawk* will call at Weymouth to pick up some cargo. All your belongings in London will be on her. Mr. Worley will see to that. I met and spoke with Captain Ramshaw, and paid for your passage. He has set aside a cabin for you, and you will dine with him more often than you won't." He paused. "You are going to Philadelphia, Hugh. It is the custom of planters and merchants in the colonies to send their sons to schools here for education or to learn their fathers' business. I have decided that you will go to the colonies, to work for Mr. Talbot, and absorb that end of the business. I've already sent him a letter advising him of your due arrival. It went by packet two days ago. There is an academy in Philadelphia. I have learned that it is not a disgrace to complete one's education there. Mr. Talbot himself is an alumnus. You will stay with him and his family. I will give you money and some bills of exchange for expenses, and you will get an allowance every few months. You will be gone for two years or so. I entertain no hope that anything will have changed during that time. Except, perhaps, that this war will have ended."

"When you return," said the Baroness, "our new home ought to be finished, and that is where you will stay."

"At least until you and Reverdy are married," added the Baron.

There was nothing more to be said on the subject. A wall clock ticked on, and birds feuded in the shrubbery outside the orangery window. Neither the father, the mother, nor the son spoke for a while. They allowed the silence to absorb their fears, thoughts, and dashed hopes.

Hugh broke the silence first. He rose and said, "I sketched likenesses of my friends. I'll go and fetch them. You should, at least, have an idea of the reason...for my leaving." He smiled. "Why, I think I shall do sketches of you both, and of Alice, and Roger, too, to take with me to Philadelphia."

"And not of Reverdy?" asked the Baroness.

Hugh laughed. "I have more than enough likenesses of her." He did not elaborate. Effney Kenrick knew nothing of her son's plans to erect a temple.

*   *   *

Many considerations entered into Garnet Kenrick's decision to send Hugh away—away from the Earl, beyond his brother's threat to expose him, away from the corruption—and away from his own complicity in the corruption he knew his son despised. He could sense only an indistinct figure on the horizon of Hugh's life. He wished Hugh to become whatever that figure was, but cleanly, without the odor of shame or disgust. His son was becoming something he was not. He was willing to see him become that thing, independently, inevitably, even if it meant, someday, that his son would become his enemy and harshest critic.

His decision was vindicated when Hugh brought the drawings into the orangery and spread them over the table. The Baron studied them, and pointing to one figure, asked, "Is that William Horlick, the noted fabulist?"

"Noted by some," remarked Hugh.

"And he turned against his friends—and you?"

"Yes."

"What a fool! And this black fellow: He is the one who was your special friend, the one who died trying to protect you on the pillory?"

"Yes. That is he."

The Baroness remarked, "They look like elevated company, Hugh, except, I suppose for Mr. Horlick, who apparently chose to descend from the heights." She saw Hugh look at her with an oddly pleased smile; she did not know the significance of her words. "I'm sorry, Hugh, that you have lost such friends."

Later, in private, the Baron inquired about the T on William Horlick's cheek. "It looks like a branding. How did he get it?"

"I put it there," said Hugh. "He had gone to the pillory to see the men he betrayed. He threw the first stone. I ensured that it was his last."

The Baron frowned and said softly, "Oh, Hugh, that was cruel!"

"It was justice, Father," said Hugh. "There is no law that commands punishment for his crime. I made amends for its absence. That is all." The finality of his words forbad pursuit of the subject.

This was the son Garnet Kenrick was certain would face him in the future, when Hugh was a man.

*   *   *

Hugh called on Reverdy the next day to inform her of his departure and destination. "Have you told your parents yet about why I am here?"

"No," said the girl. "But they have wondered why your family have returned."

"Now that you know when and where I am going, you must tell them."

"I will, Hugh. Today."

Hugh rose from the divan and paced once before Reverdy. After a moment, he asked, "Has your mother or father ever expressed doubts about our marriage?"

"Not to me," said the girl. "James has alluded to it, to me, in private, but if Mother has not spoken to me about any doubts she and Father may have, then they cannot be serious."

Hugh picked up the portfolio he brought with him. "I have something for you, Reverdy." He took out a drawing. It was a self-portrait in crayon. "I did it last night." He handed it to her. "For you to remember me by—for the next two years."

She studied the picture, then threw it down, jumped up, and embraced Hugh, burying her face in his shoulder. "Weymouth...in two weeks...you will be gone..."

They kissed.

Hugh said, when they had finished, "When I am back, the two years will seem like only two weeks."

"Damn your uncle!" whispered Reverdy.

"Yes," replied Hugh. "Damn him."

Reverdy disengaged herself from Hugh's embrace, and sat down again. "How long is the voyage?"

"Two months, most likely. With a good, constant wind, perhaps six weeks. That's what Captain Ramshaw told my father." Hugh resumed his seat next to Reverdy. "My ship will probably stop at Falmouth after Weymouth, then join a convoy at Plymouth. Father says that the only danger will come from privateers, not the French navy. The *Sparrowhawk*, though, has always beaten off her attackers, and there have been many."

"I had forgotten that danger."

Hugh smiled. "Never fear. If I find myself confronted with an armed Frenchman, I will tell him that his countrymen write better than they fight." He smiled when Reverdy grinned against her will. He said, "Reverdy, promise me that you will come to Weymouth. This is not merely my invitation. My mother has invited you to ride in our carriage, with us. Your parents may follow in their own."

Reverdy said, "I promise, Hugh. I will come even if my parents do not."

*   *   *

The two weeks passed swiftly. The Kenricks were preoccupied with new homes—the Baron and Baroness, with seeing that the Milgram house in Danvers was repaired and cleaned, and Hugh with selecting what things to take with him on the voyage to Philadelphia.

Five days before he and his family were to leave for Weymouth, where they would stay at an inn to await the arrival of the *Sparrowhawk*, a letter came for him from London, dated nearly two weeks before. It was from Sir Dogmael Jones:

"Milord Kenrick: I write you with the information that, after a diligent search for a means to rescue your friends from the morbid caresses of our delicate English prisons, I found that means. Very recently I met by arrangement in a tavern near the Cornhill Exchange Captain Charles Musto, who commands the *Charon*, a brig-sized merchantman. He is a fellow whose sole exports from this country are redemptioners, emigrants, and convicts. He and his partner in Charleston in Carolina have made this a business for years. I told him about your friends (neglecting to mention your name) and what cheap tutors these educated fellows might make for the colonial bashaws who might buy them. Without weighing into details, their indentures, which are for seven years, were procured, and Captain Musto has purchased them. When they will depart on the *Charon*, I do not know. I called on them at Newgate and they expressed their gratitude. I am certain that they will fare far better instructing colonial children in the rudiments of things than breaking stone or fashioning spars at Blackwell or Deptford. They have asked me to convey to you their thanks for your gesture at Charing Cross, and also that they share the sorrow for losing Mr. Swain, who acted and died gallantly. It is their mutual hope that you and they may meet again some day.

Your most obedient servant, Dogmael Jones."

This news overjoyed Hugh, who immediately penned a reply, thanking Jones for the information and mentioning the fact that he, too, was going to the colonies. "Your efforts on behalf of my friends," he wrote, "will not be forgotten. I have related to my father your efforts throughout the matter, and he is appreciative. If there is anything he or I could do for you, please do not hesitate to write either of us."

Two nights before they were to set out for Weymouth, the Kenricks invited the Brunes and the Tallmadges to a farewell supper in Hugh's honor. The gay affair was dampened somewhat by Mrs. Brune's announcement to the Baroness that her family would not be able to journey to Weymouth. "Regrettably, we have been invited to spend a week or so with the McDougals in Surrey," she said, "and if we are to arrive there in a decent time, we must embark on the very day you are going to Weymouth. It would be utterly impossible to try to fit in two protracted journeys. Had we known earlier about your plans, we might have written to the McDougals, postponing our arrival one or two days. But Reverdy did not inform us of Hugh's departure until it was too late. I am very sorry."

Effney Kenrick sensed that there was more to it than conflicting agendas, but she said nothing. She did not allow the news to affect her role as the happy and gracious hostess. She was only sorry that she had been right about the effect that Hugh's actions had apparently had on the Brunes. And she saw, by Hugh's and Reverdy's demeanors that evening, that Hugh also knew and that the girl was not happy with the change in plans. She did her best to give the pair as much time together alone as possible. When the guests were gone, she waited until Hugh raised the subject.

He said, "We shall write each other," he commented. "Mr. Tallmadge has given Roger permission to come with us to Weymouth, instead."

"Roger is always welcome, Hugh," said the Baroness.

Hugh noted the concerned look on his mother's face. He smiled. "She's promised not to allow her mother to marry her off to someone else," he said. "And when I return, if necessary, we shall elope. That is all there is to that."

By silent agreement, nothing more was said on the subject.

*   *   *

It was with a sense of disappointment that the Kenricks waited a mere one day for the *Sparrowhawk* to drop anchor in Weymouth Harbor. They had hoped for two or three days.

And it was a brave, self-controlled party that stood on the breezy, busy dock mid-morning the next day. Once the last goodbyes, embraces, reassurances, and promises had been exchanged, Hugh turned and walked up the gang-board. He had, for a final time, grimly shaken hands with his father, traded lingering busses with his mother and sister, and shaken hands with Roger Tallmadge. He carried his friend's farewell gift, an army officer's long-glass. When Roger presented it to him, his friend stammered, "An aid for my farsighted and soon-to-be-faraway friend." He had added, "I spent all last night making that up, and I bought the glass in a shop in Poole. My father repaired it."

The *Sparrowhawk* had matured over the years. She was a vessel of commerce, and still, out of necessity, a vessel of war. Gone were the Quakers, the "phony guns"; she now boasted thirty, alternating four- and six-pounders, each manned by an expert crew. She carried on this voyage chiefly cargo, mostly manufactures from England, together with woven and liquid products from Spain and Portugal, disguised on altered cockets as items of English origin. There were only eleven passengers, including three officials and their wives traveling to the colonies to assume government posts there, and five paying passengers. The crew of eighty outnumbered them. This was one of the rare voyages on which the frigate-sized vessel carried no redemptioners, indentures, or felons.

Captain John Ramshaw met Hugh as he stepped on deck off the gang-board. "Welcome aboard, Mr. Kenrick," he said, shaking his guest passenger's hand.

"Thank you, sir."

"We will get under way shortly, sir." Ramshaw studied Hugh for a moment, trying to reconcile his passenger with what little Garnet Kenrick had told him in Benjamin Worley's office at Lion Key. He said, "I usually tell my passengers to go below to their quarters, to be out of the crew's way. You may stay here, if you wish. Your berth is ready. It was an officer's berth that we had been using for extra space, but it has been cleaned out and made comfortable. I hope you find it acceptable." Ramshaw reached into his coat and handed Hugh a key. "Be sure to lock its gate when you leave the berth, or when you sleep. My crew is honest, but I won't vouch for the other passengers or for the limpets."

"Limpets, sir?"

"Never heard the term at Lion Key?" Ramshaw chuckled. "That's our name for bureaucrats, and customs officials, and other two-legged albatrosses."

Hugh smiled. "I expect to enlarge my vocabulary on this voyage, under your tutelage, sir."

"Hmmm…a vocabulary, which, if what your father the Baron has told me about you is true, should match your own reputation."

"I am certain that he exaggerated, sir."

"We shall see," said Ramshaw. "Well, over there, sir," he said, nodding to some shrouds. "Take a last look at your family, and let them have a last look at you."

Ten minutes later the Weymouth postmaster and two clerks arrived to deliver mail Ramshaw was taking to Philadelphia. Twenty minutes later the port pilot, his job done, climbed down the rope ladder on the side to his gig and pushed off. The *Sparrowhawk* crept out to sea on a mild breeze, bound for Falmouth, and then Plymouth, the great naval base on the south coast of Cornwall.

Hugh watched from the main deck until the town became an indistinct blur, then disappeared as the *Sparrowhawk* rounded the Isle of Portland, whose quarries were the source of the stone that was going into the construction of Blackfriars Bridge in London, and had gone into so many great houses in England, including the spacious place he had once called home.

Epilogue: The Voyage

HIS BERTH WAS MORE A CELL THAN WAS HIS BILLET IN THE TOWER OF London. There was a bunk with some blankets and drawers below it, a table, a chair, and a small bureau, all crammed together in a space little more than five feet by five, between the iron bars and the side of the ship. A lantern swung from a beam over the table, on which sat a single tin candleholder. Stashed in a corner were his valises and two trunks. The remainder of his luggage was in the hold. Next to his berth was that of Mr. Iverson, the surgeon, and across the way those of Mr. Haynie, the bursar, and Mr. Dietz, the ship's master, Ramshaw's second-in-command. At the end of the passage were Ramshaw's cabin and the companionway stairs leading to the deck above.

The other passengers' berths consisted of hammocks strung from overhead beams, with a common table for meals. Some of the wives had rigged partitioning sheets to separate their and their husbands' berths from the others for privacy.

Except for the initial introductions to the other passengers, and occasional conversations with them, Hugh did not associate with them. He supped more often with Ramshaw and his officers than he did with the other passengers, when the captain was receptive to company; at other times, he was served his meals in his berth by the cook's mate. He kept to himself, reading, or writing in the journal he bought in Weymouth, or going above to watch the crew at work, or to think. Most of the crew and all of the passengers knew who he was, but not why he was on board. His solitary demeanor whetted their curiosity, but did not embolden it to discreet enquiry. When he wished to be alone, he was left alone.

On the first night out of Weymouth, Ramshaw had him to supper in the cabin. Replying to the captain's tactful queries, Hugh told him why he was going to the colonies.

"Well, imagine that!" said Ramshaw. "Thumbing one's nose at the Crown! And over a band of freethinkers! I mean nothing darkish, sir, but you are a curiosity. So, it is not merely a clash of temperaments between you and your uncle?"

"No, sir."

"Well, I must assure you that you are always welcome at my table—but, I don't advise that you regale the crew or passengers with your tale. Someone may not appreciate the valor, or the tragedy."

"I had not intended to, sir."

Ramshaw rose and renewed their glasses with Montrachet wine. "I like your father, sir, and not merely for the depth of his purse. Seems to be a hard-dealing man with a greater knowledge of my business than I would credit any, well, peer with having. I could do more business with him, if he were of a mind."

"He is not a peer, and won't be until my uncle expires." Hugh paused. "I will write him of your interest, once I am settled in Philadelphia."

"Thank you, sir."

Hugh had glanced at Ramshaw's bookcase. He did not see *Hyperborea* among the titles. He inquired about it.

"Oh, that? I have a house in Norfolk, sir, and I rotate my library. The sea air, you know, can be so cruel on books. Why do you ask?"

"It is a particular favorite of mine. I do not meet many men who have read it, or display it."

"I see." Ramshaw studied his guest for a moment. "What are your views on smuggling, Mr. Kenrick?"

Hugh shrugged. "It is an activity that would not be necessary if there were no taxes on imports, or on manufactures that go out from a country. I suppose that someday, when I am Earl of Danvers and am able to sit in Lords, I shall oppose every tax bill that comes up from the Commons, and argue and vote for the repeal of existing ones."

"Why so thorough a dislike, sir?"

"For justice, and the eradication of limpets."

"I see," repeated Ramshaw. He spent some time lighting a pipe, then said, "I knew the author, slightly, of your particular favorite."

Hugh's jaw dropped. "You knew Romney Marsh?"

"Yes. That was one of his many names."

Hugh leaned forward eagerly. "He was a criminal, was he not?"

Ramshaw shook his head. "No. He was a smuggler. Knew most of the Skelly gang, I did—but you're not to let that go about."

Hugh was beside himself with joy. "I envy you, sir!" He asked Ramshaw for more details.

Ramshaw obliged, ending with, "The only survivor was Jack. Jack Frake. He was transported to Virginia on this very ship. Sat where you're sitting now. Found him in the Falmouth jail, and bought his indenture, and sold him for a penny to a planter in Queen Anne. Now he's a planter himself. Saved his master's life during the Braddock disaster, in Pennsylvania, though Virginia still claims that whole area. Massie—John Massie—he was a captain of a company of militia, who lost two sons there. Well, the last I heard, Jack's indenture was nearly up, and he was to marry Captain Massie's daughter, Jane. He's not done badly as a transported convict. I might call on him after I put up at Yorktown." Ramshaw grinned broadly. "Jack, you see, helped Marsh to copy out that book, when he was with the gang. I thought you might treasure that little item."

"I do," said Hugh. "That book is among several others I set aside to read on this voyage. Thank you." He smiled at the captain. "Here is to your health, sir, and to smugglers, and to transported felons of the more valorous suasion."

Ramshaw laughed, and touched his glass to his guest's. "To your health, sir!"

*   *   *

When the *Sparrowhawk* reached Plymouth, Ramshaw had only enough time to attend a conference of merchantmen's captains, called by the naval authorities, to receive instructions on formations, signals, and policies, and then be rowed back to his vessel to prepare to rendezvous two miles out to join the convoy. There were twenty-one merchantmen in it, in addition to two navy transports carrying troops and supplies to Massachusetts. The convoy was escorted by three ships of the line: two frigates of forty guns each, the *Helios* and the *Jason*, and a third-rate frigate of seventy-four guns, the *Zeus*. The *Helios* led the way, the *Jason* took a position in the middle of the procession, while the *Zeus* brought up the rear.

Ramshaw and the other captains were especially pleased with the presence of the *Zeus*; no single privateer would think of tackling her or any vessel she protected, not unless it was working with other privateers or accompanied by a French man-of-war of similar size. Allowing for troublesome winds and sea conditions, the convoy was to keep in a two-column formation, the smaller vessels in front behind the *Helios*, the larger vessels following in order of size. No privateer or enemy vessel would try to capture a merchantman if its captain knew that a line of larger, armed ships would soon bear down on it; fighting a merchantman and taking it as a prize was too risky and time-consuming an operation. Any merchantman that strayed more than a mile from the convoy, regardless of sea conditions or other circumstances, would not be defended or assisted by the frigates, if it was attacked. This was made clear by the commander of the convoy, Post-Captain Timothy Farbrace. The convoy would break up once the mainland was sighted, and the merchantmen would be free to go their separate ways.

Ramshaw brought back on board with him copies of the orders and rules of the convoy, and also a list of all the vessels in it. Among the lighter ships was the *Charon*, a brig-sized merchantman, captained by Charles Musto. She carried more than one hundred men, women, and children. Three-quarters of these were redemptioners, or "indenteds"; the rest were convicts of both sexes and a variety of ages, including an eleven-year-old girl sentenced for stealing a pair of ladies' hose, and a sixty-two-year-old man sentenced for hawking untaxed port in Dover.

Among the frigate-sized vessels was the *Manx*, owned by the Royal African Company, which carried three hundred slaves. This vessel arrived from Bristol, and had been anchored at Plymouth for over a month, waiting for a convoy to assemble. There had been four hundred slaves, but every day several of them died of disease, starvation, or heat prostration, and her captain was ordered by authorities on shore to sail five miles out to sea to dispose of the bodies, so that none would wash up on the tide anywhere near the town.

There was no reason for Ramshaw to share this information with any of the passengers, and so Hugh did not learn of the *Charon* until one month into the voyage.

*   *   *

The rigors of the sea voyage were such that Hugh was temporarily cured of the melancholy of leaving far behind everyone and everything he ever cared for; his energies were channeled into surviving the boredom, monotony, and claustrophobia. He soon learned that, in such unrelenting close quarters, a balance must be struck between sociability and solitude; that is, to know when to seek the company of others, and when to leave them alone. He absorbed this lesson quickly, and it made the experience tolerable. Aiding him was his status as an aristocrat; no one but Ramshaw and his officers spoke to him, unless spoken to by him. He allowed no one else to become familiar with him. For the first time in his life, Hugh was pleased with the deference paid his rank. It spared him the annoyance of contrived small talk with tiresome people.

The voyage was blessed with fair winds and little in the way of rough seas. "This very likely will be the last pleasant crossing of the year," Ramshaw remarked to him one day on the main deck. "In the fall, the ocean prepares to make itself an obstructive harridan." The convoy managed to retain its formation. Sails had been sighted on the horizon; whether they belonged to friendly or hostile ships, no one could say, for they were not seen again. The *Sparrowhawk* occupied a place near the rear, two vessels away from the formidable *Zeus*. Even so, Ramshaw ordered battle drills twice a week. Hugh was astounded with the efficiency of the crew and with how quickly the ship could be made battle-ready.

"Can you handle a musket, sir?" the captain inquired during one of the drills.

"Yes, sir."

"Good. You will be given one, if the necessity arises." Ramshaw pointed to a swivel gun on the quarterdeck above them. "See that, Mr. Kenrick? Jack Frake helped crew that very gun. He saved this ship when we were assaulted by a French privateer. Blew the captain's head off with it."

In late September, a brief easterly squall struck the convoy, scattering the ships widely in a torrential rain and with winds that tried to drive them back to England. It was a dangerous predicament. The thick gray curtain of rain reduced visibility to a few score yards on any side of the *Sparrowhawk*, which could ram the vessel ahead of her, or be rammed by it or the one behind. The squall moved on, and just as suddenly, the sea was calm and the skies blue.

The *Zeus* signaled her charges to reform, then flew special flags to the *Jason* to count the ships, a message that was in turn relayed to the *Helios*, once she was back in signaling range. Hours later, a lieutenant reported to the convoy commander that two merchantmen were casualties of the squall: the *Manx*, whose upturned keel could be seen bobbing in the water over a mile north of the *Jason*, with survivors clinging to her; and a sloop, *George's Pleasure*, a mile south of the *Helios*, listing on her larboard side with damaged masts. The *Charon*, too, was driven far away from the convoy. Though she appeared undamaged and was in a position to assist *George's Pleasure*, the *Helios* reported that the *Charon* seemed inclined neither to give aid to the sloop nor to rejoin the formation with any haste, though she was paralleling the convoy and edging back in its direction. The convoy commander instructed his lieutenant to repeat the formation order, and to add the caution that any vessel breaking formation to aid one of the disabled ships or rescue its crew would do so at its own risk.

Ramshaw was on deck, observing the progress of the crew as it repaired some minor tears in the spanker and staysail. The bursar, a decommissioned midshipman from the last war, was able to read the *Zeus*'s signals. He handed the captain a transcription of the communications to the other warships. "The *Manx* and *George's Pleasure*?" remarked Ramshaw. "Caught with their topsails down, I'll wager." He sighed. "Well, at least those black devils on the *Manx* have been spared a worse death. Heard they were being taken to the Carolinas to work rice." He paused, then strode across the deck to larboard and raised his spyglass. "There's *George*," he said, "and that must be the *Charon*. Yes, that's her. Can just make out her name."

"What an odd name," said the bursar.

"It was once the *Pelican*," said Ramshaw. "But Musto takes so many souls to the colonies that he renamed her after the fellow who rows the dead across the Styx to Hades—for a fee, of course. Queer sense of humor, I'd say."

"Well," chuckled the bursar, "at least he's read a book or two."

"What name did you say?"

Ramshaw and the bursar turned to the questioner. Hugh stood there. After the squall passed, he had reappeared on deck. He had removed his frock coat and waistcoat, and offered to help clean up the deck. Ramshaw had refused him the request. "Thank you for the interest, sir, and no offense intended, but you wouldn't know where to put things." Now he answered, "The *Charon*."

"Where?"

Ramshaw handed him the spyglass and pointed.

Hugh raised the glass and after a moment found the vessel. He gave the glass back to Ramshaw, who noted the look of joy on his passenger's face.

"Why do you ask, sir?" asked the captain.

"My three friends are on her." Hugh's face brightened a little. "Think of it! Four Pippins have been banished to… *Hyperborea*!"

"How do you know they are on her?"

"Their attorney wrote me that their indentures were purchased by a Captain Musto, of the *Charon*, almost a month before you came to Weymouth."

Ramshaw grinned ironically. "Well, they had better be praying that Musto falls back into line with this convoy, sir, else the *Charon* may be picked off by a privateer and towed to the Barbary. The folks in that part of the world never tire of slaves. There would be no working off their indentures then."

*   *   *

An hour later the lookout shouted down, "Sails ahoy! To the southwest, bearing down on a stray!"

Ramshaw rushed up the steps of the quarterdeck and raised his glass. *George's Pleasure* had been left far behind. Through the glass he could see, a little less than a mile to the southwest, two sets of sails, both belonging to two-masted brig-sized ships. One flew the red ensign, the other the gold and white of France, whose yellow border and fleurs-de-lis glinted occasionally in the sunlight.

"Why such predators should sail under so pretty a flag is something I will never understand," Ramshaw said to himself. To his ship's master, he said, "Ready the larboard guns, Mr. Dietz, but don't load just yet."

A cabin boy soon appeared with a drum and beat the alert. The crew of the *Sparrowhawk* jumped to life and the deck swarmed with men who cleared the deck for action and prepared the guns to be loaded.

Hugh had remained on deck to watch the *Charon*. Now he rushed below to his berth and fetched the long-glass Roger Tallmadge had given him. He joined Ramshaw and the others on the quarterdeck to be out of the way of the gun crews. Through his glass he could see the French privateer close in on the English brig.

The convoy was sailing in a southwestern direction, bringing the vessels in the rear of it closer to the tableau. The gun crews on the larboard side stood braced to act the moment Ramshaw gave the word. All the other passengers had gathered in mid-deck to watch what was about to happen.

"It's begun," said Ramshaw.

Through his glass Hugh saw white puffs of smoke rise from between the two distant vessels, then drift across the water. The privateer was firing from its starboard side into the *Charon*'s larboard, and not much else could be seen. A moment later the reports of the two ships' guns reached the *Sparrowhawk*.

Haynie, the bursar, said, "Musto's not going to surrender without a fight. Maybe he thinks the *Zeus* will rescue him. But I do believe the *Charon* is vastly outclassed."

Iverson, the surgeon, also had a spyglass. "Mr. Ramshaw, did you happen to see the Frenchman's name?"

"No," said the captain. "He was too far away."

"Bad choice for a prize," commented Haynie. "A cargo of redemptioners won't fetch a sou in France. They'll have to sail the *Charon* clear to Tunis, or let her go after they take all the money on board and their pick of the women."

Ramshaw gasped. "The Frenchman's leaving off! What the deuce—?"

The two vessels traded second broadsides. Other guns on the privateer must also have fired grape and chain at the *Charon*'s masts. Canvas fore and aft shredded, and lines and shrouds on both its masts fell to the deck.

And then they all saw the reason why the privateer was quitting. On their left the *Zeus,* under full sail, had broken formation and was speeding in the direction of the fight.

"Wonder if the Frenchman could read signals from such a distance," speculated Iverson. "That would explain why he thought the *Charon* was easy prey."

"Whatever he thought," remarked Ramshaw, "it was wrong."

As the privateer disengaged in order to escape being trapped between the *Charon* and the *Zeus*, it fired one last broadside into the brig, as though out of spite.

Defiantly, the *Charon* answered with another.

The reports from this last exchange had just reached the spectator's ears when there was another explosion. Abruptly, the bowsprit and part of the *Charon*'s bow were neatly severed from the rest of the vessel, and the foremast, partly secured by lines to the bow and bowsprit, bent, cracked, and fell with them.

"Good God!" exclaimed Ramshaw. "The damned fool must have stored powder above the water line!"

"You're right, sir!" answered Haynie. "That's the only thing that could do that! A French ball from that last broadside must have found a gun port and shot straight through to it!"

The *Sparrowhawk* was little more than half a mile away now. Her observers could see men swarming over the deck of the *Charon*, and other figures emerging with the billowing smoke from her hatches. Some of these were women and children. As they watched, the bow sank and the truck and masthead of the foremast dipped into the choppy waves. Flames shot up through the shattered foredeck, but were quickly extinguished as water flooded into the vessel. The *Charon*'s stern rose out of the water as the vessel began a swift descent. Rigging, guns, crew, and passengers slid or tumbled down the deck and splashed into the waves. In less than a minute, only the aft cabin was visible. Then the water broke and gushed through its paneled glass. The red ensign, wrapped around the lanyard, was the last thing to be swallowed by the waves. Then the *Charon* was gone, leaving behind bodies and debris.

The sea was quiet. Even the privateer seemed to pause in horror of what its crew had just witnessed. Ramshaw and his officers swept the site with their glasses for signs of survivors. None were to be seen.

"There were over a hundred people on the *Charon*," remarked the surgeon in a near-whisper. "Counting convicts and crews."

Ramshaw glanced at Hugh. Hugh stood with an expression frozen in disbelief, and tears rolled down his cheeks.

The captain stepped over to him and said, "If they were lucky or God was merciful, Mr. Kenrick, they were fettered somewhere below the powder, or close to it, and they died quickly. Most of the others had to settle for drowning."

"I can see the name now!" said Iverson. "*Le Voleur*! 'The Thief!'"

The *Zeus* swiftly approached *Le Voleur*'s stern. All of her starboard gun ports were open and that side of the warship bristled with the black noses of guns. The *Sparrowhawk* was now directly opposite the *Zeus* and the privateer.

Ramshaw glanced at Hugh again, and saw him sitting on a pile of coiled rope near the tiller. "Mr. Kenrick," he said, "you may want to see this." Hugh looked up, then rose and rejoined the men at the railing.

"She's going to rake the stern!" said Iverson.

The *Zeus* fired. Two decks of guns blazed in consecutive pairs at the rear of *Le Voleur* as the warship glided past. Debris flew out from the disintegrating aft cabin.

"That is hellish gunnery!" exclaimed Haynie. "If only a third of those balls go through, they'll rip her to pieces inside clear up to the bow!"

"Who is the captain of the *Zeus*?" asked Iverson.

"Our convoy commander, Post-Captain Farbrace," answered Ramshaw, still peering through his glass. "Timothy Farbrace. Though there is nothing timid about that gentleman."

"There goes the rudder! The Frenchman is done for!"

They saw two crewmen on the privateer scramble to haul down the white and gold banner. "She's striking her colors! Bravo!" cried Haynie.

The crew and passengers of the *Sparrowhawk* cheered.

The *Zeus* tacked sharply starboard and maneuvered alongside the privateer. "By God, he is good!" said Ramshaw in admiration.

Then they heard the thunder of a broadside as the *Zeus* proceeded to pound the larboard side of *Le Voleur*. They could even discern the crackle of small arms.

"He's going to finish her off!" cried Haynie.

Again, the spectators watched in amazement. The warship fired five broadsides into the privateer, then tacked starboard again to rake the bow. The top half of *Le Voleur*'s mizzenmast collapsed and fell to the deck. Grape and chain shot pierced the canvasses of her foremast. Brown smoke began to creep in wisps from the gun ports on the starboard side. The privateer began to list on her larboard side.

The *Zeus* tacked starboard again and in a minute blocked the view of the spectators on the *Sparrowhawk* as the warship rode through the debris of the *Charon*. Through gaps in the smoke they could see the frigate's crew working the guns on the main deck as the warship delivered more broadsides, while others worked her sails. Crewmen and red-jacketed marines were busy pouring musket fire into the unfortunate privateer.

Ramshaw said, "It seems that our Mr. Farbrace is intent on punishing those Frenchmen for Captain Musto's folly. That is not abiding by the rules."

"Perhaps not," remarked Haynie. "But, look! There is a better explanation!" he pointed to the southwest. The group trained their glasses in that direction. On the horizon, they saw sails, two sets of them. One set seemed to indicate a frigate, the other, another brig.

"Prudence, then, governs Mr. Farbrace," sighed Ramshaw. "Forgive me for impugning your character, sir."

Once more the *Zeus* tacked, but more slowly. They saw now that *Le Voleur* had capsized and was lying on her larboard side, showing half of her hull. Men flailed desperately in the water around her, and others clung to floating debris. Still others were trying to get a foothold on the slippery, barnacle-pitted hull.

"She is finished, Mr. Farbrace," said Ramshaw to himself, "and she's not put a scratch on your lovely ship. Pick up some of those rascals and perhaps they will tell you who else is lurking in these parts."

But again, the *Zeus* loosed another full broadside. Some balls glanced off the hull, but others found weak spots and dented or shattered the wood. The men on the *Sparrowhawk* imagined they could hear the Frenchmen on the hull curse the *Zeus*. They could see them shaking their fists at her before they dived back into the water. One Frenchman was caught in midair as he dived and cut in half by a shot from the *Zeus*.

Water shot up through the new holes in the hull, and *Le Voleur* slipped quietly beneath the waves.

"The thief will sleep with the suicide," remarked Iverson.

"That is more cruelty than I saw at Charing Cross," said Hugh. "That ship was no match for the *Zeus*. What was the purpose in destroying her?"

Ramshaw did not immediately answer. He watched the *Zeus* tack around the debris and survivors—making no attempt to pick up the few men who still splashed in the water—and saw the spongers swab the barrels of the warship's guns. One by one, the gun ports dropped shut.

"The purpose, Mr. Kenrick?" said the captain, lowering his glass and tucking it under his arm. "To make an example of her, for the benefit of those chaps there." He nodded in the direction of the new sails. "They won't worry us now. Won't even bother to follow us."

Hugh gestured vaguely in the direction of the carnage. "What about all those passengers from the *Charon*? I can see...their bodies in the water. We can't just...leave them..."

Haynie said, "There's nothing to be done for them, sir. We don't know who they were, and we would simply need to toss them back in."

Ramshaw gave his crew the order to stand down, but stopped before he descended to the main deck. "I am very sorry that you lost your friends, Mr. Kenrick." He patted one of Hugh's shoulders. "Have supper with me this evening. Sea-pie on Sheffield plate. Washed down with a quart or more of Madeira. That will help you sleep...and accept it...and forget it."

"I won't forget," said Hugh. He glanced once more out at the debris. The *Zeus* was cutting through it to rejoin the formation. "I am the last of the Pippins," he added, more to himself than to Ramshaw.

A stiff breeze whipped through his shirt and filled the sails of the *Sparrowhawk*. The bodies, the debris, and the survivors from *Le Voleur* vanished behind the waves.

*   *   *

Hugh Kenrick withdrew into himself and remained withdrawn for the rest of the voyage. He said little, ate little, but wrote extensively in his journal, describing, among many other things, the terrible fates of the *Charon* and *Le Voleur*. His sleep was interrupted now and then by unbidden, recurring nightmares, in which he or one of his perished friends was chained to a wall in the hold of a sinking ship, or strapped to a cask of gunpowder while vague, laughing faces tossed lit matches at him. He did not scream, but thought he had when he woke up in a sweat. Ramshaw tried to draw him out of the mood, but was unsuccessful.

There were no further incidents. The sails on the horizon disappeared, and the convoy headed west without further molestation by man or weather. The convoy commander invited Ramshaw and Hugh to supper on the *Zeus*. The post-captain had observed Ramshaw's battle drills with appreciation, and word had also reached him that the *Sparrowhawk* carried nobility. Hugh declined the invitation, and asked Ramshaw to convey his thanks and apologies. He did not wish to meet the man who had punished the Frenchmen of *Le Voleur*, even though he was convinced by Ramshaw that it had been the right thing to do.

Hugh came back to life only when Iverson came by his berth to inform him that the mainland had been sighted. Hugh smiled for the first time in weeks. He found his long-glass and went up to the quarterdeck and, for the rest of the morning, surveyed the shores of the alien continent. Only three other merchantmen remained from the convoy. The others, including the warships and the transports, had already gone their separate ways.

A day later, the *Sparrowhawk* rounded Cape May, entered Delaware Bay, and sailed placidly up its river. Hugh paced excitedly up and down the deck, unable to believe the immensity of the place, and believing it at the same time. From the deck he could see tobacco fields, and fields of corn and wheat, and great houses, and sleepy river towns, and rivers that meandered west to vanish into unending carpets of forests. A mountain range far in that direction ran from one invisible point north to another south. The earth seemed larger here. He felt equal to the challenge of all its possibilities.

John Ramshaw watched his special passenger, and was glad.

Another day passed, and the *Sparrowhawk* welcomed aboard the pilot who would take the merchantman into port. Through his long-glass, Hugh

Kenrick could see the steeples of the city of Philadelphia.

The voyage begun by him long ago in the halls of Danvers was nearly over. There lay his future, and England was far away.

Acknowledgments

I am indebted, first and foremost, to two individuals, no longer with us. One confirmed my approach to life, the other confirmed its direction: Ayn Rand, the novelist-philosopher, whose novels I discovered, when a teenager, in the vandalized library of a suburban Pittsburgh boys' home; and David Lean, the British director, whose *Lawrence of Arabia* I saw the same year, an event that cemented my ambition to become a novelist.

Special fond thanks go to Wayne Barrett, former editor of the *Colonial Williamsburg Journal*, who was certain this novel would see the light of day after having read the first page long ago; and to the BookPress in Williamsburg, whose partners, John Ballinger and John Curtis, also encouraged me and allowed me to rummage through their valuable stock on the track of ideas and materials.

Further debts of thanks are owed to the staff and past and current directors of the John D. Rockefeller, Jr. Library at Colonial Williamsburg for their assistance; to many of Colonial Williamsburg's costumed "interpreters," too numerous to name here, for the passion, lore, and information they imparted; and to the staff of the Earl Gregg Swem Library at the College of William & Mary, Williamsburg.

Pat Walsh, editor, together with Robert Tindall and Emily McManus, have my gratitude for their incisive suggestions and innumerable corrections, and for sharing my confidence that this novel will find a large and appreciative readership.

Lastly, I owe a debt of thanks to the Founders for having given me something worth writing about, and a country in which to write it.